SOUL CRYSTALS: THE MASK OF TRAGEDY

LATROBE BARNITZ

PRIVATE DRAGON
Publishing

SNAPSHOTS

6 MONTHS **Ago**

The metal mass creaked and shrieked from the pressure. For anyone unaccustomed to the claustrophobic space, those sounds would have been jarring. It was like the world was caving in on you, and it was doing it in near-total darkness.

A young man, who had only introduced himself as, "Zeke," flung his arms out to brace himself. Still, he had enough sense not to touch any of the sensitive instruments.

That trepidation gave Jules DuPont more satisfaction than it should have. In the short time they had known each other, the mysterious stranger had been far from good company. The twenty-something, who spoke in what the Frenchman discerned as either an American or English Canadian accent, had shown so little emotion so far that his presence felt more than a little disconcerting. He was either suspiciously tight-lipped or simply a bore in DuPont's eyes.

"Relax," DuPont soothed with a hint of smugness.

After all, he could not let this amateur touch any of the instruments by accident.

As the submersible expert methodically checked the current readings, he thought back to their meeting and the strange request that had preceded it.

Jules had been obsessed with submarines since he had been a small child. After all, he shared a first name with Jules Verne. Those childhood dreams had led him to an engineering degree and time in the French navy. With the expertise gained and connections made, he had used a portion of his family's considerable assets on a craft of his own. Decades had led to the creation of La Sirène, a true underwater craft that Jules piloted for scientists and the like. It had already studied leagues along the floors of the Mediterranean and eastern Atlantic.

Dupont had been contacted out of the blue by an organization whose focus was typically far away from underwater exploration. It was A.R.C., Amulus Regional Containment, that had come calling. Apparently, they had reason to believe that unclaimed anima crystals were dwelling just off of Spain's southern coast. If this was true, they would be the first pure crystals ever found in modern times and would be helpful to A.R.C.'s research. It was an important expedition. DuPont was unsure why there was so little fanfare for it. There was barely even a team assembled. There was DuPont's usual crew monitoring the goings-on in the boat. Before-hand, they had been the ones to launch the sub and would be hoisting it back onto the boat afterward via a crane. From A.R.C., there were only two.

There was another young man, Kade, observing with DuPont's team. Like Zeke, DuPont had rarely seen his eyes since they were nearly always covered by sunglasses. It reminded the Frenchman of something that he had heard about border troops at Korea's D.M.Z. Apparently, many of the men posted there tend to wear sunglasses to hide their emotions so that no looks can be interpreted as provocative by the opposing side. Zeke had not removed his pair until just before climbing into the cramped sub.

Throughout the journey down, Zeke was paying close attention to the camera feed showcasing view from the sub's bottom There was good reason in this. At A.R.C.'s request, the sub had been outfitted with a needle-like appendage underneath. They had explained that this device would essentially inject a radar scanner into the seafloor. Supposedly, A.R.C. had researchers at another location who would be surveying the results. The purpose of the mission made sense to DuPont. Still, he did not like outsiders making modifications to the craft he had spent so much time, money, and effort into constructing. Besides, it made the vehicle look ugly. It was now a mosquito with a long proboscis. At the end was now some sort of pressurized tube.

At the current depth, it was pitch black outside the submarine. Just like in a car driving at night, the interior of the vehicle was kept dark while powerful lights illuminated the immediate area on the outside. There were light switches near the instruments if necessary.

Taking in the moment, DuPont relished his views of the water around him. It was quite empty of life and had been for some time during the journey. The world knew about the fascinating life forms of the deep sea, but those were often rare. DuPont knew that more dives were greeted by blank sea and sand rather than discoveries. To him, the modifications to his prized creation only slightly dampened his mood. Being this far from everyone else in a futuristic-looking craft made him feel like an astronaut. It mattered only a little that the normally sleek vehicle now had a long, ugly nose. Exploration alone was a thrill.

Zeke was beginning to become impatient. It was clear in his body language how his index finger repeated tapped his opposite bicep and how his eyes narrowed. However, the stoicism in his speech remained. DuPont knew that the journey would take time. Good exploration and science were both meticulous and methodological. In these conditions, safety was obviously paramount.

Finally, the camera feed caught sight of the bottom. Zeke rose slightly from his seat in excitement. It was the most emotion DuPont had seen from him. Still, the young man could not move very far in the cramped space.

On camera, the ocean floor looked more like a dusty cloud that was now growing. In minutes, gravity and ocean pressure had dropped the sub to the bottom with the machine appendage contacting first. This caused more creaking and rocking, but those effects gradually ceased.

Zeke was now half-standing, half-sitting, as much as the limited room would allow. A change had come over him. His legs shook in place. His mouth hung slightly open while his eyes grew even wider.

On the first inspection in the dim light, DuPont thought this was a fear-filled reaction. Indeed, whatever had come over the formally stone-faced man seemed to be as primal as fight-or-flight instinct. DuPont could just make out the curves around the younger man's mouth. No, this was excitement. It was childlike and intense. Zeke reminded DuPont of his own children opening presents on Christmas morning. It was the intention-consuming anticipation of something great and good.

DuPont opened his mouth to speak but realized that he was unsure of what to say. The sudden change and current expression of Zeke unnerved him. Even in the darkened interior, the whites of his eyes seemed to glow with maniacal light.

The submarine jolted sideways, hard and fast. DuPont bumped his head on metal siding. Both the physical jolt and the shock of surprise left him shaking. Never before had the sub behaved like that.

The next moment, the sub was bouncing as if whacked by a giant baseball bat from below. Visibility went to zero. A churning wave of angry sand and sentiment enveloped all the windows and camera feeds.

DuPont was bashed around the inside, unable to even grip the controls or compose his frantic mind. His brain was only filled with a sense of dread and doom. Dents started to appear in the pressurized walls. From there, the tightening and closing of the walls were unstoppable as DuPont and Zeke were squeezed.

DuPont realized that Zeke was fanatically chanting, "It's coming! It's coming!"

With his last breath, DuPont screamed. "What was in that tube?"

———

There was a slow, maddening drip from the curved ceiling. Both the ceiling and the sloping walls were made of one whole stone of a cloudy gray color. Voices echoed from far enough away that they were unintelligible. They were just a bunch of syllables spit into the spacious air of the place.

Interrupting the monotony of stone was a metal door along the wall. It was cracked open slightly, revealing a hard, yellow light. From behind it, more voices were ringing.

The room was furnished only with cots and few sets of tables and chairs. A few young men with shaved heads were dozing or half-dozing on the cots, despite the noisy occupants of the tables. The latter group was wearing tan uniforms, but many of the buttons were undone. There were more than a few wrinkled fronts and sleeves.

"Tell me this, lads," a young man with only a bruise of dark hair on his head said as he shuffled playing cards to his partners, "Tawny's a Welshman. Grove's from the North. Mac's a Scotsman, and I'm an Irishman. The question is, what are we doin' under a rock in the south of Spain?"

The other soldiers just studied their cards.

"The answer is, no one has a clue."

The other card players only gave short grumbles at the bad joke. In the ensuing moments, some cards were dropped while others were held. More than a few curses were murmured lowly.

Abruptly, one of the men who had been laying on a cot stood up and slowly made his way across the stone floor in bare feet. He stopped at the table.

It took several moments for his presence to distract them from their game.

"Can't sleep, Hendrickson?" the Irishman asked. "Or is it that you want in?"

Hendrickson shook his head. "Do you hear it? There's this loud drippin'. It's keeping me awake."

The table's four occupants allowed a quiet to fall. There was the faintest pitter-patter coming from somewhere far away.

"I hear it," the Irishman agreed, "but, I think you'd have to be like the princess from 'The Princess and the Pea' to let that get to yah."

"Probably condensation," Tawny theorized. "Cool rock tends to do that. What's odd is that someone was saying the tide was way down a little earlier."

A sudden barrage of alarms roared in their ears. Each one of the card players let their cards fall from their grip without a thought. All the sleeping men shot up and were standing with their boots on within seconds.

"A bloody drill!" someone shouted loud enough that the blaring did not drown him out.

Without missing a step, each of the trained soldiers was ready to march out the door.

Grove, the first man in line, stopped abruptly, breaking the well-organized formation.

"What the—"

The Englishman stooped down to within centimeters of the ground. He swirled his fingertips around in brown water.

"A pipe's burst?"

"Explains the alarm," Mac noted.

The other men in front pushed the door the rest of the way open. Several inches of water were covering the cavernous corridor.

"That's a lot of water given the space," Mac noticed.

"Franky's been clogging up the loo again," some from the back of the line snickered.

"Actually, seems pretty serious," Tawny scolded the man. "Wait. Quiet down, everyone."

There was a small, rhythmic sound of water lapping against stone. Without warning, a wave of several more centimeters in height cascaded down the hall.

"Don't like this," Grove murmured as he reached for the metal door.

He tugged it shut, sealing the room. The other men still stood behind him.

"Wha—was that the right protocol?" someone asked.

Grove shrugged. "Just didn't want to get wet. Besides, someone'll send us a message soon enough."

This insistence was greeted by mostly nods. The soldiers held their formation, although slightly more unsure now.

There was the sound of another wave from the other side of the door. This one did not sound like the previous one. It had all the rushing sounds of a wave breaking against the shore. Stunned, the wide-eyed men stared at the secured metal door. The first booming sound was followed by a second. After that, it did not let up.

The soldiers stayed planted where they were. One by one, their heads silently and apprehensively turned towards a series of growing damp spots to the sides of the door.

The dripping started there, too.

CHAPTER 1
IN THE DEN

LEONARD HOWE WAS BLEEDING BADLY. It was maddening, the soft dribbling on his neck from the horribly painful spot on his ear.

He cursed, not for the first time, and muttered, "He got my ear. All he had was a little dagger, and he got my ear. Took the communicator clean out, too! McGreevy's gonna have a laugh. Not that I didn't get him worse."

Howe kicked the tanto knife, and it clattered across the tile floor. Its blue crystal had turned to dust and then into nothing moments ago.

"Clean-up crew will be here soon," he told the body against the wall. "Hate being alone during raids like this. I end up talking to the dead people."

He heard the elevator power up towards the well-lit room. It had been a secret, but its entrance was now exposed through a smashed-open set of cabinets. It came up slowly.

Howe pressed his hand harder against his dripping ear.

"Lights are making my head hurt even worse."

Finally, a grim-faced boy with black hair stepped into the lobby without a word. His shirt was red and slick. However, neither his body nor clothes were torn. His head turned towards Howe slowly. Although the teen's posture was loose and cool, his brown eyes were intense and unsettling.

"No need for suspense," declared Howe. "What's the news down there? See? My communicator got busted off."

"It's like we thought," Jason Saito breathed in a chilly voice. "There

1

were civilian prisoners, probably A.R.C. family members. Some guards but not much resistance."

"How about-"

"Still no sign."

Howe shook his head. "The frowner won't be happy. He never is anyway, though. Where's McGreevy? I better patch up this ear before he comes up and laughs at me for getting cut by a kid."

"He won't be coming back up," Jason reported flatly.

Howe's head drooped. "You said there wasn't much resistance?"

"There was some resistance."

Howe cursed lowly. "We were at this for a long time together. Both came out of Belfast after The Troubles. Gonna need a smoke now. Not like that poison inhalation hurts people like us, right?"

Jason slowly rounded the lobby desk to stand beside Howe.

"Before he died," Jason remarked bitterly, "he told me some interesting things."

Howe's brow became sprinkled with sweat. His hands clutched his battle-axe a little tighter. The red crystal near the head flickered faintly.

"Did he now?" asked Howe with a heavy breath. "Any dying words for an old friend?"

He did not intend to hear an answer. He wretched the heavy ax upward.

A second later, it was on the ground along with his hands.

"That's the problem with axes," mentioned Jason matter-of-factly. "The follow-through is strong, but starting the stroke takes longer than it does to swing a sword because of the unbalanced weight."

Howe scrambled, weeping, and ended up leaning on the front desk.

Jason stooped down to look at him.

"I know almost everything. There are still a few things though."

"And what did McGreevy not know that you think I do?" begged Howe against the ripening pain.

"I just want to know who gave the order," stated Jason. "Then, it will be over for you."

Howe grunted and spat. "I-I should have known. Just like The Rat, you are. I should have done you like your mother. I could have stamped you out then. You filthy traitor!"

Jason tugged on the man's streaming wrist, forcing him to throw his head back and howl.

"Who?" he demanded again.

"Y-You already know who!" sniveled Howe.

"I need you to say it."

"J-Jackson!" he coughed.

Jason let go of Howe.

"What are you going to do now!" questioned the fast-bleeding man. "You've killed A.R.C. and A.I.M. Neither will take you in when they hear."

"Eventually," agreed Jason. "As for now, you've just been killed by that A.I.M. guard lying over there. I think, in time, I will have a place. You'll never see that, though."

It was over with another flash of the red-glowing saber.

Jason tapped the communicator in his ear.

"I can confirm the safety of the prisoners," he relayed dryly. "There was stiff resistance. Two agents are down."

CHAPTER 2
THE MASK OF TRAGEDY

THIS AREA of Tokyo's Koto Ward bustled during the day. Unlike the warehouse districts of other cities, this place was not too far off from the foot-traffic of museums, gardens, and corporate centers. The outer facades of the buildings were remarkably clean, with well-kept trunks parked beside them or in garages. The majority of people had long gone home after a long workday. The machines that had hummed during all daylight hours now were quiet. A few could listen to the hidden barbarity going on in one warehouse.

There, metal brutally scraped metal, making clashes of a sound not unlike fingernails on a chalkboard. Sparks leaped furiously off two gleaming weapons as they met again and again. One was a blue, shimmering kusarigama. It was a wicked-looking samurai weapon consisting of a ball, chain, and sickle. The ball circled its opponents, probing despite blocks coming from a wakizashi short sword. The man with the sword batted the metal ball aside repeatedly with the side of his wave-striped blade. His arms worked furiously as they bulged through his partially unbuttoned dress shirt. The younger man with the kusarigama worked the chain with his anima, spinning it far faster than he could with his wrists. In the fight from a distance, this man in urban camo had a hard-pressing advantage. Any hints of confidence were hiding behind bandana the same colors of his outfit.

Still, the simplicity of the short blade with its red sparks let the older man be more fluid. He gained ground slowly, working his way towards a path of his own advantage. A number of men watched from behind shipping containers and wooden crates. None said a word of encouragement or discouragement. One said matched their champion's mottled gray. The others looked as if they had just stepped out of a board meeting.

As he zoned in, the swordsman made a barely visible flick of his fingers. One of the men on his side of the warehouse tossed him a slender shape. With his free hand, the man flicked off the scabbard of another wakizashi. This one showed a lazy purple.

The young man was surprised, and it showed. Two anima weapons? It was impossible! An Amulus had one crystal and a crystal had one master.

In the shadows of the roof beams above, a new figure emerged. Without warning, it landed just to the side of the Japanese swordsman. The shrouded male figure landed on his feet like a cat—without breaking his stride.

"Where?" it whispered to itself in a husky voice.

A chorus of shouting came from the swordsman's side as well as himself. They pointed angrily at this figure in a dark blue coat and gray mask. Rows of men lit up their anima crystals. It was like the Aurora Borealis emerging from both sides of the building. Metal blades and wooden yumi bows aimed threateningly at the newcomer. Based on the figure's body language, he felt no pressure from the waves of anima building up around him. His mask did not reveal his own eyes, giving him only a blank stare made of black felt circles. Painted partway down the face was an upturned, grimacing mouth.

Despite the commotion, no one directly approached the sleek intruder. However, the match had screeched to a halt as both combatants focused on the man in the frowning mask. The man with the two swords threatened to be the first to move. His fingers twitched along his wakizashi. Only some sort of nervous apprehension prevented him from apprehending the source of the disruption.

Ignoring everyone else, the newcomer's scabbard swung about as he strode purposefully towards a wooden crate. He gave it an ear-shattering kick. A man spilled out before skidding on the ground. He came to a rest in a heap of arms and legs only after putting a dent in a shipping container. Echoes of a purple glow faded from the unconscious man and one of the swords the one fighter held.

The swordsman's side ceased their outcry. It was now louder on the other side as the men came close to entering the battlefield. The man with the chain weapon held them back with a wave. He then used the opportunity to ensnare the swordsman with the chain. The swordsman tried to fight back but was pulled in. With his arms pinned, he made weak swings toward the other man who blocked with his sickle.

The younger fighter used his angle to his advantage as he flicked the sickle blade deep into the wrist of the arm holding the red crystal sword. At the same time, he kicked the other, faded wakizashi aside with ease. The swordsman sunk to his knees with an agonizing cry. With the blade inside him, he dared not move. It was even difficult for an Amulus to survive a severed artery. Without a word, his men filed out of the building. No one followed them.

The swordsman's eyes were not fixed on the man who held him in checkmate, but on the shadowy figure who had come down from the ceiling.

"Why the mask?" he asked defiantly, in perfect English. "Most of us know who you are."

Checking on the injured man draped on the shipping container, the masked man did not answer.

"It's funny," the swordsman continued, giving no indication of the pain he was enduring. "This American savior of A.R.C. coming to Japan with a nihonto. It reminds me of something. When my father first went to America to get investors for his company, he dressed like a cowboy. He had a bolo tie and hat. After all, America was the Old West in movies. People laughed at him then. I should be laughing at you now."

The gray mask slid out his sword and rested it on the businessman's shoulder.

Disregarding the man's jibes, he questioned in a monotone voice. "Where are the other hostage locations in Japan?"

He received only a stubborn glare.

"I need to know," it was less of a demand and more of a statement of fact. "Where are the other hostage locations?"

"You don't scare me," the businessman growled.

The man with the katana let a green flame burn down his captive's shirt.

"I did the research," he relayed. "I checked your books. The real ones on those hard drives from the last place we hit. How will the public react when they learn where your father got the seed money for the company?"

The remainder of the man's shirt dipped to reveal a red dragon skin tattoo encircling his entire torso. From the chest, the willowy Asian dragon looked up with burning eyes and an open mouth.

The gray mask continued. "You said that you lost part of your pinkie during a skiing accident when you were young. I'm guessing that is a lie."

"There are yakuza groups older than your home country!" declared the businessman.

"You are forgetting that we represent A.R.C.," asserted the camo mask. "Now, tell us. At least your company's name will survive. Your children will have futures. That is more than we can say about some of the children you took from our agents."

Takahashi Hideo, C.E.O. of Taka Corp Electronics, relented. "You've hit them all. All the ones in Japan. I know what you seek, and you will not find them here, young man."

"Then, where?" barked the gray mask, finally letting his feelings boil.

"I do not know. That is the truth."

The gray mask held his sword back, readying a cut on the unarmed enemy. His upper arm shook with tension. He paused, studied Takashi's eyes, and backed down.

By then, a cavalcade of agents in jet-black vans and S.U.V.s had surrounded the building. A procession of masked people surrounded the group. The agent holding the blade impaled in Takahashi's wrist let the sickle slide out. The businessman's arm fell slack to the ground. The group of agents pulled him away as one readied a bandage for the bleeding arm. A stretch hurriedly made its way to the man denting the metal shipping container.

"We will find them," assured the camo fighter with his mask billowing forward as he spoke. "We have my word."

"I'm sorry, Kishi," the man in the gray mask apologized. "I think you had it covered. I just had to make sure."

Kishi shook his head. "Better to make sure. I appreciate your concern for me. Our job was done. Takahashi and A.I.M. were humiliated for cheating. More reparations will be demanded and received. We could not have asked for a more successful mission. And, I could not have asked for a better subordinate."

"I'll be going then," notified the gray mask as if he had not heard the compliment.

"Where are you off to?" asked Kishi. "The mission was mine. The report is mine."

"I'm heading back to the U.S., anyway," clarified the young man with the katana. "We still have our source."

As he made to leave, Kishi clung to his shoulder for a moment.

"Afterwards, rest. That is an order."

"Right."

———

The hooded and masked young man made his way towards the plane. In ordinary circumstances, no one would have gotten near an airplane with their identity hidden. However, this was one of A.R.C.'s private jets, marked for special use and kept in a special section of the airport. Special taskforces had their privileges.

A black-haired youth stood next to the airstairs.

"You won't like this," he announced through a smirk. "There is a stowaway problem, and she's angry."

The gray mask stopped for a moment, confused. He regained his stride quickly.

I had a feeling this day was coming.

He dragged himself up the stairs to meet a girl with a wavy, dark ponytail. She said nothing at first, only staring at him intently and disapprovingly. She swung out a hand. The masked young man had to struggle against his superhuman instincts to not react. In one motion, she yanked off the frowning, unhappy mask on his face.

"Paul Engel," Camilla scolded as her large brown eyes narrowed.

The yank was followed up by a heavy, resounding slap from her opposite hand.

CHAPTER 3
UNMASKED

PAUL STOOD THERE BLANKLY. His head remained in the same position as it had before the slap.

"At least make it look like it hurt!" complained Camilla. "I don't care what you have in your veins."

"Hi, Cam," Paul greeted her quickly in a low voice.

"Six months!" she shouted. "You cut everyone that cares about you out of your life for six months, and you just say, 'Hi?'"

Paul averted his gaze. "I'm sorry."

Cam shook her head. "Paul, what isn't getting through to you? Six months ago, I thought you might be dead. Then, I heard you survived, but you were horrifically tortured. Next, I get transferred, and they tell me that I'm not allowed to contact you. Here's the last straw. You're not the only one who's detail-oriented enough to constantly run through reports. I found one saying you were behind the transfers. Not just mine, but Robby's and Alice's."

"I thought that you always wanted to be in disaster relief," Paul said in his defense.

"I did, eventually!" Camilla shot back. "I was going to earn the promotion myself. Plus, I definitely wasn't going to leave when my team was in a crisis. Luper died, Alice went off the rails, and you got screwed up!"

"How did you get here?" asked Paul, uncomfortably trying to change the subject.

"Apparently," Camilla responded, "when people know that you are friends with the Mask of Tragedy, they give you some clout. I said that I wanted to get a private plane to assess possible seismic activity in Japan, they just said, 'perfect, there's a jet about to head out.'"

"The plane needs to take off soon," Paul informed, trying again. "We should get inside."

"Great!" exclaimed Camilla with upfront sarcasm. "I can yell at you in there."

The interior of the aircraft was outfitted with hardwood paneling and a velvety carpet. There were a couple of sets of comfortable recliners and even baskets filled with reading material. Most of the space was dwarfed by a massive TV. Paul caught his own beleaguered expression in the dark reflection.

This is unnecessary for me. A cargo plane with some seats would have been fine.

"You know how I know something's wrong?" Camilla asked before answering herself. "Because I got in touch with Robby. Apparently, you won't see him either, and he's worried. Robby Swanson, the guy who never worries about anything, is worried! How could you cut us all out?"

"I had to," Paul responded quietly.

"Bullshit!"

"Because you died. You all died."

Camilla, taken aback, sunk into her seat.

"You all died from my perspective," Paul explained, tension leaping into his haggard voice. "I know you didn't, but when I was told that, it seemed real. The Scientist didn't just convince me then. He made the scene so realistic. It really could have happened. It could still happen, especially now that I'm a target."

"It wasn't your fault," related Camilla in a softer tone. "It never would be."

Paul shook his head. "I've learned that the only thing I can control is myself. That means that I have to do all I can to do good. I have to do things myself."

"You blame yourself," Camilla realized. "Paul, when someone pulls the trigger, it's their fault. It's not the fault of the person who couldn't dive in front of the bullet in time."

"What matters is what happens in the end," Paul argued.

"Even it ends with you destroying yourself physically and mentally?" prodded Camilla.

Paul did not respond, but the affirmation was there.

Camilla looked over to Jason in the corner. "Did you just stand by while he got like this?"

"This isn't a game," Jason put it coolly. "We can't always afford to think about everything happening on the outside. What matters is what comes next."

Giving up on Jason, Camilla cried out. "Look, Paul! Whatever happened, it wasn't your call to cut us out. We put our lives on the line ourselves. It isn't fair to torture us or yourself with this. At least tell me that you'll at least call Robby and Alice. Until then, I won't be leaving you alone."

"I'll think about it," murmured Paul.

Camilla swore at the air. "Paul, you've changed, and I hate it. What did this screwed up world do to you?"

Paul let the conversation hang like rotting fruit in front of his nose.

I can't afford to even think like that. Not the way she does. Not the way I used to just months ago.

"So, when's the last time you slept?" Camilla finally questioned. "You look terrible. You know that you still need to sleep, even if you're stronger than before."

"I was planning on sleeping on the plane ride back," replied Paul. "It is a long flight."

"That's not what I asked."

Camilla then sighed and let it slide.

"Fine. I'll make sure you do."

Self-conscious, Paul put his mask down as he climbed onto a leaned-back recliner at the other end of the cabin. He felt very tired. Only the shapeless dread outweighed that heavy feeling. There were anxious feelings that Paul feared would form into full thoughts now that he was alone in his own head.

I've learned to hate this part.

The thoughts took hold. There were the usual ones springing up again.

You can't rest, not until Aunt Morgan and Uncle Nick are found! Think about all they've done for you! They raised you as their own child as the most loving parents! You probably don't need to sleep like a normal person. You're an Alpha Amulus.

No! I need to sleep! I need to sleep now! I have to rest and be fresh for what-ever comes next! Should I even be out doing things like this? If A.I.M. has it figured out who I am behind the mask, what will they do to Aunt Morgan and Uncle Nick if I keep messing with them?

There were new doubts, too.

Cam's right! I've hurt the people closest to me!

No! I did it to protect them! I can unequivocally say that their lives are better without me, especially now with what's happening to me. They would be better off if they never met me! So, just forget me already!

Oh, God! That man inside the crate… a little more force, and he would be another in my body count. I even held back! Is he crippled now? Even as an Amulus, is he crippled for life? I'm losing it. Every day, I'm losing it a little more.

He was distracted by his own heart beating. It was banging in his chest so hard, the skin around his ribcage was rubbing against the inside of his shirt.

I wonder if it looks like I'm asleep to Cam.

Somehow, impossibly, he was able to stop thinking and drift off due to the sheer exhaustion.

CHAPTER 4
THE BUILDER

"THAT'S IT FOR TODAY, GUYS," Dr. Allison declared abruptly as she turned off the humming projector. "I do have your latest tests. You can pick them up on the way out. I'll be honest, this one was a back-breaker. In fact, in these abbreviated summer courses, I usually curve the grade off of the highest score with that person getting a hundred. This time, that bought up everyone a whopping two points, so I had to do some finagling by throwing out some questions. You can decide if you want to thank me after you pick yours up. Have a good weekend, everyone!"

"Oooh," moaned Betty anxiously. "I don't want to see this car crash, but I kind of want to, too."

The rest of the class slid out from their desks slowly before approaching the front desk in anticipatory silence. There was an almost mechanized sound of the repeated flipping of paper as each student took one and left the classroom without a word.

"Whatcha get? Watcha get?" questioned Betty as she hopping absent mindedly on the white tile floor. "Are we going to suffer together?"

"Not great," Jasmine replied grimly. "This won't kill me... I'll just... I'll just..."

Her voice trailed off as she schemed.

"Oh, I'll just study with the smartest person like I usually do. I just have to find the person at the top of the curve this time."

She and Betty stared down the line of revealed papers with little indiscretion. They interrogated the others who had their papers hidden, often in heart-throbbing shame.

"Who?" Jasmine asked herself.

She looked through the crowd to see only dismayed faces. Just beyond them, she saw a slight, blonde girl rounding the corner towards the gray back stairwell. She disappeared behind a set of double doors like a shadow through a crack.

"Hey!" shouted Jasmine with legs pumping. "Wait up!"

Betty followed close behind her, nearly clinging onto her backpack as they navigated the crowd. The two of them burst through the doors, catching the girl with a foot on the first stair.

"You! You!" Jasmine addressed her as she caught her breath.

The girl turned two large, dreary eyes towards her.

"I'm sorry," Jasmin panted. "Just wanted to ask what you got on the test. I mean… just for reference."

The girl held up her paper with a blank expression. There was a "98" written in red across the top with a "100" circled beside it.

"So, it *was* you!" Jasmine exclaimed. "I'm sorry, my friend here and I were wondering if you wanted to study with us sometime. You're… Your name was… uh…"

"Alice!" finished Betty as she waved cheerfully. "I'm good with names."

"Right, right," Jasmine said, as if she had just come up with the name before Betty's intrusion. "So, what do you say?"

The girl simply stared at them for several seconds. It seemed to Jasmine as if Alice were really agonizing over this casual decision for whatever reason. After all, this was a normal thing that college students did. She could not remember this girl ever speaking in class. This was strange to her since it now seemed that this girl could probably answer all the professor's questions based on her test score.

"I suppose," she answered, almost whispering.

"Great!" responded Jasmine. "You know what? I'll buy you a coffee for helping us out."

Alice froze again for several seconds.

"I believe that I prefer tea," she amended cautiously.

"Tea it is then!"

———

Jasmine nervously stirred her latte, while Betty tried not to slurp her smoothie concoction too noisily. Alice sat in front of them with arms at her side. She had barely touched the tea in front of her. The steam coming off of it was coming in lighter wisps now. Her eyes were downcast, and she had not said a word about anything. Jasmine was struck by how much she did not know about this girl. She typically learned at least a superficial background fact about each classmate when the class was this small. She was not even sure where this young-looking girl was from.

"So, what made you want to get into architecture?" queried Jasmin pleasantly.

"I think that I would like to design gardens," Alice replied slowly, almost unsurely. "I have a degree in botany."

"You already have a degree?" questioned Jasmin surprisedly and rhetorically.

"Hey, are you one of those people who looks like a teenager but is exactly thirty-something?" Betty asked curiously.

"No," answered Alice. "I am not in my thirties."

Alice's phone vibrated, and she pulled it out of her pocket before its third spasm.

"Yes. I see. I appreciate your telling me. No. No. Goodbye," was all that was said on her end.

"Guy problem?" Betty blurted out. "Girl problem?"

"Betty!" interrupted Jasmine.

"Hey, I'm only that short with my exes," Betty justified.

"I do not understand," Alice stated.

"You know," Betty elaborated. "Someone is giving you trouble. That type of thing."

"It's not our business," Jasmine interjected.

Alice thought for a moment. "I believe that I am the cause of some trouble. There is a difficult situation."

"We'll leave it…" Jasmine started to say.

Betty continued. "If that's the case, just apologize if it's your fault. If it no one's fault, just say that it's a screwed-up situation. It's about the honesty. The more you lie to someone or yourself, the more stress you get under trying to keep up the lie."

Jasmine sighed. "Wow, this has been… intrusive. I'll understand if you won't tutor us… or talk to us again.

Alice shook her head. "No, I will tutor you. I prize your advice. You both remind me of some people I know."

CHAPTER 5
SLIPPING

———

THE DARK-HAIRED BOY shoved the door repeatedly. It stayed perfectly bolted.

"You can't keep me in here!" he cried. "I know what I can do!"

The rest of the children in the room had formerly been talking among themselves on large beanbag chairs. They now looked apprehensively at the disturbed newcomer.

"Give me back my sword!" he continued. "It's mine! It chose me! Do you know what I've been through with it?"

The rest of the windowless room stood in opposition to the harsh, metal door. The carpet and whimsical chairs were patterned with light shades of red and blue squares. Across the checkerboard floor, there was even a blank TV with a black gaming console underneath. Both were situated on a movable metal fixture with wheels.

"Come on!" he shouted as he punched the door this time.

Despite the blows from the small, yet superhuman fists, the heavy metal still held without even losing its shape.

"What's this thing made of?" he then murmured to himself.

He noticed the young faces staring at him disapprovingly.

"What?" he yelled back at them.

"Hey, hey," a short-haired girl said as she approached him. "You're a real rebel aren'tcha?"

"Go away," he hissed lowly. "I don't need you. I don't need anyone here! I was just fine on my own!"

"You know?" the girl started, unfazed. "I think I like you."

This outburst broke his concentration. His face went from red in anger to red in embarrassment.

"Don't make fun of me!" he threatened.

"I'm serious!" the girl giggled. "Plus, I think you're wrong about us. Not about this place, but just us in here. I think we can help you."

"I help myself," he snarled. "Have any of you killed anyone? Have you watched anyone die? 'Cause that's what life's like for is! If you don't like it, fine. Just hide in here for the rest of your lives. Me, I have things to do."

"Nope," the girl with the cheery brown eyes disagreed. "I think I can help you. Just let me."

"You're going to help me kill everyone I want to kill?" he asked without caring for an answer.

"Yes," she confirmed, surprisingly.

The dour boy thought for a moment.

"Let's fight then," he challenged. "If I'm just stuck in here, then it's like I'm not to be doing anything. I'm going to prove to the people on the other side of that door that they should let me out. They'll have to when you need a doctor."

"Count me in!" the girl cheered through a smile.

There was a chorus of warnings from the beanbags.

"Oh no," one boy said. "I know you're a newbie. You don't fight Ling. Trust me. You just don't."

"I still have the scars!" another announced overdramatically. "I mean… kind of."

"Ling's the best," the youngest-looking girl in the room put it simply.

Ling made an imaginary line of the floor with her foot.

"We can start right here," she informed. "Whoever gives up first, loses."

The rest of the kids preemptively took their beanbags to the far corners of the playroom. Most of their heads rested on their hands as they looked on attentively with eyes gleaming.

The boy wasted no time in rushing the girl. He would tackle her to the ground, and that would make her shut up. He zipped forward with arms raised straight like Frankenstein's movie monster.

He registered a tap on the elbow, and then Ling was gone. His head swiveled breathlessly from side to side before he was on the ground. Someone unseen was pulling his arm upwards. The boy heard nothing but giggles above him.

"That's why you don't fight Ling," one of the boys repeated for obvious emphasis.

"I'm not giving up," the boy grunted.

He bucked his legs, but they did not want to straighten.

"She's like a bull rider!" laughed the youngest girl.

The boy shook from side to side. He crept along with just his fingers. Still, he could not get rid of the weight on his back. Finally, he lay still to catch his breath.

The weight departed.

"I didn't give! I didn't g-" insisted the boy, scrambling.

Judging by everyone else's reactions, the judgment had been made. The boy only conceded with his silence.

Ling was still beaming behind him.

"I knew you were fun!"

Spinning around to confront her, he demanded, "How did you even do that?"

Ling tapped her head with a finger.

"I'm a Psychic, yah see?" she explained. "I just gave you a thought that said that I wasn't there when I still was. I was invisible to you. The rest was history."

The boy brushed lint from the carpet off of himself.

"You won't do that to me again," Jason warned.

"Yeah, let's do it again sometime!" Ling cheered.

———

Paul woke up in a hurricane in his head.

There was that girl there! There was that boy! Jason was… who's Jason again? The playroom! Everything was there, but now it's not. Where is here? This room… have I been here?

Wait! Who? Who am I? What's my name? It's important! Really important! Am I Jason? Maybe… maybe… it was his memory. No. No!

I…I…I…

I'm Paul.

He took a deep, rib-quaking breath. He felt his body tossing side-to-side. The material underneath him was warm from the friction.

My name is Paul. Paul Michael Engel. I'm from Pallisville, Pennsylvania. My parents died when I was young. An aunt and uncle, Morgan and Nick, raised me. I have a friend named Robby. I have other friends. Their names are…

They are Camilla and Alice. I'm an Amulus working for A.R.C. I'm strong and important, but I'm too dangerous.

Yes.

It was coming back now. That did not mean all the worrying had ceased.

It felt longer this time. I can't say for certain, though. I have no way to time these symptoms. I just have to think of this as another deadline. I have to do everything before I lose my mind.

Paul sat up normally, carefully attempting to show that nothing was wrong. He heard Jason and Camilla chatting quietly at the other part of the cabin. *I never thought of Jason having someone to connect with when he first joined A.R.C. He always seemed like a loner. He never talks about himself much, so I guess there is a lot I don't know about him. I wonder where Ling and those other kids are now. The Observer must be sending me another important piece of information about my teammate. Does this help or hurt what my own anima is doing to my head? I wish he would stop being so cryptic. He only gives me tiny threads of information from the memories he sends. I don't even know who or where he is. The way he connected with me on that mental plane made him seem so... inhuman.*

Forcing himself back to alertness, he rejoined Camilla and Jason. Camilla's brown eyes still looked full of worry for him. Paul hated to be causing someone to feel that way because of him. *I'm not worth it. Let me go.*

"I'm sorry I didn't ask about this earlier," Paul started carefully. "How is your family, Cam? So much happened to the east coast. All of those tidal waves from the seismic activity... I heard it wasn't as bad as Europe or Africa, but still..."

"So, I got calls for the first time in forever," she answered, finally shifting her concentration from Paul. "Both parents. They all got out. Dad and them are with family upstate. Mom's side is cooped up in a hotel with other people displaced by the waves. They'll be allowed to go back soon... maybe even in a few days, but they still don't know what the damage is to their homes is. I mean... the east coast, Western Europe, Africa... the cost is in the trillions. Thank God, there was such an early warning for us in the US. Most people got out. Who knows who didn't? Did we really have something to do with this?"

"We're digging," replied Jason. "Paul and I have been trying to figure that out when we have the time. Jackson really upped our access, but not to everything. If we find someone at fault, they'll pay. A.I.M. or A.R.C., it doesn't matter."

"Just warn me before you turn both of them against you," said Camilla.

With the inner turmoil and the conversation going, Paul barely felt the plane land. They exited and headed for a special section of the airport, which A.R.C. had in its deep pockets. Here, they passed by unchecked despite carrying some of the most dangerous weapons on earth.

"What are you two doing next?" Camilla questioned as they entered a van.

"Back to base," answered Jason.

"You're still using the actual A.R.C. buildings?" Camilla wondered, surprised.

Jason shook his head.

"It's too clogged with protesters at most times of the day. There is a new spot downtown."

"I'm coming with you guys," she insisted. "I'll check in my department from there."

CHAPTER 6
DEEP DOWN

A.R.C. NOW HID underneath the city. They were nearly under the feet of their own protesters. Blocks away, hidden among the loud neon of fast-food places, coffee shops, and ATMs, were a group of old alleyways where stone still bobbed a sea of cement. Past a few doors were chipped stairs that led to places deeper than basements.

The Seattle Underground was a legend that had been forgotten and rediscovered. The original city, built of wood, had once burned. While businessmen waited for the building to come back, they desperately needed ways to dig themselves out of their collective hole. Since the city's surface was wreckage, they went underneath. When the city came back, people went back up top. Only stories and the experiences of people who had found linkages in alleys and basements had remained. Tourists became interested, along with A.R.C. and A.I.M. The closed-off section of the underground around the official building let operatives move through the city quickly by avoiding traffic. With the base overrun, the occupants simply moved underneath the street. Their new space was nearly decrepit in some places, but gave much wider space for barracks and labs. Seattle was a goldmine of secrecy, and A.R.C. was glad to currently hold it.

Paul used Camilla's breaking away for her phone call to slip into narrow, barely lit stretch. The musky smell of mold and dust on top of mold and dust took hold of the air. It was like sniffing an old mushroom. Neither of the walls seemed to have a single, fully intact brick between them. Nevertheless, the base's operatives had told him that it was safe.

Paul stepped into the next section of the base. It looked as if the original builders of the underground had stumbled upon a spaceship. Built right into the brick sidings were meters-thick metal walls dotted with fingerprint scanners. The only indication that there were doors were the slight indents in the metal. Beyond them was a metal desk covered with monitors. Each was trained on a separate person in the narrow spaces behind the bunker walls. One did push-ups. Another read a thick book on an uncomfortable wooden chair. The last one under white sheets on a small bed.

This was a prison for some of the most powerful beings on the planet. Both A.R.C. and A.I.M. had long been coming up with ways to imprison enemy agents. At this time, at least in A.R.C.'s case, the solution was to keep the prisoners locked deep underground in the most secure of tight spaces. Crystals were separated from their users. They were kept as far away as possible to diminish the Amulus' power. These prisoners, for instance, currently had their jewelry and weapons hidden away somewhere in China.

On the other hand, A.R.C. was not above throwing the crystals of the most dangerous captives down to the bottom of the sea. Only those who may still be converted to the cause had their sources of power kept where human hands could reach.

The implication at this Seattle base was clear. Even if an Amulus prisoner was strong enough to break through the layers of steel, the underground collapse would not spare even the strongest superhuman. Even if the prisoners did not do as advised, then this place was already their grave.

Paul waved at the guard at the desk, a girl of barely twenty who was trying to make it look like she was surveying the monitors instead of perusing the magazine on her lap.

"Sup, boss?" she asked casually.

Paul did not have the same problems the rest of the base's inhabitants had with Callie. She had been a failed trainee, an Amulus who had no head for battle. Paul felt no blame towards her. *If I hadn't become an Alpha, then I could have ended up like her. Being bonded to a crystal can be a cruel thing. It can thrust the nicest of people into a never-ending war.*

He could never stop himself from staring at her crystal. It was purple and was connected to a broach which marked her as a Psychic. As her story went, she had simply started off by clipping it into her clothes. However, an A.R.C. instructor had once been incensed at her nonchalant attitude towards combat training. He had impaled and fastened the clasp on the skin near the girl's collarbone as a reminder that she would always be an Amulus. As a powerful anima artifact, it had stayed in place. Not even its user could muster up the strength to unclasp it. So, it stayed as a piercing.

I was lucky that Luper was rough but fair. No, he was beyond fair. He actively put his trainees beyond everything else. He died rescuing me, after all.

The no-longer painful reminder never seemed to put a damper on the girl's attitude.

I don't deserve to be called, "boss." She's older than I am.

Paul silently shook away his feelings.

"03," he stated. "I need to see him again."

"Ugh," moaned Callie. "Can't stand him. You sure you want to go in alone?"

"I'm sure."

"Righto!" Callie blurted as she hit a series of buttons. "Don't let him know I'm here. He's too cocky for someone locked up in a secret prison. It's creepy."

After putting on his mask and tapping the scanner, he slid in through a crack in the metal before it hissed shut.

A bad case of blonde bed-hair leaned sideways from its resting place to study him. A hand smoothed out the unruliness by grabbing it deep in its knuckles. The young man flopped out of bed, wearing what could have been messy, white pajamas. He swung his legs around a nearby chair, one of the few other pieces of furniture in the room. That was Jake Olson's whole world ever since losing his one-sided duel with Gregory Luper.

"Yo," he greeted the visitor. "Frowny-face. That's a good sign."

Paul rested a hand on the opposite chair without sitting down. His index finger ticked like a running clock on the metal. He let the prisoner continue talking.

"You don't have to play around with me," the young man put it confidently. "I get what you're always doing. The spiral guy's the bad cop. You've got the frown, but you're the good cop. I've watched those shows, too. So, good news this time, right? The stuff I said before must have really paid off."

"I need more locations," stated Paul coolly.

The prisoner wiggled his fingers.

"Okay, okay. Let me think. It's been a while, remember? I remember the maps. I've given you all that. There might have been rumors of more places. I think I gave you all those."

Paul's hands were now fully around his chair. "More!"

"Listen!" insisted Olsen. "I've got nothin' I'd keep from you! A.I.M. had me burned, right? They barely trained me, stuck me as a guard over the normals. Then, they put me in the fights. They let some monster break my knees and elbows and left me to die! I hate 'em!"

"There has to be more."

The black-green coloration was seeping through Paul's veins, making his skin almost translucent. His eyes glowed the same colors from behind the mask. Olsen cowered behind them like a deer in headlights.

"Man, what's your problem?" he yelled shakily. "I've said everything! If you ask me, I deserve…"

Paul was inches from him. More than Olsen's voice was shaking now.

"Alright! Alright!" he cried, tears welling. "I know I'm soft. I grew up with a lot of money. Mom was a model. Look! I'm stupid, okay? I'll say whatever, but I said it all!"

A rush of green anima knocked a towering stack of magazines off of the unmade bed. They fluttered so intensely that they shredded.

An arm struck Olsen like a swinging metal bar. He flew into the side of his metal bed frame.

"No!" he whimpered. "No!"

"More," breathed the Alpha as he crept towards the bed. "More."

A pair of burning hands pressed Olsen harder and harder to the bedframe. He stopped talking as the air continued to leave his lungs painfully.

A rough hand on his shoulder tore the Alpha away.

"Paul!"

Jason's dark brown eyes were bulging behind his mesh mask. Paul realized his hand was on his sword pommel. He took it away, staring at it like it was a creature stuck to the end of his wrist. Jason pulled him outside and let the door click shut. A wide-eyed Callie stood up from behind the monitors.

"I-I'm sorry, Paul, I…" she stammered.

Paul let his head hang as low as it could reach. "Don't apologize."

"What were you thinking?" shouted Jason into his face.

Paul was silent. His eyes stayed below Jason's furious gaze.

"You!" Jason continued loudly before lowering his voice slightly. "With you, I don't have to worry about this stuff. I just don't get it. I mean, we worked him over. We got him to the point where he trusted you. What were you even doing in there without me?"

"There have to be more locations," Paul breathed meekly.

"Yeah!" Jason agreed. "And what you did in there is not helping us find them!"

Paul lightly brushed Jason's arm off of himself. "I just need time to think."

He began striding away hurriedly.

"Look!" interjected Jason. "I didn't get what Cam was saying about you until now. I think she's right. You need to fix whatever is going on with you, or you *are* going to let everyone down!"

Paul kept his back turned and only increased his pace, leaving Jason behind to curse under his breath. He only wanted to get away. Seeing another person looking at him at that disapproving manner would be more than he could take. He wandered aimlessly at first, but then headed towards the deserted annex of the underground complex. He ended up scampering through backrooms and closets.

I just need a place… a place away from everyone. I need time. I just need time.

He found the closet in the base's furthest corner away from the main atrium. He closed the door behind him and knelt down in the dusty darkness.

My name is Paul. Paul Michael Engel. I'm from Pallisville, Pennsylvania. I'm seventeen years old. That's who I am. Remember! That's who I am.

I am also an Alpha Amulus. That is what I have to be. I hold lives in my hands. Futures will or won't come about based on what I do. I can't let it all slip until I do everything I need to. Jason's right. I can't let everyone down. I can't let anyone down.

I'll keep it together… just a little longer.

CHAPTER 7
DEBRIEF

PAUL DID his best to avoid both Jason and Camilla after he emerged from the closet. He nibbled on a flavorless ham sandwich as he peered over a large map in his otherwise bleak office. It glittered with stars. The stars did not mark something bright, however. They were the locations of A.I.M.'s hostages, their leverage on A.R.C.'s agents. Every star was now marked with an added dark line. The map was the only color in the plain, white-walled room. He did not want to devote the time to decorate it. Time was precious when you were out to rescue the people you loved. Besides, if he were to hang old pictures, most of them would contain the very people he was searching for.

There has to be more! Paul insisted to himself. *There must a pattern, a reasoning behind the locations. There has to be something that indicates where others would be.*

He began skirting each star with a protractor. *What is it? Triangulation? A certain distance in between? Randomization based on a certain formula? No, probably something not mathematical. City population size? City square footage? Does the randomization involve one of those things as a factor for calculation?*

He saw that he was beginning to put a hole in the map. *It's maddening!*

There was a light knock on his door. He opened it to find Callie, who still struggled to meet his gaze.

"I-I'm really sorry about earlier," he apologized again.

"It's just that kind of job," she said without a smile. "Here."

She handed him a glowing tablet.

"Engel," came a deep, commanding voice from behind the screen.

"Jackson," greeted Paul.

Gareth Jackson was close to an old man now. His hair was artic white in spots of his military-style crew cut. Yet, his face was thin and tight, almost without wrinkles. A large pair of shoulders and a bulging neck made him look anything but frail. He wore a gray suit now, but Paul guessed that felt the former S.A.S. soldier always felt more comfortable in camo fatigues.

Paul felt like his saliva was glue in his mouth. *I hope no one has told him what just happened. More than anyone, he has to think that I have this all together.*

"Agent Sakurai has reported a successful mission," he stated with no warmth. "Well done."

"It was all because of Kishi," Paul praised, attempting to shift Jackson's focus. "It was his op, and he executed."

"Yes, I will note your praise for him in the file."

Paul could not stand to look into the man's eyes. They were an intense, piercing blue. Paul felt like they were always about to accuse him of something, even on the days everything was going smoothly. The bulging veins in his neck were enough to scare his eyes away, too.

"Right," the military man continued. "Are you alone?"

Paul peered around. He was still half-crouched over in an empty back room. *That's never a good sign.*

"Yes."

"You're certain?"

"Yes," Paul repeated, feeling like he was talking to a teacher who would not give his students a chance to be correct.

"It's best you stay that way for now," warned Jackson. "There's been some sensitive, troubling intel."

Paul gulped quietly. *What would scare even Jackson? He's careful and sometimes overly so, but not like this.*

"It's Whaley," Jackson explained. "I will send the file on time-delete. He has been spotted close to your location. In the wood, to be precise. He is a vital target. He is linked to the mysterious A.I.M. leader, Red Mask, and is an enhanced Amuli like yourself. One of the few. It would be a great victory to take him off of the board. "

"I don't understand," Paul said half-frantically. "We hold Seattle, and no battle has been called. For someone so recognized to show his face... it could be war."

"Careful, Engel!" barked Jackson. "We jump to no conclusions. I will not have that word even said until the situation would be upon us. We do not know what this is. You will find out. Alone."

Paul understood the implication. Whaley was an enhanced Amuli and an ordinary Amuli would only be a liability for Paul. Amuli were A.R.C.'s most precious commodity. They could not just throw one away against an impossible enemy. *Even if Jackson won't admit it, that is a part of war. To view human lives as commodities.*

"What do I tell the others?" Paul questioned.

"You tell them the truth," ordered Jackson. "You have a personal order from me that is on a need-to-know basis. You are the only one who needs to know."

Paul nodded. "Send me the coordinates. I'm on my way now."

Not now! Not when Cam is here! Not when I still have to find them! I can't afford to get sidetracked like this!

Only Paul's rapid footsteps betrayed his frustrations.

CHAPTER 8
THE WANDERING POET

PAUL STEPPED out of the car slowly. It was a gray sedan, not the typical ride of a secret agent in the movies. Those stood out. This did not. People forgot about nondescript sedans as soon as they passed by. The more boring, the better. Like a secret agent, however, there was more under the hood. A.R.C. had their engines tuned like police cars in both speed and all-important durability. To Paul, this was more daunting than assuring. He had never yet tested these cars to their fullest extent. After all, he should have been only a beginner driver.

I like being in control. I can control my own two feet. Car wheels can be a different matter.

It was strange being in this forest. Paul had essentially grown up in one. This one was just unique enough to feel alien. The tree trunks seemed wider and rounder. Their leaves were just a different shade of green. There was more space between them as well. In western Pennsylvania, it was hard to find woods that was not choked with dead leaves and bushes. To the south, he could see the white edge of Mount Rainier, sitting on the horizon like a bowl of vanilla ice cream. Seeing a peak topped with white instead of green, brown, and gray was an adjustment as well.

There were even flowers. Alice would have been able to tell him the names. She probably would like this place. *No. Don't think about her. Know that she is one of the people that you are doing this for. Keep your distance. She is better off without you… just like everyone else.*

Paul slipped from the campground into the tree line. He slid his mask over his face, ignoring the ever-present tremors in his hand. They reminded him of how thin his grip over himself had become.

He'll be away from the crowds of the campgrounds and hiking trails. I just need to be careful not to get lost myself.

The wind was rushing around him now as he took each quick step carefully. He always landed on his toes. If his heel needed to land for balance, he let the front of the foot cushion it first. The smaller amount of brush meant less of a danger of stepping on noisy sticks. Still, he kept an eye on the ground. He was getting closer to spot Jackson's analysts had estimated the spot that the drone camera had zoomed in on. He did not envy their job of searching through every photograph of the forest for a match down to the nearest tree.

He trod onward, hoping that there would be no hikers or campers between him and Whaley.

He heard a sound like the air itself was cracking. He was struck into spinning by an unseen blast to his back.

Paul did not let himself fall from his feet. He put a wide tree between himself and the direction of the blast. His senses went into overdrive, listening to every crunch and eyes flittering toward every movement.

Careless! He berated himself. *What if he wasn't actually caught? What if he wanted to be spotted? He wanted to draw me out here! He wasn't careless. I was!*

Paul groped around behind himself, searching his own back. His stomach sunk low.

The backpack containing his sword was yards away from him. Its straps were shorn off, and it lay will beyond his reach from his pinned-down position. Paul was aware that he was still a potential killing machine without his sword. Still, he was a soldier without his weapon, and he felt naked without it.

Unbelievably, Emerson Whaley stepped casually into view. Paul was nearly dumbfounded. *Why? When a sniper or long-distance fighter gives up their position, isn't that like losing the battle for them?*

If this was a trap, Paul would spring it on his own terms. He darted between trees, sprinting a dizzying zigzag. *It's easiest to hit a still target. It's hardest to hit a randomly moving, speedy target!*

Paul was close enough to see his opponent's metal-rimmed glasses. Without his sword, he took up a fluid stance. If the blood had not been pounding relentlessly in his ears, he might have smiled to himself. *On instinct, I went for Robby's favorite.*

Robby had been showing off his collection of Bruce Lee movies for years. He had been delighted to learn later that Lee's method of Jeet-

Kune-Do was, in fact, a real martial art with real practitioners. Moreover, its resourcefulness and penchant for realism made it stand up to even A.R.C.'s handbooks of martial arts training. During Paul's short time with A.R.C.-Human, Robby had enthusiastically taught him some pointers.

Most stances started with the dominant arm forward. In the real world, where speed was everything, it paid to be able to get in a quick, strong jab to force an opponent off balance. The body was maneuvered almost sideways, like Jason's fencing technique, to shrink the target area. The ankles stayed loose with the feet in constant motion like a boxer. In short, it was a blend of practicality that felt comforting to Paul.

Paul advanced in the free-flowing stance. He varied his movement to prevent Whaley from locking on. He just had to get closer. Close combat was his domain. Strangely, Whaley did little to hinder him, only aiming steadily with the blue-glowing bow. A sky-colored arrow of energy sat ever ready.

With only a few feet to go, Paul planted a foot on a sturdy tree trunk, just above the roots. He sprang, not high in the air, but forward and slightly sideways. He rushed toward Whaley like a missile spouting green flame, but kept the ground within reach of his foot in case he needed to suddenly shift direction. His fist glowed with a lattice of black-green veins. It rebounded hard off the crystal-strengthened bow as Whaley went to block.

Paul had anticipated this. Luper had once taught him that, in close combat with weapons, the person who strikes first sometimes hits last. That was the technique of the counter, the parry-riposte. People tended to put them all behind one attack, not thinking about the future. If their momentum was jarringly halted, they were at a hard disadvantage. That was the bread and butter of a swordsman.

This was a feint, and the attack was half-hearted, only attempting to trigger a reaction. Paul anticipated the block. He only pretended to fall prey to the parry-riposte. His second hand was already on its way before Whaley could think of a riposte.

Paul could see right into his opponent's eyes now. Like the rest of his body, they were remarkably calm. Paul imagined that his own eyes blazed ferociously behind his mask.

Paul grabbed Whaley just underneath the shirt collar with his free hand. It was time to switch martial arts. He pulled Whaley off the ground upwards and then sideways while using his hip as a fulcrum, to the ground in a variation of judo's Tsurikomi Goshi throw. Whaley was evidently well-versed in the same styles of fighting. From the ground, he planted a foot in Paul's abdomen before using his arms to send Paul tumbling over him with a move reminiscent of judo's Tomoe Nage reversal. Instead of falling up with a pin or hold, Whaley rolled clear to stare back at him with his calm, almost-mocking eyes.

Paul could feel the frustration seeping deep into his bones. It was the beginning of the rage that he had was become all too accustomed to. He could feel the tidal waves of angry anima. It now felt like someone was screaming in his ears. Maybe it was just the voice in his head.

Some of the waves broke to the surface. Green flashes shot from Paul's back like a pair of giant wings.

I am Paul Engel, he struggled to tell himself. *I... I...*

The Alpha Amulus now hurled himself forward.

Whaley's mouth spewed spittle when a foot took him like a rocket into the nearest tree. The person before him had expressionless eyes of only burning green. An elbow was coming next.

Even pinned to the tree, Whaley dodged with a twist of his neck. The blazing elbow sent half of the trunk splintering.

Whaley dropped to his knees before a fist crashed through the remainder of the trunk. He then rolling, spitting from the dust and tearing up from the heat of his enemy's anima. Paul felt as though his own anima was tearing his body apart. He could not even stand straight.

The tree's branches landed with a series of thuds. With every thud, Paul doubled over farther and farther. Every boom was bringing him back to his senses. He hugged himself so hard that it hurt his chest and sides.

"P-Paul..." he whispered aloud. "I..."

Whaley only watched on in apparent concern. He did nothing to advance on his stricken opponent.

Paul caught his breath but could not stop the shaking.

"I had prayed that it would have been different for you."

Paul looked up to see Whaley resting nonchalantly against a tree.

"Shall we stop fighting now and talk about why I called you out here?"

CHAPTER 9
A BRANCH

"YOU DIDN'T CALL ME..."

Paul's voice trailed off as he thought. *Yes. It was too easy to find him. I thought it was a straightforward trap, but it's something different. That doesn't mean that there's not a trap at the end.*

"Yes, you see," applauded Emerson Whaley, "I knew you were intelligent, Paul. No, don't worry. There is no one else here to hurt you or even to hear me reveal your name."

"Forgive me if I don't trust you," blurted Paul with eyes on his forest surroundings.

"You don't necessarily have to trust me. Apologies for the shock as well. I thought it best to separate you from your weapon hidden in that backpack. I didn't want this to come to a situation that either of us regrets."

"So, what is this?" asked Paul.

There's no way Jackson would allow this. Talking to an enemy is not his protocol. You capture or kill, and that's it. Yet I'm not him.

"I will start by saying that we have some common ground," began Whaley.

He held up a hand, letting Paul see the back. Blue shades in the veins shimmered off and on. Each time they flickered, the hand trembled violently. Whaley grimaced as he put the hand down. The flashes stopped, but the tremors only slowed.

"As I said," the studious-looking man continued, "I had hopes that the same thing would not be happening to you. I hypothesized that, perhaps, you would not be suffering the same side effects as the other enhanced Amuli due to your added… quirks."

Am I really that easy to read? It's a problem to be so transparent in front of an enemy. He's not talking like an enemy, though.

"We were but rats in a lab," Whaley pointed out. "I am sure you were well aware of that. That perverted scientist was not as much a perfectionist as he let on. No, he failed to look at the long-term effects of enhancing an Amulus. I have a name for you to find. Bernardo Rodrigues, the only other enhanced Amuli left. Pray that you find only the name and not the man."

"Why tell me?" questioned Paul, who had just been comforted by spotting his sword on the ground. "Are you betraying A.I.M.?"

Whaley nodded slyly. "Betraying, but not leaving. It is a tougher life in this supernatural world to be a turncoat or a rogue. No, I am not leaving my comfort zone. I want to make this evident, there are those in A.I.M. that doubt A.I.M. I would bet everything that there are those in A.R.C. who doubt A.R.C., maybe even you."

Paul hardened his expression to prevent any cracks. "It's going to take more than that for me to turn away from A.R.C."

"Wise," commended Whaley. "Now, here is the real reason for this meeting. There is a man that once helped you. Now, he is very much in need of your help."

Paul only stared back, puzzled.

"You were once on your deathbed," explained Whaley. "One person stood up for you. He caused a commotion that gave you time and depleted your enemy's manpower, albeit unwittingly."

"Carson Colter," realized Paul.

Whaley nodded with a grin. "Yes. You may have been on the receiving end of his wrath, but I know that you find him to be an honorable man. He is a man of violence with a one-track mind. He is also a fine friend, a father, and an honest man. How many of the latter have you seen in this business?"

"You want A.R.C. to help a man who's killed A.R.C. operatives?" Paul shot back.

"No," answered Whaley with a knowing look. "I want you to help a man who needs it. I know that you have the mobility and the directive to act on your own. You can help him without anyone else knowing. I do not currently have that luxury. A certain man with a scary mask is nearly always looking over my shoulder these days."

Even though he was trying to keep his face blank, Paul knew that Whaley could read what he was thinking.

"What would you have me do?"

Whaley answered, "Primarily, it would be a simple warfare check. He tends to forget about the boring, everyday things in life. Leave him alone for too long and he basically stops taking care of himself. Remember that one-track mind. Food and supplies can be hard to come by where he is stationed. The only other thing would be to let him know if he needs to move and where he can go. He knows the safe spots to hide from A.I.M. but not the ones to hide from A.R.C."

"Where is he?" asked Paul, finally probing the level of trust.

"Someplace, you know very well. Where can you hide where everyone least expects it? His answer was somewhere where cover was already blown."

Paul nodded as the words clicked. "Why are you doing all this?"

Whaley threw his head back to embrace the blue sky. "I think that I have already implied that I feel the day that the current status quo is undone is coming. With the steps being taken by Red Mask, I am sure of that. His is a mad plan, creating chaos by making his own organization the enemy. No doubt he will rebrand it without the public's knowledge and pass it off as a new solution to the Amulus crisis. That is what I have gleaned. More than that, however, I need someone to help my friend. Now, you won't find two more different people than the two of us, but that is the beauty of it. I have always listened to my head, while Colter listens to his heart and emotions."

Just like Robby and I. "What do I get out of it?" he asked aloud.

Whaley answered. "In his early career, Colter would not listen to anyone. Because of that, he was often tasked with petty guard duty. Well, I know that you are looking for some prisoners."

Paul almost-absentmindedly slid back into a defensive stance. The hair stood raised on his fresh goosebumps.

Whaley raised a hand. "Relax. Believe me, relax. Not only will you get information, but I think you are far different from the usual operative. I can see an altruistic spirit in you. I can even feel it deep in your anima. You still want to be a good person. Most people I know have forgotten that feeling. It is refreshing to see."

Paul still eyed him with apprehension.

"Even now, you are focused on protecting the innocent. Please, help me get back to that. Make me feel like I am doing good again. It is all for a friend."

"I'll think about it," Paul answered honestly.

Whaley's ensuing nod was confident but not ecstatic.

"I think I would have liked to know you, Paul," he complimented.

"You know, before I became an Amulus, I was a tutor then. Wealthy parents paid me large amounts of money to make sure their children did well on the SATs and got into the best colleges. In a way, I was doing something I enjoyed. I was in the world of knowledge. My dissatisfaction came from the fact that my students did not share that passion. To them, knowledge was only a means to an end. They wanted a top college and to be let into the family business. They did not care what they learned, just as long as they learned it. I don't sense that feeling from you at all, Paul. I think that I would have much rather had a student like you. Alas, maybe someday."

Whaley melded into the brush. Paul could have followed him, but he did not.

CHAPTER 10
RUNNER

PAUL FELT like he was tearing through the underground base. Other agents stepped out of his way. Their eyes were wide with anticipation of some outburst from this superhuman of superhumans.

I hate that look. I think that, more than anything else, the worst feeling in the world happens when people look at you in a way that you don't want them to. I once stumbled over my words, and people thought I was stupid or socially inept. Now that I'm losing control, people look at me like I'm dangerous. Maybe I am. I don't want to be.

He then found someone in front of him who was worried for a different reason.

"Where have you been?" Camilla demanded. "It's been hours!"

Paul sighed, a gesture playing at confidence. "A mission from Jackson. It had to be kept secret, but it's over now."

"Well, tell him to buzz off sometimes," advised Camilla. "What? It's not like he can fire you from your team. You're now an Alpha Amulus, after all, and that carries weight. If you're being run ragged, you'll be less of a help to him, anyway."

Time to see how well I can act. I've never been good at it or even enthusiastic about trying it.

"You know what?' asked Paul rhetorically. "I've been thinking about what we've been talking about. I think that you're probably right. I should take some time to… regroup, at least. I might try going back to Pittsburgh for a while to see Robby."

If she ends up talking to Robby about this later, I will have burned down this friendship. It's for the best either way. The more distance I get from people, the better.

"Oh?" Camilla responded with an eyebrow confusedly twitching. "This isn't what... I thought you would take more convincing."

"I just need to get my mind off of things," Paul declared only slightly unsurely. "Robby is good at that."

"I guess he is," she admitted slowly. "Do you want me to come along?"

"I think that I have kept you long enough," answered Paul sincerely. "I'm guessing that your department is really busy."

"It is," she confirmed. "But... I think I made it clear that I put my friends first."

"Really," Paul said with the lies now weighing deep into his gut. "It's okay."

"If you say so. I'm just glad you're taking steps. I will give you some space then."

She watched Paul carefully as he went to confirm his plans at the desk.

Paul was glad not to be facing her anymore. His face was now red, and he could feel beads of moisture forming underneath his hair follicles. *I'm not sure if I will be able to face her again. It's the right thing to do, but all I feel is guilt.*

His fingers clenched the desk tightly as he spoke to Callie, "I need another plane. This one to Pittsburgh or as close as you can get me, given the circumstances."

"The east coast is a little... hard now," she pondered aloud as she tapped the keys. "I guess Pittsburgh is far enough inland that it's a little less hectic right now. I think I can get you one."

Paul could not help looking back at Camilla one last time before leaving to collect his things. In his office, he clicked on his tablet. Jackson's face was waiting.

"Well?"

Paul took a deep breath. *No lies this time. He'll see through them. I just need to tell as much of the truth as I can safely.*

"I encountered Whaley," Paul reported. "There was a... misunderstanding and a scuffle. He ended up getting away, but he dropped information."

"I thought that it was well within your abilities as the Alpha to capture or put down any lone Amuli, enhanced or otherwise," interrupted Jackson disapprovingly.

"He got the drop on me," explained Paul, succeeding in taking any hint of whining out of his tone.

"I suppose that I can understand that," relented Jackson with no change in his deep voice. "Some things in battle never change, even as things grow stranger."

Paul nodded, relieved, as if a cool drop of water was soothing his back.

"We spoke," Paul continued. "He did drop some hints."

"Hints like what?" demanded Jackson.

There's no beating around the bush with him.

"I took it with a lot of speculation, but he may not be as onboard with A.I.M. as he appears."

Jackson finally glanced away from Paul as he thought.

"It would be strange to suddenly grow a conscience," he murmured. "A.I.M. operatives are typically so indoctrinated. Still, Whaley is an academic, and they often do not yield to the established order. Your speculation is wise. I can't say that we wouldn't welcome someone of his power level into A.R.C."

"I got the sense that he wouldn't stand with A.R.C. either," added Paul.

"Rubbish!" Jackson brushed off. "Rogue Amuli with no structure are a threat to others and to themselves. Wolves survive better in a pack than alone."

There's more," continued Paul, eager for Jackson's negativity to end. "Whaley gave me a lead on an A.I.M. agent who used to be a guard. Apparently, he's close to my old base."

"Why would he tell you this?" questioned Jackson.

Paul shrugged. "I guess I'm a better actor than I let on."

"Deception's never been my way," Jackson admitted. "I prefer it when everything is straightforward and makes sense. Let me guess, you wish to scope this out yourself?"

"Yes," answered Paul quickly. "I know the area and need the mobility. I've already seen about booking a flight."

Jackson responded after intensely drumming his thumbs for a few moments. "Granted. Power and mobility are what this strike force is made of. One thing to be wary of, however. I would not be so trusting of the words of A.I.M. operatives. As you've experienced, most are brainwashed and some are half-mad. You could well be walking into another trap. If so, spring it, run or fight, and let no one trick you again. I have faith in your venture to decide whether Whaley's words are falsehoods or truths."

The screen flickered to black.

Paul let out a deep sigh, but a deep, gnawing feeling would not let him relax. It seemed to always be there now for one reason or another.

Now, it's time to walk into a trap or deal with Carson Colter. I'm not sure which is worse.

CHAPTER 11
HOMECOMING

PAUL HAD BARELY DRIVEN in the area around his hometown. After all, he had not even had his license for a year before he joined A.R.C. An outsider may have found the roads ridged by nothing but trees and steep hills claustrophobic. To Paul, it was comforting. It was like being embraced by a familiar blanket.

It was only while driving that he would understand the local complaints about the roads. The months of snow and ice every year chipped into the pavement and left loose gravel and potholes. Between that and the ups and downs of the hills, it was almost a roller coaster at times.

He stopped to make way for deer more than once. Before, he could not have imagined being a hunter. Still, he had respect for those who put deer on tables and out of car grills. Those were the top two enemies of everyone in the area, deer and whose ever job it was to fix the roads.

I need to stop being nostalgic and distracted. I need to focus on the mission. Just the mission.

There were more flashbacks to come, however, when he pulled up to a general store. Despite himself, he wondered if Lou was nearby as he exited the car. There was no truck and the stained-wood building appeared closed for the day. *This place is so a tight-knit area that any new car will probably stick out here, but it would stick out more if I abandoned it at the side of a road.*

Oddly enough, he seemed to sense the direction of the abandoned bunker. *I've always had a good memory. That's the only reason I always did well in school.*

He took off into the trees and brush. Once again, he felt like this could have been months ago. Luper would be waiting for a report at the bunker before providing some wise advice. Camilla would be waiting for conversation at the improvised dinner table. Alice would be tending her plants. Jason would still be in one of the workout rooms, pounding away on some poor wooden post. When reality sunk in, he realized how far he had gone to keep himself alone.

He lost sense of time amongst the scraggly bushes. There was a monotony to the woodsy surroundings. Sticks, leaves, and dirt just repeated before him ad nauseam. The last clearing emerged before he knew it.

What had once been the shed was now lumber, halfway into the sunk ground. Moss was already growing over it, and the grass was poking out among some of the splinters. Paul knew that the next winter would probably eliminate all trace. There would nothing to mark the compound underneath of it all.

Paul tried to remember where the opening had been. Clearly, when A.R.C. had left, they let the ground reclaim it. *I may have to do some digging.*

He suddenly felt a strange, forceful nudge against his back.

"Stop right there!"

But I didn't sense any anima.

With one motion of his arm, he drew his sword and struck behind him. This was Batto Jutsu, the art of sword drawing, which could more aptly be named, "the art of sword drawing and slashing at the same time."

A metal gun barrel when flying before Paul's masked face as he spun around.

Paul stopped any follow-up when he saw the shocked face before him.

"Ja-" Paul began shouting before stopping himself.

Jack Dawson's arms shot straight up. His wide eyes looked like only marbles while still.

Paul lowered his katana from his former classmate's throat. *What is he even doing here? This is my old school bully, and he's just randomly here? We're miles from town! This is just like Robby finding me in that sewer.*

It took him a second to realize that his mask was on and that his identity was safe.

"Easy now," Jack braved in a whisper. "Don't mean any harm."

You just held a gun to me!

Paul's heart beat rapidly, and his mind worked quickly. The rest of his body was frozen. *He might know…*

Paul abruptly coughed a few times, trying to make his voice harsher. He could not risk testing his voice out before actually speaking.

"Where is he?" Paul barked in a voice far deeper than his usual one.

He tried to rein it in to keep it from being too cartoonish.

"Who?" asked Jack.

From the twitches in his face, Paul could see that he was playing.

"You know," Paul murmured gruffly as he brought the sword back up, adding a tongue of flame for good measure.

"Yeah! Alright! Alright!" he cracked. "Down in the hole."

"Show me."

Jack uncovered some cracked boards to reveal what remained of the hatch. The locking mechanism no longer functioned, but the trapdoor still opened and shut.

The two traversed the rungs, where Paul discovered that more than a few were now missing. The same could be said for the lights on the ground floor.

Jack led Paul towards the pantry. From the corners of his vision, he could see the workout equipment, chairs, tables, and computers were all overturned with many straying far from their original locations. They had to side-step a couple of cracked monitors. Paul knew that all computers, hard drives, and hard records would be gone—swept up by the A.R.C. clean-up crew.

Jack opened up the still-functional door to the pantry. The hulking figure of Carson Colter sat at the edge of a bed.

My old bed. Paul realized with a hint of amusement.

The former-A.I.M. operative's face lit up with a slow smile.

"Yo!" he waved. "Fancy meeting you here, frowny face. You know I know what ya look like, right?"

Paul kept the mask on his face.

Colter shrugged. "Suite yourself. You come to bring me into A.R.C.? Gonna give me a good fight than like the last time?"

"I need information," Paul demanded gravely. "I heard you used to be a guard over normals."

"Maybe I was," said Colter playfully. "What are you gonna do for me?"

"I can track down your kid," informed Paul. "You can see him."

Colter shook his head. "And scare the ex-wife away, too? Nah. If she's around, any visit's gonna be short."

Colter stretched his legs after sliding off the bed.

"I've got a better idea. You gave me a good fight one time. I appreciate that. Let's do it again. After, I'll tell ya about when I guarded normies if you win."

"One of us may not walk away," scoffed Paul.

"No," disagreed Colter. "We'll do it smart. No weapons. We'll toss them on the surface and fight down here. If I win... geez, I don't know... maybe you'll end up hanging around here a couple of days and fight me again. It's your old stomping grounds, so you'll be cozy."

"Fine."

As strong as Colter is, he's not enhanced, and he's not an Alpha. The odds are in my favor. I don't have to worry about Jack running off with my sword. Even away from me, that crystal will burn hotter than a normal person can handle during the fight. Still, this feels like another pointless fight. Another waste of time.

"Kid," Colter addressed Jack. "Get out of here for a while. With everything that'll be flying around down there, you'd be killed in two seconds flat. Bunker walls don't protect you when you're locked in with the danger. Come back when you stop hearing the sounds of booms and hitting."

"I kinda want to see it," complained Jack.

Colter itched his neck.

"I guess... you can look down from the hole. Just don't get your head blown off by flying anima."

With Jack taking katana and claymore to the surface, Paul settled into position. He decided it was time for more Jeet-Kune-Do. When he had started as an Amulus fighter, he may have opted to start with judo or ju-jitsu straightaway to compensate for the size difference between himself and Colter. That would have used his opponent's weight against himself. Now, Paul's strength had outgrown his size. He wanted speed and a quick end.

He paced in place.

Colter looked more like a boxer. Both fists were raised.

People see Colter is an airhead. He's quite intelligent in the one thing he likes, fighting.

Not one for subtlety, Colter charged ahead.

Somewhere, despite his focus, Paul felt the world begin to change. At first, he thought it was the numbing, overwhelming stress he had been experiencing lately. This feeling took him to a new place altogether.

Not now! Why are you sending this to me now? Do you want me to die?

———

Gareth Jackson slid a keycard into an electronic lock. His hair had more black in it but only at the very top. The man inside the cell cowered when the light struck him. He wriggled off of his bed.

"You have my say-so," Jackson announced grimly. "We have little choice but to use your plan, doctor. Just know that you are A.I.M. We are A.R.C. What you do today will not expunge your filth.

The Scientist scurried forward excitedly.

"I only wish to-"

"Silence!" interrupted Jackson. "You will do nothing that you have not been ordered to do. Frankly, my men would be ashamed of me for letting you out."

He swung the man roughly by the arm as he brought him to another locked room with a heavy, metal door.

There was something muffled behind the door. It was strangely high-pitched and pleasant, like birds chirping.

There were two young girls sitting on metal chairs inside. The one who had been talking stopped upon seeing their approach. Her expression hardened as she nervously smoothed out a pant leg.

The other one had been silent. She was hooked into a contraption full of I.V. bags and tubes. Her expression was listless. Her blue eyes were as still as an ocean without currents.

The Scientist pointed to the cluster of medical equipment without speaking.

"Yes?" said Jackson impatiently.

"The amount will need to be decreased," The Scientist explained. "A high dose will cloud the effects of the procedure."

"I suppose if she kills you, you are expendable anyway."

The Scientist took down some of the bags of liquid. He then motioned for Ling to touch the golden star crystal around Alice's neck. He had Alice do the same to Ling's red crystal.

"Atlantean," The Scientist addressed Alice. "You will concentrate all of your Psychic energy on the girl's crystal. You may begin. Do not stop."

"Is that all?" questioned Jackson skeptically.

"It is a hypothesis," warned The Scientist. "Through my research, I believe that the gold crystal has properties far different from yours or mine. It has already taken on anima from multiple Amuli in the past. It both releases, as a regular crystal does, and stores. Perhaps then, the power can be shared. If shared power may decrease the amount of strain on the Atlantean. It may even be halved. I warn you, however, it is only a hypothesis as I said. If only there were more subjects!"

Jackson raised a firm hand. "Enough!"

Alice's hand was eradicating Ling's crystal with golden light. Ling twitched in her chair for a moment, apparently in discomfort.

As the golden light gradually overwhelmed the red one, Ling began squirming. Eventually, she was sobbing. Even Alice's sedated and stoic expression changed to one of worry as she saw the look on her partner's face.

"Continue!" shouted The Scientist excitedly.

Jackson said nothing.

Finally, Ling grew rigid. Her back was straight, and her expression was pure blankness.

The Scientist rushed in to observe her. He pulled up her chin to gaze into her eyes. There was no longer any brown. There was only black and white.

Jackson caught The Scientist with a backhand, sending him spinning to the floor.

"A Dead Eyes!" he cried. "You turned a promising Psychic into a damn Dead Eyes!"

"I... I... s... said that it was merely... a hypothesis," stammered The Scientist.

Jackson shook his head. "I should have known! You're all damn cult members!"

He pressed a heavy boot on the man's ribs.

"You're going in a hole," Jackson threatened. "I'm putting you on a transport, and then they will throw you down in a hole. You will suffer worse than this girl did."

————

As the vision ended, Paul could feel the air rushing off Colter's thick fist.

CHAPTER 12
POINTLESS

PAUL REACTED JUST in time to block Colter's speeding fist with his forearm. That was, perhaps, the real strength of Jeet-Kune-Do, the ability to absorb an impact and counter. *Be like water.* Robby had mentioned that quote enough times for Paul to grow sick of it. Nevertheless, the principle was true.

Even as the fist painfully impacted, Paul let the kinetic energy rush through him. He let his body go fluid. He would not let himself be like a wooden board that would break. He had to be something closer to Jell-O.

Colter's fist was tied up after his punch, and that meant his momentum and one striking limb were briefly stopped. Paul would have countered. Here was the opportunity for parry-riposte again. However, he was distracted, and now his stomach was bundled tight.

Jackson! He used the Scientist to—that was disgusting! How could you ever trust that madman! What he—they—did to Ling was unforgivable! Does Jason know what happened? Why didn't Alice tell me? I guess I never gave her the chance. No wonder she's never wanted to be close to anyone. Jackson! The Scientist! What they did to Ling and Alice! And I've been working for Jackson…

Colter followed up with his other fist. His fighting style was like a train. He would pound through full-speed-ahead or derail. That risky technique was part of the thrill for him.

Paul turned to block the other one. Still, he did not counter. *I have to be careful, too. I can win, but he has to be able to talk afterward. I don't even know if I can risk knocking him out. I may lose too much time! I have… I have to…*

The tightness spread from his stomach. It was in his chest. It was in his shoulder and arms. He could swear that it was pulling muscles without his consent. He did not notice the green anima raising from him. Its flares were rimmed with black.

He was being pulled tighter, and it hurt. His mind was going blank. He could not remember what he had been thinking the previous moment. The anima was becoming a swirling inferno.

My name is Paul Engel! He tried desperately to rein it in. *I can't lose it… I can't…*

Colter was struck by a burning tidal wave. He slid backward, shielding himself by raising his forearms in an "X." By the time he put them down, they were bright red and throbbing.

"Kid," the large man awed.

An anima storm was enveloping the entire bunker. Black-green fire and lightning split the wooden doorways. Some pieces of debris flung upwards, and others were incinerated. Colter had to squint his eyes within the bursts of flaming wind. He could not even make out what had been a teenage boy in front of him.

"This is what I've been waiting my whole life see!" Colter cried. "Something as awesome as this."

Then he sensed the feeling on the anima. It was frustration, confusion, and aimlessness. Just feeling it made him want to pace around.

"Kid!" Colter called worriedly. "Are you even in there?"

A figure made of anima fire surged out of the hurricane.

Colter was hit by a shoulder, and his own ribs crackled. He found himself in a crater where a wall had been. The figure loomed over him.

From his back, Colter dodged just in time for a fist to create a second crater. He scurried to his feet and put distance between himself and the figure.

It seemed confused. Colter was no longer there, but it kept pounding the wall and was now rupturing concrete. Then it stopped.

It still burned, but sat on its knees with its arms on the floor.

"Kid," addressed Colter. "What did they do to ya?"

Seizing the silence, he begrudgingly made his way to the disheveled rungs. He was not followed.

He caught his breath as he emerged in the summer air. He then bent down, clutching the metal hatch with both hands. The metal steamed until it went yellow. Colter let it melt together, erasing the opening.

"The hell was that?" shouted Jack while inches from his face.

Colter caught his breath.

"N-never. I've never run from a fight like that. No, it wasn't a fight anyway. What did they do?"

"So, that's not normal with Amuli?" asked Jack. "I thought super-strength and energy explosions were big things with you guys."

Colter shook his head.

"Never seen anything like it. Yeah, that stuff happens, but never to this degree. The energy. The intensity. He lost his mind. I know they experimented on him. I know about Dead Eyes, but not something like this."

Carson finally looked the sweaty Jack over.

"I see my sword. Where's his?"

"I... I..." stammered Jack, wincing. "When he went nuclear, his sword started burning me. I kinda dropped it down the hole."

"Now, there's no way anyone's getting down there!" exclaimed Colter. "He may burn it all out of him, but he's so different from other Amuli and that may not happen soon. This is bad news. Real bad news."

"So, what we do? demanded Jack. "I mean, my curfew's even coming up soon."

Colter cursed. He was about to rub sweat off of his face, but now realized how bad his burnt arms were hurting.

"I've been trying to avoid everyone out here. I said that if anyone came, at least I get a good fight til the end. Now, I gotta call someone or someones. Get out your phone."

"Uh," moaned Jack. "No service. I mean, think about where we are."

Colter cursed again. He roughly grabbed Jack by the waist.

"Hey! Hey! Put me down! Whatcha doing?"

"We're going to town," he answered, almost complaining. "Everything'll be faster if I carry ya. You'll even make your curfew."

CHAPTER 13
THE MISSING

"MORE GAS!" shouted a man from behind a computer monitor.

"You don't have to tell me!"

The young man who answered was saddled on the back of a motor-cycle without a paint job. The gray urban camouflage and helmet that the youth wore blended into the bare metal. The cycle was without wheels and wires zigzagged into the engine.

"Right there!"

"She can take more!"

The machine began humming at a higher pitch. It then whined before grinding.

The young man stepped away from the motorcycle as the engine faded.

"I said it was good at that RPM," admonished the man behind the computer before taking a swig of soda from a Styrofoam cup.

Robby Swanson took off his helmet before patting the man on the shoulder.

"I thought we were testing how much she could take," he explained with his ever-present grin. "We weren't just seeing what she's good at."

The worker sighed. "You're going to fix whatever went wrong this time. Now, I've got to look through my log of the readings."

Robby tinkered with a bolt.

"I think we're going too hard on the engine," he thought aloud.

"You mean you're going too hard on it," clarified the man clicking the keyboard.

"No, that's not what I mean," explained Robby. "It's the size. She's giving all she's got, but it's not enough."

The worker sighed again. "You want us to throw out the whole design again? Look, we either have a weight problem or a speed problem. That's what you get with electric motors. They are just too heavy. We just want to be able to maneuver, right?"

"You ever fought an Amulus?" Robby questioned.

"No," admitted the man.

"Then trust me," insisted Robby, "when things go south, you'll want to get out of there in a hurry."

"All I hear is more work," his assistant murmured.

Robby playfully slapped him on the back, harder than he was expecting. He coughed on a swig from his straw.

"Just think, we'll be the ones who solved this problem for all bikers. Well, for A.R.C.-Human bikers for now… and for the foreseeable future. But, someday, bikers everywhere!"

"I'm not even a biker," complained the man.

They were interrupted by a self-assured voice at the doorway.

"Well, well, well. Robby Swanson. Always playing with his toys."

Robby's permanent smile grew wider.

"Cam 'The Bella' Bellano."

The girl with streaming, dark hair stifled a laugh.

"Did you just call me the 'girl' or the 'beautiful?' I'm Italian and Colombian, remember?"

Robby shook his head emphatically. "Why not both?"

Camilla coughed, not wanting him to hear her laugh.

"Take five, Blake," said Robby to the assistant. "Anyway, Cam, you should see the new drones!"

Blake half-stumbled away, still sucking down on his straw. Camilla recognized in his beleaguered expression that he must have been subjected to working with Robby Swanson for a while now. Robby himself was stroking the side of a drone with two large propellers and a porcelain white finish. The entire rig, complete with gun placements, was larger than he was.

"So, what's that on your lip?" she questioned, walking closer to observe Robby's face.

"As you can see," he said as he stroked his fuzzy upper lip. "I've become a man in both age and physical form."

"I thought it was dirt at first," admitted Camilla playfully. "I can tell that Paul hasn't been around you much lately. It seems like one of the things that he'd talk you out of."

"He has the book smarts," Robby explained. "I have the street smarts."

"Many people on the street have a dirt-stache?"

"Tons!" bragged Robby.

"All right, enough of you. Where's Paul?"

Robby scratched his forehead with a wrench. "That's something I would like to know."

"Wait! He's not here?" asked Camilla, surprised.

"He's been around here?" said Robby as he impatiently jogged towards the doorway. "Let's go find him then!"

"Hold up!" Camilla exclaimed, stopping him with a tug of his shirt. "If he hasn't been around to see you, then he isn't here. Weird. I thought he was going to. He isn't the type to lie. That's more your speed."

"What did he tell you exactly?" queried Robby.

"He said that he was coming here to see you because he needed a break. Clearly, you're someone who can disconnect anyone from reality. He left way before me. He should have been here by now. I was just stopping by since it's pretty hard to get a plane straight into the east coast right now."

"That's trouble," pointed out Robby. "The only time when Paul lies is when he knows that he's taking on too much himself. It's like this. Back in school, he let everyone copy his homework during first period. That's like lying to teachers, right? Well, one person would pass the homework straight on to the next person, and that kept going. So, during the break before second period when he needed the homework, Paul had to scramble to ask everyone in our grade about who had his homework at that point. You know how much Paul loves to get up and talk to someone he doesn't know or barely knows."

"That sounds like him," affirmed Camilla. "Basically, Paul always wants to solve everyone else's problems but in the background. That reminds me of something he said to me. He talked about how A.I.M. convinced him that all of us were dead. He told me that we had all once died to him. Now that he has us back, he doesn't want to lose us."

"It's not that," Robby disagreed, losing his smile. "He's okay not being around us. He's used to being a loner. He just wants to know that we are okay."

"Basically, he is a really smart, caring guy who has over thought himself into doing something stupid," summed up Camilla. "For once, he's the one doing something stupid. So, where do we find him?"

"Hmm," Robby thought. "That's the problem with smart people, they're good at things like hiding. Is there anyone who knows where he could be?"

"He's on a special strike force directly under Speaker Jackson," related Camilla. "Everything is on a need-to-know-basis at that point."

"Do we know anyone else on the strike force?"

"One," gulped Camilla.

————

"No," answered Jason quickly.

"You have no idea where he is?" questioned Camilla from the other side of the phone.

"No."

"Do you know anyone who does?" pressed Camilla.

"Jackson. Probably."

"He's not really on option, right?"

"Nope."

"Urgh," moaned Camilla as she hung up the closed-system phone. "He was a great conversation, like always."

Robby's cell phone vibrated noisily from his pocket for the third time.

"You going to get that?" complained Camilla. "I thought that A.R.C. banned non-official means of communication between agents."

Robby shrugged as he went to answer. "I can't help it if I'm popular."

"Safety be damned, right?"

Robby's eyebrows went strangely uneven while he listened. "So, this isn't about computer class homework?"

After a few minutes of strange wincing and answering, Robby slid the phone back into his pocket.

"I found him," Robby finally announced, looking more worried than Camilla had ever seen him. "We're going to have to find someone else first."

CHAPTER 14
GET THE GIRL

"I HAVE A PLAN," declared Robby.

"Is it as crazy as any of your other plans?"

"I don't do any other type of plan."

"So, let me get this straight," Camilla began, "the situation is crazy already. Carson Colter and a kid from your high school called the official A.R.C. hotline, saying that an agent, Paul, was in trouble. Your cousin, Jess, passed him off to you after his name popped up on caller ID because she was used to hearing you complain about him. Apparently, Paul is out of control because of whatever they did to him at A.I.M., and now he's locked in our old, underground bunker. Is there any way this doesn't get any more messed up?"

"It's about to," Robby said. "We can't let Jackson know. He'll end up scrapping whatever Paul was doing and throw him a cell. We need some people that we can trust to help out."

"How do we help him?" questioned Camilla. "We don't know what A.I.M. did to him."

"But," started Robby, "we do know someone who seems to know a lot about weird Amulus powers."

"Alice," realized Camilla. "She would help Paul, but we don't even know where she is."

"Who does?"

"That's another encrypted file," relayed Camilla. "Any higher-up could look at it."

"Are there any higher-ups that you trust?"

"You mean, besides your cousin."

Robby shook his head. "A.R.C. files and A.R.C.-Human files are sepa-rate. You don't think that I haven't already used her credentials to find what Paul's been up to?"

"I guess I should know you better than that," admitted Camilla slyly. "As far as people I trust go. Sometimes, I forget what a shady business this is. I can't think of many. Grady would be number one, but he's only a city leader and doesn't have that level of clearance. I know Adam Avery helped us out of the mess at the bunker. He was also the only one who was nice to us and seemed to care during the oversight investigation. Still, that may have just been putting on a face."

Robby smoothed over his fuzzy mustache as he thought.

"I remember Paul talking about someone he knows in the Research Division. There is a guy who was friends with his parents."

"Those are both half-leads, though," Camilla pointed out. "There is one guy that would have the information that we don't totally trust. There is another guy who works on a completely different type of assign-ment and only might have the information, but we can probably trust him."

"They both fit into the plan, though," formulated Robby. "They both can have their roles. We can tell the research guy what is really going on and make him keep it a secret in the name of Paul's safety. He can put out feelers and help out but can only do so much. He's like a backup plan. With Avery, we don't even have to explain to him that we're looking for Alice to help Paul. We can just say that we want to see her for… her birthday or something. When's her birthday, anyway?"

"I don't know," admitted Camilla. "I kind of feel bad about that."

"You were fighting together like sisters-in-arms for like a year, and you never figured out her birthday?"

Camilla shrugged. "I mean, you've met Alice."

"Well," relented Robby, "I guess we can just make up an excuse along the way. I'm good at improv."

"Is this one of the things that you just say you're good at impressing me?" pressed Camilla. "Still, the way you cooked up this plan so fast, it's almost scary. Do you secretly play mind games with people all the time?"

Robby smiled as he made a show of putting his hands on his hips. "I'm a con-man. It's all about the con."

"This really isn't a con."

———

"Uh huh," Robby nodded despite talking over the phone. "Right, Mr. Avery. We were supposed to meet up for a surprise party, but we lost her contact information."

A few steps away, Camilla muttered, "Why did I agree to let him do the talking?"

"Oh, it's because it's classified. That explains a lot."

Camilla started staring daggers at him.

"Yes, Mr. Avery, group bonding is important. I agree. That's why this visit is important. Yes, we are helping her with her social skills. Does Paul know? Hhmmm."

"Change the topic!" Camilla hissed.

"Well, he's busy with Speaker Jackson's team and all that."

Robby was quiet for a few moments before Camilla heard him again.

"Yes, thank you, Mr. Avery. Oh, I mean Adam. Yes, I will call you Adam. And, hey, Adam, this is kind of a weird question, but I heard that Paul knows someone from your research division. Do you know who that might be? He knew his parents or something. His name was like Ham or Hammy or something."

Camilla was now surprised that she was not sweating.

"Why do I need to know that? Um…" Robby thought aloud. "You know, Paul is working so hard. We thought another doing another get-together with him. That's probably something will talk about with Alice. Yeah, it's kind of a lot of get-togethers, but work is stressful. Not that you give us too much to do, but we are still teenagers, kinda."

Sensing Camilla looking at him, Robby gave her a confidant wink.

"Yes, I do realize that it will be hard to convince Jackson. You know, we're just gonna try."

Robby motioned for Camilla to hand him the pen and paper on the nearby desk.

"Right. Right. Thanks, Adam."

Robby said goodbye and hung up. He held up Alice's address and Dr. Hamilton's phone number.

"Well, it's time for phone call number two!"

Camilla reached over and snatched the phone from a surprised Robby.

"Oh no. That last call almost gave me a heart attack. I'm handling this one."

———

"You know," Robby began. "I really thought college was all about crazy parties. Seeing this is all really disappointing."

"This is the summer term," sighed Camilla. "Of course, there is next to no one here."

The building smelled like new carpet in the hallways and Pine-Sol in the common areas. Camilla and Robby passed one common area with glass on all sides. Instead of letting in light, it let in the shadow of the adjacent building. In the hallways, bulletin boards overflowed with old club flyers and campus advertisements.

"It's pretty nice," commented Camilla as she surveyed the bright blue walls.

"I thought that college dorms were supposed to be rundown," complained Robby. "You know, full of character. That's why everyone moves into frat houses."

"You watch too many movies," realized Camilla.

Alice's name was posted on her door in the form of a heart poster.

"Oh no," Robby started sarcastically. "She's changed, too. That wasn't her style."

"The RA's make those," explained Camilla. "Have you seriously never been invited into a college dorm?"

"Ouch."

They knocked on the door. The door only cracked open.

"Yes?"

"Surprise!" shouted Robby.

"This is actually kind of serious," berated Camilla.

"Welcome," said Alice somberly.

The suite had one simple bed on one side. The other side was filled with vine plants. One snaked over a windowsill which was dotted with flowerpots. Two desks were pushed together with a single blue floor plan draped over them. It was held down by a teacup.

"May I help you to some…" Alice surveyed the room and only found the teacup. "… green tea or water?"

"I'm good," answered Robby, trying not to be creeped out by Alice's blank expression and tone.

"No thanks," gulped Camilla.

"Forgive me," apologized Alice with her head downcast. "I am still learning the intricacies of friendly communication. It is far more complex than I previously thought."

"It's all right," said Camilla. "Really."

"You said 'surprise,'" Alice thought aloud. "I believe that indicates a social occasion. A surprise party, for example. Though, it is not my birthday. That is in December. A surprise from friends? Then, that means I should continue the conversation. How is your relationship?"

Camilla let out something between an exhale and a scream.

"Great!" replied Robby.

"Excuse me!" exclaimed Camilla before she let her face turn back from red. "You are reading too much into this."

Alice lowered her head again.

"I apologize," she said sincerely. "As I said, I am still new to social graces. Two of my classmates have been aiding me by showing me movies. I have learned that, in romances, the couple typically treats each other with distrust and sometimes contempt at first. The circumstances of their lives then forced them together. Both occurrences have happened in your cases. I see now that I was mistaken in my perception of these trends."

Camilla kept a hand over her eyes. "I really want to know who your new friends are and what movies they've been showing you. What you've been seeing are called movie tropes."

"I appreciate your knowledge," thanked Alice as she produced a notebook and began jotting something down.

"You don't need to…" Camilla started. "In all seriousness, there is something major going on, and we need you."

She and Robby explained Paul's predicament based on all the knowledge they had. By the end, Alice was sitting on her bed. Her expression reminded Camilla of the Alice she had first met. Her large, blue eyes were nearly vacant. They seemed to be welling but never produced a running tear.

"This was my greatest fear," she finally spoke faintly. "I am beyond selfish. My very existence and actions cause nothing but pain to good people."

"Hey," Camilla interrupted softly. "Don't say that. Don't ever say something like that. We all know that it's hard for you. I can say that everyone I know who has been around you does not think like that."

"That is because you do not even know what I am," Alice said. "A.R.C. has kept truths, and I have kept truths. You would not say those words if you knew the truth about my existence."

"Tell us then," Camilla cajoled her. "I'll be the judge of that, but I can tell you that it won't change a thing. We've fought together as teammates."

Alice responded by pulling up the metal string around her pale neck.

"Whoa!" shouted Robby. "What happened to your crystal? I thought they were connected to stuff like forever."

Alice responded huskily. "Paul has it now."

"That's not possible," Camilla disagreed in disbelief. "Everyone knows that it's one crystal, one Amulus."

"It is for every crystal except the one I had," Alice explained. "It was not even my crystal."

"But, you're an Amulus, so you have a crystal somewhere, right?" Robby questioned. Alice continued without meeting their eyes. "You could say that I am not human. I am neither a human nor a normal Amulus. What I am goes back to how Amuli began."

"I'm getting goosebumps," admitted Robby.

"You both understand that both A.R.C. and A.I.M. hide many things from the greater world," Alice continued. "They hide even more from their own operatives. Amuli did not first emerge during the Cold War. They have existed for centuries as legends at the outskirts of societies. Only as the world became more interconnected, did they have the chance to come to power in the forms of A.R.C. and A.I.M. The most prevalent use of anima weapons came from a society only recently discovered by A.R.C. They have kept most of the information about that place secret."

"Atlantis!" inferred Robby. "You know, I did a report on it in school."

Alice nodded. "From the information I was given, it seems that the Atlanteans used anima crystals as part of their daily lives. They did this for centuries and incorporated a number of rituals that A.I.M. now undertakes. Anima crystals somehow were incorporated into their very DNA, which was passed from parent to child. Those Atlanteans were my ancestors."

"You were an Amulus from the beginning," realized Camilla. "How many Atlanteans are there?"

"As I understand it," Alice replied stoically. "I am the only one remaining."

"Where did they all go?" questioned Robby.

Alice answered. "It seems that the less Atlantean genes one has, the less likely it is for her or him to manifest powers naturally. There may be other descendants of the Atlanteans, but they do not present the recessive genes."

"To put this... delicately," Robby stammered with morbid curiosity. "Nothing Lannister-esque happened, did it?

"Not in the past several generations to my knowledge," Alice replied without embarrassment. "I appreciate your willingness to quiz me on today's pop culture. No, I am told that my father's family fled to the United States long ago to escape witch-hunts. My mother's family did likewise by first moving to remote northern Scandinavia before coming to the United States as well. They were the last two of their kind and were matched for the preservation of the line."

"That… shouldn't happen," struggled Camilla. "Today, people shouldn't be forced like that. I'm guessing it was tough for you."

"I did not know them truly," Alice stated. "They perished before I could even form memories. It seems that they finally fought for control over their own lives and died."

For once, Robby was speechless. Camilla tried.

"I don't believe it," she breathed hoarsely. "Things like that happened in the background of everyone's daily lives? I was going to kindergarten, while you were an A.R.C. test subject?"

"I do not know if my life was good or bad for me," Alice articulated. "It was all I knew. I can say, however, that my life has not been good for others."

"So," Robby finally ventured. "What does this have to do with the Paul situation?"

Alice touched her empty necklace again. Her eyes looked far away from them in shame.

"As you know, I once did have a crystal. It was a free crystal that only magnifies Atlantean powers, one passed down on my mother's side of the family. It was the only one that I know of that has been activated without an Amulus. It is possibly a remnant of Atlantis. When I found Paul, it seems that an A.I.M. researcher had somehow found a way to break anima crystals. I am sure that you thought that this was another impossibility. He was using the broken shards to increase the power of other Amuli by injecting the shards into their bloodstreams. Paul's crystal was broken, and he was dying. My life probably seems very strange to you because of this, but this is the first time I felt despair. I decided to force the free crystal to bond to Paul. It listened."

"So, what's happening now?" Camilla wondered. "Is it rejecting him?"

"Not quite," Alice analyzed. "Anima use in any way is probably unnatural. It causes strain on both the body and mind. The free crystal contains residual anima from all of its previous holders. That is where the amplification comes from. The combination of the crystal injection and free crystal must be wreaking havoc on Paul's mind, and he did not even grow up with the crystal as I did. The crystal had a very negative impact on my own mind. I can only speculate what is happening to Paul. It is all my fault."

"No way!" disagreed Camilla. "From what you just said, you're the one who kept him alive."

"Yes," Alice answered meekly. "I also cursed him and then left him."

"He's the one who has been pushing everyone away, including you," reminded Camilla. "He thinks he's protecting us, but he's just hurting himself."

"I take it that you would get on a plane with us?" guessed Robby. "As soon as possible?"

Alice fervently nodded.

"I wonder if A.R.C. has frequent flyer miles," quipped Camilla.

CHAPTER 15
BENEATH

"IF THAT'S how you drive a car, then I'd hate to see how you drive a motorcycle!" Camilla shouted as she stepped out of the sedan.

"It's the roads," Robby blamed after a neck scratch. "Ask anyone around here. They exist to murder you. The same thing with the kamikaze deer."

Another individual was climbing out of a similar dark-colored vehicle. His thin arms hung about him as his suit sleeves flapped in the breeze. He produced a stack of manilla folders from the car's trunk.

Camilla and Robby walked towards him side-by-side.

"What a minute!" Camilla interrupted as she gestured toward Robby. "Standing next to you it's like... did you get taller? Did you actually get taller? You're almost as tall as me!"

"Told you," sneered Robby as he streaked his barely-there mustache. "I'm a man now."

The thin man looked up from his papers long enough to give both of them a quick handshake.

"Dr. Hamilton Barnes. I feel really glad that you called me in to help. Paul is the last piece I have of two of my closest friends. With him being as you described, it beyond breaks my heart. I'm glad to know that he has friends like the three of you."

He peered toward Alice, who was shyly bringing up the rear.

"You're her," he realized. "Alice, Abby's daughter. I only met your mother once, but she was a very kind and pleasant person to be around. I know a little about her life and yours. It wasn't fair. I know that's putting it too lightly."

Alice barely nodded.

Dr. Barnes took in the whole group.

"Now, you've done something that I probably would not have. Is it true that we're about to meet with Carson Colter?"

"In the flesh!" Colter announced as he and a rifle-armed Jack came striding out of the woods.

"C-Colter!"

Dr. Barnes looked as if he was about to make a break for his car. He had never been a combat agent and never had envisioned himself working away from a desk. Willpower halted his feet from running. Meanwhile, Camilla turned her back before slipping on her mask as Robby did the same with his full-face helmet.

"I-I understand you're in this to help a friend of mine," Dr. Barnes stammered bravely.

"He's a good kid," Colter confirmed. "I want to fight him again, but fairly. Not with all this nonsense that's been going on with him."

"W-What does that mean?"

"Ya know, just fighting."

"Right," Dr. Barnes moved on while still apprehensive. "We will cross that bridge, eventually. Now, I'm come up with an option for us. Keep in mind, we are very much in the dark as far as what is happening to Paul. The crystal that is affecting him is the only one of its kind."

He spilled his folders on his car's roof to let the others view his comprehensive notes.

"My idea is fairly simple but will likely be difficult to implement," he explained. "The only person who has any power over this crystal other than Paul is Alice. Even though, she has little knowledge of its intricacies herself. We just need Alice to get close to Paul in order to assert some kind of control over the crystal. She may be able to damper its effects. Do you feel that is possible?"

Alice nodded. "I cannot say that it will work for sure. So much of it is based on feelings, something that I am not good at. I will just do whatever I have to do for Paul."

"How about this?" started Colter. "You're forgetting that he's like an animal down there on a warpath. I think he'll go for whoever comes near."

Dr. Barnes continued his plan. "That is the difficult part. We will need people to distract him while Alice gets close."

"That's me for sure," declared Colter. "It'll be a crazy fight down there. I'm game for it."

"Paul's a friend," said Camilla. "I have to go, too. We'll need Amuli down there. We're the only ones who can even hold up."

"And me," added Robby.

The entire group turned to him without speaking.

"I know how much you want to help him," stressed Camilla. "You have your suit, but the energy he will be giving off down there will be beyond what it can take. We don't know what his mindset is. The Paul we know might not be the one in the bunker."

"I don't think you get it," Robby asserted.

His face was far from its usual grin. His forehead was creased, and his eyes seemed narrower. They focused dead on Camilla, who almost recoiled.

"Paul is a friend of everyone here. I know that. Well, he's my best friend. Did any of you grow up with him? I did. You know I've got a brain full of crappy jokes because that's how my mind works. I've got ADHD and can't focus on anything. As a kid, and even now, I can barely sit through a class. I couldn't run track unless someone was screaming in my ear to keep me on track. My parents, heck my whole family, think I'm a screwup. They've always seen me ending up as a janitor at one of their plants. You know the one person I've known for almost as long as I can remember who has never thought anything remotely like that about me? Paul. He's the opposite of me. He's the type of kid my parents wanted. That doesn't bother me one bit. He's the guy who always laughed with me and not at me. I think he wanted to be more like me, while I wanted to be like him. He got me out of jams with bullies and teachers, and I did the same for him. Neither of us ever asked each other for help. We just gave it like it was expected. When I couldn't take my parents, I would sleepover at his house. It felt more like my home than my parents' house. Paul has no ego. It's a blessing and curse because he thinks the world of everyone else and nothing about himself. I'll ask everyone this, how the hell would I not go down there to help someone like that? If someone wants to stop me, you'll have to kill me. I don't care what it will be like down there."

To Camilla, Robby appeared to have a different light in his eyes behind the tinted visor. It was as if he, too, had anima blazing there.

"Wait a minute!" interrupted Jack. "That Paul!"

Everyone now turned towards the relative bystander whose eyes swirled around as if they there looking for a solution in the air.

He spoke again, pointing a finger at Robby. "Swanson? I'd recognize that annoying voice anywhere, even behind the mask! And the guy down there, that's Engel, isn't it? He's your only friend, so it has to be him. The hell is going on here?"

Robby pressed a button on his helmet that lifted his visor up. "Yeah, Paul's an Amulus. I'm in A.R.C., too. That's where we went when we disappeared from town."

Jack grabbed two fistfuls of his hair. "Gah, I shoulda figured that out!"

"If it makes you feel better," interjected Camilla. "You weren't supposed to figure it out."

"What are you doing here?" demanded Robby.

"Okay, Okay," Jack started with raised arms. "I was in the area around here. I was doing some… pre-season scouting for a deer spot. My dad's tree-stand isn't too far from here. And well, without you or Engel to tutor me, I got kicked out of Schwert and into public school. After that, my dad doesn't seem to care much about me. Just as long as I get in by curfew, so—"

"Not your life's story!" shouted Robby, reveling in making his former bully shrink.

"Right, Right," Jack continued. "I found the wood all over the ground here, and there was this guy close to starving. I had some snacks, so I gave 'em those. Turns out, he's an Amulus on the run. We actually have stuff in common. Plus, he's got cool stuff he can do, so we pal around."

"I thought you hated Amuli," reminded Robby.

"I… uh…" pondered Jack. "Yah know, I kind of did. I guess getting to know one wasn't so bad. I think just don't like A.I.M. and A.R.C. We don't have like a free country because of them. I mean… that's like what Carson said."

"But, we're in A.R.C.," pointed out Robby."

"Well, what am I supposed to do?" Jack asked rhetorically. "They got powers and you got more guns, and like armor or sumpin'."

"All right," Robby relented. "Forget you. I'm going to get my friend. You just stay out of the way."

"What's the strategy?" Camilla asked the group.

Colter stepped farther into the makeshift circle. "I'm goin' in first. I need to get all I can out of the kid while this is happening. Everyone can just follow me and see if they hold up."

"He's the tank then," agreed Robby. "We just need to get Alice in close to work her magic. She can follow the tank. I'm up after that. Cam can bring up the rear since she's got the range."

Silence affirmed the group's agreement. They walked warily toward the welded hatch, staring it down like an entrance into the unknown. Colter applied more melting heat to the metal until it dripped like hot mercury.

"Last one down shuts the door."

CHAPTER 16
LOST BOY

WHERE THERE HAD BEEN debris before, there was now ash. Black piles sloped against the walls, while dark brown spots littered the broken floor. The bunker smelled like the inside of an old, grimy oven with a hint of fresh sweat. The scents hung on air which had now cooled.

At the end of the bunker hallway, a solitary figure sat slumped against the wall. None of the Amuli detected any anima coming from him.

Robby quickened his stride. Without turning, Colter held back a hand to give his chest a light push. They continued in their formation at a steady pace.

It was slight at first. Anima started trickling into the smelly air. Only the Amuli felt a small sinking feeling, like a minor stomachache at first. The feeling grew with every footstep. Weights rattled against their chests, sucking air and energy away. Robby even flipped a switch on his helmet that let his suit read his vitals.

Paul's mask was partially broken. His mouth and one closed eye were exposed. Camilla peered nervously from behind the group as they approached.

Colter sunk into a squat, surveying the unconscious Amulus.

"Kid," he whispered softly. "Kid."

He gently tapped his shoe into Paul's. He kept one hand on his massive sword.

A burning, dark green eye flew open. The white had been swallowed by a mix of green with a black outline.

A splatter of blood flung upwards. The entire group recoiled from the slash. Colter threw himself backward. A thin, red line traced up his entire abdomen. It began to seep.

"He's got his damn sword!" Colter exclaimed.

Even with the wound, Colter raised his claymore in defense.

No follow-up came. Paul's sword-arm stayed extended upward.

Alice rushed to Colter's side.

"It's not deep," Colter informed her while brushing her back. "Wait a minute here."

Colter leaned as close to Paul as he dared. He fixed on the exposed, glowing eye. It was steady, like a candle in a windless room, and just as lifeless. There was no indication of movement or recognition within it.

"I don't think he's conscious," Colter noted. "It's like he's doing this all on instinct. He just won't let us in close."

He then nodded at Alice. "'Kay, I'll distract him and you move in."

He swung downward, intending to stop short if no resistance was given.

His sword was sailing over his head in the next moment. Colter staying focused just long enough to see Paul standing. A fierce kick to his stomach sent Colter smacking into the opposite wall. His spittle and blood, from a bitten tongue, had sprayed over Paul's damaged mask as the large man had flown. With Colter on the ground, it was clear that his long cut was now a problem.

"Paul!" screamed Alice as Robby cursed behind her.

Robby took over.

"We're gonna overwhelm him!" he told Alice. "We both go in at once. I'll go just before, so if he gets someone, it'll just be me."

"What are you saying, Robby!" screamed Camilla from behind them.

Robby did not wait for the girls to agree to his on-the-spot plan. He readied his stun baton and stabbed forward. Alice followed, reaching out both arms to grab Paul.

There was a horrible, wailing scream.

Alice stopped her reach short, swiveling her head to see Robby. He was looking down at his right arm, but his eyes were glazed, not comprehending anything. Where his hand had been, there was now only a bunch of crimson.

Camilla screamed next. Despite the tears in her eyes and the horror on her face, she sprinted forward, abandoning her position. She pulled the stunned Robby backward as she slunk away.

"Alice!" she cried. "We're getting out of here!"

She clung to Robby as she whisked him backward on her retreat.

"Alice!" she yelled again as she reached the ladder, hoisting Robby upwards.

She shouted the name again as she, too, vaulted up the ladder.

Alice now focused on Paul. His head was down, and his arm was splayed outward in the air. He was like a marionette on strings with his anima pulling him along. Alice stepped closer.

Paul's sword-arm shot out like a snake. Alice shrunk back in time, only allowing the katana to graze her clothes.

She realized something beyond Paul's lack of pursuit and follow-through. He was being sloppy. She knew Paul was a stickler to martial arts and weapon forms, almost to his own detriment. This husk was not powered by Paul's conscious mind at all. It was some animal.

Another slash came when she advanced again, only to shrink back. Now, she had the timing. There was little variance to this simple mind's movement. It relied too heavily on keeping its sword-arm rigidly straight.

She strode forward again. As the stabbing attack surging past her, she grabbed the arm, twisting it. The dangerous sword had been stopped.

Still holding Paul's arm, Alice contorted her body in place to dodge the fist that had been about to club her. The fist then straightened before grabbing at her collar. She did not dodge this time. The steel-like arm hoisted her upwards. It did not matter. Alice had the skin-to-skin contact she needed. This way, it was easiest to get inside of his head.

Alice closed her eyes as a screaming pressure enveloped her.

CHAPTER 17
BLANK

A COUPLE JOKED CONTENTLY JUST above the sound of the breeze from the open windows. The woman's long, dark hair streamed along like a cloud as a light smile touched her face. The man's sides were shaking with laughter. He had a large grin and giggling blue eyes. There was fresh, pesky stubble on the back of his neck, growing back after a recent haircut.

"You know, Sam..." he started saying.

He stopped suddenly, and his face tightened. He had a bad feeling, something gross and terrifying. It felt like his gut was being drained. He focused on a figure emerging, coming up on the side of the road.

Everything went blindingly bright and then dark.

The man was crawling along the gravel before he was aware of being out of the car. He turned his sore neck to see smoke and chunks of metal. Paint flakes and cracked fiberglass were mixed into the gravel.

"Sam!" he moaned, not hearing his own voice. "Sam!"

He grabbed awkwardly for the necklace around his neck. His fingers rubbed a blue crystal, offering only the slightest relief in his hazy mind. He called the name out again, even though he would not have heard a reply over the buzzing in his ears.

It took too much energy to keep his head up and crawl at the same time. He inched along until his hand felt a hard boot.

He slowly cranked his neck upward until he saw a tired face above him. The man's eyes had red veins popping out of the whites. A patchy, scraggly beard protruded in in hairy chunks along his jawline.

"Engel," he called down through clenched teeth.

"A-Aiden?" croaked Michael Engel, now finding his voice in full.

He had a difficult time keeping his head steady. Aiden seemed to fade out and in because of the sun's glare.

"How could you?" Aiden moaned somberly. "Not just Abigail… Alice too…"

Michael had to spit out chunks of dirt to keep talking.

"Aiden…" he wheezed. "Y-You don't understand. It's not… I didn't…"

Aiden did not seem to be listening.

"W-where's Sam?" asked Michael desperately. "Where is she?"

"It's going to be over soon," assured Aiden, still staring at empty space. "But, it's never going to be okay…"

"I-I," tried Michael. "I would never. Not Sam. Not Ham. Think!"

Aiden's hand lit a golden fire. His fingers were straight, turning his hand into a flaming blade.

"Just me!" Michael pleaded with all the hoarse voice he could muster. "Just me! Swear that you'll leave Sam alone! Don't go after Paul! They've done nothing!"

Aiden stabbed downward. It ended quickly.

Aiden staggered as if in a trance. He kneeled down beside the body, reaching for dripping blood. Two of his fingers became covered as if by a wax seal. With his unsoiled hand, he reached into a package he had been carrying. A sword slid out. It was a katana with black silk wrapped around the handle. The silk's series of gaps were arranged in a diamond pattern. Fitted into one of these gaps was a faint green crystal. Ritualistically, Aiden smeared the blood across the crystal.

"A curse," he murmured in a crazed tone. "My mother told me about one… not sure if it's true. She said that blood is important. Atlanteans like me have crystal permeated into it. One of her stories was that the last lifeblood has special properties, too. You put a dying man's blood on a crystal, the rest of his line is bound to that crystal. My final revenge. My daughter didn't get to live. Your son's life will be hell. Just like ours was. Many times, he will wish he was dead."

A new car pulled towards Aiden. It was a gleaming black SUV. A single man stepped out, holding a bo staff.

Greg Luper surveyed the scene. He sprinted towards the first body, checking for any sign of life. He turned towards Aiden.

"You have gone this far," Luper breathed, readying his staff.

"Putting things right," mumbled Aiden.

"You have not," corrected Luper. "I should have put you down long ago. You will not live to regret this. I will."

"You can kill an Alpha?" Aiden wondered.

"I can kill a sorry excuse for one."

Luper charged, blasting Aiden in the ribs with the blue-glowing staff. Aiden staggered backward as if drunk. He tried to aim a punch, but it was like he was moving in slow-motion compared to Luper. The man in the suit had one hand on Aiden's back and one on his staff. Both hands pushed inward. Aiden's barrier was thick, but Luper was well inside the range.

Aiden barely struggled, only flailing his arms. His eyes were dead long before his heart was crushed.

The staff came out the other end, right into Luper's free hand.

Moments later, after radioing in, Luper grasped his bloody staff in a daze.

"Aiden came here to die after he got his misplaced revenge," he realized aloud. "What has this world done to all of us?"

———

Alice was sobbing in the corner of a room. She had never heard her own body make those sounds. She surprised herself. Her throat was gasping as if hiccupping, and likewise, would not stop when she bid it to.

Feeling the carpet with her tear-stained fingers, she began to get a sense of the room. There was a large desk towards the center. Computer monitors were spaced out evenly along a series of tables. There were more empty tables and chairs across from the large desk. The rest of the room was filled with bookshelves. Most were only about chest-high, but larger ones lined the far walls. There were windows, but they were shuttered by blinds. The room smelled of dust, glue, and old paper.

Alice thought that she was alone at first. She then caught a glimpse of a figure on the far side of the room. He was frantically dumping books from the shelves onto the farthest table.

Still hugging herself, Alice cautiously approached Paul. Pages fluttered loosely through his fingers as he turned them. He did not seem to notice her. She got closer, but his head stayed down.

Between setting one book down and picking up another, Paul glanced upward at her.

"Uh… I-I'm sorry," he addressed her, almost startled. "C-Could… um… could you help me with this?"

Alice did not say anything. She looked deep into Paul's hollow eyes. She could tell that they did not recognize her. She peered down at the stacks of books, some of which were open.

They were all blank. Some pages were a pristine white, while others had yellowed or browned. There was not an illustration or word to be seen on any of them. Not even the glossy, white bindings displayed anything.

"I think… I think…" Paul started nervously as he rubbed his temples with one hand and flipped empty pages with another. "I think I'm supposed to know something. Maybe, I'm supposed to find something. I know it's something important. I just can't find anything."

Alice silently went about helping him. She built up a stack of books from shelves around the whole library. Quick skims through showed that they were the same as the ones Paul had already searched through. She stopped after a few minutes, her worried, teary gaze staying on Paul.

Finally, she walked to the large desk in the center of the room. She reached a hand into its cubby-holes until she drew out a pencil. She sat down in a wooden chair across from Paul.

"I am unsure as to what I am supposed to do," Alice apologized bluntly. "I may be able to try something."

"Anything!" exclaimed Paul excitedly. "Anything would help me out."

Alice let out a deep breath before beginning the soft patter of pencil on paper.

"I have never been creative," Alice apologized. "All my life, I did what I was asked to do. I have trouble deciding to do things on my own imitative. I will do my best to write a story."

Paul's warm, brown eyes focused on her deeply, pleading for her to start.

She began as she wrote the same words. "I once knew a boy. He lost nearly everything when he was young. That was my family's fault. That was something that I discovered later. I have always been terrified for him to find out and to see the monster that I am. Despite all that, this boy grew up to be smart and kind. However, he still blamed himself for all his faults. This made him feel as if he had to make up for his failings by trying so hard at everything. Putting out the effort made him feel like he was worthwhile to the rest of humanity. This earnest boy was drawn into conflict with two warring factions by sheer, unfortunate coincidence. I first met him then. I tried to keep him away from it, even though I knew it was in vain. I had never behaved so irrationally in my life. It was because I had never felt an energy like his.

"We went through many trials together. Along the way, he taught me how normal people feel. He taught me how they struggle. I failed to notice how lost and inhuman he began to feel. He pushed away his friends, including me, in order to protect us from himself. I do not think he understood how badly we wanted to stand beside him. It was not his work that made us stay around him. It was simply him. It was his personality. It was his kindness. It was his propensity to illuminate aspects of the world to others. We wanted to shoulder his burden because he taught us that is what friends do. Now, I am afraid that he is very lost. I do not know the way back to him. It makes me very sad. I can't tell him how much he means to me. I can't tell him how much I care about him. I can't tell him... that I have fallen in love with him."

Paul was looking at her as she lifted her head away from the book with tears in her eyes. His usual eyes were back. They acknowledged the crying girl in front of her. The innocence had been replaced with deep regret.

"Alice..."

———

Paul opened his brown eyes. His ragged mask was tugging at his hair, so he stripped it off. At first, he thought that he was being supported by only a warm coat wrapped around him. He then caught a glimpse of Alice's blonde hair and pale hands.

He felt weakness and tiredness racking his body. His stomach growled embarrassingly loud. He closed his eyes and blushed.

CHAPTER 18
THE DEPTHS

"ALL RIGHT," began Jessica Swanson. "Let me get this straight. The reason why Robby just went through hours of surgery on his arm and is down a normal hand is because of Paul. I'm only going to ask this once. What is Paul, the most important Amulus apparently, doing asleep in our infirmary when I was never notified?"

Robby, lying in his hospital bed, opened his mouth.

"And don't say it's because he's tired," she snapped before Robby could speak.

Camilla explained after rolling her eyes at Robby. "Yeah, he's strong. Apparently, he's too strong, and it messes with his head. Memory loss. Bursts of aggression and dissociation. It's a whole deal. Alice, who dealt with a similar type of thing, has to work on it with him. She can like… siphon some of the anima away from him and get into his head. We brought him here because we trust you. We can't let A.R.C., as a whole, know what is going on with him."

"It's because Jackson is a tool who'd throw Paul into confinement or something if he'd ever find out," Robby added.

"I'm actually sort of impressed," Jessica said to Robby. "That's a decent line of thinking. So, what's the next step? You do realize that Jackson is the Speaker, and we're going to need to make reports to him."

"We just lie," Robby blurted.

Jessica sighed. "It's going to have to be a series of good ones. Anyway, Paul's a good kid. There's that and the fact that he's damn important to this organization. You all can work through what you need to here. Just don't endanger my men."

She strode away, but not before giving Robby a serious stare down directly in the eyes.

"H-hey," Paul squeaked humbly as he appeared in the doorway.

He was still paler than usual, but he walked steadily and evenly. The way he slightly outstretched his shaky arms hinted at nervous apprehension.

"Someone's been hitting the Chinese food," noticed Robby.

"I..." Paul breathed, "I can't believe... I'm sorry. I'm so sorry. Robby, your arm..."

Robby held up the black prosthetic that sprang from his wrist. Each of its robot fingers wiggled slightly. For the circuitry alone, the cost was in the tens of thousands. After all, A.R.C. had all the money in the world, almost literally. The inner wires simulated nerve endings and connected directly to the nervous system. It was another application of the technology that went into the A.R.C.-Human suits. The contrast was that the suits functioned on something like a neural Wi-Fi signal, while Robby's hand had the full ethernet connection. That did not mean that the adjustment was seamless for him. It still felt like all of his fingers had suddenly been replaced with clumsy building blocks.

"Nah, it's okay," Robby forgave him. "You've got the burning green sword, but now I'm Luke Skywalker."

Paul was not listening.

"Everything... so much is my fault."

"Hey," interjected Camilla. "We've gotten past it. But, we need to talk about how we got into this mess in the first place."

"I screwed everything up!" Paul shouted.

They should be mad! They should be furious! They shouldn't even want to talk to me!

"You did one thing wrong," admitted Camilla calmly. "You didn't trust us to let us know what was going on. We knew everything that was going on with your aunt and uncle, but you could have told us the rest. You could have told us anything."

"I wanted to protect you all," Paul explained. "I wanted Alice to live a normal life. I didn't want you or Robby to get hurt anymore."

"Paul, I appreciate the sentiment," Camilla relented. "But it's not your place to decide that for us. We have minds of our own. We know what we do can get us hurt or worse. It doesn't matter. We've made our calls. And now, we're here together. We're going to move forward together."

"I don't get it," Paul declared. "You both should be screaming at me! Alice, too."

"Paul, you need to kick your addiction to broccoli!" played Robby. "Did that work for you?"

"It's a start, I guess," relented Paul, succumbing to Robby's humor. "But is everyone absolutely sure? Everyone really wants to get into all the dangerous stuff I've been doing? It's... uh... going to get worse from here on... probably."

"Of course," agreed Camilla. "Just for curiosity's sake, how crazy are we talking?"

Paul grimaced and closed his eyes. "I've been thinking that the best course of action, in order to... do the most good we can, might be to investigate our own organization. We might be making enemies of people that are currently are allies, well because there is a lot of... shadiness and worse."

"Who are we going after, exactly?" questioned Camilla.

"Jackson," groaned Paul without opening his eyes.

"Okay," sighed Camilla. "This is going to take a moment to sink in. You were, and now we, are going to be digging up dirt on the man who is running your task force... and basically our whole operation."

"Please, don't be mad," winced Paul. "You did say that you would help me with what I'm going to do next. It's just that... there have been things that Jackson has done and is probably still doing that I can't stomach. I might need Alice to help explain it all. I think that it's just making this whole world murkier. If we get to the bottom of everything, I think we will dredge up a lot of important things. I don't have any other leads, so my aunt and uncle's location might be one of them. I want to go to the depths of both A.R.C. and A.I.M. to find all we can."

He let Camilla and Robby think. They were both deep in thought for several moments, judging by Robby's squinting of his playful, brown eyes.

"If you're back to the Paul I remember, then I know that you already have a plan," Camilla finally insinuated. "Maybe some back-up plans, too."

"We're going to have to change a few things," said Paul, glancing between his two friends to make sure they were still on-board. "No department in A.R.C. has the level of access that the Research Division has, outside of the Council and the Speaker's strike force, that is. I'm on the strike for, but the rest of you aren't. Luckily, we have an in with the Research Division. I'm thinking of asking Ham—Dr. Barnes of adding the two of you. I... uh... know that won't make either of you two very happy. Cam, you're doing what you wanted to in the Search and Rescue Division. Robby, you're basically a founding part of A.R.C.-Human. I can't ask either of you two to-"

"Of course, we'll do it," interjected Camilla. "Search and Rescue will still be there whenever we pull through whatever this is."

"I'm taking my bike though," Robby informed.

"What are you going to do?" asked Camilla to Paul.

"I'm… a little lucky," gulped Paul convincingly. "I do have some freedom from being on the strike team. Since my duties lately have been tracking down Whaley and Colter, I can just keep feeding the message that I am on these false leads. Hopefully, that holds up until we find… whatever we find. It might be a fight, but I might be able to pull Jason into this. I think his duty is to his own sense of justice."

"We've got one more important person," pointed out Robby.

"Right," acknowledged Paul. "If Alice is in, we're going to need to do some maneuvering. I've been thinking about that. So, Dr. Barnes is specifically in charge of the North American Research Division. Technically, he only answers to Adam Avery. Jackson is the Speaker, but in terms of his powers, he can only set general Council agenda and grant agents special powers and privileges. In other matters, he is equal to the other members of A.R.C. The North American Research Division is under Avery, and Alice is a North American agent on North American soil. She may have special R-and-R orders from Jackson, but if she wants to go back into the field, she could place herself under Avery. We just need Avery to agree. Remember, that would mean he would be getting something, and he's helped us out a little in the past. He was even Luper's ally, so he might give his former trainees preferential treatment."

"Coming up with a devious plan so quickly sounds a lot like me," remarked Robby. "You do need to work on your slick conman skills, though. Oh yeah, where is Alice anyway?"

"You know, it's weird," Paul answered, "I heard that she's here, but I haven't seen her once."

"She has the room next to mine," Camilla relayed. "You know, I don't remember seeing her come out of it. Do you think she's okay? I mean… after what went down at the bunker?"

———

"Alice," called Camilla as she quickly rapped on the door. "It's… um… all of us. Everything okay?"

There was no answer as Camilla tried the cold door again.

"Alice, I'm sure you saw some… messed up stuff in my head and my memories," Paul admitted. "If that did anything, I'm really sorry."

"Please leave!" ordered a shaky voice from the other side of the door.

The three friends stared in brief shock at the blank door. None of them had ever heard such emotion creep into Alice's voice before. There was nothing robotic about it. There was only a deep sense of hurt, tugging the voice down.

"Are you sure?" Camilla asked soothingly.

"None of you should have need of me."

"Maybe we don't 'need of you,' but we do want to see you," Robby elaborated.

"I cannot understand why."

Camilla explained. "Because we're all friends, and we're not going to leave until you, at least, open up the door."

The door cracked open. One red-rimmed blue eye peered out like a spot of light.

"I am not a friend," Alice said. "Friends do not keep important things from each other."

"Everyone's got their secrets," Camilla pointed out.

"People do not have secrets like mine," Alice confessed. "Paul, you saw. I have known for some time. I had seen the memory. It was so horrible, and I kept it from you."

Alice could not keep herself from accidentally sending bits of images. *There was Aiden, wading through scraps of a burning car. He seemed so distraught that he was forcing his legs to move as if by a lever.*

Alice regained control.

"What?" blurted out Camilla and Robby in unison surprise.

Paul looked down at his shoes. He focused on them, begging the tears not to come and his throat not to tighten.

"I can see why you kept that inside," he acknowledged softly. "It's something so bad. Who would want to talk about it? There was probably a right time and place to tell me, but I don't think we ever had one, or maybe, I never gave you one."

"No!" Alice snapped. "You can see now! You can see why I was caged for years. You can see that I am a monster as well. There was not only that one in my mind. I am Atlantean, and that is not human. I have the same blood and the same genes as my father. I am his offspring. I am the daughter of your parents' murderer. I cannot be allowed to be your friend!"

"You're not him," corrected Paul. "You're you, Alice. You're just you, a human named Alice. You had nothing to do with that. When I look at you, I don't see Aiden. I just see you. I saw your mother once and if anything, you seem more like her. The way you talk sounds like Luper. If our parents were enemies, but so what? We were both fresh slates."

"Without my family, yours would still be alive."

"It's not on you. Don't blame yourself. It's not fair."

"I am still unconvinced. I am unsure why you would still behave warmly towards me."

Paul thought for a moment before answering: "If you want to do something to atone, I have something. I want you to live your life as Alice and not as your dad or some mindless test subject. I want you to do things that keep you happy and healthy. I want you to be our friend and to never blame yourself for who you are and where you came from. If you do those things, we will be even."

Alice finally took a step out. She was still cautious and had a sleeved arm covering her face. She gave a slight nod towards the group.

CHAPTER 19
DREDGE

"MY EYES HURT," Robby whined for the third time. "I'm gonna need glasses soon. I don't have your super eyes."

The rest of the group ignored him for the third time. Their faces were also buried in computer monitors. The only other sounds were tapping and clicking. Within A.R.C., the Research Division had access to almost everything. In order to do its job in providing a clear picture of intelligence for agents, it needed all the bandwidth it could get. The usernames and passwords of division members carried some weight. Paul realized, in half-dismay and half-amusement, that the exploits of his strike team were absent from even the most updated files. He shrugged his shoulders after several minutes of furious typing.

I guess superhumans can get cramps, too.

Paul was just about to scroll below a line of text that he had barely skimmed when he stopped.

"Bernardo Rodrigues," he murmured.

"Who?" asked Camilla and Robby in unison.

"When I talked with Emerson Whaley," Paul began. "He mentioned that name. He is, apparently, the only other enhanced Amulus still living. I knew that there was one more, but no one in A.R.C. has ever told me who. Whaley said to look out for him because he's dangerous. I just found a few references about him. He was an A.I.M. operative but has not been active lately. Just like with me, the enhancement seems to have done something to him mentally. It is thought that his instability is the reason for his lack of appearances recently."

"How does that help us?" questioned Camilla.

"According to Whaley, he's a part of this whole unraveling process," Paul explained. "Whaley has questionable loyalty to A.I.M., and that's not because he likes A.R.C. He told me so, and all of the information he gave me supports that idea. He wanted for me to avoid him physically but to investigate him. He could be the key to moving forward."

"So, where is this scary guy?" Robby wondered.

"Uh," Paul exhaled. "That is not good news. Speculation is that A.I.M. has a secret facility in Centralia. The fact that no one would want to go there is the reason why it is still hidden and has not been confirmed by A.R.C."

"So, I used to sleep through geography lessons in social studies, along with most of social studies," Robby admitted. "What's up with that place you just talked about?"

"Yeah," agreed Camilla with some hesitation. "I used to pass notes during social studies, so I was only half-listening. Still, I've never heard of that place."

"Well," started Paul as Robby saw him proudly morphing into his know-it-all mode. "Centralia was a mining town in Pennsylvania. They mined coal which is obviously very flammable since burning it starts off the process of getting power from it. In Centralia, there was a fire in the mine that spread to the vein of coal itself, and it was really big. It was so big that part of it ran under the town itself. The fire underground made streets and buildings collapse and drove just about all the residents out. Fire even shot out of the ground. Here's the thing, it's still burning after decades. The coal and other debris underground are still on fire. You know there are other conditions where fire can burn underground like during wildfires when-"

"Save it," interrupted Robby. "So, basically, we have to go to a town that is hell on earth?"

"Pretty much," acknowledged Paul. "You have to worry about smoke inhalation and the possibility of being sunk into a fiery sinkhole just by walking around. Amuli can survive a lot of things. I doubt that an almost never-ending coal fire is one of them."

"I'm sure they have great postcards there," joked Camilla. "So, how did A.I.M. build anything there?"

"I guess if they set up a building on the extreme outskirts and took really good readings," Paul speculated. "They could have built or taken over a place without having to defend it since no one would want to go there. You would have to really not care about your agents to send them there, and, well, we know that A.I.M. doesn't. The building could be safe today but not be safe tomorrow or maybe ten years from now."

"You know, this has been strange to me for a while," Camilla switched gears. "The way A.R.C. is run. Fake executives act for the general public, but there are visible leaders to people on the inside. We know the A.R.C. Council, and they're famous enough that most A.I.M. agents probably know them, too. With A.I.M. though, it's like they don't even have a structure outside of their fake one. Maybe, they just keep it really well hidden."

"Luper thought that A.I.M. is more of a loose confederation of bases," Paul proposed. "Base leaders probably have a lot of freedom. The information we gleaned from captives seems to point in that direction. Still, they seem to be almost like... heroes or icons. Their people like The Rat and his group, who tend to tie the bases together based on merit. If they ever become more unified, well, that's a scary thing to think about."

"Shall I request cars?" blurted Alice, steering back the conversation.

"Yeah," notified Camilla. "We're all going to 'hell.'"

"We still need a plan," pointed out Paul. "We don't even know how to find this place safely."

"My time to shine," Robby announced as he successfully rubbed his hands together after several attempts. "I really wanted to use the big one though."

Robby drummed on his keyboard, staring in apparent delight with at the laptop screen. "Oh man, someone should make a video game like this!"

Paul peered over his shoulder. The view was whizzing from close up to far-away, yet Robby's eyes seemed to be tracking it all.

I really don't want to set foot in there.

It was a surreal scene on the screen. The feed was like a disaster movie unfolding. Some houses stood plainly, albeit with fading or chipped paint. Others had half-tumbled over, spewing bricks and wood. The intact structures had been bandaged with support buttresses. Old model cars with thick, metal bodies rusted away. A few lawns were littered with children's bicycles and balls. Those were the more pleasant sites.

The streets and driveways seemed to be alive. They exhaled smoke like steamy breath in some areas through their cracked webs. Age and smoke had left them all ashy gray. Even after several hours of staring, neither the sky nor the air itself seemed to change from that same color. There had been blue skies during the drive in.

"You know, I can multitask," Robby bragged. "We can talk while I look. I was even thinking of firing up a game in another browser."

"Cam would punch you if she heard you say that," Paul claimed with honesty. "She probably wouldn't kill you, but it might be close.

"So... uh, what went down in that bunker?" Robby queried in a more serious tone. "It sounds like some serious stuff. Look, you don't have to explain everything if you don't want to. I got some of the gist from what Alice said."

"It's okay."

Robby knows basically everything else about me.

"It's all going to sound really weird."

"What about our lives doesn't sound weird at this point?"

Paul recounted in the clearest way he could. "Using Alice's crystal and having my old crystal in my veins has put a lot a stress on my mind. Not all of the time. Just when I use them too much. You probably guessed that. I mean, your hand..."

He could not help from looking at Robby's new appendage. Robby did not seem to mind.

He continued, "It all turned my brain into mush. I literally couldn't remember anything about myself. I think my brain was trying to make sense of it all, Then Alice established a telepathic link. We met inside my head. To explain it, I guess Alice can sometimes create almost mental planes. She can use her powers to control your sensations and make your brain think it's somewhere that doesn't actually exist in the real world. Anyway, we met up in a library in my head."

"The horror," Robby interrupted.

"I didn't recognize her. Something was prompting me to just look through empty book after empty book. I think that those books were supposed to symbolize my memories. I'm not sure if Alice did that on purpose or not. Alice helped me out by writing her recollections of me in one of the books. It was very sweet. She said that she loved me, not a big deal and it's not what you'd think. After that, my brain kind of just settled. I felt better and remembered everything. Then, I woke up."

"Whoa! Whoa! Whoa!" Robby shouted after letting Paul finish. "Back up the truck! What was that last part?"

Paul shrugged. "What part? A lot of things happened."

"You know," Robby exclaimed as he excitedly nudged Paul in the ribs, "the part about the girl falling in love with you!"

"What are you going on about?" Paul wondered, honestly confused.

"Duh!"

Paul thought for a minute before exhaling. "Oh. You thought it was that? No, I'm pretty sure that it was more like a 'I've fallen in love with you as a friend' type thing. You know how there is a bond between friends?"

Robby rubbed his eyes. "You are the dumbest smart person I know."

"What?"

"No one says 'I've fallen in love with you as a friend!'"

"Right," admitted Paul. "But, you kind of think it. It's just a different way to express a friendly bond. Alice talks a little bit differently from most people. It's not her fault at all, and it's fine."

"So," Robby started as his eyes narrowed, "would you say that you've fallen in love with me as a friend?"

"No! No!" Paul replied while waving his hands. "We're just friends. I wouldn't say it like that."

"Exactly! No one would!"

Paul thumped his seat with frustration, while he thought of something that would sound convincing.

"It's like how in Greek, well definitely in Ancient Greek, there is more than one word for love," Paul argued. "Different words describe different types of love. The one you're thinking about is eros which is romantic love. I'm talking about philia which like the brother/sister/friend bond."

"I get it," realized Robby. "You don't know this, but that is just your low self-esteem rationalizing again. You don't like you, so you can't imagine anyone else loving you. You can't even comprehend it. Well, get with it. It's happening."

"It would be unbelievable," Paul shot back. "If it was true! I mean, Alice is like… ridiculously hot, incredibly interesting, unconsciously self-sacrificing, super giving, really smart, tremendously powerful, a great fighter, and, plus, she has a very interesting way of looking at the world. It's somehow both childlike and wise at the same time. She really makes you take a step back and evaluate yourself and everything around you. Why would she ever be interested in me in a romantic way? It's some miracle that she calls herself my friend."

Paul found himself wanting to smack the grin from Robby's face.

"How 'bout this?" Robby began with the smuggest expression imaginable. "She's just over in the other car, waiting for us. Why don't you go over there and ask her which of those Greek loves she was talking about?"

Paul's face went from red to maroon. His breath came steamy hot from his nose, while his heart was punching the inside of his ribcage.

"I… uh… I don't need to. Like I said, I know."

"Take it this way," Robby began with a smirk, "you just used all those words to describe her. If there's even a tiny chance that it was the lovey-dovey love she was talking about, don't you think you owe it to her to respond in some way?"

Paul stared intensely at the ground outside the car window, now wanting to be swallowed by it. "Can you just go back to you bragging about the drone? I liked talking about that a lot more."

"Fine," relented Robby. "I'm definitely familiar with that 'eros' word though, if you ever want to go back to that topic."

Paul thought he caught a flash of the drone's glare then. It was hard to tell. Its clear, plastic body and propellers allowed the observer to look right through it. The motor and computer chips were visible but had been built small enough that they could barely been seen unless the drone was within feet of the onlooker. That was if someone was already looking for it. The propellers ran as quiet and quick as a hummingbird's wings as it hovered around.

Paul's mind wondered towards the abandoned highway and roads leading up to the empty town. It too was severely cracked but had much more color than the decrepit roads inside the town. Almost every inch had been tagged. There was everything, including names, stick figures, dirty words, pleasant words, symbols, and elaborate pictures.

It's a real mass of humanity, Paul realized. *People put down whatever was in their minds and hearts, even if it was just a joke. There's something really honest about that. I can't say that I would come here to do that though.*

"There's that one guy again," Robby reported as he pointed towards the front window of one, intact house on the screen.

An older, bald man moved to the armchair in his living room. He appeared to have a book, but the two boys could not make out the cover.

"We'll keep an eye on him, I guess," responded Paul. "We do have to remember that a handful of people still live here, even if this is the least populated town in the state."

"Why?"

"I supposed some of the residents of the town just stayed," Paul hypothesized. "Home can be a hard place to leave when you have a family history there. The other reason is the same reason A.I.M. is probably here, the privacy. There are no wandering eyes, and you're left alone. There's no postal code even. I mean, there used to be back when it wasn't on fire. If you want to get off the grid or if you're overly paranoid about the government and postmen, you can come here. There is just the added risk of a quick death from falling into a burning pit or a slow death from smoke inhalation."

"Some people," sighed Robby. "I guess we can't go up and ask him either. If he sees two teenagers coming up to his house, he'll probably think that we're going to tag that too. I would not be surprised if everyone living here has some guns. They could be trouble, even for you guys, if they got too close."

"This does give me an idea, though," Paul said as he chewed his thumbnail. "The last few residents are probably very observant or even paranoid about whatever goes on in town. I doubt that A.I.M. can hide people coming and going forever. They've probably seen them. If they are paranoid, it wouldn't be out of the ballpark for them to be wary of or cast glances at what may be A.I.M.'s base. It's a stretch, but it's the only lead we have."

"Aye, aye," answered Robby. "It's more spying on crazy old people, then."

Paul struggled with boredom and complacency for the next few minutes, while Robby chewed on a candy bar that he had gotten from the last gas station stop.

"You know, people in this part of the state actually say soda instead of pop," Robby mumbled with a mouth full of chocolate, "I don't get it. Why are things so different in every part of this weird state? One city even throws snowballs at Santa Claus when they're winning a football game."

"It's an old state made of settlers from all over," Paul replied in a dull voice. "It's the same in other places. There are parts of Spain where the native language isn't even… wait… hey!"

Paul bumped Robby's shoulder in order to point at the screen, causing a brief fit of coughing chocolate chunks from the latter.

"That building. See it? The one with the white siding. The supports are a slightly different shade that the ones on the other buildings. It looks newer. I could swear that the guy in the chair has glanced at it over his book more than once. It even sits far enough away from the rest of the buildings that it might be on more solid ground."

Robby put down his chocolate bar.

"What's the plan?

CHAPTER 20
THROUGH THE ASHES

"IT'S FRUSTRATING," noted Camilla in the now-crowded car. "Boarded-up windows. Unsteady ground. It's hard to see inside or even to approach carefully."

Robby shook his head. "I should have brought the big boy drone. It has a better camera and infrared. The little guy's camera is just too small."

"It's only about a million times more noticeable," disagreed Camilla. "Really, what are we going to do?"

Paul was uncomfortably aware of Alice sitting behind him. She too was studying the screen with her hazy blue eyes. It was as if her smell was strangely filling up the sedan. It was floral tinged with sweetness. No one else seemed to even notice it.

It's all in my head. It's weird. It's weird. I was finally getting to understand Alice and feeling comfortable about around her. Now, I have to think about all this stuff. This is just going to be one more thing to stress me out! Is this how it's always going to be?

"Our senses," stated Alice slowly.

Paul was now forced to look at her directly.

Don't do too much eye contact. Don't do too little eye contact. I could... give something away... or not seem cool.

"They are unable to keep anything hidden underground in this location," Alice elaborated. "There are too many problems with the soil. All facilities have to be above ground. A.R.C. and A.I.M. facilities are typically underground in other locations. That prevents ordinary humans from finding them as well as blocking the special senses shared by Amuli. Here, there can be no such protection."

"You guys want to go out based on feel?" questioned Robby. "I'm not really equipped or trained in that stuff like the rest of you."

"I think it checks out," declared Camilla. "An anima presence as strong as Rodrigues won't be easy to hide from other Amuli. Robby doesn't have to go in. He's still getting used to his new arm anyway. He can continue to observe with the drone from here. What do you think Paul?"

"I think it can work," Paul affirmed. "The risk is being seen. They probably have cameras, even if we can't see them from the drone. We just have to go in at angles that they likely wouldn't see and keep our individual anima presences low."

————

Paul, Alice, and Camilla each stood in position on the tiled roof. The tiles felt strangely rough and alien under their feet. It was clear that they were not meant to walked on. Each Amuli had on their respective masks. Alice had the white masquerade. Camilla's was purple and tight around her cheekbones. Paul had a copy of his old mask.

I swear it looks like the frown is slightly straighter on this one.

"Ready?" whispered Camilla.

There were nods before they all jumped in unison. The space in-between the two structures was over twenty feet. For Amuli, that was just within range. Alice and Paul cleared far towards the inner part of the roof. Camilla landed on the edge.

All three of us landing at once can be loud, Paul analyzed. *Still, one bump can be discounted. Three successive bumps can make someone think it's a trend. People tend not to worry about harmless noises if they are not repeated.*

They started the next part of the operation. Camilla stayed on the roof. If the occupants came outside, she could easily pick them off from the roof. Alice and Paul slid down from opposite sides of the roof. Pressed right up against the sidings, the two were in obvious camera blind zones. Cameras attached to a building typically did not record the sidings themselves, but, instead, everything in front of them. The steep drop-off meant little to their superpowered bodies. As they perused the sides, they made sure to hug the width tightly, staying hidden on the same principles as the slide down.

Paul had felt that something was off after just being in the vicinity of the building. It was similar to what he had felt from Whaley and Li. It was rage but mostly confusion. There was a haziness to it as well. It was like being in an angry thundercloud. Now, he just had to pinpoint the location. Finding Rodrigues himself was the first part of the battle.

Other than the intensity prickling his skin, the building appeared surprisingly normal. It reminded Paul of buildings in his hometown where large, old houses had been converted into dentist offices.

"There's no movement," reported Robby from the earpiece. "I'd say that you guys are invisible right now."

"*Camilla says likewise,*" Alice rang into Paul's head.

From the outset, Paul felt a sinking feeling in his stomach. He was unsure if this was the usual pre-mission nerves, the atmosphere of his smoking, empty surroundings, or the presence of Rodrigues's anima. Now as he crept around the building, he could feel it eating at his stomach. Anima in the air was violating his skin like crawling spiders.

"*This is some of the worst I've felt.*"

"*Here,*" Alice relayed calmly. "*The anima is much thicker here.*"

Paul stepped towards her with his back scraping the paneling. He could pick out Alice's anima. It felt less glassy than when he had first felt it months ago. It was nearly soft and cotton-like now. The presence of the other, more menacing anima made it hard to focus on anything else as he came closer. The spiders had become pythons, constricting his body while weighing it down.

He found Alice, seemingly unperturbed by the anima, peering up at a second-floor window.

"*We can move in,*" she suggested in a thought towards him.

He nodded gravely.

Alice's fingers lit up as if covered by liquid gold. She pressed them into the building at a place at the top of her reach. She released the hand for a moment, letting the newly formed handhold cool before reinserting. After creating the next hold, she swung her way up, creating more holes as she went.

Paul first tried to put his hands through the marks Alice hand made. He found his fingers to be significantly larger than hers. He followed her lead and made his own. He gripped the building underneath her as she reached the window which had been heavily boarded. With blazing fingers, she silently sliced through the wood. She passed the loose pieces to Paul who let them gently go to the ground. After some quick work, the widow was clear. No one had appeared inside it.

"Good luck," said Robby in a rare, serious tone.

Alice rolled inside and Paul followed.

The room was bare of people and nearly of furniture. A wooden table sat against a wall with mismatched chairs unevenly pushed in. Frayed carpeting extended from the open doorway and below the widows. It stopped abruptly partway through the room to expose the wooden floor. It was the structure taking up the opposite side of the room that took up all of the intruders' attention.

Metal walls closed off that portion. The only entrance to the sub-room was metal door which was tightly clasped. It looked like an industrial freezer. Every step closer to it even made Paul feel far chillier.

"He is being sedated in there," Alice notified. *"I can feel very cloudy thoughts."*

Paul noticed the apprehension as her thoughts brushed his mind. He remembered that Alice had once been kept in a very similar situation.

"I will search the lower floors," she insisted. *"We have found him, and he is restrained. Now, it is time to find anyone else how might interfere."*

Paul realized that this likely left him only an attic to search through. Alice had the more difficult job. *I would offer to take the harder role but that would be an insult to Alice and her abilities.*

He replied, *"Call if you need me. I will be there."*

Paul took a deep breath, attempting to slow down his heart, as he skirted the stairwell with a raised sword. There was no movement other than Alice's methodical descent. Paul moved likewise, snaking his way upstairs.

The attic was in similar shape as the floor below. Only here, the floor creaked, forcing Paul into a light shuffle on his toes. The only thing in the attic was a desk sans chair.

There were no notes or computer equipment on the surface. Paul gingerly opened the drawers but found them similarly empty. As he slid back the bottom drawer after a scouring, he heard a new sound: paper being crinkled. He stuck a hand in the thin area between the drawers and the backboard of the desk and came away with a single sheet of paper.

Paul eyed the scrap in the light of a sunbeam. There were two holes at the top where staples had seemingly been stripped out as if torn from a packet. Rodrigues's picture stared up at him from the page. The eyes were glazed, under obvious sedation. The neck muscles bulged almost painfully. The head was nearly square. The man had the look of a body-builder. Paul had already seen most of the contents of the page before. It chronicled the man's past in Brazil and his time in A.I.M. as well as the modification that had led to his deteriorated mental state.

It's strange. It's all so familiar…

A thought from Alice came in then. *"It appears to be empty."*

Rather than relieved, Paul was still paranoid.

"*I don't like this,*" he let Alice know. "*This could be a trap. They could be listening or have a hideaway somewhere. Maybe, they saw us coming, left, and are coming back with help.*"

The two pondered the possibilities on their own for a minute.

"*If we have a chance, perhaps we should be out quickly,*" Alice formulated. "*If there are no other sources of information, that leaves us with Rodrigues himself, if he is still beyond the door.*"

Paul agreed with the logic. "*We'll head there but stay careful.*"

They met up at the metal door again. Both of them felt around the metal.

"*Weird,*" Paul noticed. "*There doesn't seem to be a way to communicate inside or even see inside. The only way to know if he's in there is to get in there.*"

"*That is likely the next move,*" Alice acknowledged.

Paul thrummed his fingers on his pants to his heartbeat. He sighed as loud as he dared. "*I guess we have to.*"

"*He is likely sedated if he is here,*" Alice assured him. "*If it comes to it, we must trust each other's strengths as we are strong.*"

Paul tried to think confidently. "*We'll go together.*"

Alice produced a key she had found on the bottom floor. Obviously, the occupants of this building had been more concerned with the person inside the prison having access to the key than any person outside of it. The door squeaked open, much too loud for Paul's nerves.

Like the outside, the inside of the room was lined with metal. Stepping through the doorway, Paul could see the thickness.

I wonder what kind of metal this is, Paul pondered to himself. *How was it built to hold back one of the strongest Amuli?*

Paul could not feel his heartbeat when he noticed the occupied chair in the corner. He raised his katana, bracing it against himself. Deep down, he had hoped that this chamber would have been as empty as the rest of the building. Either that or he wished the sinister anima was simply a false alarm for a much less dangerous Amuli.

Bernardo Rodrigues lay on what looked to be a dentist's chair. It was leaning the whole way back, making the hulking man's face obscured to Paul and Alice. His frame far overlapped the sides of the skinny chair. It seemed ready to collapse under him.

Both Alice and Paul stood in primed position. They were in defensive stance, waiting for the still body to make a move. Paul forced himself to breath naturally for the chance that he was about to need his lungs for some greater exertion.

No movement came. The crossing networks of tubes running from large bags into Rodrigues signified that sedatives were still being emptied into him.

With a quick glance at each other, the two knew that they had to get closer. The search thus far had been frustratingly fruitless. Rodrigues himself was the final lead.

"We have the advantage," Alice stated her analysis. *"He is unconscious and will likely be drowsy if he awakes. We outnumber him and have similar strength levels."*

"Alright," Paul admitted. *"We just need to be careful. His advantage is his unpredictability. We have no idea what is left of his mind. He could be like a wounded animal."*

Alice's stoic face showed that she had long since made the same conclusions.

Rodrigues's sleeping face was not that of a monster. It was placid with soft breathing. The eyebrows were loose and relaxed.

"He's quite out of it," Paul surmised. *"That's good. We just have to hold down this place until we can call for a containment team and it gets here."*

Alice stood, transfixed on the body but listless in her posture. Paul could see a storm behind her eyes, even though they remained dreamy on the surface.

Paul turned to the network of tubs and bags. *"I wonder how much is left in the bags. How long has he been here alone and why?"*

He took a step closer to the stand. With a bobbing finger, he counted the bags to confirm something.

"Alice," His thoughts were as chilled as his rigid body. *"All of the bags are empty."*

Two bloodshot, red eyes flung open.

CHAPTER 21
SINK

PAUL WAS BARELY able to brace himself when the shockwave hit. The maelstrom of red energy created a fog the color of blood spray. Paul lost sight of Alice in its wake. The storm seemed to bend and shift. Paul found himself in an opening.

The fog was retreating through the door. Alice and Rodrigues were gone.

Paul dashed for the doorway. His feet moved so fast that he lost traction on the scraps of carpet for a moment. The constant shockwaves were now pounded the stairs and below. Paul managed to stay just within the waves' edge, though they tore his shirt. He found Alice and her opponent in what may have once been a waiting room or large living room.

Alice had surrounded herself with a giant ball made of her gold anima. Rodrigues pounded mindlessly away at it. Paul's heart sank even lower than it had been.

Rodrigues was not hammering with his fists but with his anima weapon. Paul recognized it as a nagamaki, a bladed weapon not far from his own katana. The two were similar in construction with a handle of rayskin wrapped over by silk and a folded-metal blade with surgical sharpness. The difference was in the proportion of the two swords. Rodrigues's weapon had a far longer hilt. It was nearly the length of the shaft of a spear. The weapon may have been built closer to a glaive than a sword, but it was made for slashing. They were supposedly able to take horseman off of his horse and maybe bring the horse down with him. Paul had the advantage in lightness and speed, but Rodrigues had greater reach, leverage, and power with his weapon. That is, if his mind had been intact.

Rodrigues's loud hammering showed little recognition for what his was doing. It was pure confusion and rage at everything around him.

The more he wore on, the more blackness tinged into his red anima along the edges.

That's the enhancement power.

Catching a glimpse of the man's eyes, Paul could see that the whites had been replaced by black, so that they were red on black like blood on a decaying wound.

Paul's own anima turned dark green and black as he concentrated. He could only hold that focus for a moment.

———

A tall, skinny man was walking down a cramped alleyway. Above him, small balconies seemed to be stacked on top of each other. Clothes were draped off many of them, while others were occupied by people or by an occasional potted plant. The white paint on the twin apartment complexes was losing a war to patches of gray concrete.

The narrow pavement was nearly full of people. Many of them sweated in the blustery humidity. The thin man was no different. Occasionally on his walk, a group of young men would pass by him. They pointed and smiled at him, giggling amongst themselves cruelly. Inevitably, at least one member of each group would nudge him or push him roughly before sending a joke his way. It was clear that he was familiar with them and they with him.

He finally emerged towards more open air but then more people. These ones did not seem to notice him. He had to awkwardly dance his way through passersby to cross the street. Accidently jostled by an elbow towards a building, he found himself looking into window.

The inner floor of the place was made up of light blue padding. The people standing towards the center of the room had either white or blue robe-like garments. They were fighting, but not roughly. A couple of them grappling before one tossed the other by one arm but let the opponent land gently on the padding. The victor then helped the fallen one up. The surrounding crowd, who stood along the walls and windows raised arms and cheered, though the skinny man could not hear them. Some of these people were similarly dressed, while others wore sweaty T-shirts like the man who was watching from outside.

On the far wall, there was a sword on display. Surprisingly, its handle nearly seemed longer than the sheathed blade. The wrapping was black silk crisscrossing a red diamond-like patter.

The skinny man had worked his way from the window to the clear, glass door. He stared deeply at the weapon that was drawing him inside like a magnet.

———

Paul was back to see Alice still guarding herself from Rodrigues's blows.

I hate it. When I come back, no time passes, but I still feel thrown off. Observer, why now? I don't know if you can hear me. I can understand you showing me this, but why in the middle of the fight?

He darted in towards Rodrigues's open back. The man's white T-shirt was barely holding together as his shoulder muscles flexed with every swing.

Paul turned his sword sideways as if positioning a block but swung towards the large man's back.

Rodrigues's anima barrier slowed the katana down so that it gave him little more than a pat.

I have to be forceful. I don't want to injure him badly, but he needs to be taken down.

Paul followed up. He cut from the other side, powering the blade with green and black anima through the red mist barrier. This time, it struck between the ripped man's shoulder blades, causing him to stumble.

Rodrigues's focus shifted to Paul. He spun around, aiming an upward chop at Paul's head. Paul leaned backwards, helping the nagamaki upwards with a nick of his sword. The ribs were open, and Paul struck.

A raised hand barely stopped the flat of the blade. Had Paul meant to cut and injure, it would have gone through the hand and to the body.

Paul felt the storm rising with red gusts.

It's hard. I can't find the middle ground. I could kill him, but I can't seem to capture him. Maybe, burning through all that anima will tire him out.

Paul dodged backwards again and again as more haphazard slashes came. One took out a bannister of the stairwell.

He's enhanced. There's no telling how much anima he has in there.

Paul could feel the ugly, bubbling frustration within him. His veins now ran the colors of him anima. His thoughts grew cloudy.

"Paul!"

The thought was forceful. It reminded Paul of when Robby would give him an exaggerated slap on the back.

"Paul, you don't have to do it alone."

Even amidst the battle and the constant, fiery swings, Paul could feel his thoughts and heart settling. Alice had scrambled to his side.

"Together."

With one word, Paul could completely understand what she meant. Side-by-side, their green and gold anima blended together. Paul could feel the burden of the enhancement and free crystal being lightened. Alice was shouldering the heaviness with him, both the pain of emotion from the crystal residue in his blood and the weight of the lives poured into the free crystal. It was all quieter for a moment.

Paul raised his sword in one arm as Alice helped to brace it with hers. Paul's green-glowing arm had gold fluttering around it.

"Together," their thought was in unison.

Anima blasted forward like a laser cannon. It carried Rodrigues into the wall where it exploded in a cloud of dust, wood chips, and paint. Moments later, Paul and Alice were coughing in the choking air while staring a hole leading to the outside.

"I just hope it wasn't too much," Paul blurted aloud. *"For both his health and our cover,"* he added mentally.

They both clambered out of the building's wound.

Rodrigues was slowly up-righting himself on the rugged, cracked street. Both Alice and Paul feared to venture out that far. It was too close to the town proper and the hell below. There was no telling where the latter started. They went only towards the edge of the lawn. Paul realized that he had spent a large supply of his anima. Still, his augmentations meant that there was still power left in his reserve. His body and mind just had to catch up.

Steam was rising from red burns on Rodrigues's torso. The shock of the blast had obviously confused him. It took him several attempts to grasp the nagamaki that had landed in the crack next to him after his hand repeatedly missed it.

Some steam came from his own hurricane of anima which was picking up again. Paul worried that the effect was masking steam coming from the ground. He did not know what to do nor where to move. The ground itself was too much of an unknown.

Rodrigues's red-black eyes found them again. He waddled over towards them with his legs spread wide. As he went, he slammed his sword into the ground repeatedly, adding to the maze of cracks. It was clear that his broken mind's only emotion was currently frustration.

"Wait!" Paul warned aloud. "Stop that! It's dangerous."

The enhanced Amulus kept coming.

"Please," begged Paul. "You don't know what you're doing! I don't know if you're still in there, but you have to stop this!"

"I have tried his mind," Alice notified. "He can only project feelings, dark feelings. I do not think there is a way of getting through."

Paul gritted his teeth.

It began when Rodrigues was within yards of them. The cracks grew larger. They formed faster and faster until pavement and gravel were fading away. Rodrigues was slipping. It was as if the ground had become liquid, like a rough and uneven ocean. He was now on all-fours, pawing the ground for grip. His fingers dug in like claws.

A barrage of smoke caught Paul right under his chin. He could barely see through singeing tears. It felt like he had shoved his head into a campfire. The scraping and rumbling from the collapsing pavement were deafening. All of his senses were consumed by the hellscape emerging before him.

"Paul!"

"*Paul!*"

Alice was forcefully tugging at his shoulder, leaning him partway backwards.

"We must retreat!"

"*We must retreat.*"

Paul shrugged her off.

"Rodrigues!" he choked through a burning throat. "Bernardo!"

Just below a black cloud, he could just see the large man stumbling on his knees. Paul took careful steps toward him. He extended an arm to full reach.

"Grab on! You have to grab on."

Rodrigues's weight was causing an upslope on the opposite side of the crumbling ground which now reached towards Paul. Rodrigues slid at the other end. Paul tried reaching over it.

On the other side, he could not see the fire itself. There was only black smoke, and the dirt and gravel that had turned yellow-hot. Rodrigues was skimming downwards. He dug in with his sword and fingernails like a desperate animal using its claws. He could not stop. The fiery hole was gaping open.

Paul lost him in the smoke before Rodrigues sunk downward.

Finally, Alice hefted Paul by the waist, pulling him backwards as far as she could while still keeping her breath amidst the heavy smoke.

When they reached relative safety, Paul was still staring at the smoking mess of street in shock. He was only brought back to the present moment by a fit of coughing. Even his saliva and mucus burned.

"No!" he wheezed. "No!"

He beat a fist against his leg.

"It can't be," he whispered. "I... I c-couldn't do anything."

CHAPTER 22
SEEK

PAUL SAT HUNCHED over in the backseat of the otherwise empty sedan. They had come in two cars. There was less of a chance of something going wrong with two vehicles than a single one. Being in A.R.C., one always prepared a getaway option. In this moment, Paul wanted to get away. Somehow, he knew that this feeling would not leave him no matter how far we got away from this place.

I have all this power. I had Alice at my side. Still, I feel so useless. It's like nothing's changed from back when I first became an Amulus. I still fail. My incompetence got someone killed. People are always getting hurt when they're near me. I should just start driving away by myself. The only thing keeping me here is my guilt of everything that they went through to get me back.

Camilla and Robby were talking outside. In his mind, Paul assumed that they were complaining about him.

Why do I always do that? I always think that the people that care about me think the worst of me. It's like the way I think is broken. But what else has kept me alive other than my brain… and my friends?

He looked down at his shoes, feeling some strange need to untie them and retie them over and over, anything to put his mind onto something else.

The door slid open gently. Alice silently sat down into the seat beside Paul who had only glanced for a moment to see who was entering the car. They sat in the quiet for several moments, both staring at the seat in front of them with blank eyes.

Without a word, she put both arms around him. Paul lost his heartbeat for a moment. He slowly reciprocated, letting his arms wrap around her.

I never knew someone could feel so warm. Are girls' hoodies always this soft?

It was like placing a hand over the gentle heat of a candle. With his head well above the short girl's shoulder, he peered out the window for a moment.

Robby, please don't be watching this.

He did not want the soothing moment to end.

Okay, is there such a thing as too long? No…no, don't complain. Am I supposed to break away first? If I take too long, does that make it creepy or too forward?

As suddenly as it started, Alice slipped away and out of the car. Paul checked his face and found it flushed.

I hope she didn't see that.

Strangely, it still felt like she was there with him. He could still feel the warmness.

Oh, no. Oh, no. What if Robby was right? Then, what am I supposed to do? No, no, I can take heart. I strongly believe that I have never been attractive to one single person, nor do I have any right to put any girl through the hell of dating anyone as messed up as me.

Still, it would be absurdly nice.

No! That's selfish. I would get everything, and she would get nothing.

But Alice is so great!

Shut up! Shut up! I know! I need to find a book. Someone has to have written advice about this exact type of situation.

No, they haven't.

Paul sighed.

Alright. I need to shut it down. All the voices and desires in my head will have to take a break. I have serious work to do.

Before climbing out of the car, he gulped heavily. *Wait a minute. Alice once said that she only hears thoughts that are projected to her, but there are exceptions when the thoughts or feelings are exceptionally powerfully.*

As he thought, he absentmindedly rummaged through his pockets. He was surprised to feel and hear a crinkle. He pulled out a piece of hastily folded paper.

I'm surprised it didn't burn up in the anima or fall out of my pocket at some point. Is this the only thing we have to show? I guess it's better than the nothing I had a second ago.

"Okay," said Dr. Hamilton Barnes over the secure line. "I'm just loading up the image you sent me."

"Right," Paul affirmed as he glanced over the wrinkled paper in his hands.

He stared with regret at Rodrigues's portrait above the text. *What a life of torment, and it ends because of my actions. If it weren't me, maybe someone else would have given him a chance to recover his mind and free will.*

"Oh, sorry," apologized the voice from the other side of the phone. "I think I clicked on the wrong link."

Paul could hear a fervent series of clicks in the background noise.

"No, wait. That is what you sent me. You sent me a copy of a file we already had on Rodrigues?"

I thought it looked familiar.

Paul could feel his throat tighten as the realization sunk in further.

"I sent a picture of the exact document I found inside the base."

Dr. Barnes stayed silent for more than a few seconds. Paul could feel the nervous energy from the other side of the call.

"I can think of several hypotheses," he finally stated with mustered professionalism. "Each one of them would be a nightmare. The first is that A.I.M. has access to our computer system and that printed out the report. The second is that there is a mole who has passed on that information to the other side. The third one, which would be the best bad situation, would be that this document was left behind during a base turnover and is, hopefully, the only A.R.C. document to reach A.I.M.'s hands. This will require investigation immediately. Information is our lifeblood. If its leaking, it could be a mortal wound."

"I've thought of an alternative theory," Paul ventured. "What if A.R.C. agents have already been here? Look, I know that there has never been paperwork filed for a mission here, but what if a covert team has been here? One that is more influential and top-secret than Jackson's strike-force. A team that has never been on the books. They may have left something behind."

"Are you talking about a conspiracy?" asked Dr. Barnes, worried.

"I think that we're functioning like an internal affairs department right now. That's the angle we've been probing."

Dr. Barnes sighed. "My advice? Go up the chain of command for now but do it smart. If you've fingered Jackson for something, don't raise his suspicions. I'm assuming that you've come to the realization that he would be the only leader in A.R.C. who would do something like that. It fits his gung-ho, militaristic MO. He also has a legion of agents completely loyal to him who can keep secrets. You aren't actually standing on his turf anyway. That would be Avery's territory. Avery isn't someone who is comfortable with the old guard either. He's a young mover-and-shaker like your group. He was the only one to oppose Jackson in the last Speaker election. He had my vote. I can set up a meeting with him that would be on the sensitive, quieter side. Anyway, I'm sure he would be thrilled that you're bringing the information on Rodrigues to him first."

As we've thought, Avery is our best shot for help from the top. It would have been much better if I were on his strike-team.

"Paul, I know that you're a careful agent. In this case, please be extra careful. I think you are about to pit Avery and Jackson against each other while playing both sides. A.R.C. is not A.I.M., but it is not usually a comfortable place to work, especially for those who spar with council members."

"I will," answered Paul. "Ham, thank you for everything. I'm afraid that I've also put you in a terrible position."

"I'm in the position that I want to be in. I want to be helping out a friend."

They said their goodbyes.

Paul looked up with slight embarrassment to see that his nonofficial team had gathered around him with eager looks. *When did they all get here?*

"You're … uh… you're all kind of staring at me," he pointed out, finding himself unable to look Alice in the face specifically.

"Well, yeah!" Robby exclaimed. "You've become the 'plan-man.' You're the one who is always coming up with things."

"So, it's my call? You all caught the gist of all that?"

"It's simple," summed up Camilla. "We go to Avery. He investigates what's up. He uncovers whatever shady stuff is going on within A.R.C. and then we move on together. We just want your say-so."

"Alright then," Paul moaned. "We just have to investigate possibly the most powerful organization on earth without them turning them against us, or better yet never let them know what we're doing."

"Simple," Alice agreed with Camilla.

"So," started Paul as he tried to figure out what to say next. "First, it looks like we're going to somewhere Cam knows well."

"Oh joy," Camilla whined.

"Um… actually, before that," Paul corrected himself, "I want to do something first."

He stared deeply down at the pavement. This was a nearly bare stretch, away from the jokes and names spray-painted a few feet away.

He slowly unleashed his sword, letting the violent green flame sprout from the katana's stip.

Paul brought it down on the pavement, tracing a pattern of burning heat. Eventually, he stopped while the rest of the group peered down.

There were now dark, ashy grooves in the asphalt that formed the shapes of letters. They read: "Bernardo Rodrigues."

CHAPTER 23
IDEOLOGY

PAUL COULD JUST MAKE out the scenes from blocks away. In places, the city nearly looked like parts of Centralia. Fire had destroyed that city, but water had damaged this one. Rusty cars huddled in groups on sidewalks and some streets had buildings with a barely a window between them on the lower floors. Some old bricks had made a dusty impression on the sidewalk after their falls. Everywhere, there was a dark dampness that seemed to have sunk permanently into every building and area of street.

It's strange. People are bustling just a few streets away.

His friends walked with him up until a nondescript building loomed over them.

Paul rubbed the back of his neck anxiously.

"You know," he started slowly, "you could all come with me for... um... maybe solidarity's sake."

Please, don't leave me.

"Nuh uh," disagreed Camilla. "He called for you alone. We'll be there in spirit."

"Yeah, you're Mr. Important," said Robby. "Look at you. You look all grown up and confident in that suit like a businessman going to a board meeting."

"Alright," Paul sighed.

"So," Robby began, "where are the rest of us off to? We're in the big city with nothing to do."

"If you say, 'the big city' or 'we're in the city' again, I'm going to punch you," complained Camilla. "No one here talks like that. Actually, no one talks like that outside of travel commercials. Anyway, I've got some stuff to take care of. It's actually family stuff. Like on-my-own stuff."

"Perhaps, I can see Central Park," Alice wondered.

"Go for it," Camilla said. "Just keep Robby out of trouble."

"Alice," Robby said to her. "Let's get in so much trouble."

"It's almost time," Paul observed.

After taps on the shoulder from Camilla and Robby, Paul found himself inside an elevator. The button had a secret fingerprint scanner. If someone other than a member of A.R.C. had tried the elevator controls, they might have become frustrated by the lack of response.

On the chosen floor, Paul found the hallways stacked with filled boxes. Several people milled about, too busy to even give him a look. The scraping sound of wood being dragged over linoleum erupted from several of the doorways he passed by.

Either things are being moved in or moved out quickly.

Paul studied the door number at the end of the hall. It matched the, "42" he remembered. To his dismay, a group of people lingered by the open doorway, talking quickly and laughing off-and-on all at once.

"Excuse me. Excuse me."

Paul angled his body and awkwardly waded through them to reach the front.

The interior consisted of only a couple tables, a large monitor on the wall, and dual-screen computer setup. Adam Avery stood over the one table, tracing a line on what seemed to be a map. Paul shifted his weight uncomfortably as he waited for the North American Council Member to notice him.

"Ah, I sense some new anima," Avery finally declared as he stood up straight to nod at Paul. "Anyway, guys, I have a meeting now. I think you each can move forward with what we talked about."

The warm crowd dispersed slowly.

"Alright, Paul," Avery addressed him while rolling up a map followed by a set of blueprints. "Do you mind if I shut the door? I heard from Hamilton what's bothering you. It's some... sensitive stuff, and it's actually bothering me, too."

"Sure."

"Ugh," grunted Avery after closing the door and surveying the room. "I would offer you something to sit on, but I guess not. It's been pretty crazy here. This isn't the usual New York building. That's still being repaired. We were originally pushed farther away, but the city is making progress, so we moved closer to the old spot. The idea was to show strength, but I'll let you be the judge of that. It's a wonder that A.I.M. hasn't made a move on us. We're pretty vulnerable."

Paul was struck by his candor. *He definitely isn't Jackson.*

Adam Avery was a tall man. He was muscular but still slim. His hair was slicked back, and his face showed a thin layer of even stubble. His expressive eyes had a movie star glint in them.

He looks every bit the part his reputation says he is. I feel like a plain nobody in comparison.

"Everything has just gone so sideways," Avery continued. "If this building was labeled like our other ones, the protests probably would be the thickest here. On the other hand, I'd say that a little accountability might be a good thing."

He's bold. Paul realized. *I guess that suits his reputation, too.*

"After all, that's why we've come together here isn't it?"

"Right," squeaked Paul as he failed to meet Avery's confidence level.

Avery's handsome face sank into a graver expression. His eyes seemed to lose some life and sink into their sockets.

"Hamilton has let me know about Centralia," Avery reported. "It's troubling."

"It is," chimed Paul, unsure of what to add.

"Follow me over to the computer," Avery insisted. "It's a bit cramped because of the hasty setup here."

Paul followed to find Canadian, maple leaf flag wallpaper on both monitors.

"I have to represent," Avery joked. "I spend too much time in the U.S. now."

He quickly brought up a file before resting his hands nonchalantly on the desk from his standing position.

Paul could see pictures strongholds and safehouses in secluded locations. There were some on snow-topped mountains, others in deserts, and more in rundown city corners. They each had the hallmarks of A.R.C. or A.I.M. occupation. There were metal-lined rooms and holding cells. Windows were thick with glass which was beyond bullet resistant. Large control panels and elaborate computer displays enveloped most of some rooms. Some were merely dusty, while others had been smashed enthusiastically.

"A.I.M. bases," Paul ponder aloud.

"You would think," answered Avery. "There hasn't been any trace of them in these locations. These places were not taken by force. They were simply stumbled across after being hastily abandoned."

"What about Hunters?" guessed Paul. "Or government ops?"

Avery shook his head. "Look at the computers. The only Hunters who were this advanced were the Swanson's, and they're on our side now. Plus, we've got the governments in our pocket. They said that these sites weren't theirs, and they are too terrified to lie."

Paul put the pieces together.

"You think that someone in A.R.C. has gone rogue."

"It's a terrifying theory isn't it?" Avery admitted somberly. "It could be anyone of influence in A.R.C. I'll ask you, who does this most sound like?"

"You really think it's Jackson," Paul remarked, now shock to see his suspicions were shared. "That was my theory about Centralia. I found an A.R.C. file there that points to A.R.C. involvement there at some point. I can't say for sure, but maybe A.R.C. operatives just had a mission there before we came. Or maybe, A.R.C. had already taken over that base without anyone's knowledge. That makes the presence of the file all the more likely. If the base had been taken, it should have been in our records. If it involved someone as powerful and important as Rodrigues, it should have been fairly widely known within A.R.C. Also, if it was just a mission, why was Rodrigues not taken in and moved from Centralia? Maybe, because it was it was A.R.C. who had already contained him there. It all points to a secret mission to take over and operate Centralia. The only A.R.C. member with that the pull and authority to do something like that would be Jackson. Even the assembling for his strike force hints at his dislike of notifying the rest of A.R.C. of his activities."

Paul continued. "The angles Jackson runs are usually borderline within A.R.C. rules. The strike-team is one of those angles. Anyway, he's been on the Council for the longest. He has the most influence. But what do you think he's doing? What is he hiding at secret locations?"

"I'd love to know," Avery commented. "It makes you wonder. Jackson typically has everything done within the rules. What is so shocking that he needs to skirt them? People call A.R.C. shady, and I will admit that we are in many ways. What is shadier than shady?"

Paul felt like there was phlegm in throat. He was not sure if it was real or imagined from the pressure, but he coughed anyway.

"I have dreams," Paul revealed shakily, feeling the power in what he was about to say. "Sometimes, they come when I am asleep, and sometimes they occur when I feel strong anima from someone. I guess I don't have to tell you about that. With your highest level of clearance, you've definitely heard of Amuli like that before. Anyway, there was one with Jackson. He had an A.I.M. scientist at A.R.C. secretly. It was a twisted one he kept hidden away. I checked the records, and there is nothing about it.

I think he was desperate. Alice wasn't panning out the way he hoped, and it's no wonder with the way she was treated. He needed to reign her in. So, he brought in the scientist and a young Amulus. The theory was that they could have Alice transfer some of her power to the other Amulus. Ling was her name. It didn't work. I don't know if that scientist betrayed him or what, but it was... beyond horrible. She became a Dead Eyes. The experiment had failed and devolved into that ritual. None of this was written down."

Avery hand on the desk had turned into a fist.

"These dreams you have, have you ever had any that were authenticated? Do you really dream what really has happened?"

"Yes," Paul whispered, still reeling. "I have had multiple memory dreams corroborated by people who were actually present in those moments. The other ones have all fit in with stories I've been told. I haven't had any reason to doubt them."

"It's so much worse than I thought," Avery declared with his emotions rising to his usually cool exterior. "Jackson talks about much he opposes A.I.M.'s methods. He claims his whole gung-ho rationale is to prevent A.I.M. from doing its damage to innocents. To think he was doing the same thing, even if it was only for a time."

"I-I didn't want to be the one to tell you," Paul admitted. "I know what it might... er... does mean."

Both of Avery's fists were now clenched as he stared at them with intensity. His eyes burned purple, and Paul was sure the rapier at his side was doing likewise.

"I can't express how much it means for you to give me this information," Avery praised. "I am, no A.R.C., is in your debt. For now, I think you can rest assured. A.R.C. will not come undone at right this moment. I would need more proof. Pictures of empty buildings and dreams are not going to convince the rest of the Council to move to action. There are provisions for removal from the Council in A.R.C.'s charter, but it has never been done before."

"You want me to find proof," Paul surmised.

"Oh, no," relented Avery graciously. "By all means, give me proof if you stumble across it, but I will do the heavy lifting. I do not put A.R.C. operatives in harm's way lightly. You would put yourself at odds with one of the most powerful men in the world and his supporters. Remember, you have your current status by his approval. You came to the right place. I will take this from here. This will not happen overnight. You have my word that I will be methodical and precise. When Jackson goes down, it will be with the support of everyone in A.R.C."

Paul felt in shoulders relaxing. *I feel like I shouldn't be letting my guard down, but I've just heard everything I hoped that I would.*

Avery seemed to have loosened up as well, and his aura became one of clarity.

"It always comes down to things like this," he remarked thoughtfully. "Governmental philosophy and politics. A.R.C. and A.I.M. has essentially replaced governments but have become tied up with similar power struggles. It is now Jackson's philosophy versus the less militaristic members of A.R.C. It reminds me of a history lesson. Forgive me if this is out of place. I don't mean to put you on the spot, but you're a smart kid, Paul. Sorry, a smart agent. I've read your files and reports, but more importantly, I've seen you in action. Tell me, do you know the origin of the word 'tyrant.'"

"It's from the Greek, *tyrannos*," Paul answered quickly.

"Go on. What did that word mean in its original sense?"

"Well," Paul started as he put the information together in his brain. "It makes sense when you look at it this way, some ancient Greek thinkers thought that governments changed cyclically based on what they had observed in city-states. For instance, a city-state may start with a monarchy with a monarch at the top. Then, the people would rebel for themselves and form a democracy where they had the power themselves. But eventually, a few rich or affluent individuals or families would seize power and form an oligarchy, a government ruled by a few. After that, the *tyrannos* would emerge. One oligarch would promise the people benefits and power if they supported the *tyrannos* in overthrowing the other oligarchs and become sole ruler. In time, that oligarch or his successors would be the new monarch as the cycle began again."

"I couldn't have said it better," Avery complimented. "It's funny. The word tyrant has come to describe an evil, power-hungry despot. A *tyrannos* was not that necessarily. Instead, they were patrons of the people. They acted in their interest. I know about one theory on why the word's meaning changed so much. Who wrote down the histories? The general mass of people did not have the leisure time because they were just trying to sustain themselves, and the *tyrannos* rarely did because they were busy ruling. It was the aristocrats who wrote things down. It was the oligarchs or potential oligarchs who portrayed tyrants in such a way. History is written by the winners and also the rich."

"You think Jackson thinks of himself as a *tyrannos*?" Paul ventured.

Avery smirked. "I'm merely saying that politics is a dirty business, and I don't like it. Still, I'll do what I must. It might surprise you that I've already started."

"What?" Paul blurted with a raised eyebrow.

"You're not the only operative to come to me with concerns about Jackson," Avery explained. "He sent an agent to check up on me. Lucky for me, he's just as concerned about the future of A.R.C. as you and is just as wary of anyway wannabe despots who would hurt the public at large. I actually have him running the beginning of the research downstairs. I'll call him up for us."

"Really, you don't have to waste his time with me," Paul insisted bashfully.

"It's fine, Paul," Avery said as he tapped a message into the closed computer system. "He may be happy to work with you again. I know that I am."

Who? Paul scoured his mind for all A.R.C. operatives with loyalty to Avery. There were too many faces he had passed casually in the halls and the files over the past few months.

There was a quick, solid knock.

"C'mon in," greeted Avery.

Paul observed the doorway with curiosity.

Jason slipped through and immediately shut the door.

"Hey," he breathed their direction.

Jason! I'm relieved its him! I was afraid that we would end up on opposite sides of this. We have our differences, but to say that I respect him is an under-statement.

"He's probably already told why I'm here," Jason said abruptly. "The orders for the strike-force, well, they didn't sit right with me. I have to say that you've done a good job to keep Jackson out of your hair. I guess he just respects power over all else."

He's changed. Paul realized. *I should have realized that over the past few months we've been working together. He got his revenge on The Rat. I guess he had to pick a new mission in life. This is so different from when he implied that he was ready to die to kill The Rat.*

"This is an opportunity for us," Avery implored. "You are both part of Jackson's inner circle now. You have a level of access to him and his plans. I've given you both the same directive. Let me handle the bulk of it. Just let me know if stumble across anything else that seems suspicious. We can work though Ham who's technically under me. Jackson might notice, but he will probably write it off. He doesn't show respect to the non-Amuli, and you can probably come up with good excuses to talk to Ham. He is the head of the North American Research division, after all. We will get him when we get him. That's all."

Paul felt a sudden rush upon being dismissed. He clutched the door-knob to steady himself was things went dark.

———

It was pitch black except for a thin, vertical line of faintly yellow light.

From the inside of the supply closet, the light shined just enough to show the figure of a teenage boy. On the outside, the barely cracked-open door gave no hint of the occupant behind it. Had the boy been full-grown, there probably would not have been enough space to hide in-between the door and the stack of sheets, cloth, and disinfectants behind him.

A few nurses crowded behind their station, oblivious to the nearby closet's occupant. Their voices were clear from the hiding place.

"Oh, Mark," one addressed a fellow scrub-dressed figure. "Since you're new, there's a small, little situation that sometimes goes on here. It's no big deal, but you should probably know."

"You're scaring me," Mark joked to the female nurse.

She continued. "The girl in 448, she has a brother who's around here a lot."

"But that's not a problem, is it?"

"Oh no, not really," she admitted. "He's a good boy, well-behaved. It's just that he sticks around after visiting hours sometimes. We've caught him hiding in her room from time to time."

"How old is he?"

"Oh, they're twins those two. You wouldn't know from the look of them. They're not identical. He's just a kid."

"So, it's actually kind of sweet."

"Oh, it is. It's just that we can't have kids running around at all hours. I mean, he's not making trouble, but if we let him stay past hours, then everyone will want to. Patients need time to rest, and staff need time to work."

"Gotcha. What about mom and dad for those two?"

"Oh, the dad's never been in the picture, apparently," she scoffed. "The poor kids. The mom, well… she's in here sometimes. Doesn't do a great job of taking care of herself, or them. I think the boy is the one who actually holds it all together. At his age. I'm guessing she leaves him with the boyfriend-flavor-of-the-month sometimes, but they don't care too much about keeping track of him."

"That's rough," the male nurse said. "What's her story again?"

"She was born unlucky, the poor thing," the female nurse sighed.

"Weak heart. Weak lungs. It was a difficult birth. The brother came out first, and he was healthy and strong. She just didn't get the same chance. She's been in and out of here most of her life."

"You hate to hear stories like that. I'm just glad she has someone."

"Yes, don't we all wish we had someone like that."

The woman wrestled her Styrofoam cup of coffee from in-between the stacks of papers on the station bench.

"I hate to leave you with that in mind, but it's my break. I'll be down the hall if you need me. Thankfully, it's been quiet tonight."

"Yeah, have fun," the new nurse said before putting his head into a file.

The boy in the closet knew how to creak open the door and close it without a sound. He also knew that if someone practically crawled along the floor, the nurses could not see over the station to catch them. And so, he slowly stepped his way to room 448 and slid through the door.

The girl lying in the bed stirred. She always seemed to sense when he was there. She took a deep breath from the tubes in her nose but stayed still. Only her eyes flickering open showed that she was awake.

"How do you always know?" he whispered, only being slightly sure that he was out of earshot of the nurses' station.

"I've been here so long, I'm used to the normal sounds," she murmured sleepily. "When I hear a new one, I know it's you."

She had fallen asleep with the curtains open. Just enough light came in for the two siblings to see each other.

The girl was rail-thin with circles under her eyes that looked like thick bruises. Her skin was pale which contrasted with her straight, black hair that lay splayed about her pillow. It was obvious that no hairdressers had not been called to the room lately. Despite her weak appearance, she had soulful brown eyes and an expressive mouth above a dainty chin. Every so often, there was the mechanical hiss of oxygen being pumped into her nose through a clear tube.

"Geez, stop looking at me," she half-complained with a light chuckle. "What are you even doing here?"

The boy shrugged. "I don't know. Mom's at Grant's house again. I'm bored."

He struggled with one of his jacket pockets to pull out a foil-covered rectangle.

"Plus, I brought this. Cookies and cream. The kind you like."

"I'll have to get to it later," she said as her brother placed the candy bar on a tray by the bed.

The boy seemed slightly dejected. His sister did not even have the strength to reach over and pick up a candy bar.

"Not trying to be mean," the sister started. "Don't you have friends or something that you can hang out with?"

"Yeah," he admitted. "But being here seems important. It's like something I have to do."

"Adam, Adam," the girl repeated softly. "I'm not that important. You don't have to keep coming in all the time. Do something fun instead. Don't just say that this is one of those twin-connection things."

"If I were… like you, wouldn't you visit me all the time?" Adam asked.

"You'd never be like me," she answered. "You're too determined. You would have found a way to get yourself out of this bed."

"Don't you ever think you're weak, Sarah! Something will come up. This can't last forever. Your body will get stronger. It has to. I know! Do you know how doctors are studying those superhuman Amulus guys? Maybe that will make them come up with something."

Sarah shook her head as much as the tubes would allow. "You know other doctors come in sometimes. You know… like the…um…the ones for your head. I'm not supposed to talk about what we say to each other, but they sometimes say stuff about controlling what you can control and not what you can't. I can't help being here, so why worry? I can let it get me down, but I won't. Otherwise, how could I even live? Think about it like this, you can't do anything about me. Why think about it? Just keep being a good person like you already are. It's called making peace."

Adam's eyes inflated with tears made of some anger but mostly bitterness. "I'm sorry. I don't believe you! There has to be something! Something…"

"Just believe it. For me."

Adam shut his eyes tightly, trying to hide the tears.

Sarah spoke again with her voice growing even weaker. "I'm sorry. I'm just really tired right now."

———

Paul exited the office while taking one last look at Avery.

So, is that what drives him? Where is Sarah now? That must have been so much to take on while they were that young. I wish I could talk more with the people whose memories I see, but they usually seem too painful for me to even bring up.

As Paul stepped away, Avery was back to his work. For a moment, Paul thought he caught a glimpse of the young Adam in his face.

CHAPTER 24
REDIRECTION

"TWO HUNDRED AND FORTY-FOUR," Paul chanted under his breath again as he craned his neck at the row of connected houses. "Two hundred and forty-four."

"You've got it memorized?" Jason asked sarcastically before pounding on a door without hesitation.

There was a clear fumbling with the doorknob and a slight commotion before the door swung open.

Camilla struggled outward as a young boy dangled from one arm. He giggled and kicked his feet in the air.

"Ow, Sebi!" she complained to the stowaway. "Sebi, let go. That hurts. Sebastian, let go!"

She finally wiggled him off, and he scampered inside.

"Sorry about that," she apologized meekly.

Why does she look embarrassed? Paul wondered.

"Uh, come in," she said. "Everyone's here. Actually, too many people are in here."

The inside walls were painted a bright blue, and yellow decorative places dotted the walls. They seemed just out of reach for small hands.

Robby was sitting on a couch, holding up a video game controller like a trophy.

"I told yah!" he boasted. "That's how you beat that water level."

A boy with the front end of his black hair spiked matched Robby's smile.

"Wow, man!"

In the connected kitchen, Alice sat on a stool with arms at her side as she studied a cup in front of her.

From somewhere unseen, a short woman with Camilla's hair color and eyes put herself in front of the two new arrivals.

"Good to see you two," she greeted warmly with a slight accent. "You must be Paul and… um… you are Jason. I'm glad to meet Cami's teammates. Do you want anything?"

Camilla pushed herself through the room.

"Mom, mom, stop it for a second. We all need to talk in private for a moment."

Her mother began to leave but lingered slightly.

"Ugh," Camilla sighed. "Anyway, this is my mom. The little one clinging to me is Sebastian. The one Robby is playing with is David. Here's my stepdad, Eddy."

A man with the same, albeit graying, hair as David came out of a hallway to shake the hands of the new arrivals.

Paul thought back to the memories he had glimpsed from Camilla previously. *This is so different. Everything's so… happy and normal.*

Camilla sighed again. "Well, they're going to say 'hi' and 'bye,' because we're all leaving."

She turned to Paul and Jason as Alice got up from her chair.

"There's a little park down the street. It's usually quiet there."

They made their way out of the small living to the door.

"Robby?" Camilla called, exacerbated.

"Alright, coming," Robby said after taking notice of them. "Anyway, it's been real. Remember, check around all the rooms. If you find a short-cut, take that first."

———

The playground smelled of the fresh woodchips around the slide and jungle-gym. The small trees planted on the far sides of the park seemed to block the industrial smells of the city. It was empty save for the group at the picnic tables. Still, each of them looked over their shoulder more than once. That was just the world A.R.C. agents lived in.

"I thought they seemed nice," Robby commented honestly. "Though David needs to work on his platforming."

"Quite pleasant," Alice agreed.

"Yeah, well," Camilla started. "We've done some patching up lately. Almost losing them to tidal waves and flooding would bring anyone closer. It's just that I forget how much family it is at times, you know? Two brothers from my mom and Eddy. Two sisters from my dad and his wife."

"I do not know what having a sibling is like," Alice pointed out. "In my familial situation, that may have been a mercy."

"I don't have any siblings either," Paul said, pulling the conversation out of a darker place.

"It's weird," Camilla summed up. "It's like you have mini-clones of yourself that want to copy everything about you, and then one day, they became their own person out of the blue."

Robby crossed his arms exaggeratedly. "Spoken like a true big sister."

Camilla sighed. "I should have known that you were your family's baby."

Jason tapped his palms against the picnic table before having to brush away the splinters.

"This is a great reunion," he admitted. "But we need to get to the point."

"Yeah, like why you're suddenly here," realized Robby.

"You don't think that you're the only ones who know that Jackson's been up to something shady? I caught wind of some off-the-books bases. Along with the questionable orders I've been getting, I had the same idea. I just went to Avery first."

"So, Avery's in," Camilla deciphered.

"You could say he's in' and 'we're out,'" Paul summarized. "He'll take the lead. We did our jobs. We took things up the chain of command. It's out of our hands for now."

"Wait!" Robby interjected. "You mean we're done with this?"

"It was dangerous enough," Paul countered. "We have always had Hunters and A.I.M. to deal with. We can't put Jackson on our plate too. We've been at the risk of going rogue already. Plus, we only know that Jackson is hiding something. We don't know what he's hiding. If Jason and I continue to work with him, we might find out. It's innocent until proven guilty. With Avery on our side, the mysteries will start to unravel. When things are clearer, I'll know what I have to work toward to get my aunt and uncle back."

Camilla massaged her cheek as she thought.

"Alright," she said calmly. "I understand the logic in backing off a little now. Still, it feels like one of those times where you're trying to take on everything on your own, Paul. So, I'm sticking with the Research Division for now. It will keep us in contact and give me an excuse to keep up with you two."

"Well then, me too," Robby added.

"I will do likewise," agreed Alice.

"We also have the other big thing," Jason stated. "It's what you guys did in Pennsylvania."

"Here's my thoughts," Paul began. "Jackson really can't say that was his base or if his men were just there first. Even if he knows what we did, he can't do anything. We weren't supposed to be there, but he really wasn't either. There weren't any logs for a mission to an A.I.M. base in Centralia, let alone a base takeover. The fact that I found an A.R.C. record there speaks to the fact that it had become an A.R.C. entirely. It will make things uncomfortable though, if he knows that we have dirt on him. We just have to hope that he really does need Jason and me. We can also see if he acts any different after what happened."

"I'd be ticked," relayed Robby. "He set up a whole project there. He had that crazy guy with a barrel chest locked up there. Plus, he can't even show that he's mad about it, or it will show that he had something to do with it. Man, we are cold-blooded."

"We still don't know why it was abandoned," Camilla pointed out. "Except for Rodrigues, of course."

"He may have been aware of our coming," Alice hypothesized. "Rodrigues would have been difficult to move quickly, due to the risk of him regaining consciousness."

"Well, that's bad," Robby said glumly. "That means he's onto us."

"It's unnerving," Paul agreed. "On the other hand, he can't do anything to us since he's in the wrong. If he were to do something like kicking Jason or me off of the strike-force, it would look suspicious."

"Anyway, he may have known that someone was onto him but didn't know it was us," Camilla guessed. "Or maybe he knows we were there but doesn't know that we think he was involved."

"It's a lot of unknowns," Jason said. "I might be the last person to say this, but we probably have to wait and see where the chips fall."

Each of them ran the whole conversation through again in their heads. It seemed too important to stop thinking about it.

Whenever there are unknowns, that's when my mind wanders to the worst possibilities. The next conversation with Jackson will be key. It feels so strange that I am still on his team when I'm investigating him. I think these were the type of politics that Luper liked to stay away from.

"I guess I should ask how you feel, Paul," Camilla finally addressed him. "This has to be the hardest on you. You're using deception to get to what's important to you."

"You know," Paul deflected with a slight blush, "I pretty much feel like I always do."

Basically, every day since I joined A.R.C.

"We're all in this," Camilla declared passionately. "We're going to dig through all the crap to get your family back."

CHAPTER 25
OTHER SIDE

"COUNCILMEN AVERY HAS INFORMED me of your report to him on the whereabouts of Carson Colter," Jackson's floating head on the video screen informed.

So, that's the cover that Avery thought up, Paul surmised.

Jackson continued. "While I appreciate the initiative, please contact me before traveling such a distance. You have the freedom, but this is a team after all. Our communication is key. Remember this also, your position enables you to move without being bogged down by bureaucracy, so reporting to Avery as well may have been redundant."

I've gotten off easy so far. If he knows it was me in Centralia, he isn't showing it. I wish I could read his mind, but even Psychics can't do that fully.

"I believe that I must commend you," Jackson declared as Paul's mouth slightly opened in barely hidden surprise. "You have encountered two enhanced Amuli in Carson and Whaley. They may not be in A.R.C. cells at this point, however, they are not causing trouble either. Clearly, you have caused them to retreat. That is not a final victory but it is a victory, nonetheless. As such, I am putting you on point for a new mission. I think that it is well-suited for your skills."

So, he trusts me. Or does he?

"There is an issue in the American heartland," Jackson explained. "Rogue Amuli have taken control of a motorway service area. They have surrounded the place with large vehicles and set themselves up inside. We estimate at least three individuals. There have been only a few clear pictures taken by drones. That is all we know at the moment. This will be suited for the strike-force since speed is of the essence. We do not need bad publicity, or any publicity at all, for that matter. We are now under intense scrutiny thanks to that outlandish plan from A.I.M. It has always been best for us to blend into the background of the world's perception. We should be seen as simply a government-like agency, boring and nothing more. So, I ask you, take care of the situation before the reporters and cameras come. Don't be the one to draw them in either. Apprehend the rogues and turn them over to the nearest prison base. You are the lead as I said previously. Your friend Saito, Sakurai, and Robeson will join you."

Paul ran a hand through his hair. *On top of all this, I have to worry about leading people who are more experienced than me. That's most of the strike-force.*

"You have a ticket for a flight to Topeka. Take it to the mission area."

———

It was a van this time.

I have a weird dislike for vans now, Paul admitted to himself. *Nondescript sedans don't attract attention. People don't think about them after they pass. Plus, they accelerate quickly. Larger vehicles draw the eyes. Someone sees a van and wonders if it's for a business or a large family. They think about it. Or maybe just my obsessive and paranoid mind does. Still, with the supplies needed for a possible siege, it can't be helped.*

Brandon Robeson was at the wheel. He had short dark hair parted slightly on one side. His face had the same look as many of the other upper-level agents Paul had encountered. It was somewhere between professional and brooding. Neither aspect invited conversation, not that Paul was eager. On the other hand, the more talkative people in his life had made him all too aware of long or awkward silences by pointing them out whenever one occurred. The current one in the van felt like both.

Robeson was young, as was the rest of the strike-force. Barely twenty, he had been a ringer in this region, winning several Midwestern cities for A.R.C. Topeka was still held thanks to his efforts just before his inclusion into the strike-force.

Well out into the country now, the surroundings were beginning to look alien to Paul. Nearly all of his travel during recent months had left him with only brief stops to new places. None of them really sank in. He still looked out every window expecting to see large hills and forests in the background. Only recently had he even gotten accustomed to being surrounded by city skylines.

Here, he could see farther out than he ever had before on land. With his anima-enhanced eyes, that was quite far. There was grass everywhere, and it was quite thick at close inspection. The monotony was only broken up by a rare tree or tiny incline. In some areas, it looked to be an inhospitable dessert save for the yellowing grass and sandy clumps or dirt.

Visibility is a plus, Paul switched from aesthetics to analytics. *It's just that the enemy has it, too. The plains are a different environment than I'm used to.*

The van slowed as they passed a sign for a truck stop. A hanging piece of fabric below it informed that it was closed. It looked anything but official, with the word "closed" hastily formed by spray-paint.

"That'll be it," Robeson said as he steered the car in that direction.

Paul felt the familiar, heavy thump of his heart before a mission. His teeth seemed to clench hard enough that he had to use more than the usual effort to even open his mouth.

I wonder if this feeling will ever change. Part of me wishes it would, but another part of me thinks I will have lost myself at that point.

"Do we want them to know that we're here?" asked Robeson as it got to crunch time.

"Somewhat," Paul answered. "It will be negotiation first. If you're okay with it, Brandon and I will try to get through by talking. They have to know at least a little of what they're up against, so they might want a way out. Meanwhile, Kishi and Jason will use that as cover to sneak around behind. I know that's a challenge with the lack of cover here. You two will only move in if things take a turn. We will only fight if we have to, and if we do, we should have the advantage since we have the drop on them. But I mean… what do you guys think? It's your lives on the line, too."

"Fine with me," agreed Robeson.

"I have confidence in the plan," Kishi reported.

Jason just grunted his approval.

The quick mobilization of this team means that we didn't have time to practice. Plus, our Psychic, Ben, is on another mission. That doesn't help with communication.

The fact that something was wrong at the truck stop was not hidden. Several trailers were turned on their sides. They were arranged in a rough triangle around the main building. Seeing through the windows, the inside appeared to be barricaded with furniture and vending machines.

Fortification, Paul observed.

"I think we've found our cover," Jason commented.

He and Kishi waited patiently in the backseat as Paul and Robeson got ready.

"Leaving your sword?" Jason questioned. "You can't leave your powers behind."

Paul did feel less comfortable without the katana at his waist.

"I was thinking of the psychological effect," Paul explained. "A show of good faith."

"What about me?" Robeson wondered as his heavy eyebrows knitted in near-skepticism.

"I was thinking that your shield looks innocuous enough," Paul pointed out. "That's not to say… uh…. God knows that it's powerful. It's just…"

"I get it," Robeson muttered gruffly. "It looks like stretched fabric."

"I think that we all know Paul is strong enough even without the sword," Kishi complimented.

Paul graciously nodded. "If we're ready. We'll start."

Paul was out of the vehicle quickly.

I can't start hesitating now. I can't fall back into old, bad habits.

The overturned trailers were not a difficult climb for an Amulus. Paul and Robeson were quickly over them and heading for the entrance at a steady pace. They kept their eyes, ears, and six senses ready in case of a projectile-based Amulus.

There's just too little information about this mission.

Paul kept his hands away from his sides strategically. He wanted to make a show of being unarmed.

As they got closer to the hastily blocked doors. They could hear a commotion inside. Chairs were screeching across a floor. Paul felt the familiar tingle of anima in the air. This one was unpleasant like a wailing soundwave reverberating against his skin. *It's hostile.*

Robeson readied his shield. Paul continued with caution toward the door. The barricade was not going to be a problem for him.

Suddenly, there was the sound of crashing and breaking inside. Chairs and tables at the top of the pile clattered into the floor. A shadow squeezed through flew outside with surprising speed.

Paul easily dodged a purple-glowing fist with a single step back. He could see it was a man with a thin face and a wiry goatee.

The other fist followed up as Paul sidestepped.

"Please," Paul interjected as he dodged yet more poorly aimed punches. "We can talk this out."

The only response was more desperate attacks.

I really wanted to be hands-off.

With the next fist, Paul let the punch slip by him before grabbing at the wrist.

"I'm not here to hurt you," he explained to the attacker who would not meet his gaze.

The reply was a punch at point-blank range. Well before impact, Paul twisted the man's body around by the wrist. It was a simple, self-defense move.

"Please, stop," Paul commanded calmly.

The man used Paul's lack of aggression to his slight advantage. In a couple of twists, he wrenched himself free. Dripping with sweat, he eyed Paul up for another run.

He then hit the ground with a smattering of blue anima bouncing off of him.

Paul turned to Robeson.

"Well, I was getting tired of that," he informed. "Sometimes, there's no getting through to people. Really though, sending out your Psychic first? These must be real amateurs."

Paul saw the lack of weapon on the man and realized that the unpleasant invasion of anima had stopped. He stooped without hesitation to check the man's vitals. They were fine.

I guess I can't control every action of my teammates. Lucky, the 'no-kill if possible' policy got through to Brandon.

"Maybe his friends will be smarter," guessed Robeson as he scrambled through the fallen furniture inside the glass doors.

They entered the barren lobby with both agents checking out a different end of the building. Paul crept towards an empty convenience store portion. On the other end, Robeson headed for the restaurant end.

"Got them," the latter relayed quickly.

Paul turned towards the restaurant. At one of the only tables remaining, two people sat calmly behind bottled drinks.

"What do we do?" Robeson questioned. "I have an easy shot on both of them."

Paul looked at Robeson's anima weapon. It was a shield, but dangerous, nonetheless. Robeson sometimes used it as an extra barrier, a blunt weapon, or the source of a powerful blast. For a defense implement, it could cause some surprising damage as Paul had seen outside.

Some Native American groups believed that their medicine shields gave them special power in ceremonies. They were right about this one. I wonder how many of them were actually anima weapons. That may have been where the legends began.

Paul abruptly ended his reflection.

"I'll go talk to them first. I think that's what they want. Maybe, that's why they're waiting patiently. If you see Kishi or Jason on their approach, signal them to hold back unless it gets violent."

With sweaty palms, Paul crossed over to the tile floor. *I'm so weird. I'm not sure if I'm more anxious about a possible fight or because I'm about to meet new people.*

He got a good look at them early with his perceptive eyes. The one pointed towards him was a man in red flannel and jeans. He was slightly overweight and had his large, hammy hands on the table. The other was a similarly dressed girl. She was Paul's age or maybe older. Looking back over her shoulder, she swept dark brown hair out of her blue eyes as she eyed his approach with disapproval.

"C'mon in," the man addressed Paul pleasantly with a homey Midwestern accent.

Paul drew closer to the table.

"Well, sit down," offered the man who had scruffy stubble. "I'll admit. Masks make me nervous."

"Forgot I had it on," Paul admitted, grasping his mask below the frown.

He hesitated for a moment. *I guess I did want to be open. That was the plan.*

"See, that's better," said the man. "Now, how about the friend who came in with you. Does he need a rest?"

One, 'friend.' Good. That means he doesn't know about Kishi and Jason at the other entrance.

"I think he feels like standing," Paul replied honestly in a low enough voice that he hoped Robeson would not hear.

"He can suit himself then," the man said nonchalantly. "I have your face, how about a name?"

You can find out a lot with a face. You can find out a lot with a name. Both of them together... I think I've hurt enough people with my full identity being revealed. It might seem flaky though.

"Well... call me 'Green' for now," Paul ventured as lit a tiny green flame on his finger for a moment while flashing the unnatural eyes of the same color.

"That's a neat party trick," complimented the man only somewhat sarcastically.

How about mine?

The alien thought rattled around Paul's head as he stared into the man's now blue eyes.

"I'll stick to the less-freaky talking," the man followed up as his eyes dimmed. "Mr. Green will have to do. I'm Joe. This is Kim."

Kim looked less than pleased that her name had been revealed. Then again, the sour look had never left her face.

"We've been wondering when someone would show up," Joe sighed. "Which are you, A.R.C. or A.I.M.?"

"A.R.C.," Paul answered.

"I hope you'll forgive me if I've always thought of them as one and the same," Joe revealed. "I don't know heads-or-tails of either one."

"They're pretty different," Paul informed them cryptically.

"It's been a bad break for the both of us," Joe confessed. "Both of us have similar stories. I'm a truck driver, not that Kim here was. I picked up a trinket for my wife at a little roadside gift shop. Now, I've got all these special things I can do but don't feel like I can go home. Don't want to drag the wife into this. I don't know how much Kim wants me to say since she doesn't talk much herself. Apparently, she got hers in a similar way and ran from home."

"Joe's been taking care of me since he picked me up on the side of the road," Kim finally spoke in a low voice. "And it's not what you think. Joe's a good guy. He's more of a dad to me than my dad was when he was around."

Paul steered the conversation back to the issues at hand. "Who was the man at the door?"

"That's Hardy," Joe replied. "I'm guessing he's dead now?"

"Unconscious," Paul corrected.

"Probably missing at least a few teeth though or some brain cells."

Paul did not let the comment faze him. It really had not in the first place.

"I don't know his first name," Joe relayed. "I think he was a drifter mostly. This plan and this place were his ideas. He was another guy I bumped into on the road with a similar story. He was paranoid but so were we. You have to admit, those data leaks are something. Everyone is reading up on what you guys and those other guys are supposedly doing. If half of it were true, we wanted to stay out of it. We didn't want to get involved in someone else's war. Maybe it was a stupid plan, but we thought that if we were already running then we could keep running. Hardy thought someone was on our tail and decided to make a stand. We on the other hand didn't want to abandon him, but we didn't want to fight either. So, here we are."

They are so like me at the beginning. I wanted no part in the fighting. But I did… what I thought I had to. Seeming these two here makes them seem so innocent, while I feel so guilty.

Paul sighed, feeling the uncomfortable nostalgia. "I'm going to level with you. Those leaks, everything posted online, it's all true other than the fact that Red Mask is the worst of us and not the hero he makes himself out to be. A.R.C. and A.I.M. have all the power in the world behind the scenes, and they're at war. Amuli have all had to pick a side."

"It's just as I've been saying, then," Joe shrugged. "It's dangerous and violent that life. I don't want any part of it, and I don't think Kim wants it either. Leave us out of it."

Kim shook her head bitterly.

"You don't get it," Paul disagreed with urgency. "What I'm saying is that you both are already a part of it. The second you are discovered, it's either A.R.C. or A.I.M. Believe me, A.R.C. isn't the greatest, but A.I.M. is worse. They are *the* worst. They use their cover as a medical agency to perform human experiments."

Paul let his veins build up the black and green mixture. He pointed to a prominent one in his neck.

"I was an A.I.M. prisoner once. They did things to me that I'm still trying to understand. You don't have to be like me. A.R.C. can take you in and protect you and your loved ones."

Paul felt the irony of the last sentence like an ulcer on his tongue.

"How dare you!" Kim shouted as she looked Paul fully in the face for the first time. "You keep talking about your experience and what you've been through. You don't know the first thing about us. Just because something has been good for you doesn't mean that it will be good for us. You don't know where we came from and how we came to be here!"

Joe made a half-hearted "stop" motion but then saw that it was no use.

"I mean, look at you!" she blasted. "You barge in here with a mask on after taking out one of our friends? You said that you want to want to level with us? How far do you think you are above us?"

Paul's skin went cold as he started feeling droplets along his armpits. *I'm not cut out for this. That's why I feel like such an imposter all the time. Really, I should just be reading in a corner of the school library right now. I don't belong here doing this.*

Paul was suddenly aware of the seconds ticking by.

He finally stammered, "I-I don't… I-I understand…"

Paul was aware of the fist coming. Even when fighting Amuli now, everything slowed down for him. He even had time to think of whether he should dodge. *No. It's like that time with Cam. I need to feel this, and she needs to get it out… I think.*

Kim hit him in the nose. Paul did not flinch. With his enhanced durability, there was no red mark or blood. *I don't think she really meant to injure me anyway.*

Joe had jumped from his chair, knocking over as he raced around the table toward Kim. However, she was already walking away towards the restroom doors with her back turned. Her fingers sent Paul an unflattering message.

"She's really a good girl," Joe apologized, looking sincerely sorry. "She just has fight in her and all this fire. I don't think she meant to…"

"I know," Paul interjected while absentmindedly rubbing his unharmed nose.

Joe sighed. "I gotta…"

A cylinder-like blast caught the trucker in the ribs. He hurtled to the ground and splayed out painfully.

Paul reached for a sword that was not there while turning towards the anima's direction. Meanwhile, Kim came rushing back.

"Joe!" she screamed as she slid towards him on the floor. "What did you do? Why?"

Robeson put down his shield as he entered the dining area.

CHAPTER 26
AGAINST THE GOOD

PAUL KNOCKED over his chair as he stared down at his teammate.

"Why?" he simply shouted.

"You were attacked," Robeson pointed out coolly. "I was ensuring your safety."

"It wasn't like that," Paul gritted.

He felt and saw the black and green rising in his veins. Without thinking, he massaged his neck along the dark streaks as he forced the feelings back down.

Paul knelt at the unconscious Joe's feet. "How is he?"

"Stay away!" Kim yelled hard enough that Paul could feel her hot, angry breath.

Paul backed away. Robeson now seemed annoyed. One of his eyebrows twitched intermittently.

"It wasn't enough to kill him," he muttered.

"That's not the point," Paul murmured as he tried to peer around Kim to get a good glance at Joe.

He then heard the faintest of footsteps. Jason and Kishi had come from the other side of the room with weapons out.

"We heard a commotion," Kishi explained while lowering his kusarigama after surveying the scene.

Jason responded solemnly in kind with his saber.

Robeson stared down his nose at Kim. "Are you coming with us standing, or are you coming unconscious like him?"

Kim flashed her red-rimmed eyes his way. Surprisingly, she slowly put her hands on her head kneeled on the floor. She gave everyone in the room the same glare. Robeson caught the dirtiest looks.

"What?" he complained. "I did what the mission called for. Things were getting out of control, and I settled it. The mission is successfully completed with no causalities."

Paul swallowed hard. He had too many things to say to speak. Much of it would have been to Kim. The harsher words would have gone to Robeson.

Robeson could not shake the stares.

"What do you all want from me? None of you had the drive to end things. Remember, we work for Jackson. He wants things down quickly and efficiently with no harm to A.R.C. agents. That's how we'll do things. The only ones I care about are the guys who have my back. Do you really have my back or what?"

They knew better than to answer.

Paul still boiled. *That's the problem. That's the problem with Jackson and the people loyal to him. They will do anything for the sake of A.R.C. What about everyone not in A.R.C.? What about collateral damage?*

The squad then followed their duty. Paul found it strange that it was Jason who gently led Kim to the van by guiding her by the shoulder. *I guess he knows all about kids' pain when their parent-figures are hurt.*

Kishi and Paul carefully carried Joe on a table before laying him down on the backseat of the van.

————

They had stopped at a gas station. Even A.R.C. vans needed fuel, and even Amuli needed food. Robeson and Kishi were inside. Jason was pumping gas, while Paul stood in the much-needed air. It was well past dark, and they were still miles from the airport.

The ride had been almost unbearable for Paul. He had sat by Joe, checking his condition. He had been stirring but was not awake yet and was now being watched by Kim inside the van. Paul still wanted to come up with something to say to her. Nothing he thought up seemed to make up for what his team and his mission had done. Looking Robeson's way, he could feel the dark bitterness in his veins.

He could still feel it. He wanted it to leave him, to explode out of him at once to give him that relief. He barely paid attention to what he was doing now. He ripped off a few of the strands of long grass from the encircling field. Green and black fire consumed them and the seeds at the end popped. It was Paul's act of rebellion, and it felt pathetic to him.

"Careful," Jason warned as he came upon him. "You'll set everything on fire."

Paul let the ashes fall and did not add to them.

"I feel like such a villain," Paul moaned, not wasting words. "I've felt like this so often now, but I'm still not used to it. Specifically, I feel like an imposter playing a villain. I'm just a stupid kid who's hurting people. How can I be doing the right thing?"

Jason shook his head. "Sometimes, you're still that naïve kid."

"I think that role was better for me. It came naturally."

"You didn't always act like it."

Paul did not respond to the truthful words. *I did act nervous all of the time because everything was so new. You can't really mentally prepare yourself for a life like this.*

He addressed Jason as he kicked at a loose stone. "I feel like I'm missing part of what I used to be. I don't think that I can get it back. I want to see the world like I used to."

Jason gave Paul a modest jab to the shoulder, not even wanting to cause a flinch.

"It's pandora's box at times," Jason philosophized. "Once all that negativity escapes from inside of you, you can't put it back. Once you see things, you can never go back. That doesn't mean you can't find a place that's comfortable once again. Time is a weird thing."

Is that what life has been like for Jason? He had everything taken away and then he got his revenge. He fulfilled the goal that had been gnawing away at all of his being. After all of that, did he find a new headspace? Is he really more emotionally connected to us than he leads on?

Jason continued as he gazed soulfully up at the stars. "The thing is, sometimes you just have to get to that place on your own. The world doesn't lay it out for you. You have to make it happen yourself."

"I wish things would just fall into place," Paul admitted. "I wish a white cowboy hat would just fall on my head. I don't know where to start."

"You want my advice?" Jason quipped rhetorically. "I think you know some good people. You know the ones I'm talking about. Stick with them and maybe it will rub off on you. The good feelings, I mean."

Paul smiled. "If Cam and Robby could hear you right now-"

"Please," Jason scoffed. "I'm only talking about you. You've seen stuff. I've seen stuff. I kind of get it. It's just about moving on despite everything weighing you down."

Paul felt a strange exhilaration from having this guarded person open up to him.

"I think you may be right," he said slowly. "I have to make good things happen. No more excuses. After this, I'm meeting with Jackson face-to-face. I going to use whatever off-the-books resources he has to find my aunt and uncle. I need to do something good again, even if it's selfish."

"You're right," Jason agreed as he finished at the pump. "That's exactly what you're going to do."

Paul ventured a joke. "When did you grow a heart?"

Jason smirked. "It's always been there. I just haven't felt it beating in a long time."

CHAPTER 27
THE LOCK

"JACKSON'S SENT THE DROP-OFF LOCATION," Brandon Robeson informed from the passenger seat. "It's now on the GPS."

"I recognize it," Kishi replied from behind the wheel.

Jason and Paul were quiet in the row behind them, as were Joe and Kim in the farthest seats. Jason looked to be sleeping with his arms crossed over his chest.

Paul envied him. *I wish I had the inner peace to catch some sleep on a mission.*

It was an eerie night. There were no other vehicles on the road, save for an occasional semi-truck. Being stuck in a closed space with people he had just wronged did little to help Paul's mood.

They were several miles from the glow of a town when Kishi turned onto a once-paved road. It was clear, even in the black of night, that it had not been repaired for some time.

Strange, Paul thought restlessly. *I don't remember a base location here. It's not like I have them all memorized though. Still, there aren't a lot of good hiding places on the plains in terms of forests and mountainsides. Distance from civilization might be the only way to do it.*

The van pulled up to an old gate that had once been painted entirely white, along with the connected guard station.

Kishi rolled down his window, letting breezy, warm air in. Paul nearly jumped when the station's intercom system showed itself to be working.

"We have been notified of your drop-off," a can voice informed them. "You may proceed."

The gate worked as well, and it swung upward to let them pass onto a long driveway which was in the same condition as the adjoining road.

A large brick building quickly came into view as they rounded a turn. Paul noted its seemingly utilitarian nature. *It looks like an old hospital or maybe a sanitorium. The latter would explain the guard station. Funny, it used to be a place for people to get better. What's it doing now?*

The front double-doors were initially still during the drive but eventually opened let an agent pass. He was dressed in combat-ready brown camo and wielded an iron war-hammer with a long shaft. He kept both hands on it on his way to the car.

It feels strangely unnerving that the weapon looks so much like the tool, Paul thought glumly. *A tool for building turned into a tool for killing.*

Kishi and Robeson let their windows roll down. Jason somehow awoke on queue.

"I'll take them now," the guard informed the group.

"Hold on," Jason ordered as he undid his seatbelt. "I'd like to walk these two in. You know, just for the added assurance."

The guard's face, although slightly obscured in the night, appeared confused.

"That would be... irregular and unnecessary. We can handle it."

Jason was already out the door.

"What are you even doing?" wondered an annoyed Robeson. "Now, you're just wasting time. There's no reason for us to go in there."

Jason shrugged. "It will give me a chance to stretch my legs."

He then raised his eyebrows at Paul who had caught on. Paul climbed out of the van as well.

"I was given the lead on the mission, and I say it's okay. After all, the more aspects of A.R.C. we involve ourselves in, the better we can understand the whole operation. It will just be a quick walk in and out."

"Ugh," moaned Robeson. "Count me out. I'd rather just drop them and leave like we're supposed to. Jackson hates time-wasting."

Kishi waved them away. "If you're going to take a walk, just do it."

The guard seemed slightly hesitant to have Jason and Paul come along but relented. Joe, now conscious but still out of it, leaned on Kim as they walked in the middle of the group. Their heads were down as they trudged dejectedly.

Paul could not stand the sight. *Two people who don't want to hurt anyone. Now, they're being locked up for making an enemy of A.R.C. We have to make something good come of this at least by exploring what is really going on at this place. I just hate to leave Joe and Kim like this.*

The guard with the war-hammer opened the doors for the group.

Another guard stood inside the lobby which, judging by the stacks of cushioned chairs piled against a wallpapered wall, had obviously once housed a waiting room. This other guard was similarly dressed as the first and also wielded a hammer. This one was a maul, another medieval weapon that was a mixture between an ax and a hammer. The design had come from tools used to split logs. It was another tool that had transitioned to kill.

The hammer bros, Paul thought wryly. *That's the joke Robby would make. God, after hanging around him all of these years, he's started to rub off on me.*

Still, he did not feel like smiling. A still-functioning elevator took them to an upper floor.

This hallway had the same chipped, white paint and cream-colored wallpaper as the other floors. Obviously, no one had thought of making an aesthetic repair. The same could not be said about the doors on this level. They were bulky and metal with a series of latches, the ones Paul had seen Amuli imprisoned behind. There was no doubt that the walls had been enforced as well.

It's a sound enough holding area for superhumans, Paul analyzed coldly. *Even if the metal reinforcement breaks during an escape attempt, it will create enough noise to alert all the guards. With being on a higher floor, most Amuli could not come out of a fall from the window unscathed.*

The guard leading them stopped at a room with a perceived vacancy.

"Wait!" Paul interjected without a real idea of what to say next.

The guard's annoyed face restricted even more.

"Uhhhmmm…" Paul murmured as he collected his thoughts. "I'm not sure if you got the memo, but these prisoners are VIPs. That comes straight from Jackson. Don't you have somewhere nicer?"

Joe and Kim glanced at each other in surprise.

The guard was less amused.

"These two? I thought that…"

Jason interrupted him this time. "Please, don't make things hard on us. You know us. We're the strike-force, Speaker Jackson's personal strike-force. If you want to pull something worse than guard duty, just do as we say. It will save us all a lot of trouble."

The guard nervously scratched his chin and relented. "Whatever. I guess there's a lounge area that we aren't using ourselves."

"Take us there," Jason ordered him.

They were then taken to another former waiting room. This one had intact, cushioned chairs and couches.

"I guess we'll just keep a guard at the door," the uneasy guard offered.

Paul watched Kim and Joe as the door shut on them. *The guilt physically hurts. I feel sick. I want to say something, but I don't know what, and the guard's watching.*

Kim still seemed bitter as ever. After hearing Jason's demands, Joe's face hinted at gratitude but still seemed pained overall. Paul could only give them a nod.

Then, they were in the rickety elevator again. Paul's stomach lurched as he heard the unseen cables groaning and complaining. After an uneasy moment, the elevator stopped and the lights of its panel flickered.

The guard swore as he rattled the panel. "Again? Don't know why I don't just use the stairs every time."

After some forceful button pushing, the doors squeaked open.

"We'll…uh… have to walk the rest of the way down," the guard announced.

The three of them squeezed through the barely open doors.

It was obvious that this floor had been given different alterations than the ones above. Doors had been pried away from their old frames and had been replaced. Vertical, metal bars had been put in their place. Similarly, metal cages hung protectively around the windows inside each room. In both cases, Paul found the metal bars jarring. There was no hiding their purpose.

Now this feels like a traditional prison. A prison that is off-the-grid, even for A.R.C. Still, just the metal bars? You would think that they would be outfitted like the rooms on the upper floors if they were to hold Amuli.

Here, the prisoners were visible. There was one per makeshift cell. Their clothes were clean and intact, and they did not appear to be malnourished. However, there was an unmistakable sense of hollow despair in each of their eyes. The majority of them stared blankly into space. Some had been afforded televisions. The flashing lights in front of them only highlighted their faces which were starving for freedom. At one point, Paul had to grip the wall to concentrate on something other than the mounting queasiness and guilt in his aching stomach.

It was Jason who fully caught onto the situation first. He split off from the guard to stare one of the prisoners in the face. The prisoner shied away at first, falling back from the intense gaze. Finally, he could no longer ignore the Amulus before him and looked back at Jason but made no attempt to say anything.

The prisoner was a man in perhaps his late thirties or early forties. His hair and stubble showed signs of gray around the edges. It was clear that he had not been offered a razor in some time.

"You," Jason addressed the prisoner simply. "Why are you here?"

The guard turned to him, dumbfounded. "What are doing? How is this even necessary?"

"Relax," Jason shot back, but the red seeping into his eyes made the guard do anything but.

The prisoner seemed too nervous to respond. He only gulped hard enough to move his Adam's apple.

"Well? Say something."

Paul moved closer to the prisoner, offering him a friendlier face than Jason or the guard.

"Please," he pleaded. "Tell us about yourself. My friend and I are new to this place. We just want to know what's going on here."

"I… uh…" the prisoner half-choked in a shaky voice. "I… don't know what this is, but please don't hurt me and don't hurt Emma. She's just a girl."

"Who is Emma?" asked Paul.

"This is so…" the guard began to complain.

"Quiet!" Jason barked at him. "I told you that we are Jackson's strike-force. You do what we say."

"Please, it's just that I thought you would know… or something. She's my daughter. I don't know what kind of game this is, but I know she's an Amulus. I know that some people don't like that and Amuli have their own rules about things. I know I'm here because of that."

"Wait! You're not an Amulus yourself?" Jason questioned him.

The man shook his head. "No, no, just Emma. Just please tell me she's safe."

Paul felt his heart pumping red-hot as his face grew warm.

"You're imprisoning non-Amuli here?" he interrogated the guard as he boiled.

The guard was now fed up. He angrily shoved an index finger towards Paul's face.

"Enough!" he cried. "I find it hard to believe that Speaker Jackson's strike-force would treat me and this facility in this way! I have half a mind to call him. Not only are you wasting everyone's time, but you are questioning the Speaker's own directives.

Jason shrugged. "Go ahead. Call him. I'm sure he'd be thrilled. Like you said, he loves it when people waste his time."

The guard closed his mouth but his lip still quivered

Paul dropped his head low, a shadow seemed to cover his face.

"We'll go then."

Jason, taken aback, tried to meet his gaze.

"We're going," Paul stressed again.

Jason let a steaming exhale escape his nostrils. "Fine."

The guard and Jason started on, but Paul lagged slightly behind.

"Please!" the prisoner called from behind the bars. "Her name is Emma Jean St. John! Just please don't hurt her! I don't know if you hold my bank accounts already, but I'll give you everything in them. Just let her be safe! None of this is her fault!"

With the gaze of the guard off of him, Paul veered towards the bars as he walked past them.

"This is awful," he whispered. "I know. I can't say how sorry I am. I really am the scum of the earth. I'll come back. I swear. I'll try to find Emma."

He could not leave without driving his point home. With little more than his hand and an almost unseen flick of his wrist, he struck a bar in a flash. A crack appeared. If one was not looking straight at it, one would have t thought the metal was still perfectly intact. However, Paul and the prisoner could see the hairline crack that would give way if pulled upon. One destroyed bar would not let the man escape, but it did give him a sign of sincerity.

I mean it. You will be free and with your daughter.

Paul then briskly and purposefully followed behind the frustrated guard.

CHAPTER 28
RUNNING COLD

THE TABLET COMPUTER was shaking in Paul's hands. Jason gave him a slightly annoyed look before Paul handed it over. Paul then let Jason do most of the talking.

I barely kept it together when I reported back to Jackson on the previous call, Paul thought bitterly. *All the anger, guilt, and frustration, they weigh on me like everything else now.*

Adam Avery waited for him to finish before speaking. Even he appeared to be close to losing his composure at times.

"I guess it's time, then," Avery said in a low, grave voice when Jason had completed his whistleblowing account. "I was afraid of this day. I didn't want it to come. For A.R.C. to come to war with itself in this situation…"

Avery then took a breath.

"But it must be done. I hope both of you are in agreement. I will contact the other members of the Council. There is a provision for removal from the Council, but it has never been done. There is no precedent."

"What about evidence?" Paul wondered.

"I have my own men," answered Avery. "They can scout the locations you've both seen. Also, I may need to call on the two of you as witnesses. Now, I in no way ask that lightly. It may turn you against some of your friends and allies, people you've fought beside."

"We have to do it," Jason summed up. "Justice has to be done. It never gets done by just wishing it."

Paul nodded slowly. "These past few months, I've done a lot of things that I'm not proud of. I just want to do something good, even if it's hard."

We'll have so many people against us. Brandon already doesn't like us. Kishi and Ben, though, they've always seemed alright. Will they all feel betrayed by their former strike-force members? Will they be loyal to Jackson?

"The next step is to call a Council meeting," Avery explained. "It would do no good to just barge into Jackson's office with accusations. Like in a courtroom, we have to bring a mountain of evidence to the Council. Even then, who knows? Will they see the ethical side of things or will they support Jackson for doing whatever it takes to support A.R.C."

"Okay, how do we help you?" Paul asked anxiously.

"You can start with that name you gave me," Avery said. "That girl, Emma. You can try to find her in the database of known A.I.M. agents. It's always hard to identify people who always wear masks, but it's worth it if we can give more credence to the story."

Paul shook his head. "That's just it. I searched the databases. There wasn't a record, which isn't surprising for a young A.I.M. agent that A.R.C. hasn't encountered yet."

"He searched," murmured Jason. "Exhaustively for hours. It was more than a little OCD and annoying."

Paul shrugged.

Avery tapped the arms of his office chair as he thought. "I wonder..."

It took him only a few taps at the keyboard of his computer, separate from his video screen. Then, his fingers and face froze like those of a pale statue. It took him a moment to find the words.

"You were checking the wrong databases, I'm afraid," he gulped.

"Really?" Jason wondered.

Avery explained with heavy somberness. "Emma Jean St. John is not in our database of A.I.M. agents or independent Amuli. She's in the A.R.C. database."

"T-The A.R.C. agent database?" Paul barely breathed it out.

Avery nodded slowly.

No one, on either side of the screen, knew what to say next. Paul felt faint as the blood seemed to drain out of his head.

"Well," Jason finally croaked as he aggressively put a hand on the saber at his waist, "I guess we know where we're going next."

Avery shook his head again before running a hand through his hair as he thought.

"It may be unfair... No, it may be impossible to ask this," he began. "We still need to exercise caution. Jackson is probably the most powerful man in A.R.C. This just has to be another boulder on that pile of evidence."

What if... What if... Paul's whole mouth quivered as he tried to collect himself.

"I can guess the reason behind this," Paul said as he forced calmness into his tone. "He's been capturing A.R.C. family members and telling the agents that they were captured by A.I.M. That makes... them fight harder. God knows if he ever intends to return them. It's pure manipulation. Anything to strengthen A.R.C. Any human cost."

Both Avery and Jason gave him looks that they knew what he was on to.

"You can try to stop me, but I'm going to get my aunt and uncle," Paul asserted. "The reason why they have never turned up in an A.I.M. prison must be because they are in an A.R.C. prison. The only hole in my theory is the video that I was shown by that A.I.M. scientist who shouldn't have had the footage. On the other hand, it's not like he didn't show me any other doctored pieces of evidence to manipulate my mind. There's also the possibility of a mole leaking the footage."

Avery sighed. "I know you're smart, Paul. Just... keep being smart about this. Don't get every anima weapon in the world pointed at you."

"What's your plan?" questioned Jason. "I know you always come up with one."

"It's reasonable that the others on the strike-force know of secret locations that might be prisons. I'll ask one of them about them."

"Who do we trust, then?" Jason asked. "Definitely not Robeson. He's Jackson's lackey through-and-through."

"Not Brandon," Paul agreed. "That leaves Ben and Kishi. We know them. They're not bad people. I don't think they've been going along with Jackson's off-the-books activities. Anyway, we just have to ask about secret drop-offs, rumors, and anything they've seen out of the ordinary... well... ordinary for us."

Avery tapped on his separate computer screen again.

"Since we've started the internal investigation, I've been trying to track the other members of your team," he explained. "Ben is in route to the States now."

"So, Kishi then," Jason said. "He's down the hall. We'll just have to distract Brandon with something else. Even asking questions might set him off."

Paul sighed. "I'm sure he'd be thrilled if we tell him to get us some takeout. Maybe if we use our A.R.C. allowances to get him something..."

"I'll say it again, caution," stressed Avery. "Where are you guys, anyway? How did you get out of earshot of those super-powered ears?"

"We're in like a basement," Paul admitted. "We're in an old hotel, and Jason and I kind of stumbled into it when we were looking for a place to hide. That's why it's dark, and there's a weird dripping sound in the background."

———

Kishi sat cross-legged at the end of his hotel-room bed. Even in perceived safety, he liked to keep the chain of his kusarigama coiled around his arm.

"First off," he started. "Don't act like I'm stupid. You know I'm not. I know you're not. Get that out of the way. I know, maybe, a little about what you two are doing. That secret prison isn't sitting right with you, and you want to know what I know. That's also why you sent Brandon to the Thai place for takeout so you could talk to me alone."

Jason's hand crept nervously as if he wanted it to drift towards his sword.

"Basically," Paul replied to Jason's surprise. "I mean… has any of this stuff lately been sitting right with you?"

"Not really," Kishi admitted. "But what can you do? Jackson's on the Council. He's the Speaker. That means he has all the power. If we do too much of what he doesn't like, he could get rid of us easily."

"What if there was something that you could do?" Paul asked him, trying to sound inspiring.

"Is it a sure thing?" Kishi wondered. "You really have something to offset the most powerful man there is?"

"Well," Paul began while scratching his neck, "We have Avery's support."

"The rest of the Council?"

Paul sighed. "We're working on it."

"Why not give it time, then?" Kishi questioned. "Get support from the rest of them."

"I'm not sure if I can wait," Paul informed him desperately. "You see, I think he has my aunt and uncle somewhere. My only family."

"Geez," Kishi exhaled before muttering something in Japanese.

"That's not to mention all the innocents he has in other places," Jason added passionately.

Stone-faced, Kishi thought it over for a moment.

"Information," he then said. "I'll tell you what I know. You don't let anyone know what I told you, understand? If it comes to fighting, I will keep my distance."

"Not even for a cause like this?" Jason shot back.

"No," Kishi answered calmly. "Don't misunderstand. I like the both of you. You are good teammates. Good people. It's just… I can't be of help to anyone if I'm dead. Don't mistake it. Jackson's enemies tend to die."

Paul nodded. "Anything you can give us is enough. I know this isn't easy."

Kishi nodded back. "Okay. I'll tell you about a place. There was a drop-off like the one we just had. It was strange, not in the records. I couldn't sense anima from some of the prisoners. I did not think much of it then, but what we just saw is making me reflect on it now. The thing is, it's almost in plain sight. It's so obvious no one would look there. In the old A.R.C. headquarters in New York, there's a basement that goes way down. You'll find some of Jackson's personal prisoners there, I'm sure."

Paul put a fist on the wall and slowly pushed it in frustration.

"The old A.R.C. headquarters," Paul breathed. "That was on the edge of the tidal wave range! There was some damage. If they were underground…"

He began dashing out of the room without a thought. Paul was about to descend the nearest stairwell when Jason forcefully caught him by the upper arm.

"You know it's bad when I'm telling you to slow down," Jason murmured in his ear. "You need backup. Call Camilla and the others, or she'll slap you again when she finds out you went off half-cocked without her. I'll make the arrangements and give Jackson some sort of bull excuse that he'll buy. You just take a breather and wait for our ride."

"I just want to find out what happened when the waves hit," Paul murmured half to himself and half to Jason. "If they were there… I just want to know."

Dealing with Jackson comes later.

CHAPTER 29
IN THE AIR

THE CABIN of the private plane traveling from Pittsburgh to New York was tense. Each of the passengers had their eyes forward. Their eyes, however, were not focused on the plane's interior. They were locked into the mission.

Paul had positioned himself closest to the door. His legs were barely under control and ready to race for the descending stairway as soon as the plane landed. It was like there was no one else but him in this space. It was even hard for him to nail down concrete thoughts or plans after arrival. The "thoughts" were all more feelings of dread than anything.

He barely noticed Camilla as she leaned over the back of his seat.

"Hey, we'll get them," she encouraged him warmly. "Have some faith."

I guess I don't put faith in enough things. I get too wrapped up in trying to do everything myself. I just never want to put those burdens onto anyone else. In this world, those burdens are heavy.

Jason chimed in after hearing them. "It will be just like when we barged into that place near Topeka. We'll just throw our weight around again. If we have to fight, we fight. We're strong anyway. Jackson will be wrapped up in the Council meeting that Avery just called. I hear the rest of those guys are on their own planes as we speak."

"We just have to pray that Jackson isn't onto anything," Paul mused pessimistically. "Not what we're doing, and not what that meeting is going to be about. It's a gamble. All of this."

Jessica had taken a break from the cockpit with Antonio now in command. Like the rest of the cabin, she heard the conversation as she strolled in.

"In my experience," she started. "Most good things in life come from a gamble. Hey, trusting Greg Luper a while ago was a gamble for me, and that's why we're all here. Besides, even if the Council doesn't take your side, you've got A.R.C.-Human backing you up now. I don't have a Council position, but I do have my own division of hungry, non-super-human soldiers. Plus, you have something rare in war, a moral high ground. I tend to think that people fight better when they're doing something that they think is right."

"I say this all the time," Robby began as he took his turn. "You're the smartest person I know, but you think some stupid things sometimes. You've been worried lately about being pulled down in all the crap that goes on. Well, now you've pulled yourself out of that crap-pool. You got back to the good stuff. Just keep things simple. That's what I do."

Camilla sighed. "Just keep in mind that it's not the same kind of 'simple' that means 'dumb.' This guy gets those confused."

"Okay, Cami."

"Geez. You should have never met my mother."

"Did you make transport arrangements... for everyone we might find," Paul asked Jessica.

No matter what kind of words were said to him, his mind always went back to the mission.

She nodded. "I called for some buses to stand by before we took off. They're on their way."

"You know, I kind of wanted to be a bus driver when I was little," Robby thought aloud while changing the subject to something lighter. "Then, I realized that I don't like country music. That seems to be the only thing that they can pick up on their radios."

"I thought you wanted to be a Transformer that turned into a school bus," countered Jessica.

Robby, like always, found a way to put Paul's mind onto something less stressful.

"You know," Paul said, "I think that's how I remember it too."

"Well, I guess that was the ideal situation," Robby admitted playfully.

Jason rubbed his forehead and sighed. "You people."

"What you mean *you people*?" Robby sarcastically demanded. "You're one of us."

"That's true," Camilla agreed. "We're all stuck together now. We're traitors, heroes, or whatever the case may be."

Paul felt himself increasingly pulled into the background as the conversation wore on. *It's always been strangely comforting to melt away into other people's voices. I've been called quiet, but I like to hang around talkers like Robby and Cam. I feel strange when words aren't flowing in the air. I just don't always feel like I have to add to them.*

He got up to use the restroom and passed by Alice in the back row. She kept to herself, as usual, with her eyes drifting out the window. Like him, she had tight lines of dread on her face.

She's doing better with emotions, Paul realized. *I can almost read her at times now. I just wish that she wasn't feeling this particular emotion right now.*

"Are you doing okay?" he asked her, hoping to at least put some mock confidence in his voice. "You know, we… we'll all get through this."

I wish that had sounded convincing.

"Do you feel it?" she questioned him back.

"Well, I feel um…"

"I cannot describe it," she explained. "There is a feeling hanging on the air, like anima. I feel something like change coming. There is an opportunity there in the newness, but there is something uncomfortable as well."

"Is it from your abilities as a psychic?"

"I do not know," she answered. "I do not like that I do not know."

There has to be something comforting I can say.

"So, you're scared, and I'm terrified. There's something I always think of. It was back when we first met. I said that we were acquaintances. Later, I realized that was stupid, and I said we were friends. Now, I'm thinking, with all of us here, it's more than that. We're family. We're family because we sacrifice for each other. I don't know much about family. I only ever had a really small one. I just think that I feel the best when I'm fighting beside you and everyone on this plane. I feel like I'm on the right side of things. If I die being by your side, well, I'll die knowing that I did the right thing."

Alice only blinked several times in response. With each blink, Paul could see the emotions coming to her. *It is getting easier for her. Is it really easy though? To let yourself feel more? To open yourself up when you never did before?*

She finally spoke in a husky voice. "I did not even understand the concept of family for the longest time. I believe that I still don't. I only know that I'm glad I found one, and I'm glad it's you."

Paul nodded. "Me too."

———

Paul's secure line was blowing up even as he touched down. He picked it up and barely had time to utter a, "Hello?"

"Paul! The situation… it's the worst! It's the worst thing we could have imagined."

Adam Avery sounded out of breath and desperate. The tone was chilling coming from the usual powerful and confident A.R.C. leader.

"W-What?" Paul murmured.

"It's the Council!" Avery yelled hard enough for a loud vibration to course through the phone. "They were coming in on separate planes. Someone got to them! All of them! They were all sabotaged!"

A crowd had gathered around Paul, who could barely hide his shaking.

"What are you saying?"

"They're gone. All of them. The Council is just Jackson and me now."

"Y-You're sure?"

Of course, he's sure! He's Adam Avery! He wouldn't give me misinformation on something this important!

"Yes!"

"Oh, God! W-What d-do we do?"

"I… uh… first put everyone on speaker. They have to know!"

Paul did as he was told, but he was also sure that the desperate message had already leaked through the phone. All of the plane's passengers were leaning in with horror-struck faces.

"W-Who?" Paul stammered. "Who could have done this?"

"Something like this… I can't say for certain. A.I.M. is getting bolder. You, unfortunately, know that firsthand. This is beyond bold. Hunters have been quiet. They are splintered, and that has made most of the groups weak. Something of this scale is almost beyond them. Then, there's the question of how they knew about which planes to hit. How did the information leak?"

Paul did not know if Avery was purposely leading him in the direction that was now occurring to him. The theory forming in his mind somehow seemed the most plausible… and possibly the most frightening.

"J-Jackson," he whimpered. "What if…. What if he's been onto us? You've said, and I've seen, that he would do anything for the sake of A.R.C. Hasn't he always thought that he himself was best for A.R.C. If he knew that our group and the Council were planning to remove him, how would he react? Would he do something this terrible?"

There was a long pause. The surrounding group on the plane was coming to their own conclusions now. It seemed all but certain.

"We cannot afford to not be smart about this," declared Avery. "A.R.C. is now hurtling towards destruction, and with it, the balance of this world. We must protect it. I will protect my agents. We have to prepare for every possibility, even the horrible one that you described. If we don't move fast, the world as we know it could be gone in hours."

"I think we have to go," Jason blurted.

Paul nodded gravely. "We have to confront him. Even if it's not him, we have to see him to figure this out. I know that this is going to be nothing but hostile. If he even thinks that we are remotely accusing him of something, it could get ugly."

"That's why it's the two of us going," Jason insisted. "The rest of you will go to the prison, while Paul and I will go to where I think he is. That's a secret office he keeps a few miles away. Jackson's tough. You can see it in his eyes that he hasn't lost that while sitting behind a desk. He will always be that S.A.S. soldier at heart. But if it comes to it, I'll take one of the world's strongest Amuli at my side to face him."

"What about the rest of us?" Camilla questioned. "Who knows what kind of numbers he has right beside him? Shouldn't you two have backup?"

Jason disagreed. "We're still technically his men, so it won't cause a scene when we get in there. We know that we can get right to him face-to-face. If we bring too many, he'll be suspicious right off the bat."

"Cam," Paul addressed her softly, "I get it. None of us wanted to split up at this point, but we have more than one objective. You know, there's nobody I trust more to rescue my aunt and uncle. You were on rescue teams before... in one of the worst disasters of all time, no less. Plus, you help people. I think that's just a part of you."

Blushing, Camilla let the words hang for a moment as she considered Paul's words.

With a clear face, she said, "Just tell me that this isn't about something deeper. This isn't because you don't want to face them, right? God, Paul, I know you always think the worst of yourself, and it's not fair to you. No matter what you think you've done to ruin yourself, they will be there for you. I mean... I don't know them, but I've been getting better at family stuff lately. If they raised someone like you, they won't forsake you. Sometimes, we just need to adjust our picture of someone. We don't need to freak out and throw it out altogether."

"I promise that I'm going to do what is best for everyone at this second," Paul answered.

"Just include yourself in that, buddy," Robby reminded him.

Paul looked around at all the faces. *I don't deserve all of them. I guess they wouldn't want me to think like that.*

"I've got cars here at the airport," Jessica reported. "The buses will come after we get to the prison. Then, they'll keep themselves hidden from any crossfire if a battle breaks out. The important thing is that we have a getaway strategy ready for both us and anyone we rescue."

She headed back to the cockpit while the others strapped themselves to their seats. Paul found himself struggling with the seatbelt for a moment with his nervous hands and wandering mind. *I am about to something that will have a profound change in the world, and I can't even buckle myself.*

As the exit stairs were brought up beside the plane, Antonio joined them after leaving his cockpit.

"It's just another day," he said to them after sensing the mood. "We know what we do. We do the mission and get it done. At the end of the day, we'll kick back. That's how it's always gone, and that's how it will go today. No worries."

Paul appreciated the sentiment but could not even envision himself letting go of the anxiety. *With this severity and pressure, it would almost feel wrong to shrug it off. It's too important.*

As everyone readied to leave, Paul felt like he was going in slow motion. The others were focused and ready. *My mind always wanders to all the wrong places.*

He found himself as being almost the last person remaining on the plane. Only Alice stood behind him.

"P-Paul?"

He turned around.

In the time that we had known her, he'd only seen a few emotions come over her face. The absence of one, which had long been her base, seemed almost an emotion in of itself. Other than that, he had seen her sad. There was always the hint of that in her gaze. He had seen her concerned for the happenings of a mission. However, he had never seen her flustered. There was now the uncertain look of something gnawing away at her. She shuffled from foot to foot.

"I have to say something important. I do not really know how…"

She trailed off for a moment before continuing.

"It's just that things might change after today. I do not know if I will have the chance to explain this again, or possibly not for a very long time. This may be long-winded, but I believe that I have to say this all in full."

Is she worried about the outcome of all this? We don't know what the world will look like after today.

She took a breath.

"Nearly all my life, I think that I was doing the bare minimum of living. I ate and drank. I worked. I kept myself physically conditioned. It was practical things only. I just thought of humans as any other animal. I survived, and that was it. I worked for A.R.C. because they let me survive. When I first encountered Camilla…. Cam and Jason, I first noticed a strange complication in myself. When I met you, it grew. It is hard to explain. My mind, which had only been devoted to the minimum and the rational, now felt irrational. I felt things at times, and they drove me. Luper taught me what that meant and how that fits into life. It is hard to feel. It is hard to be open. It's painful, but I can no longer imagine a different world. I cannot go back."

Alice… did we really do all that for her? I don't think we meant to, but it happened. I'm glad it did.

She continued, her blue eyes growing misty. "The night I saw you, everything changed."

"It has been a strange ride since then," Paul agreed.

She shook her head. "You don't understand something. I tracked the package that day. I encountered A.I.M. agents, but they were nothing. I got through and saw you. I saw you walk down the street with Robby. I saw you get the package. I felt something that whole time."

"I don't really understand…" his voice trailed off.

"People who are not Amuli have anima too," she explained. "I know you have felt that. It is not as intense, but it is there. With an Amulus, you can always feel it. If it is strong enough, you can feel it coming from a normal human, just leaking out. When I was near you, before you even opened that package, I sensed something from you. It was pure and earnest. It was clear water in my muddy world. I had never felt that from someone. There was a desire to be good and kind for their own sake. It was honest. When you awoke as an Amulus, I felt those feelings again but stronger. Then, it was mixed in with doubt and fear, but they were still there. They were all emotions that were new to me… as were most emotions. But these… I had never even thought that someone could feel that way. It was new then, but I still feel it now."

Strangely, Paul's thoughts did not drift as they did at most times. He was in this moment.

Alice went on. "It was strategy to separate you from your sword that night. I sensed other enemies in the area. Diluting your powers by removing the sword from you may have hidden you from them. I don't think that is why I did it though. It felt so strange to act on emotion. I barely knew what I was doing. Really, I just wanted you to stay separate from this world. I wanted you to stay pure and safe. I so foolishly thought that without your anima crystal, you may stop being an Amulus. You would wake up and think that it had all been a dream. It was so irrational and out of the realm of everything I had known."

Paul felt a warmness in his cheeks. Likewise, there was a rosiness now running down Alice's pale face.

"I had no idea," he murmured. "I know that Luper said that it was just procedure. I'm sorry that I made you act so far out of your comfort zone."

Alice shook her head. "As I said, you are too pure. I am still beginning to understand what I am feeling now. A little while ago, I had some friends who helped me with that. It is still so confusing to act on feelings. That is why, before anything else changes, I want you to know…"

It all hit Paul at once, like sunshine bursting through a line of trees. There was the reason why Alice was blushing. There was a reason why his face matched hers.

Then it was all so quick. She was leaning in while her chin turned upward. Her heavy lashes seemed to weigh down her eyes.

It felt like flower peddles brushing his lips at first. He managed to gain some self-awareness. Just like he had seen in movies, he had the good sense to close his own eyes and to lightly embrace her back. He did not know if the rushing in his ears was fast-moving blood or a crashing tidal wave.

As her head pulled away, he felt the soft, warm breath from her nostrils on his neck. For a moment, she held him tightly while burying her head in his chest. Paul wished that time could move slower for just this one moment.

Eventually, Paul saw her give him one last look and exit the plane for the stairs. He did not know how much time passed with him standing alone and watching her leave. It felt like a long time, but it could have been seconds just as easily.

I don't think… I don't think I really did anything noteworthy in life until just now. I think there will be my life before this moment and my life after it.

Heart still pounding, he began walking with cement-filled shoes.

Wait! What am I supposed to do now… after that? What am I supposed to say?

A more rational voice in his head interjected.

Stupid! You don't have to think nervous thoughts right now. That was great! Enjoy it!

Paul nodded to no one and exited the plane.

CHAPTER 30
THE GUARDS

JASON WAS BEHIND THE WHEEL. He had already warned Paul about nervously tapping his fingers on the window.

I always hate the car ride to something important. It's like the steady, numbing rhythm of the wheels on the pavement and the rushing wind are trying to lure me into a false sense of complacency. It's like I have to fight against my mind going blank when I need it to stay focused.

When he thought back to the last moments before he left the plane, his stomach filled with a different group of butterflies.

"Something happened on the plane after everyone else left," Jason guessed pointedly.

It was not like him to talk about anything other than the mission at hand. For Jason, there was only that and the training leading up to a mission to focus on.

Paul's face went maroon. He waved his arms frantically. "Uh... um... no? It was a... um..." he stammered. "W-Why do you ask?"

Would Alice want other people to know? Do I? Should we make some kind of agreement? Wait, that sounds too formal.

"I usually don't get into other people's business when it doesn't affect what I do," Jason said as he kept his eyes trained on the street. "I'm only asking because it was freakin' obvious that something was coming."

"It was?"

That is seriously news to me. Do other people also think so? Maybe, but they should have told me! Or maybe I would have gotten too worked up beforehand and freaked out like I usually do.

"I don't know much about that kind of stuff," Jason admitted. "Sometimes the people in that situation are the last to realize it."

This is… new. Did Jason ever have someone?

He thought for a moment as Jason's words hung. *The only one that I can think of is Ling. Oh God, does he know what happened to her? Should I say?*

"Relax," Jason relented. "I'm not going to scold you for letting things get personal. Sometimes, I think that it's important to have someone or something. You have to see that thing or person in the distance because that's your goal to reach. It doesn't matter what hurdles there are between you and the goal then. You'll get over them because you have to. It's more than a motivator, it's a piece of you. It's what makes you tick."

I haven't even thought about that. It's hard to think about the future sometimes when you could get killed on any given day. But, yes, Alice is a goal now. I want my world to get quieter. I want things to get less crazy. I want to have the time and mindset to take her on dates. I want to get to know her and be a normal couple. Maybe normal isn't the right word for the two of us. Maybe there is something better than normal. Alice is already better than normal.

"It used to be revenge for me," Jason explained. "But I used to see my mom in the distance, too. I thought that if I killed everyone at fault, the distance would close. I'm not sure if it did or not. I'll just say that I think your goal is now better than mine was. Revenge is poison. When you live for it, it just runs through your veins and makes everything agony."

"What about now?" Paul ventured, picking up on Jason's rare, sharing mood.

Jason sighed. "Now, I just want to push for a world where no one ends up as messed up as me."

"You know what? Same here. I don't want anyone to have to live like me."

"Christ," Jason breathed in exasperation. "I think you'll always be naïve."

Paul snorted a laugh was surprised to hear Jason do likewise.

I think he means that I'll always be annoying to him. That's fine. Friends annoy each other sometimes. Robby is the king of that.

The conversation lifted Paul's spirits until the building came into view.

"That's it," Jason surmised. "Jackson has an office in there. As the Speaker, he's been setting up shop in the other Council members' territories to keep an eye on them. Notice that he didn't put it in Avery's office. He wanted to be close enough to spy but far enough to not make it look obvious."

There was a crane attached to one side of the building where some siding was missing.

"He put a safehouse in a building that didn't seem official enough for an entity like A.R.C.," Paul assumed.

They pulled in towards it without having to worry about the usual lines of traffic. The city was mostly safe now and was a far cry from when the disaster hit only months ago. The water had retreated. Construction crews had fixed electrical lines and pumped water out of basements. Still, the aura of tragedy seemed to hang around this dim section of the city. All of the water damage which had left permanent, shadowlike stains on lower walls.

The secret base had the usual hallmarks of an A.R.C. city compound. A nearby, residential-looking garage door led to an actual underground parking garage which connected to the base. The computer chips inside Jason and Paul's car opened a divider for them. From there, it was a downward slope to a dingy basement.

I wonder who got stuck with the menial duty of pumping this out. Maybe Jackson got someone from A.R.C.-Human to do it. He tends to not think much of the non-Amuli.

Judging by the large puddles in several areas, the job had not been done too enthusiastically.

A military man like Jackson would hate that. Now I really wonder who he cursed out.

From a distance, Paul saw two figures near the passenger elevator that served as an entrance into the base proper.

It's time, he thought as his stomach tightened.

Seeing the faces of the young men guarding the door squeezed his stomach even tighter. Jason barely acknowledged them as he quickly exited the car.

"You know what I hate the most?" asked Brandon Robeson, breaking the tense silence. "Ungrateful People. They're just as bad as traitors."

Paul approached him while staying tightlipped.

"That's right," Robeson taunted. "I have access to a private plane, too. It's one of the many things Speaker Jackson has done for us, if you can remember that."

"Oh my God," Jason breathed. "Shut up!"

Paul waved him off.

"I know what you two are up to," Robeson threatened. "I should have known after the way you behaved at that old hospital place."

"What do you think that is?" Paul wondered.

"Some self-righteous crap that will just add to the piles of pompous sewage in the world."

"We're trying to do the right thing," Paul asserted.

"Get off your high horse," shot back Robeson. "Jason used to call you naïve, so I'm not sure what he's doing beside you now. I'd say now that you're way beyond naïve. You're an idealist. It's only about your sense of right and wrong. You ever think about how that screws things up for everyone else? You want to break the wheel and kill everyone riding it."

"I don't want anyone dead," Paul assured him.

"Too late," Robeson countered. "Whether that mess in the sky was you guys or someone else, it's raining bodies."

"Please," murmured Jason. "I think we all know who that was."

"Do we really?" asked Robeson.

"Easy, boys," Ben finally spoke.

His blonde bangs tended to bob back-and-forth over his beach-tanned forehead as he talked.

"If none of us are at fault for the Council going down, then why can't we all go back to the way things were? We're all technically still playing for the same team."

"We just need to see him," Paul pleaded.

"If that's the case," Ben said, "I'm sorry to say that he's not seeing anyone for right now. Why don't you come back later? With all that's happening, I'm sure you can understand."

"It's vital," Paul stressed. "Things could get much worse than they already are."

"What are you going to do when you see him?" Robeson asked the pointed question.

Jason chose not to answer directly. "Are you going to let us through or not?"

His hand drifted dangerously close to his saber. In response, Robeson lifted his animal-skin shield, while Ben's dangling crystal earrings flickered a lime-colored spark.

"Is this the way everyone wants it?" Paul wondered, hoping for one last chance at a resolution. "What have we come to? We were all comrades."

"Maybe you should listen to yourself," ventured Robeson. "Those are the right words, but you've got them all twisted."

Ben simply said, "Sorry, mate. Orders are orders."

Paul and Jason parted like a swinging set of doors as Robeson sent them a roaring, blue blast.

Off of a pivot, Paul found himself faced with Ben. Jason and Robeson were on his other side.

"Stop. Stop. Stop. Stop. Stop. Stop."

The thoughts thrummed into Paul's head like annoying white noise.

It's a Psychic trick. They bombard you with thoughts to confuse you and distract you. It's something to break your concentration and give them an edge.

"Stop. Stop. Stop. Stop."

There was a feeling attached to the telepathic words as well. They almost felt tiring, as if trying to dull Paul's senses.

Ben used the constant stream of empty words to cover his advance. He came in with a leg sweep. Paul stepped back to dodge.

Ben is a Muay Thai expert. He's going to use the hardest, most bony parts of his body. There are the shins, knees, elbows, and forearms. That causes a lot of damage.

He came with the elbow next, which Paul leaned away from to let it pass by him.

Ben. I don't hate him. He's just in the way. Should I really draw my sword?

To his side, Jason seemed to be having no such doubts. His glowing red sword was holding back a steady stream of blue light. Both Paul and Ben had to jog to get away from the crossfire.

Jason seemed to buckle at first, but used the change in leverage to his advantage. With his sword now at an angle, he cascaded the enduring blast over himself. With his sword tip against the ground, he stuck a long, exaggerated stroke at the floor and followed through. This kicked up chips of cement pavement, which now hurtled toward Robeson. He screamed as they buried themselves into him, skin-deep like splinters. His was bloodied and in serious pain but was not down. Jason sprung forward to keep his momentum.

Paul had to turn back to focus on Ben. Even as a Psychic, he was a capable fighter when it came to hand-to-hand combat. He was almost like Alice in that way.

"You don't want to do this. You don't want to do this. You don't want to do this. You don't want to do this. You…"

The rhythm of the invading thoughts was close to hypnotizing. To ward against it, Paul embraced the flow.

This is something I picked up. Back in the bunker when Alice went on a rampage and then with the creepy boy in the rundown house, I think Cam tried to fight the thoughts. I just let them in. To fight against them seems to create chaos and confusion.

Ben made another attempt at a sweep. This one came with the left leg. He must have known that fighting an Amuli as strong as Paul called for no hesitation. If you can move well enough, you can just hit without being hit back.

Paul put power against power. As the shin came forward, he stomped downward, catching Ben preemptively on the shin. Ben had to scamper back. That lower leg of his jeans was now a torn, bloody mess.

Ben tried for distance next. He hurtled a wave of anima as he continued backward. Paul slid to the floor before bouncing back up after the disk-like projectile had passed.

"Screw it!" Ben shouted.

Disks came rapidly now. Paul did not have room between them to dodge. He powered up green anima onto his hands and matched the volley with green fireballs of his own. Then Ben's blasts became over-matched. One of Paul's projectiles struck Ben in the shoulder and another glanced off his ankle. He half-tumbled towards the wall.

Paul sprinted forward. Ben put up a forearm to defend himself. Paul grabbed it, bent it, and locked it. Next, Ben tried to kick out his feet. Paul simple lowered his own foot, pounding the sole of his shoe into the laces of Ben's. There was a sickening crack.

Ben's grip loosened and his eyes went hazy.

"E-Enough," he wheezed.

Paul still held the arm and kept his foot painfully in place. He was too wary for a fake-out.

"Don't believe me? Really!"

Ben raised his non-pinned arm in defeat.

"C'mon! What am I gonna do? You've broken my bloody foot. Not to mention whatever you did to my shin. My bloody head is swimming. What am I going to do to yah?"

Paul finally relaxed and pulled back. However, his body stayed tense, ready in case Ben was lying.

"That's it," Ben sighed. "It's not worth it now. Do what you want. The whole world's bloody come apart, anyway. Who knows what'll happen next?"

From there, Ben seemed content to rest while wedged between the wall and the cold ground.

The fight on the other side was coming to an end as well.

A long cut along Robeson's right arm had left it immobilized and drooping. Jason barreled into his exhausted opponent and he, too, was against the wall. Jason pushed inward along Robeson's collarbone with his forearm. Robeson's face went red from the pressure.

He still had the stubbornness to talk. "Look at you two! Are you proud? You've ruined everything! You just had to do what you were told."

The proud young man's head went almost slack from the tension along his pressure points. He still would not give up.

"You think you know what it's like?" His voice was now strangely somber. "Both of you are orphans. You think you've been given the short end of the stick? How about when you were given no stick at all? You know what it's like to be born without a chance?"

With hesitant curiosity, Paul crept closer to the scene.

"Having no chance happens when you're born on a freaking reservation. You know what that is? It's what they gave us. Places no one could farm back in the day because the land sucked. Places where no one had the money to build anything. Places that weren't even close to anything. It's a lot of nothing in places like that."

Robeson had the presence of mind to shake his head, more in emotion than in a struggle to get free.

"But I had a way out. That was Jackson. He gave me a life as long as I did what I was told. It was so easy. I didn't have to think about anything other than how good it was to be free and powerful. Isn't that what everyone wants? How can you blame someone for wanting to hang on to that? What are you guys even doing?"

Jason had had enough.

"Jason!" Paul warned the young man with the raised sword.

The sword went down, but it was the end of the guard that stuck Robeson's head. He was suddenly quiet.

Wasting no time, Jason shouted over to the still-conscious Ben. "Which floor?"

"The top," Ben griped. "Hey, bring a medic when you're done!"

Paul and Jason had the way clear to the elevator. They left Ben to mumble a long, creative, Australian curse.

CHAPTER 31
AT THE TOP

IN THE ELEVATOR, Paul had smoothed his crinkled shirt and wiped some of the blood smears off of his pants. He did not care about how he was going to present himself before Jackson in a moment. He just tidied himself on reflex, and it made him feel slightly normal.

Jason simply straightened his collar and was ready.

The floor was the most boring section of an office building that Paul had ever seen. There was a tan carpet on the floors. The walls were bleached white. There was a drag, green plant every so often. *It screams normalcy. Well, it doesn't really scream anything. I guess it mutters normalcy.*

That was A.R.C., a brutal, world-conquering organization disguised as a mundane one. Judging by the surroundings, Jackson had pride in that disguise. He had the corner office, just like any CEO.

That was where he was sitting when Jason and Paul barged in. Seeing them, he simply paused his dutiful work at his keyboard. The look he gave them was a veil of businesslike blandness hiding an iciness. The latter was deep down in his eyes.

"Straight to the point," he spoke confidently. "Are Rivers and Robeson still breathing?"

"Y-Yes," Paul choked out while flexing some sweat off of his fingers.

"Well, you haven't gone that far then."

"The question is, how far have you gone?" Jason countered. "What happened with the planes?"

"You are accusing me, then?" Jackson asked coolly. "Really? I have devoted my life to A.R.C. Why would I destroy its leadership? Am I so much a fool that I would cut off my own head?"

"We've seen it all," Jason spat. "Secret prisons. Non-Amulus prisoners, including family members of A.R.C. agents. You're a war criminal."

"My family," Paul added.

"I told you!" Jackson reminded them. "I would do anything for the sake of A.R.C. It is the one wall holding back the tide of chaos in this world. Who else would keep a world with superhumans safe? A.I.M. with their terrible experiments? World governments waging their petty wars? Or, would you prefer Hunters to pick us off one by one?"

Veins budged in his muscular neck. Some were even visible under his gray, buzz-cut hair.

"How does it help to imprison the people closest to your own men!" Paul demanded.

Jackson's hand twitched in a slight, sweeping motion as if to wave Paul's words away.

"Tell me," scoffed Jackson. "With your former demeanor, would you have served A.R.C. as well as you have? What has motivated you these past months? What has given your anima the power it needs? I supplied that motivator. You may go ahead and hate me, but you must understand that."

"You know, it's too funny," Jason fake laughed. "You hate A.I.M. so much, and yet, you let one of their men turn Ling into a Dead Eyes. How are you any different?"

"I did what I had to," Jackson stressed. "That Atlantean girl was beyond control or reason. A prisoner gave us a possible solution. That's just intelligence work."

"I've never heard hypocrisy called *that* before," Jason grumbled.

"What about Alice?" Paul interrogated. "That Atlantean, who you won't even name, is a girl with thoughts and feelings. She's so much more human than a creep like you! You kept her in a cage. You denied her anything. She had no warmth, no family, no friends. A person needs those things just as much as they need food and water."

"Listen to yourself," Jackson snapped. "What do you think A.R.C. is? Do you think it's a charity that takes in little girls and gives the world some half-baked definition of happiness? How many times must I stress it? We are a force for control. We are Amulus Regional Containment!"

"Why couldn't we be?" Paul wondered. "Is it so unnecessary or inconvenient to be ethical?"

"You are someone who will never run an organization of any kind," Jackson insulted him. "However, let me provide you with some advice despite that. Things will never be everything you want them to be. You would do well to squash those sky-high dreams, right now. I brought you into the fold, you know. I took you to the highest peak with the strike force. I thought that the responsibility would have you mature, so that you would respect what I do. Granted, some may question some of the more clandestine bases, despite their obvious necessity. I can't for the life of me think why you would be one of those people. That trip to the facility in Kansas was meant to assure you that you were a part of my most sensitive operations. I pulled back the curtains for you like an equal. I gave you my trust, and you gave me only betrayal and complication. You had power and threw it all away because it didn't taste to your liking. Other agents would have killed for the privileges you were given. I didn't fail you, even if it was a miscalculation on my part. You failed yourself with all your delusions."

Jason leaned over the desk, smugly.

"I think I get you now. I can piece it all together. You keep saying that you do everything for A.R.C. You'd cross any line for it. With your ego, you think that you are the only one who knows what's best for it. If powerful members threaten that perfect picture, you set them aside. If that doesn't work, you eliminate them. You knew that Avery had you red-handed on all the off-the-books stuff. He was going to blow things open in front of the Council. Before that, you made sure that there was no more Council. No one to expel you from power. Now, it's just you versus Avery. Does that about sum it up?"

"Oh please," Jackson scoffed. "Are you two so simple-minded? I may have had disagreements with members of the Council, but there was, and still is, no chance for my removal. The facts would see me through. I was prepared for whatever concoction Avery would come up with."

Paul found that Jackson's explanation was sticking with him. *The part that doesn't make sense is whether or not Jackson would take out some of the strongest members of A.R.C. The Council members not only had political clout, but they were immensely skilled. Jackson worships strength. Would Jackson really handicap A.R.C. like that just for his own power trip?*

Jackson's face lost its redness for a moment. He now wore a look of sudden clarity, as if the gravity of the situation had refocused his mind. He stared Jason down.

"I see it now," he mused. "You, for one, have come in here with your mindset. You've already crossed the point of no return."

Jason took a step forward, but Paul stepped in the way.

"Easy. I wouldn't do anything drastic. We still have things to figure out. The rest of A.R.C. will still want proof. A.R.C. has always been more than the Council."

Jackson rose from his desk.

"You know," he said thoughtfully. "Now, that the politeness has come off. I can say what I really think. Jason, I almost admire your approach. Don't get me wrong, you're beyond misguided. That determination and doggedness are what a soldier needs. It's a pity those traits are clouded by boorishness."

He turned to Paul.

"You, however, don't have the confidence in yourself to inspire confidence in others. It is a great shame that the golden, now green, crystal fell to you. With all that might, you could have done truly great things for A.R.C. However, your timidity and probable psychosis made getting you to accomplish worthwhile tasks feel like pulling teeth. I mean, can you do anything without finding some sort of self-righteousness in it?"

"I came here for answers!" Paul snapped. "Why did those planes go down, and why did you lock my aunt and uncle in prison?"

"Were you listening?" mocked Jackson. "I've answered both questions. I have no idea and for your own good!"

Paul could not stop Jason from getting his sword out this time.

"Those happen to be the wrong answers," Jason declared as his sword blazed red. "If we can't get right to the bottom of who murdered the Council members, then it's only reasonable that we take in the most likely suspect."

"Take into whom?" Jackson scoffed. "I am the authority here."

"You're not the only Council member left," Paul reminded him before he took a long breath.

This is really going to happen. The rebellion has started, and I'm going to be striking the first blows.

"You trust him more than me?" Jackson wondered.

"He's been transparent, helpful, and on the side of good this entire time," Paul insisted.

"Well, and I thought you were intelligent enough not to become a pawn," Jackson insulted him.

Jason turned the words against him. "How many pawns have you disposed of? How many members of your beloved A.R.C. have you put in the ground? You claim to care about A.R.C. so much, but you torture and manipulate its people. I think you really only care about the name. It's really just a word that you're so hung up. You actually don't care about what A.R.C. actually is. Its people. It's a group of humans and not just some concept."

"Well, gentlemen," Jackson sighed, "is there a way around this impasse for us? All these insults are starting to get droll."

Jason pulled back his saber, torquing up for a swing.

"Jason, wait!" Paul cried.

There has to be something we can say that prevent this from becoming a full-scale battle!

In response to Jason, Jackson's hands flew back to grasp the bow behind him. In medieval times, an English longbow could punch holes in a knight's armor. This one could punch holes in Amuli. Jackson brought it forward and into position.

Jason charged the desk. Paul realized that he had long abandoned hope of a diplomatic outcome. *I'm not sure if he ever had that in mind. Is this revenge for Ling?*

In a flash, Jackson shot a purple bolt into his own desk. It exploded into a cloud of dust, splinters, and shards of metal and plastic. Jason was forced to stop his attack, while Paul pulled up his arms to brace himself from the shrapnel.

When the cloud settled, Jackson was several paces away at the other side of the office.

It was a smokescreen! Paul realized in dismay. *He wanted to get distance from us. That's where he has the advantage.*

A volley of multiple arrow blasts surged forward as Jackson wasted no time. The bolts spanned from Jason to Paul. They both dove wide to dodge. More desks and chairs exploded in a deafening crescendo.

Both Paul and Jason rolled to their feet at opposite sides of the room. In unison, they charged Jackson from opposite angles. The two young Amuli had been trained side-by-side. They knew each other's speed, timings, and fighting patterns. Luper had drilled teamwork into them. They were two pieces of the same machine.

Jackson's reaction times were quick. He fired shot after shot from his blazing bow, constantly switching sides every time to match Jason and Paul equally. The two sidestepped and slid forward under the heavy fire.

All the combatants were moving methodically. It was hard to quickly gain traction or ground. The experienced Jackson was holding his own against the young Amuli. Paul's eyes stung from the constant showers of sparks. He more or less had to feel his way along to make progress. With his sixth sense, he knew that the stronger the sense of anima, the closer he was to the enemy.

It was the ever-impatient Jason who changed tactics first. Rather than crouching and scurrying forward by sheer reaction, he stood up fully to face the anima waves. When he was shot at, he powered a red spiral from his saber back at Jackson. The opposing anima streams crashed together, rattling the entire floor.

The strategy began to work. The bashing of the anima together created explosions that Jackson could not see through either. Anima detection generally gave an Amulus only the general idea of where a living being was. For precise targeting of projectiles, an Amulus still needed his sight. Jason was now gaining ground in bounds.

Paul decided to replicate Jason's technique. As an anima arrow came near him, he would trace an anima shock wave towards it and let it fly. Jackson was now being pinched in from two sides.

Even though the light from the anima collisions was blinding, Paul could see that he was within feet of Jackson. This time, the experienced fighter changed tactics.

Jackson stopped blasting and swung his bow around. It narrowly missed the top of Paul's head, and he could feel the generated wind tug at his hair. Jason came in with a powerful downward stroke from the other side.

With impeccable timing, Jackson moved faster than the racing sword. He cloaked his entire arm in purple anima and used it to tip the side of the saber blade away. The edge bit off his sleeve, but nothing else.

Paul's mind worked quickly as he analyzed the situation. *His weapon is a bow, but that hasn't narrowed his focus, apparently. He's amazing at both distance and close-range combat!*

Seeing Jackson tied up with Jason, Paul moved for his own strike with his sword. A moment later, he found his blade rebounding off of Jackson's wooden bow. Jason next took advantage of an opening but was matched by the bow as well. The older man's reflexes were still staggeringly sharp. With normal materials, metal would have shattered wood. However, with an anima crystal attached, any material became close to unbreakable.

Paul poured it on with downward strokes just as Jason did from the other side. *He has to get tired soon. He's fighting two Amuli at once.*

He could feel it in Jackson's anima and see it in his eyes. There was still a difference between Paul and people like Jackson and even Jason. Every attack of theirs was for the kill. Any unblocked attack would deal death. There was some mental barrier in Paul's mind. He could attack to injury or disarm, but something prevented him from going for the kill. The way his body held back, it felt more than mental. Only the enhancements in his blood and the maddening power of the new crystal drove him toward the edge of that impulse at times.

I hate this, Paul's thoughts still raced coherently as his arms swung and positioned the katana over and over. *I have to dip in again. Cam, Robby, Alice… they all wouldn't want me to. I don't see another way, though. I have to feel it.*

Paul let the emotion come as he whirled his sword harder and harder. He drove it toward the man who had locked up his aunt and uncle, his only living family, for months. He was the man who had manipulated his emotions and played with his mind. He would lock up innocents. It was this man who was leading the most powerful organization in the world toward totalitarianism.

Paul could feel the blackness seeping into his blood, even before the darkened blood vessels and shadowy anima became visible. It was hot, like boiling rage. Remembering one of Ben's moves earlier, he drove his shin into Jackson's calf. With Paul's enhanced speed, Jackson had no chance to dodge this one.

Jackson's knee buckled on reflex, but only slightly. He had a look of serious pain but rebounded quickly. It was clear that he was growing weary of defending Paul's side.

The dark energy was slowly working its way into Paul's head. He could feel the haziness. His anger was becoming confused, almost animalistic, as his mind lost focus.

Then, he over-extended himself. In his recklessness, he swept too far on a horizontal slash. Jackson saw the opening. His backhand struck Paul in the chest to stun him. Then the older man pivoted and swung his bow. It cracked across Paul's face.

A surge of black and red hit Paul's eyes as he stumbled backward to fall onto a pile of wood that had once been a desk. Shaking his bruised head, he found that the rage had dissipated, and his veins were returning to their normal color.

Maybe that's for the best. It makes me stronger but numbs my head too much. I can't think right.

He saw Jackson had not escaped his maneuver unscathed. The experienced agent's own attack had left him wide open to Jason for a moment. The red saber had stung his shoulder-blade, and he now clearly favored that side. Only quick evasion had stopped Jason's attack from being a finishing move.

Paul had never seen anything approaching desperation on Jackson's face. Yet, it was there now. His mouth was a grimace and his eyes darted around, even when no attacks from Jason were incoming.

Now fighting solo, Jason poured more power into his attacks with greater urgency. That was indicated by the strained veins popping out of his wrists. Jackson matched him blow-for-blow. Bruises and scrapes from occasional impacts filled up their faces.

Paul scrambled in the debris pile, trying to get back to the fight. In their wild, chaotic dance, Jason and Jackson had unknowingly put some distance between themselves and him. Paul looked for an opening. If he could leap in at the right angle, the fight would be over.

His focus was suddenly shattered by a feeling in the air. It was so concentrated that it could only come from anima. It was not the typical discharge of the pitched battle. This was even darker and more violent. It was anger and vengeance itself, pure bloodthirst. Paul recognized it as something similar to the pain excreted by the unleashing of the enhancement powers.

And there it was. Jason's red anima was now becoming rimmed by blackness. His throbbing veins matched the color. One of his trademark anima spirals now encircled him. It pulsed and swirled in the two colors.

Paul stopped in his tracks. *Impossible...*

CHAPTER 32
TARDY

"SO, um, this is kind of an 'are we there yet?' situation," Robby remarked. "Except it's 'are they here yet?'"

The rest of the group was too on-edge to speak. They stood scattered around an empty lot. Jessica was anxiously peering up and down the adjacent street, while she shouted frustratedly into her secure-line phone. Eventually, she went silent and instead started pounding her fingers along the screen as she rejoined the main group.

"I don't get it," she complained. "I really don't get it. The buses were on their way. They only had a short drive while we were flying in. They are supposed to be here, and I'm only getting answering machines. The logistics of this were so easy, even if it was cloak-and-dagger."

"I don't suppose they stopped for-"

"Robby, no jokes right now, okay?"

"So, what happened?" Camilla wondered. "Have we been made? If so, why aren't we being apprehended right now?"

"We do have to think of the mission," Alice pointed out warily. "Paul and Jason are risking their lives right now."

That comment made even Robby nervous.

He scratched at the base of his artificial hand and said, "So, when I was on the plane. I kind of had a bad feeling. Maybe it was like the kind that Amuli get sometimes, I don't know. I may have texted for some extra help, too. I know it was stupid not to tell anyone, but it's weird. I just really don't like making anyone nervous."

Jessica shook her head. "Even if you called in more guys from A.R.C.-Human, that isn't going to create some kind of a bottle-neck effect and slow everyone down. The first wave of vans was already leaving! I checked."

"Look," interjected Camilla, "we may not be in a great situation, but I agree with Alice. We don't know what kind of time we have to work with. Who knows? Jackson may have figured us out and will be sending people to reinforce this place. Isn't there a way of getting in, getting the prisoners out, and putting them... somewhere? That's until we have something to transport them on."

"We won't be along to just march them along for miles," Jessica realized. "We don't know what their conditions are like, and that will definitely attract attention."

They each thought solemnly for a moment.

Alice finally said, "Transporting them may not be the only option. We could take the building and then hold it. Then, we would even have a defensible position. If there are only a few prisoners, we may be able to move them elsewhere by foot if need be."

"It's not a bad plan," Jessica remarked. "In fact, it's probably the best plan for this crummy situation. We take the building and then hold tight until our transports get here or the enemy, whichever group it may be, sends reinforcements. Antonio, it's time to unload the crates."

Antonio was still working on his communicator. He looked more nervous than any else there. A just-visible line of sweat traced his forehead. On Jessica's word, he stopped fidgeting and typed in a code to pop open one of the metal crates.

"The three non-Amuli will suit up," Jessica explained. "We brought scatter-shot shotguns and flashbangs. The shotguns should push them back and give them a good bruise. The flashbangs will work like they do on anyone else. It's our best shot in close quarters inside the building. We just need to be pests until Alice or Cam can take them out. It's good that this place has cells. We'll be clearing the prisoners out of them and putting the guards in them. I just wish we had drone cameras on this place, but that's risky. Odds are they would probably be seen. If we're clear, we'll breach in five."

Robby excitedly took out his gray, urban camouflage jumpsuit and matching full-face helmet.

"No peaking," he teased as he lifted his shirt to attach the built-in electrodes that would tamper the suit to his body.

He then flexed his robotic fingers as they connected to the suit's built-in computer. "Time to see what this thing can do!"

———

Robby, Camilla, and Antonio stood in the hidden base's neighboring alleyway. Antonio's face was pale as he clutched his shotgun.

"You good buddy?" Robby asked him. "C'mon, you've been on a hundred missions."

"It's a… you know… you never get used to it," Antonio replied shakily.

"You can always bring up the rear then," Robby pointed out. "I'll be the first one in for our group."

"Hold it," Camilla advised him. "I'm first. Superhuman with an energy barrier, remember?"

Robby held up his metal hand. "Well, I'm practically Mega Man."

"She's moving in!" Camilla shushed him as the group fell in line with her prescribed order.

Alice was making her way to the front doors. Jessica crouched behind a crumbling car on the street in front of the building. Like much of this area of the city, this block was still empty of people and working cars. There were marks where water had lapped at the building's stone siding.

No one appeared outside as Alice stepped toward the doors. Her face was serene, and her eyes changed to gold. She had sensed no one in the immediate vicinity of the entrance. A nod of her head was the only signal given to the rest of the team.

A torrent of gold energy tore through the building's glass doors. She then jogged inside the small chasm she had created in what had been the entryway.

Camilla's team got moving as well. With the dark-haired girl in the lead, they crashed through the low windows of the other side of the building. From there, the plan was to divide and conquer.

A pair of guards waited for them. One was a Psychic with a long, crystal pendant bouncing about his neck, and the other held a mace. The pair swiveled towards the sound of broken windows. Prior to that, it appeared that they had been peering out from their corner at the trespasser at the front doors. They had obviously been planning an ambush and had been taken by surprise by a different ambush.

The guards, one man, and one woman, barely had time to react, let alone defend themselves, before Camilla blasted them into the walls. From there, the team moved quickly and efficiently. They were set to take the stairs and any upper floors. With her firepower, Alice stayed on the ground floor to search for a possible basement. That was the most likely location for a clandestine prison which, in all likelihood, would be heavily guarded.

Camilla's team marched up the nearest stairwell. A trio of enemies met them there. On one wing of the formation was a man armed with a heavy war hammer, and on the other was a young man with a wailing flail. Both blazed in blue. Just trailing at the center was a woman with a red-crystal earring.

Camilla took the Psychic in the center first. She reasoned that it was best to take out the source of communication first. Robby and Antonio flanked out beside her, peppering the Warriors with shotgun bursts. The ricochets into their anima barriers pushed them back slightly. That was enough time for Camilla to aim anima bullets at all three. They all went down quickly.

The next floor had an open area, and one large, closed room. Camilla fired through the doorknob. As the door swung open, Robby tossed a flashbang grenade inside. The team turned their heads as the blinding white light erupted for a moment.

Inside, they found a pair of Warriors, one with a heavy, unwieldy lance and the other with an ulfberht Viking sword, now furiously rubbing their eyes. The one with the lance went down to Camilla's first blast easily. She shot another volley at the swordsman.

Surprisingly, he had the wherewithal to deflect the wave. He had obviously been trained to use his sixth sense of anima locating when his others were compromised. The ulfberht did its signature bend upon impact. That was the strength of the Viking swords. In other blades, too much movement meant warping, or a compromised sword. Ulfbherht swords were made to bend and not break. It gave them powerful, ringing blows when it came time for their attacks.

This ulfberht wielder did not have the chance to show off this Norse metallurgy. Still at a disadvantage, he dove behind an overturned table which then splintered from anima blasts and shotgun sprays. Eventually, the attacks found him as well. When the table gave way, he lay there stunned and still.

The next floor was empty. The team had their guns drawn in every doorway, but no one responded. It was the same on the next floor.

On the last floor, another group meant them at the stairs. Camilla struck the legs of a Psychic who had stuck his foot out as he had rounded a corner. As he stumbled down, another blast took him in the head. His Warrior companion with a red-glowing sickle sword charged. He had obviously been resolved to this final, risky option. Purple anima caught him in the side. As he twirled down, Camilla smacked him in the head with her revolver.

The enemy Amulus slunk down the stairs like a slinky before coming to a small landing. There, he twisted around in pain somewhere between consciousness and unconsciousness.

"Clear."

Camilla sent the thought down to Alice.

———

On the ground floor, the guards had been taken aback by Alice's initial wave of anima. Most had ducked behind desks and tables. With her over-powered senses, she could feel the anima of each person in their hiding places. Sometimes, she could catch a piece of one of their chaotic thoughts in her mind. They were not sending their thoughts knowingly; they were just that loud in their heads.

It felt all too familiar for Alice. The people were cowering and running away. Their thoughts screamed, *"Monster!"*

No, Alice told herself. *She is not with me anymore. Paul called me a human being. He does not think I am a monster.*

It was not as a monster that she meticulously cleared the floor. She accomplished it as a level-headed agent. She tossed golden orbs of anima whenever an enemy poked their head out or revealed too much of them-selves. In an adjoining room to the lobby, a man with a purple-covered spear charge her. He ran only into a golden energy barrier that sent him flying. He overturned a few chairs on his flight toward unconsciousness.

Wedged in a corner, a set of nearly hidden stairs on the side was the most heavily guarded place in the area. A quartet of Amuli stood shoulder to shoulder, forming a chain of human and anima energy. Alice formed a larger orb this time before sending it swirling towards them. It bowled all of them over in one swoop. Only one of them had enough strength to painfully get back up. Alice sent him back to the ground with a swift chop to the back of his head. She then surveyed the controlled carnage behind her.

Fifteen, she counted analytically. *I believe that each of them can make a full recovery.*

Alice found a locked, heavy door at the bottom of the stairs. She was more careful with this one. She lit her hands with anima at the ends, forming blades. In quick strokes, she ran her hands down the door's hinges, slicing right through them. As the heavy door gave way, she caught it easily before carefully setting it on the ground.

She stopped at the doorway and found that she could walk no further. *It's like… It feels like…*

There were rough concrete floors and walls. Pitiful, bare lightbulbs hung down from the high ceiling, barely lighting the way with a sad yellow glow. Then there were the bars. Alice hated them most of all. Those and the heavy, locked doors made of metal. In the cells, it was not the cold walls that held you in but the covered exits. Freedom was being blocked right before your eyes.

Alice stood motionless as the atmosphere of oppression weighed down on her. She swore the lightbulbs were gradually snaking lower. The walls and floor were getting narrower. The bars were getting thicker. She started sweating. Absentmindedly, she put a hand up to plug the trickle on her forehead. Her breath was quick but raspy.

"Alice? Alice!"

Alice came back inside of her own head. Those were Camilla's thoughts. They were always kind and careful when they worked their way inside her head.

Here, Alice finally responded as she shook the sweat and queasiness from herself. *All clear. I have located… them. This way is clear as well.*

Camilla's group descended the stairs shortly after, pausing just behind Alice. The blonde girl shuffled her feet, unsure of herself. She felt a warm hand on her shoulder. She turned to see Camilla's round, brown eyes.

"We've got this," she insisted assuredly. "You don't have to go in. I know it's tough. But look here, you're strong. You're strong because you overcame this type of crap. You're stronger than the people who ran this place because you would never put innocents in cages."

"You're pretty cool," added Robby as he followed Camilla forward.

The group moved forward through a row of empty cells. Behind the bars were simple mattresses of a short width, barely wide enough for one person. Each cell had a tiny enclosure with a door in front. One door had swung open to reveal a single metal toilet. The inner floors were scaled linoleum and were badly scratched. It was like a bathroom floor plan gone wrong.

They were almost to another set of stairs when they found the first prisoner. He was a young man, maybe in his twenties, whose hair had gone shaggy. His weight appeared healthy enough, but there were large, dark ovals under his bloodshot eyes. He viewed the newcomers with a mix of futility and resentment.

Camilla leaned against the bars.

"Hey, it's okay," she whispered. "We're getting you out."

The young man rolled his eyes.

"I'm serious," Camilla insisted.

"Look," the man spoke in a hoarse voice. "I don't really care about whatever mind games you're playing. Pick on someone else if you want your kicks."

Camilla shrugged, realizing that this man had not heard the commotion that had occurred so far above him. "Alright. Just to show you I'm serious, I'm blowing the bars away. Stand back."

She aimed her Colt revolver at one of the bars.

The man threw his hands up. "Whoa, whoa! So, you're serious? Are you like A.I.M. or other A.R.C. guys or whatever?"

Camilla thought for a moment. "You know, I'm not quite sure what we are at the moment. All I can say is that we want to get you and everyone else out of here."

"Alright, I'm game," the man replied, springing off his bed and back to life. "You know what, though? Save the anima blasting for now. You know that I'm just human, right? If something explodes near a normal person, well, that's bad."

Camilla holstered her gun.

"You've got a point. Alice, do you feel like cutting away the bars? I would, but that's not actually something I've done before with anima."

Alice took a step forward. She was still unsteady and had a vacant look in her eyes.

Camilla changed her mind. "You know what? Save your strength for now. Has anyone seen the keys to these lately?"

The man in the cell answered, "I know some of them had keys. They seemed to change around depending on the shift."

"Hey, Robby?" asked Camilla. "Do you think that guy on the stairs is awake enough to answer some questions? He didn't seem completely knocked out, just scrambled."

"Ooh!" Robby responded. "I'll go check. I've always wanted to interrogate someone."

He dashed off.

"Just don't annoy him to death before he talks," Camilla called after him.

Robby rushed up the stairs confidently while exaggeratedly swinging his arms. He came upon the young man who had wielded the half-moon sickle sword. The swordsman had made some progress in standing up. His legs were slightly stretched, but his throbbing, cloudy head was scraping the ground. His body formed an incidental, painful arch. Robby crouched down beside him.

"Hey, since you're not busy, why don't we have a conversation?"

The wobbly young man only gave him an angry moan at first.

"Okay, Okay! Could we *please* have a conversation?"

"Scuh... Screw y-you!" slurred the woozy agent.

"Alright," Robby relented. "But things will be a lot better if this isn't a one-sided conversation."

Robby reached down to his belt and pulled off a metal cylinder with a pin at the top.

"Ta-da!' he announced. "Does this make you feel like talking? I brought a present for you."

"T-That's a... a... frag?" mumbled the guard in fear.

"Oh, this isn't a-" Robby started to dismiss him but then rethought his words. "I mean... yeah. It's exactly what you just said it was."

"C-Crazy," stammered the man. "W-We're in a half-closed... stairwell. Y-You won't get way..."

Robby smugly slid his fingers up to the pin.

"Oh, I am crazy," Robby declared the best psychotic-sounding voice he could muster. "I... uh... don't doubt my commitment to the cause."

Fear finally struck the dizzy man's eyes. He began a manic, uneven crawl away from the teenager with the stun grenade.

"Hold it!"

Robby kept one hand on the flashbang and used to other to grab the injured guard by the shoulder. His new captive tried to flail his arms and legs like an insect being picked up. In his weakened state, he did not have the strength to break free of the ordinary human.

"Okay, just tell me where the cell keys are," Robby insisted while keeping his grip firm.

"Crazy!" the panicked guard repeated.

"Alright then."

Robby kept one hand on the young Amulus and one on the non-lethal grenade. He put the latter up to his mouth and put the pin between his teeth.

"Shee dish?" he managed to mutter between gritted teeth.

The guard's struggling intensified, but Robby held firm.

"Where'sh da keysh?"

"You're insane!" the guard shouted, clearly this time.

"Where'sh da keysh?"

The guard's head slunk down in resignation. "I don't know who had the main ones on them, but we always keep a spare in the desk on the second floor."

"Shank shou," Robby said as he relaxed his grip on the man. "Wash shash sho har?"

Robby then tried unclenching his teeth. He suddenly stopped.

"Oh nuh!" he breathed. "Oh nuh! Ish shuck!"

He started to fiddle with the metal pin stuck in between two teeth as much as he dared.

The guard's mouth dropped in disbelief. "Oh, God, no! You're kidding! Of all the… there's no way. No way!"

Robby ran his tongue over the lodged, thin piece of metal.

"Ahmosh. Ahmosht."

The guard was finally stumbling away with his head in his hands.

"I-"

There was a roaring pop followed by a momentary blinding light.

———

Camilla and the rest of the team heard the bang from below.

"What was…" she mouthed. "Robby!"

She bounded up the stairs, followed by the others. She threw herself up the last several steps to the landing Robby was on.

She found him stumbling around, rubbing his eyes. His feet were shuffling aimlessly on the linoleum.

"Oh, God…" he muttered with a strange calm. "Oh, God…"

Camilla rushed to him, grabbing him by his shoulders.

"Let me see!" she insisted. "Let me see!"

Robby took his hands away from his eyes, and Camilla stared deeply into them, checking them all over.

"What happened? Did he reach for your flashbang?"

"Uh, no…" he started to say before trailing off. "I mean… yeah. That's exactly what happened."

Camilla pulled him closer by the chin to get a better look at his blood-shot eyes.

"I don't see any damage on the surface," she remarked with some relief. "You should still get looked at, but I think you'll probably be okay. I mean, you have to be careful. Flashbangs can cause permanent loss of hearing or eyesight. The guy you were interrogating is even out cold! It must have been a shock to his system."

"Yeah… I… um, can hear pretty okay. I can barely see…"

"Hold on," Camilla interrupted him. "What's that?"

"Do I have something in my teeth?"

"Hold on."

Camilla reached in and, only somewhat painfully, yanked out the grenade pin from in-between Robby's teeth.

"Ow!"

Camilla looked at the small, saliva-covered pin with disgust.

"How did this…"

Robby threw up his hands, begging. "I can explain."

Camilla thought for a moment before giving him a judgmental stare down.

"Let me get this straight," she started. "You accidentally pulled the pin off of a grenade because you put it between your teeth, and it got stuck there. You almost blinded yourself by doing… that?"

"It was an advanced interrogation technique," Robby explained in a deadpan.

"Robby…" Jessica murmured in disappointment.

The rest of the group let out sighs.

"Hey, hey!" Robby interrupted. "I did get the information! Just look in the desk on the second floor and then tell me if what I did was effective or not. Plus, hey, who's to say your whole checking me over wasn't just some ploy to touch my face?"

"I'm not even going to respond to that part," Camilla muttered as the group started for the location in unison. "Anyway, you're not handling interrogations anymore."

"Wise," Alice agreed softly.

"Alice!" Robby scoffed, dumbfounded. "Not you, too!"

CHAPTER 33
DEGREES OF SEPARATION

THE BARRED door opened with a low rumble. The young man hopped down from his bed, stretching his legs as he walked out of the cell.

"So, what you in for?" Robby asked in a faux grumble.

"Robby..." Camilla responded to his lack of decorum.

"It's kind of a long story," the freed prisoner started as he now stretched his arms. "I was supposed to be getting married. Well, I was engaged. My fiancé's name is Evelyn. One day Evelyn and I were perusing a fancy store for wedding stuff. She got too close to a ring they had on display, and that turned out to be her anima crystal. A.R.C. came calling, saying that they had to take her in for her safety and mine. We both asked them if we could wait. We figured that we could at least have a wedding. Evelyn would get sent away for a little, and then she would come back and everything would be normal. Those A.R.C. guys had different ideas. They had to take her in right away. I didn't see the urgency. I made a scene. I was stupid enough to get in their faces and maybe rough them up. Big mistake. They put me here afterward. No trial or anything. I haven't heard from Evelyn since. I've been worried that she thinks I'm dead or something. Then, you guys show up."

The rest of the group took in the story, while Robby said, "Right. Here's the awkward thing. We are kind of A.R.C. agents, too. Or maybe it's 'former agents' at this point. What do you guys think?"

"It depends on how things are going on Jason and Paul's end," guessed Jessica.

"So, it's up for interpretation," Robby concluded.

Camilla moved closer to him, giving him a deep look in the eyes.

"We're also people who want things to be done differently. Our friend's family is trapped somewhere down here, so we obviously don't agree with that. A.R.C. is going to be different now. One way or another."

"We're looking for people who want change," Jessica added. "I mean, my family used to murder Amuli. We got that to change and now we work with them."

"I was locked up as a human experiment," Alice detailed. "I want to change things so that no one will have to endure what I have."

The young man was slightly taken aback.

"That's some… heavy stuff. But look, if that's all true, you've got my help. Some of the other people down here might not be as trusting when they hear you are or used to be in A.R.C. Since we've all been stuck together, I think I can do some convincing. After all, they don't have many choices down here to begin with."

Camilla nodded. "Thanks. What's your name, anyway?"

"Ken Layton. Nice to meet you all."

This set of cells was only one of many. A set of stairs led to another cellblock that ended with more stairs. There were two prisoners on this floor. A girl and a man were housed across from each other. The man sat on his bed, reading a well-thumbed car magazine. The girl was scribbling on a piece of paper in the corner of her room. They both turned to look at the new arrivals. Ken was leading the way, hungrily munching on one of the candy bars Robby had kept in his belt pack.

"Believe me," Ken said to both prisoners. "I was skeptical at first, too. But it really seems like these guys are here to free us."

The man, who was wearing an old, white T-shirt, stood up and put on the flannel jacket that had been resting on his bed.

"Well, that's a sight for sore eyes," he said cheerily.

The girl kept her head down, still working on the paper. Every once in a while, she would flash the corner of a paranoid, blue eye towards the group outside the bars.

"Well, I don't sense anything malicious coming out of your heads. My name's Joe. Her name is Kim."

"A Psychic!" Camilla exclaimed in surprise. "There are Amuli prisoners here, too?"

Curious, she tapped on one of the bars and found it denser than the others.

"Temporary holding," Alice analyzed. "Jackson evidently wants them close to him for now."

"Sorry," Joe apologized. "I'll stick to talking this way. The other way makes me feel weird, too. All I know is that we haven't been here very long... Kim or I, that is. As far as we know, I don't think either of us has felt that weird tingle from when other Amuli prisoners are around. That's not until now, I mean. Somehow, I just feel that those two young ladies have power."

"You both have powers," Jessica pointed out. "What stopped you from destroying everything else through the gaps in bars?"

"I think they took our crystals far away," Joe explained. "I think the farther they got away, the less strength I felt in me. I can still do the thought stuff, but breaking through solid steel might be different. Anyhow, there have always been guards here, too. I can't say that numbers would have been in our favor if we did get out."

"A.R.C. policy," Camilla thought aloud. "You can't destroy someone's anima crystal... or at least, you couldn't until something that happened recently. But you can take it farther away to dim down an Amulus' power. The rumor is that A.R.C. either puts them on the opposite side of the world or they just throw them into the deepest part of the ocean."

"So, we won't be seeing our crystals for a long time then," Joe surmised.

Joe stepped out the door as soon as Camilla opened it.

"Thank you, ma'am," he said graciously. "You can't imagine how bored I've been. Even if you guys are up to something, it'll sure beat hanging out down here."

"Your turn," Camilla announced as she started to slip the key into Kim's cell door.

"Save it," Kim hissed, keeping her back turned. "I'm not leaving with you guys."

"Kim," Joe addressed her softly. "What's the matter?"

"What's the matter?" she repeated back to him. "Isn't it obvious? Everything's the matter! People are the matter. All my life I've had to put up with different people's crap. They just cheat, steal, and take advantage of you. It seems like it only gets worse when they get superpowers. It all comes to the surface then. Then, they have a way of expressing all the crap they keep inside."

Camilla took a step towards the cell.

"Forgive me for being blunt, but you're a superhuman, too."

Kim shook her head.

"Oh, wow!" she shouted sarcastically. "I've never realized that!"

She shook her head and continued.

"Yeah, I'm superhuman. You know what the difference between superhumans like me and Joe and all the show-offs in A.R.C. and A.I.M.?

It's that we don't care. I don't care about my powers. I can't think of a single reason why I would want to use them. But y'all think of reasons. That's all you do. You get so obsessed with how strong you are. You gotta come up with reasons to use that strength. Other people with powers disagree with what you're doing? Well, use your powers to fight them. Some Amuli are minding their own business and don't want to join your club? Well, shoot anima at them and then throw them in jail."

"That's not…" Camilla started as she shifted her feet, frustrated. "Everyone here and so many others… we just want to use these powers to help people. We can't get rid of them, so why not make the best out of it?"

"What if the best thing to do is nothing?" Kim shot back. "Plenty of people who try to help just end up making things worse."

Camilla was about to argue something back, but Joe quietly raised a hand to stop her.

"I get what you're saying," he said softly. "I get it because I agree with just about all of it. It's just that sometimes in life, we have to do things we don't want to do. We have to hang around people we don't want to be around. I can't tell you how much time it'll take for you to get to the places you want to be and to the people you want to be with. All I can say is, you won't find it sitting in this cell."

Kim put her head down and sighed. Slowly, she rose from the bed and approached the cell door.

"Fine."

"Now, I'm not apologizing for her because I think she has something to apologize for," Joe began as Camilla swung open the door. "When you've been through the things we have, trust doesn't come easy. Actually, we were put in here after a setup. A guy calling himself 'Green' knocked me out and sent Kim into hysterics. We're both still pretty broken up about the whole thing."

"Listen, buddy…' Robby started as he pieced the story together.

Camilla stopped him.

"I'm going to clarify something," she notified them. "It's because this 'Green' guy is a friend of ours. He wouldn't have done something like that on purpose. Most likely, your attacker was acting on his own. P… err… 'Green' was probably just as surprised as you were. In fact, we're only here to rescue you because of him. He's just a nicer guy than what he was pretending to be."

Joe scratched at the bald spot on top of his head.

"Well, that makes us have to think about things differently, doesn't it?" he asked Kim rhetorically.

She only rolled her eyes.

———

The final row of cells was another floor below. Dampness had seeped down there when the waves had come. That was evidenced by the muddy stains on the walls. The air had the stuffy smell of mold. The group just prayed that there had not been prisoners this far below when the water was dripping down. Perhaps they had only been moved there once the water had receded.

They got their answer at the last remaining cell. The man and woman occupying it were pale, gaunt, and disheveled but appeared safe and dry enough. Still, the deep impressions on their two small beds revealed that they had chosen not to step onto the damp floor very often.

This time, it was Robby who led the way. He walked up to the door with little of his trademark overconfidence. The fingers of his metal hand flexed intermittently. His darkened visor meant that no one could see his exact emotions. It seemed that he wanted to hide them from the cell's occupants most of all. He kept his head down-turned as he undid the lock, feeling like the curious eyes were staring right through his helmet.

"So, what do we have here?" Morgan wondered, skeptical of the new arrivals. "Did you flood the city again? You really like to keep us on our toes with moving around."

Part of her uncombed hair stood on end. Robby chalked that up to Engel DNA.

Nick did not address them. His dark hair was also messy in some areas, and patchy hairs had sprouted from his face.

"Um, hold tight," Robby told them as he reached for his helmet. "This is gonna be weird."

"Holy…" Morgan cried when the helmet slipped off.

Nick nearly fell out of his bed.

"I can explain," Robby offered.

"Yeah," Morgan scoffed. "You'd better. The last time I heard you say, 'I can explain,' you had only broken my front window with a boomerang. Now, you're standing there dressed like a Hunter while surrounded by a bunch of Amuli."

"You'd better start with the part where you explain where Paul is," Nick advised him warily.

"You're… um… not going to like that…" Robby murmured.

"Robby!" they both yelled in unison.

"He's fighting Gareth Jackson, probably," Robby exhaled quickly.

"Either that or they are having a nice conversation. The frustrating thing is we really don't know. It's been radio silence."

"Hold it," Morgan said with a hand over her face. "You're going to have to explain all of that. Like, Paul is fighting someone? Paul? And Gareth Jackson? That A.R.C. leader my brother hated? Yeah, my brother was an Amulus, but I'm guessing you know that by now."

"So, the reason you're down here is because of Gareth Jackson," Robby told them.

"That's starting to track," Morgan responded. "Paul doesn't like fights. Trivia battles maybe, and video games, sure. But he's never liked it when people who are close to him get hurt. Remember how he got mad at the kids who called you 'shorty pants' on the playground. I think you were both six."

Camilla's mouthed twitched as she barely stifled a laugh.

"If you guys are fighting with Jackson, does that mean you're with A.I.M.?" Morgan wondered.

"Sides are confusing right now," Robby admitted. "We are definitely not a part of A.I.M. though. We are also definitely not with the Hunters. We were all with A.R.C., but then Jackson may have killed all the other leaders. We're not sure want we are right now. Paul and Jason, the grumpy one of our friend group, are kind of figuring that out right now."

Nick's brow furrowed.

"So, if Paul's always been with A.R.C., then why did Jackson lock us up?"

"I can answer that," Camilla declared as she walked forward to finally insert herself in the conversation. "Jackson's been manipulating him. He saw Paul's psychiatric profile and decided locking his family up would make him lose his innocence."

"Well, I hope Paul hits him hard then, " Morgan replied. "I'm sorry. Who are you?"

"I'm Cam," she answered. "Paul's a friend. We trained together. He's saved my butt a few times, and I've saved his. Alice has been with us the whole way, too."

Alice drifted out from behind Camilla for a moment to nod before creeping back again with a strange shyness. Camilla was surprised to see that her pale cheeks had gone slightly rosy.

"I'm glad to see that Paul's had friends throughout this whole horrible thing," Morgan thanked them sincerely. "I bawled for a long time when I heard he had become an Amulus. It was all because of what they did to Michael... and Sam. I know that the world Amuli live in is so cruel. I've seen it firsthand. I never thought it would happen to him. I used to look over the odds to calm myself. Do you know the odds for someone to be an Amulus? What about the odds for two people in one family to become Amuli? Paul drew the shortest stick, and he doesn't deserve it. He's as good of a person as I know. I'm not just saying that because he's my kid. It's like he was born with that inside of him."

"You should know that he's done a lot of amazing things," Camilla told them. "And you'll see him soon. You can all catch up."

"I have one more question, and then I want to get the heck out of here," Morgan announced. "What's with those bodysuits for Robby and... I remember you from the Swanson barbeques... you're Jessica."

"This is going to be painfully awkward," Jessica began. "The Swansons did a lot more than just drag Amuli in the press. We had Hunters in the family. Don't worry, though. Neither Robby nor I have ever been on that side. Robby didn't even know about it until recently. We both signed up with A.R.C. when we could."

"You're right," Nick partially agreed. "That's... something to think about. It's also a comforting thought. The son of an Amulus grew up close with the son of a Hunter family and became friends."

"Yeah, I've always thought that you've fallen pretty far from the tree, Robby," Morgan informed. "Heck, we practically raised you as an honorary Engel."

The conversation took a long enough pause for the group to hear a rumbling from above. It was accompanied by the mechanical rhythm of diesel engines.

"Oh, finally," Jessica mouthed, relieved. "The buses are here. We can finally get you guys out of here."

CHAPTER 34
TRUE COLORS

THIS CAN'T BE HAPPENING.

Yet, there it was, the shadowy sign of anima enhancement. The kind that always involved a human sacrifice in the form of crystal breaking. Paul remembered the excruciating pain of his own life force being sucked out as if into a void. It had hurt his entire being and left him feeling so cold.

The Scientist... wasn't he the only one who knew how. But he... And I...

He stood up gingerly but hesitated on taking a step further.

When did it even happen? When did Jason have the time?

There were a lot of things Paul wanted to say. Instead, he only croaked out, "Jason..."

"Leave it for now," Jason advised him with an odd note of understanding in his voice. It almost sounded like regret.

"How..." Paul insisted.

The battle was still on, however.

Sensing a break in Jason's concentration, Jackson let fly. Barely moving his body, Jason easily swept the anima arrow into the ceiling with his sword. Dust and ceiling tiles rained down. Jason sped forward in a red and black blur. Jackson just held up his bow in time for a block, but Jason's momentum sent him into a wall. With Jackson pinned, Jason next aimed a furious, downward stroke. Jackson raised his bow high this time, catching the blade with it.

With his enhancements speeding up his reflexes, Jason pounced on the opening. He kicked with full force into Jackson's exposed midsection.

Jackson flew further this time, now out of his own control. The force of the kick sent him straight through the drywall. Jason followed him through the human-sized hole.

Paul shook some of his apprehension away and scrambled towards the gap. The air was even thicker with dust and debris splinters. He could just see that the battle had spilled out into the hallway beyond. Paul followed and slipped through the cough-inducing cloud.

Jason was hammering away at Jackson. The older man was still defending, but his arms were now slouching. They were not moving at the speed his brain was bidding them. Attacks were grazing through. Bloody nicks appeared all over Jackson's body.

Paul now saw the degree of difference between himself and Jason. Despite being enhanced, Paul always held back. It was not always a conscious decision. Something in his body always prevented him from wailing away at someone with all his strength. Deep down, he realized the wrongness of all the violence. There was something in violence that felt wholly unnatural to him. Violence was something that he had to force out of himself. Typically for Paul, it did not brim the surface willingly.

There was nothing that blocked Jason. That part of him had long been broken. Jason always swung for the kill. He did not simply want to win. He wanted slaughter. In his mind, that was natural, to strike down evil at any cost.

Jackson was retreating, though he seemed to realize the futility. This part of the hallway ended with a floor-to-ceiling window. There was fear and borderline madness in his eyes. It was animalistic nature. Still, he was a soldier. He had always known that death was a possibility. He had lived with that for the majority of his life. Still, it felt so strange that the end could be upon him after all these years of evading death.

The hallway ended. Jackson's back pressed up against the glass. He kept his bow raised, defiant.

Jason gave one last, powerful beat on the bow before it clattered out of Jackson's grasp. Ever the warrior, the defeated fighter's eyes remained prideful. The sentiment was backed by consternation that he lost to a boy with secret enhancements.

"It's your move now," Jackson creaked through his raw throat.

Jason pulled back his sword in preparation for a chop to the defense-less neck.

"Wait!" Paul cried as he finally caught up to them.

He had to keep rubbing the dust and ash off of his face so that his mouth would not become filled while he was speaking.

"He's done," Paul elaborated. "We have him. He can barely move, and we proved that we can beat him anytime."

Jason kept his sword at ready.

"Jason!" Paul pleaded. "Even if you don't think it's wrong to kill him while he's unarmed, think about it! He's our prisoner now! He has so much explaining to do, and he's going to do it in full view of the world. We'll have him explain what has been happening at A.R.C. We will find everyone he's put away. Everyone will see his secret prisons. A.R.C. will be able to build a new Council, one that is better than before. It will do everything the opposite of what Jackson did."

Tension was building in Jason's arm. He did not even look back at Paul.

"Jason!" Paul yelled again. "Don't undo everything we've done here."

The arm began its arc.

"Jason! For God's sake!"

The window broke from the slash's shock wave. The two pieces of Jackson's body fell out with the broken glass.

———

"Jackson!"

The younger version of Gareth Jackson barely registered the screaming in his face. His eyes were glazed over, and his drooping mouth had frozen into a deep frown. Greasepaint mixed with dried blood covered his sullied face.

His eyes slowly focused on the man in front of him, but his expression remained the same.

"What in God's name, lad?" a man in a red beret was barking spittle into his face. "What did I say? What did I say? You bloody fool! What was going through that mind?"

Jackson's lips barely moved as he spoke in a barely audible, low voice. "I just… I just…"

The commanding officer grabbed him roughly by the shoulders. His touch finally brought Jackson partway out of his stupor.

"I know you said, 'pull back,'" he whimpered. "I just… I just couldn't leave 'em!"

The officer was not swayed.

"When I say 'retreat' you retreat! You're not some bloody hero! We're all a bunch of poor bastards on this Godforsaken place at the bottom of the world."

"It's just… I could've gotten to them in time. We didn't have to leave them."

"Look at me. *Look* at me!"

Jackson did as he was told, but his neck only moved his head by cricks like it was powered by rusty gears.

"Eight men went in. We could have gotten six out! Then, you stayed! You told all of them to stay! Now, how many got out? How many?"

"Just me," Jackson sobbed.

He started furiously rubbing his hands against his short, brown hair.

"Just me… it was just because of me…"

His commanding officer shoved a pointed finger in his face. "You stop the bleeding! You here that? You don't let it all bleed out! Remember this!"

———

Paul could feel the cold, moist air clinging to him from Jackson's memory. The commanding officer's steaming breath seemed to remain as well.

As his mind reset to the present, he was hit by a wave of nausea that left him hanging on a ruined wall.

"Jason, why?" he murmured.

There was a sound of slow clapping coming from behind him. Paul turned after realizing that it had not come from more falling ceiling tiles.

"'For the love of God, Montresor!'" a man's voice quoted. "'Yes, I said, for the love of God!'"

Red Mask was strolling in slowly to join the two teenagers at the shattered window at the end of the hallway.

Paul raised his sword into position. *No! No! Not here… not now…*

Jason remained where he was. He only turned around to reveal his face speckled by Jackson's blood. He let his arms down, and his red-tipped saber hung lazily at his side.

"Why?" Paul demanded. "Why are you here?"

CHAPTER 35
BLOCKADE

"THOSE ARE NOT THE RIGHT BUSES," Robby pointed out, leaning on the wall next to one of the windows on the upper floor.

"Someone figured out what we were up to," Jessica ventured.

Mobs had streamed forth from buses located at each corner of the building. They had enveloped the building in a giant, human circle. The entirety of the crowd were Amuli, each holding a glowing weapon or trinket. Masks covered their faces. The masks were color-coordinated by the bus their wearers had stepped off of. There was orange, white, violet, and the last group was a mix of red and black.

"That's Red Mask's MO," Jessica realized. "It's after the Poe poem. The Red Death comes to an abbey and goes through colored rooms. The four are orange, white, violet, and red and black. He's taunting us."

"So, now A.I.M.'s up to something?" Camilla wondered. "Has it been them all along? Were we wrong to peg Jackson for the Council assassination?"

"It would have to be," Jessica analyzed. "They have been growing bolder, but this still doesn't seem like them. We may be in a recovering disaster area, but they are out in broad daylight. It feels like rogue Amuli and not an organization like A.R.C. or A.I.M. It's like they're inviting chaos. What is Red Mask up to?"

"*I have finished barricading the entrances,*" Alice sent the message to each of them consecutively. "*I apologize for destroying the front entrance in the first place. I thought that it may have been reinforced during my initial entry, so I applied more force than necessary.*"

Jessica replied, "*You had no way of knowing.*"

"*No worries,*" Camilla responded.

"*At least it looked cool!*" Robby added.

"I can't get any signal," Jessica told them. "They're blocking us, even the secure line and the satellite phone."

"So, we're stuck here," Camilla analyzed while nervously pacing. "No one's coming."

Robby lifted a finger in the air.

"Correction. Something is coming. I said I called some people before, and then I didn't have time to explain who. It was Blake! I'm getting something delivered!"

"Do you think it's still coming?" asked Jessica.

Robby leaned toward the window and pointed to a shape in the sky. "I'd say so."

Jessica and Camilla joined him at the window. The shape was rapidly growing bigger.

"Robby!" Jessica shouted. "Now, think! It's flying in on a signal. That's going to get interrupted at some point by whatever jammers the enemy has. It's going to crash!"

"There is a plan B," Robby explained. "We just have to hope that the signal doesn't drop until it reaches us."

"So, what is it?" Camilla questioned them.

"One of Robby's toys," Jessica explained, rolling her eyes.

Moments later, a large thud hit the roof.

"Yes!" Robby cried as he practically jumped into the air. "I'm going to go to get it!"

He raced off for the stairs as Camilla and Jessica followed.

———

The drone had made a dent in the gravel but had otherwise done nothing to compromise the integrity of the roof. The formerly flying object was several yards from beak to tail. It was painted a mix of gray and blue for camouflage within the sky. The wings were long, which, coupled with its propeller power, made it built for hovering. Under the wings, there were bunches of gas canisters. Thankfully, none had cracked open upon the crash. Its topside was covered with a detachable crate which was evenly distributed over the aircraft's weight. Robby ran to that part first.

"Well, this would have been great," Camilla observed. "Dropping a smokescreen from above would have helped us get away. Heck, this thing is big enough that almost all of us could have flown away on it."

Jessica paced the roof's perimeter, while hunched over. She had to ensure that no one in the crowd had a clear shot at them.

Strangely enough, the onlookers seemed to have spied them. However, they had done nothing apart from keeping an eye on them. No one had charged the building either. Nor had anyone shouted demands. No, they seemed to be waiting for something.

Jessica described it back to Camilla and Robby as she saw it. Robby did not seem to be listening. He was busy plugging in a code on the detachable container panel.

"Oh, man," he was whispering to himself, "I'm going to buy Blake so many slushies when I see him again!"

The lid slowly powered open.

"What is it?" Camilla questioned him. "It better be like a rocket launcher or some piece of tech that lets us send out a signal."

"It's better," Robby answered.

He finally reached in to pull it out.

"It's a... motorcycle from the future?" Camilla wondered. "How does that help us? We're stuck with nowhere to go."

The motorbike was thin and made of something resembling plastic. Only its large windshield resembled that of a high-speed, racing motorcycle. It was still obviously a prototype. The plastic was still white and the metallic, shining engine was mostly exposed.

"It's not just any motorcycle," Robby declared, imitating a used car salesman he had heard in a commercial. "It's super light, super durable, silent, and its electric battery will barely ever need to be charged. That's not even the best part."

Robby pushed down on the handlebars. The bike swiveled back and forth according to Robby's pressure. He then tilted the top component nearly horizontal, while the wheels stayed flat on the ground.

"It gyrates," Robby explained. "It always self-regulates so that the driver, me, will always stay completely upright. While going over uneven surfaces, it always self-regulates as the lower half twists and moves. That means you can drive at almost any angle. It doesn't go quite to ninety degrees, though. Gravity will still catch you there."

"So, it's the greatest motorcycle ever," Camilla pointed out impatiently. Yet it still can't get through that ground of Amuli down there."

"We don't need to," Robby replied with a devilish smile. "We can just confuse the heck out of them. I can ride around, dropping smoke. I'll be hard to hit and really annoying. We can get away in the confusion."

Camilla looked at Robby with hesitant admiration.

"That's not... the worst plan I've ever heard. It does give me an idea, though. I can add to it. It reminds me of what Luper used to teach us. It was from that samurai book Paul was always reading… oh… *The Book of Five Rings*. Anyway, the writer samurai guy in that had a strategy to use if you get completely surrounded. It doesn't do any good to just wait. All the enemies can just stab you from any angle as they close in. He said you were supposed to charge one side. You have to probe for a weakness. Even if you can't find a way out, you can change the enemy's formation so you're no longer surrounded."

"My plan exactly," Robby nodded haughtily. "I should have been a samurai, but I guess I'll let Paul have that one. So, I'll just hop on and cause heck for a while. You guys can look for an exit."

"This is still a crazy plan," Jessica said. "Like Cam, I can't say it's a terrible one. Just don't skimp on the smoke. I'll give you the rest of mine and Antonio's. Get the wind direction so you're not blowing it into your own face."

"I've got something to add," Camilla said as she took a step closer to Robby and the bike. "I'm coming, too. My firepower is a lot heavier than yours, and it comes in a small package. Two people can fit on the back of that thing, right?"

———

The masked group surrounding the building noticed a commotion at the front double doors. The space had once contained glass but was now blocked by stacks of wooden and plastic desks and chairs. It looked like a children's attempt at building a log cabin that had gone horribly wrong.

All at once, the mass of furniture came cascading downward, followed by a thick layer of gas. The whitish cloud grew furiously until it came towards the enclosed perimeter. Complacent, the armed crowd looked at each other. They had the enemy surrounded and had only expected a surrender. A literally blind cavalry charge was not what they were expecting.

Metal canisters started hitting the feet of the human circle. More smoke billowed out in some areas, while flashes of white and ear-splitting bangs rang out in others. In the confusion, the besiegers struggled just to find each other. Then purple flashes pop out.

The anima bullets were rapid, striking down several members of the small army. They had no way of pinpointing the enemy. Every once in a while, a few of their number heard the sound of wheels on pavement, but no motor.

Camilla had one arm tightly around Robby. The infrared-vision mode of Jessica's helmet let her know what was inside the smoke. However, the images were still obstructed. Vaguely human shapes were all she could make of it. On the other hand, firing into a crowd made that handicap little more than an annoyance.

With Robby driving, they worked their way to each section of enemies. That was phase one of the plan. They had to keep them guessing, taunting them with attacks that could come from anywhere. Robby swerved the cycle around for phase two.

He picked a side. The orange group was the most scattered by their preliminary attacks. They had tried regrouping in an area clear of smoke and found themselves far outside the perimeter with their backs turned to the action. In the next moment, most of them were struck down by streams of purple without ever seeing them coming.

Camilla looked back as Robby punched through the opening in the crowd. She saw new orange-yellow shapes through her helmet. Her friends were on their way. The shape in the lead had to be Alice with her uniform movement and determination. She had Morgan slung over her slender, yet powerful shoulders. Her free hand fired golden orbs of swirling energy, which dissipated the smoke in her way. More than a few hit the A.I.M. agents as well.

Joe had Nick on his back, while Kim carried Ken. Both followed Alice's lead. Without an Amuli to carry them at superhuman speed, Antonio and Jessica brought up the rear. Still, they worked as the rear guard, knocking back any pursuers with shotguns.

Robby knew that they could not go on forever. His bike had hours' worth of energy, but only Alice could have kept up for that long. The unpowered Antonio and Jessica and could not outrun the Amuli army when the pursuit began. While powered, Joe and Kim were untrained and did not have the fitness of Amuli who had been in the field as long as Alice. Right then, Robby just had to get out of range of whatever was blocking their signals. He kept going until the smoke cloud was small in his rearview and Antonio and Jessica looked exhausted.

Robby made the decision to pull into an abandoned parking garage, leading the group down to the hidden depths. They got to the floor just beyond the bottom. The slope down to the lowermost floor ran into a lake of brown, trash-filled, undissipated flood water. This was as far as they could go.

Jessica tried her coms before even catching her breath.

"Signal… signal's going through," she wheezed after finally doubling over.

"Who's listening?" Camilla asked. "People loyal to Jackson or everyone else?"

"I limited the transmission," Jessica explained. "It only went to A.R.C.-Human agents who I trust. I also put out one to Dr. Barnes in the Research Division. He should have people ready to mobilize."

"How long?" Kim demanded. "We're trapped again and there's so many!"

Jessica shook her head. "Don't know. The best shot is probably Paul and Jason finishing up with Jackson. They know where we were at least. We aren't too far from the prison, and they should be able to find us, eventually."

"We need something to get us through until then," Camilla said. "How do we hold out?"

Robby strode into the group's center.

"Here's the plan. I'm going up to be the lookout. I'll bring the bike. If I see them getting too close, I'll lead them on a chase. They won't see me until I'm on the streets, I'll make sure of that. They won't see where I came from and trace it back to you guys."

"In that case, you're getting a partner again," Camilla ventured. "I can shield you with anima from all the things they'll launch at you, at least for a little while. You don't have any smoke left, so you can't confuse them like before. They'll have easy shots. Besides, you're always prattling on about wanting to be a hero. I have to spoil your glory a little."

She held her fist forward and Robby gave it a nudge with his own.

"I couldn't ask for a better co-pilot," Robby responded with a warm grin.

"Don't get sappy on me now, Swanson," Camilla teased.

The pair sat themselves back on the motorcycle.

"Wait!" Jessica interrupted. "I can't let you two do that. What kind of person would I be? You're just kids."

"We stopped being kids a long time ago," Camilla replied as Robby switched on the silent engine.

They started off before anyone else could stop them.

Near the street-level section of the parking garage, Robby let his bike idle behind a concrete support. Neither he nor Camilla said a word as they waited for the evitable. It stood to reason that the enemy Amuli had the numbers to comb to the whole area. They would eventually be found. They just had to wait until someone came snooping.

Every second passed like a lifetime. Both Robby and Camilla knew what they were doing. They knew the chances of making it out alive or uncaptured, but chose to bottle the accompanying fear deep down to focus only on the plan. Camilla was so focused that she realized her leg had fallen asleep from non-movement. It seemed absurd, but she could not let any little annoyance distract her. Still wanting to move as little as possible in order to keep hidden, she lightly massaged her calf.

Interrupting the maddening quiet was the loud humming of a diesel engine. Then came the crunch of large wheels on gravel-strewn pavement. A bus rounded a corner at the end of the street, away from where the small group had escaped the horde.

Camilla's stronger eyes caught a glimpse of the vehicle first. It was another bus.

They were both sure then. It had to be A.I.M. reinforcements. Even if they passed the parking garage on the first go-round, the even greater number of enemies would make their discovery all the more certain.

Camilla had not even thought to consider the bus's color at first. Whereas the transports bringing the A.I.M. agents had been larger and black, this one was bright yellow.

"A school bus?" Camilla whispered in spite of herself.

She peered even closer at the siding.

"No way. Does that say, 'Schwert Academy'?"

Robby lightly raised a fist in celebration.

"Oh, yeah!" he exclaimed under his breath. "I didn't think they were going to show. It was a long shot, but we were trying to get some allies that we knew were not friends of Jackson, right? This is about that other phone call I made."

"You made a phone call? You mean the unsecured kind?"

"I'm not going to answer that, because you're just going to get mad at me."

Camilla let that go for the moment.

"Who the heck did you call?"

Robby slipped off the bike, leaving her alone on it. He then slowly crept to the parking garage entrance to wave in the oncoming bus.

"Robby!" Camilla half-yelled and half-whispered. "What are you doing?"

The driver of the bus evidently took notice of Robby and made the turn into the parking garage. The bus continued slightly past them until the yellow vehicle was also hidden in the underground portion. Its brakes evidentially screeched to a halt.

Robby walked right up to the door as it opened, while Camilla hung back in anticipation.

A large man descended the stairs to greet Robby.

"Well, well, well, little man," Carson Colter addressed Robby. "Where's this big brawl you promised?"

CHAPTER 36
BEHIND THE RED CURTAIN

"I'M REALLY GOING to miss the theatrics of this whole act," Red Mask notified Paul and Jason while reaching for his mask.

The usual mocking, sing-song voice had been replaced by a casual tone. Strangely, Paul thought he recognized it but could not remember from where. It was a confident, young man's voice that oozed charisma.

Adam Avery took the mask from his face and smiled at the two teenagers. Jason stayed standing, much like he had been. Paul's mouth quivered. His thoughts were like cars going around a racetrack. The realizations were hitting him hard enough that he had to remember to breathe.

"What is this?" Paul finally barked. "How could…"

This isn't real! It can be true!

His fingers tensed around his sword, and its crystal responded with a heavier glow.

Avery gave a slight wave of his hand.

"Relax. Honestly, I'm not going to hurt you. Why don't we just talk?"

"No, no, no!" Paul shook his head wildly. "It's not even possible. You can't lead A.I.M. and A.R.C. at the same time! Nothing about it makes sense. There's no logical way. You don't even have a red Psychic crystal like the Red Mask has, you have your rapier with a purple crystal!"

"I'd offer you a seat, but I think you three destroyed all those," Avery quipped. "First off, the red anima was a fake-out just like with the A.I.M. agents in Japan. The red was really someone else's anima. Really, relax, and I'll explain the rest."

Now, I feel so unsure about everything. He's an enemy? Should I run in while he's unfocused? I'm so tired from the fight. Would I stand a chance? Is standing here while my head explodes all I can do?

"I'm going to tell you a little about myself," Avery started while twirling his mask in his hands. "I really hate the world, or at least, the people who run it. You've seen it now, Paul. The manipulation. The lies. Leaders blocking you from doing what you know is right. The bureaucracy and the red tape. What if it all just went away?"

"You're really going to say all that when it looks like you've been the one manipulating me the whole time?" Paul shot back. "What did you make me do here?"

"Point taken," Avery relented. "No, the plan is perfect. Yes, I did want you to take out Jackson. But you can't tell me you didn't want to. I didn't make him imprison innocents, including your aunt and uncle. That was all him. I just gave you the license."

"You're with A.I.M.," Paul pointed out. "How is it even possible to play both sides?"

"I was with A.I.M., that's true," Avery answered before scrounging through his pocket.

He then tossed a bag containing broken pieces of plastic and fabric on the floor. Paul looked down to see a rainbow of mask fragments.

"You've seen A.R.C.'s list of masks, right?" Avery asked. "You've always liked researching in the databases. What can you tell me about these?"

Paul stooped down to study them closer. His eyes grew wide, but he did not answer. Avery said the words for him.

"A.I.M. was only made up of a confederation of compounds. That was the theory A.R.C. worked with, and it was true. They respected power and nothing more. Power and progress were their goals. So, when an agent challenges one of the leaders and wins, that challenger takes over the former's position. I did that again and again. Eventually, I was the only one left."

"Everyone in A.R.C. trusted you," Paul griped. "I trusted you."

"Don't confuse those two, Paul," Avery warned him. "You had trust. A.R.C. just had a blindness caused by hatred. They believed in their ideals so passionately that they would not have believed one of their higher-ups was an enemy. Every A.R.C. agent had to hate A.I.M. They could not imagine otherwise, especially that fascist, Jackson. It was a similar situation in A.I.M. I was their mole in A.R.C. They thought I risked it all for them, but my loyalties have never been with either side."

Paul felt a sick buzzing in his nerves and in his stomach. Reality itself seemed to be shaking from the revelations.

"I said that I wanted to tell you about me," reminded Avery. "That's how people come to understand each other, right? They talk it out. Well, it started early for me. I became an Amulus early on. One of my mother's boyfriends was a sword collector, and one touch of the rapier led me to this world. It was pure adventure at first. I was taken in by A.R.C. and trained as a hero in the making. That wasn't all I wanted, though. You see, I'm a twin. I had a little sister, Sarah. She was only younger than me by fifteen minutes. I was born with everything, and she was born with nothing. Her lungs and heart were stunted, and she was never able to live a normal life. She would spend a few months at home and then a fainting spell or coughing fit would put her in the hospital for the rest of the year. Me on the other hand, I got straight-A's and captained all the sports teams. I never stopped feeling guilty about that. I've always been afraid that I took something from her in the womb, like I was some kind of leech, making myself strong and killing her."

Avery looked soulfully out the window.

He continued. "When I became an Amulus, that feeling got worse. Now, I was superhuman. I could run and fight even better. Even my brain was supercharged. On the other end, Sarah was still in her hospital, coughing her life away. When it got bad, I just begged my superiors in A.R.C. to do something. We were like magicians. Surely there was something like a spell that we could cast to heal her. There had to be a ritual. Maybe I could have passed my powers on to her. They were shocked when I brought all that up. They told me that wasn't what A.R.C. did and that's not what it stood for. They didn't experiment. That would have been unclean, or some sin against nature. It could open the door to turn someone into a Dead Eyes or worse. No, that was A.I.M.'s territory, and they were the enemy. They were the boogeymen."

To illustrate the point, Avery suddenly sent a blast of purple at the bag on the floor. It was reduced to ash and burnt plastic. Paul braced himself for a possible blast coming in his direction, but Avery kept his hands at his sides.

Avery went on. "So, I flagged down A.I.M. I was already A.R.C.'s wunderkind, and they trusted me to be away on long, infiltration missions. I went into a compound and offered my services as a mole. I would do anything for Sarah. I just begged them to work their magic and use a ritual to heal her. They promised they would, but it was slow going. A.I.M. was a disjointed confederacy. All of its scientists and researchers had their own ideas for what to do next to benefit humanity or science itself. They barely had started on something when Sarah took a turn. Then, that was it for her. So, there I was, stuck between two sides. I was in A.I.M. for Sarah and I was in A.R.C. because that's how you stayed alive and out of someone's lab. Frankly, I was disgusted by both sides. There was A.R.C.'s holier-than-thou hypocrisy and A.I.M.'s blatant disregard for human decency. The deeper I got in, the more I saw that they were rotten to the core. Not only that but they had their fingers on every government, army, and business. The infection was everywhere. So, I broke it all down. I united all of A.I.M.'s compounds and labs under the Red Mask. In A.R.C., I worked my way up to Councilmen and let the rest of the Council implode. It was going to happen with Jackson's egomania and backroom activities being exposed, I just expedited the process. That brings us up to today. A.I.M. and A.R.C. are no more. The world is free of them. We can mold this new world into anything we want."

"Why are you telling us this?" Paul wondered. "We're in your way now. You just told us everything you did. The bombs on the planes, that was you, wasn't it?"

"Of course," Avery answered smugly. "I'm afraid the tidal waves were, too. Just wait until you see what we discovered in the Atlantic. It's a piece of Amuli past that will lead to our future."

Paul closed hard enough that he bit his lip in surprise.

"The earthquakes? The tidal waves? Billions! There were so many people!"

Avery nodded solemnly. "I know. It was heavy. Just try to understand that this is all a reshaping of the entire world. Alas, you cannot build a new world without breaking down the old one. You can't have two things occupying the same space. It had to happen, but we'll keep the memory of the deceased alive in what we will build next. We will honor them."

"Listen to yourself!" Paul shouted. "You killed billions! There is no justification!"

"What about the billions who will come after?" Avery countered. "They will live better than any other human beings ever have. The dead are dead. Isn't it wise to always think about future generations? It was a sacrifice to ensure the peace and prosperity of the human race."

"That's pretty grandiose," Paul insulted him.

"Is it?" Avery questioned. "Remember A.R.C. and A.I.M.'s influence. They were the world's government, even if the world didn't know it. Now, here I am. With them gone, I am the alternative. I have the power and the influence over everything. I am uploading all A.R.C. and A.I.M. records to the internet for a second, final data dump. The people will see me as the opposite version of them. I am the one to be trusted. I brought them the truth. I have become a symbol backed by real power. Here I am at the top. The people will back me. Their governments will back me. I am the one man who has united the whole human race."

"The *tyrannos*," Paul realized. "I thought that before you were saying that Jackson thought of himself as a *tyrannos*, an all-powerful leader who is seen as a benefactor to the people, but it was you. You were talking about yourself."

"Very good," Avery complimented him with admiration. "You're so quick and witty. I like that about you. Yes, a *tyrannos* is a great image. How about another one from ancient Greece? What about the philosopher-king? That was from Plato's *Republic*, not that anyone would call his proposal a Republic today. No, Plato did not want democracy. Democracy was the mob. Democracy is where the majority get together and decided to terrorize the minority. At the top of it all, Plato said that there should be a philosopher-king. The wisest one is the one that knows better. You don't ask a random group of people to give you surgery. You ask a specialist. You ask a surgeon. It's the same way for government. There should be one person who specializes in leading. It should be someone who is ethical and intelligent. It should be someone who works for the betterment of all and not just one group. We see the examples in recent history. American presidents are gaining more and more unilateral power. That's how decisions have to work. You can't wait around for votes and deliberations, especially during crises and military actions. It has to be streamlined in the modern world. Everything happens so fast. There has to be someone at the top of it all."

Paul shook his sweaty head violently, letting the beads of moisture fly everywhere.

"You!" he shouted. "You want to take everything from people. It's just your megalomania. People won't stand for it! You're talking about a world with no freedom."

"Think about it, Paul," Avery advised. "It's happened all throughout history. When people choose, they choose wrong."

"There will be rebellions," Paul disagreed. "No one will stand for it!"

Avery smoothed down his slicked-back hair.

"There may be. It will be disorganized, that's for sure. The world's governments already buckled to A.R.C. and A.I.M.'s power. I'm now stronger than both. You are not the first I've revealed all this to. There are many from the remnants of A.R.C. and A.I.M. who have backed this plan all along. They are my new army. The rest of the Amuli of the world will fall in line, or they won't stand a chance."

I've had enough! It's too much!

"Why tell us all this?" Paul questioned. "Why not just send in that army and have us killed?"

Avery looked surprised for the first time.

"Kill you?" he asked incredulously. "Why would I want to do that?"

"Don't screw around with me," Paul advised him angrily.

"I'm serious," Avery explained as he shrugged. "You're one of the people I want to rely on the most. You're very intelligent on just about every subject. I know that you have a good heart. You absolutely hate to think you're doing something wrong. I think it all boils down to the fact that you want to be of service. You want to help the people of the world. Well, with me, you can do that to a degree never seen before. I will have a monarchy that will be beyond absolute, but I can't be in all places at once. I need people like you. A philosopher-king needs his philosopher-lieutenants."

"I'm suddenly getting really tired of people telling me who I am," Paul quipped as angst dripped into his tone. "Why would I ever be on your side? All you do and all you want to do are crimes against humanity."

"Okay, okay," Avery backed off. "This isn't 'join me or die,' even though I really wish you would do the former. If you turn me down, that's fine. I'll leave you alone. You're probably really tired of all this fighting and death, so you can move on with your life. Retire from the Amulus life, even if you keep your powers. Go to school. Get a job. Get married and have kids. Live comfortably."

"And all I'll have to do is look the other way while you continue to massacre and enslave billions," Paul commented.

Avery's face suddenly grew stern and tight. A shadow seemed to pass over his handsome face.

"Don't do that," he warned through gritted teeth. "Don't do what you're implying. Don't get in the way. It will solve nothing. It will accomplish nothing but more destruction. I've had to destroy enough, Paul, and it pained me to do it. If I have to put down a futile rebellion, you're the one adding bodies to the pile. Really, I'm saying you can do anything else you want. Just don't do that."

"I know you think that the ends justify the means," Paul replied calmly and philosophically. "I always think about that idea this way: can you really see the true ends when you are just a human being? Yeah, maybe in the short run. If you kill someone in self-defense, you'll go on living. That's seeing moments ahead, though. But you're trying to see years, even lifetimes ahead. How can you know that everything will go as you plan? If I don't rebel, someone else will. There will probably be a lot of someones. Do you really want to sentence mankind to never-ending war?"

"Never-ending war is what mankind already has," argued Avery. "This is the solution. It will be seen-through because I will always be there to see it through."

"What are you saying?" Paul wondered.

"You should know this by now, Paul," Avery half-scolded him. "Nothing is impossible with anima. A.I.M. researchers have gotten deep into the science of it. They tell me that, with the artifacts we found on that seafloor, extending strength and durability won't be the only things that are improved in Amuli. Longer lives and more intelligence are now doable. My team and I will crack the aging code. I will never have to think about having my world bereft of its philosopher-king because I will always be there."

"It didn't occur to me until what you just said," Paul started. "You want to be a god, don't you?"

"I'll leave it to the people to come up with the exact titles," answered Avery. "I'll offer immortality to you as well, if you care to take it. Don't think that you will be facing the coming ages alone. I plan to make similar deals with many of your friends. There's Jason here who wanted this world to come apart so badly. Camilla Bellano has quite a heart. I can see her being at the head of charitable efforts. She's always envisioned herself doing something like that, hasn't she? Jessica Swanson actually got A.R.C. to accept regular humans in its ranks. I can see her being key in uniting the non-Amuli and making them understand what I'm doing. Last but not least, there's Alice."

"Don't you dare get near her!" Paul interrupted with venom in his voice.

Avery pretended to be physically blown back by Paul's convictions.

"Don't be so chauvinistic, Paul," he chided. "I didn't think you were the type. Don't you think she can make her own decisions?"

"Don't twist what I'm saying," Paul threatened. "Alice is the opposite of you. When she was born, she was treated like she was not human, so she felt and acted inhumanly. Now, she's worked so hard to gain that feeling. It's getting stronger in her every day. On the other hand, I think you were human once, but you've thrown that all away on purpose."

"In the future, I think we will have a much less narrow view of what being human is," Avery replied. "Anyway, I will only require her specifically for little more than a moment. Then, she's free to do what she wants. I'll give her the same choice as you have. However, in the near future, I'll need an Atlantean on Atlantis."

"What?" Paul wondered, genuinely confused.

"Oh, you haven't connected the dots yet," realized Avery arrogantly. "Forgive me. You probably heard the hypotheses months ago about the underwater island found in the Atlantic. Some people said it was Atlantis. They were right. You see, A.I.M.'s researchers have never been afraid to dig deep. Amuli in the world has not been a modern invention. It is as ancient as civilization itself. The Amuli of the past just didn't have the means to form together worldwide until modern times. In the past, they were picked off one by one as witches and black magicians. The only exception was at the dawn of the Amuli. That was on Atlantis, the lost island. They were the first to dig the crystals and built a society off of them. When the island fell, the Atlanteans spread to every corner of the world well before any European explorers. In every land, they found new Amuli to wield their crystals. It has all been a process leading up to this present moment when the ultimate wish of the Amuli is fulfilled. Amuli like us have ushered in a new, permanent era of improved humanity."

Paul's mind swirled. All the pieces of the puzzle fit as Avery had described.

"Why?" Paul asked, wavering. "Why do you need an Atlantean?"

"Oh!" Avery balked. "No, if some sort of sacrifice is what you're thinking, then that's not what I'm after. Alice's blood and very DNA are permeated with anima. The oldest records say that members of the royal family had secrets beyond the secrets of the other Atlanteans. As Atlantis's last heir, she is its queen. Her power should open things on the island that will fulfill all those promises I've been making. It will be the ultimate power in human hands. I just need her help for a little while and that will be the end of it."

"So, she's the one variable," Paul hypothesized. "She's the one thing you can't control. You need her more than anything else. She is the key to all doors on Atlantis, isn't she? There are places you can't reach, right? You need her to get you inside."

"See, Paul!" Avery exclaimed. "There's that intellect going to work, putting the picture together. You had me worried there for a second."

"I wasn't finished," Paul added. "What if she says no?"

The shadow inched over Avery's face again as it contorted ever so slightly. He was clearly holding back a grimace to stay convincing to Paul.

"We really shouldn't be going around in circles, Paul," Avery advised him. "Conversations with you are always stimulating. History, philosophy, military tactics, and government policies. I admire anyone who loves to learn and figure things out as much as you. Don't let this talk descend into sophistry. Why would she ever say no to my proposal? Why would you ever say no? I'm offering you more than anyone has ever been offered. It's not even the slightest bit selfish for you to take it since it will benefit mankind more than anything ever has!"

Avery held out his hand.

"Come on. It's all yours."

Paul presented him with a raised sword instead.

"You've killed billions and want to kill billions more," Paul answered gruffly. "You want to take every right and freedom people have away. It's strange, though. A decision this momentous usually paralyzes me. I'm really the most indecisive person I know. Yet, I'm more confident in what I'm doing right now than anything I've ever done. I don't know what powers you've gained for yourself. Just know that I'm at least going to throw my body in the way and be your speed bump."

Avery slowly pulled back his hand. He suddenly grew very stiff and cold.

"That disappoints me, Paul," he murmured emotionally. "You are someone who should be inheriting the world I will create. Instead, you're acting like you want to die before it culminates."

Paul drew in his energy in anticipation. Green anima lightly crackled around his skin.

Avery held up his hand.

"No," he said in a low voice. "Look at you. You're tired and hurt. What sense does it make for you to fight me now? Plus, I'm not going to give up on you, Paul. I'm leaving now, but we will see each other again. I really hope it happens after you gain a fresh perspective. Otherwise, our battle will come then. I'm not a tyrant who crushes people because of foolish disagreements. Sleep on it, and I'll come calling again."

It was true that Paul's legs were tired, but that did not stop him from pursuing Avery as soon as he turned his back.

"You're not leaving," Paul ordered him. "This is going to end now… before it starts."

"Oh, Paul," Avery whispered as he continued to walk away. "It's already started. My supporters are everywhere. Former A.R.C. agents, former A.I.M. agents, corporations, politicians, and activists. I already tore everything down. There's nothing in place. With A.R.C. and A.I.M. now dissolved, the governments that relied on them are going under. Even if you disagree with my methods, do you really want the world to stay in this chaos? Do you not want order?"

"You want to be the disease and the cure!" Paul surmised.

"Enough of this," Avery said, growing even more frustrated.

His open back was getting further away. Paul took a breath and readied a swing. *I've never wanted to attack someone who wasn't ready for it. This is different. I can end this evil, right now.*

Something inside him was still making him hesitate. *I know. It doesn't feel right to attack someone who doesn't want to fight back. It's just… I have to.*

Avery inclined his head back slightly.

"Coming, Jason?" he offered.

Paul then realized that Jason had not said a word during the entire exchange. He had stayed perfectly still and calm with his bloody sword at his side.

Jason slowly waded through the broken glass and passed by Paul.

Paul only looked on in disbelief.

"Jason…"

CHAPTER 37
TWO SHOTS

CAMILLA PULLED out her Colt .45 with its purple crystal ready. Colter only raised an eyebrow at the gun.

"Carson Colter!" was all Camilla shouted.

"Yeah?" Colter answered.

Robby stepped in front of Camilla.

"Hey, hey," Robby interrupted level-headedly. "Be cool. He's the other guy I called."

"You called Carson Colter?" demanded Camilla, flabbergasted. "This is the guy who you stopped from killing Paul a few months ago! He's A.I.M.!"

"Nope," Colter replied, shaking his crazy head of spiky hair. "No, on the second one, at least. Don't care about A.I.M. or A.R.C. or whatever. I'm a free man."

"It's exhilarating, isn't it?" came a voice approaching the entrance of the bus.

Emerson Whaley stepped down the stairs, fixing his black-rimmed glasses.

"Whaley, too?" Camilla shouted.

"Okay, I didn't call him," Robby admitted.

"Apparently the creep's been spying on me," Colter explained.

Whaley finally got his glasses in the place where he wanted them.

"I've been making sure you don't... well... do the things you normally do. Like rampaging, for instance," Whaley clarified. "You don't need to worry about my affiliation either. Red Mask has torn down what A.I.M.

once was. Only his loyalists remain. I believe they are the ones troubling you right now. I can't say that I like A.R.C. I only know that this current regime of A.I.M., or whatever it is, needs to be ended. It risks the exposure of everything we've all kept hidden from the world. Things that were hidden for good reason. I will ally with you in the fight against that chaos."

"Great…" Camilla moaned, not without sarcasm. "Are you actually going to explain why you called Carson freaking Colter, Robby?"

"Alright, there's a line of logic here," Robby tried putting it. "We didn't know who we had on our side at A.R.C. Like, who was going to stick with Jackson or not. So, I called reinforcements from someone totally not with A.R.C. at all. Well, I had Jack's number at least, and he talked to Colter. That's kind of why I let you guys know that I called someone but didn't say who."

"You also didn't say that you had called Blake, and we would have all been on board with him helping out," Camilla pointed out.

"Nuh-uh," Robby disagreed. "That would have ruined the bike surprise since you knew that Blake was working on the bike."

"We were coordinating strategy, Robby!" Camilla scolded. "You weren't supposed to be throwing a surprise party for yourself."

Whaley coughed lightly.

"In speaking of coordinating strategy," he butted in. "Why don't we do that instead of debating Mr. Swanson's planning ability. I will add though, it was a stroke of genius to pit the always battle-hungry Carson against your enemies here."

"You see!" Robby bragged. "You think I'm dumb, but I always get along with the smart guys like Paul and Whaley here."

"Let's meet up with everyone else again," Camilla sighed.

The newly formed group strode down to the lower level where everyone else was hunkered down.

Both Jessica and Antonio put their hands on their sidearms when they saw Colter and Whaley. Alice stood ready in battle form.

Robby waved them off. "All friendlies!"

Jessica's puzzled face was relieved after a moment of thinking.

"Those people you called," she theorized. "You really talked A.I.M.'s biggest agents into taking down A.R.C.'s leader. I know you've always been bold, but geez."

"Ex-A.I.M. agents," Whaley clarified. "No matter the circumstances, we all now find ourselves on this same side we have chosen."

"I'm here because I heard I'm going to fight an army," Colter specified. "I don't really care about anything else. I guess this Robby kid here is pretty cool though since he let me in on all this. I'll return the favor, you just tell me how, kid."

"Two for two," Robby murmured.

"Can I ask where the bus even came from?" Jessica pondered.

Colter shrugged. "I was looking for a ride. Saw it running in front of the school. Driver must've gone inside for a leak or something."

"I guess I'll say it," Camilla began cautiously. "We might have a chance of fighting our way out of this now. It's still not great, but we do have firepower and some wheels now."

"I like the sound of that," Colter agreed. "Is that what we're doing, then? Let's just go up there and give 'em hell. Once we've thinned them out enough and tired ourselves out, we'll get on the bus and go. Just... uh... don't let it get blown up."

"Guerilla-style may work best," Whaley advised. "Hit-and-run. There are a lot of places to hide in an urban landscape. Plus, we have two long-distance Warriors here."

Each member of the rag-tag group got lost in thought for a moment as they considered plans. Suddenly, there was the sound of heavy panting, and everyone turned their heads.

"Y-You're not..." Antonio stammered. "N-None of you are doing anything like that."

He had his handgun raised in shaky hands. It pointed at Jessica. Everyone had been too absorbed in thought to notice the movements of their supposed comrade.

Robby brought up his handgun on pure instinct. He pointed straight at Antonio as a look of wildness appeared in his eyes.

"Don't do anything, Robby," Jessica ordered him calmly.

Robby kept the gun trained on Antonio but made no motions toward the trigger. None of the three had their helmets on, leaving their heads exposed.

"So, what's this, Antonio?" Jessica questioned him by barely raising her voice. "Who are you really working for and how did I miss it? We've known each other a long time."

"Enough!" Colter interrupted before Antonio could answer. "This little jerk isn't going to ruin everything for me! I had such a great day planned!"

The large man took a stepped forward.

"Don't!" Camilla cried desperately. "There's no way you can get to him in time before he shoots!"

Colter shrugged and then froze in place.

"Man, I hate complicated stuff like this!" he related.

"I-It's not at all what you think," Antonio started as he perspired. "I'm A.R.C. I've always been A.R.C. I believe in Amuli and the rest of us working together. It's just… It's just that he told me what was going to happen. He had it planned so clearly. He said he only told me because the rest of you are more emotional. You might not have the guts to join him right away."

"Who?" wondered Jessica. "Jackson?"

"No!" Antonio shouted. "The opposite. It was Avery! It's always been his plan, and I agreed with it. He's going to bring the world together, and we're going to help him do it."

In addition to the sense of danger emanating from Antonio's gun, a profound sense of confusion fell over the group.

"Adam Avery?" Camilla wondered. "But we've been working with him. He was the alternative to Jackson!"

"That's mostly right," Antonio affirmed. "It's just that you've been working for him out of necessity. You don't know what he's really like. He's a genius… and so convincing… and so frightening when he's angry. It's all a game to him. He pulls the strings, playing both A.I.M. and A.R.C. You're right where he wants you… at least you were when we were all still in that siege."

"So, Avery's been the bad guy all along," Jessica realized coolly. "He pitted us against Jackson and is now ready to pick up the pieces. Is that right?"

"Not just those pieces," Antonio added. "What are the governments of the world going to do now that A.R.C. and A.I.M. are history? They were subservient to them. Now, Avery's their new master. He controls the Amuli, so he controls the entire world. With his followers from both sides, no one can stand against him. If you do, you'll be rogue, and you will be hunted."

"What happens now?" Jessica asked, not for one second letting her composure slip.

"It was perfect, just like he said!" Antonio exclaimed. "It's just… the smallest thing… it got screwed up. You see, he foresaw it all. But… but… you were supposed to stay inside that prison building. I mean… you saw those odds. You were supposed to surrender. You would all surrender and Avery would take you in. It would be painless, just like that. When you all decided to run out… I-I wanted to say something, then. I just thought that we might run for a little, but we would get caught no matter what in the end. That's when those two came. If you have even a chance of escaping, I have to stop it. So, you're all just going to walk out of here, or I'll start shooting. You'll raise your arms and march to those agents.

It's easy. Life will be good afterward. You'll see! You have to see that there's no choice. Even if Avery's wrong, there's no stopping him."

"And Avery trusted you with all this," Jessica pointed out.

"Yes," Antonio answered. "He said he could trust me. I have the stomach for this stuff. If the rest of you knew what Avery was doing, you might have freaked out. I'm here to help you. It's all done now. You don't have to worry about how we got here. Just play along."

"If this is all true," Jessica started. "Avery is a complete megalomaniac. You think we're going to go along with that? You want to live in a world where one man has all the power? Plus, think of all the people who have died in his puppet war. If he's allowed to stay in power, there's no justice… not even close."

Antonio swore as his gun shook.

"This was the problem!" Antonio shouted. "Turn off your bleeding hearts for a second. What's done is done. My option is how we get through this! It's how we survive."

"Paul and Jason," Alice murmured, speaking for the first time in a long time. "What is happening to them?"

"It's part of the plan," Antonio illuminated. "They will take out Jackson. With no one else to turn to, they will join up with Avery once he arrives. He's that convincing. So please, surrender, and I'll take you to them."

"You really think my nephew's that stupid?" Morgan questioned him from off to the side.

The non-combatants had shirked back when Antonio had first brandished his gun. Morgan was hanging back as well, but she eyed Antonio defiantly.

"You don't know, Paul," she continued. "He's the smartest person I know. He'll know a power-hungry idiot when he sees one."

"What do you even know?" Antonio demanded.

"I've probably dealt with this life longer than you," Morgan explained. "It took my brother and sister-in-law away. It's not going to take my nephew, too."

"Alright!" Antonio cried. "Shut up! Everyone, shut up! That's enough talking! Now, I'm going to start counting. If you don't start marching up the ramp, I'll shoot! You might get me if you have the stomach, Robby. But I'll get Jessica first. Can you live with that?"

"Yes, he can," Jessica answered for him while Robby said nothing. "You do what you have to do, Robby. Don't just think about me. Think about all your friends. I know you're good at doing that. What's best for them in this moment?"

"I said, shut it!" Antonio yelled. "Alright, here it goes. One."

Everyone held their breath, and no one moved.

"Two!"

Two bangs rang out almost simultaneously. Both Jessica and Antonio crumpled to the ground.

Camilla, Alice, and a shaking Robby ran to Jessica. They also gave quick glances over to where Antonio had stood.

The blood spreading darkly on the pavement was coming from his head. He was no longer a threat. He had gone before he had hit the ground.

Jessica coughed hard and painfully. The blood on her face was just a trickle coming from her inner cheek. The little bit of crimson contrasted with her pale face. She had the wherewithal to brush the dented bullet from the chest section of her armored bodysuit.

"T-That was g-good thinking, Robby," she sputtered hoarsely. "If he thought you were going to shoot, it would have been on 'one' or 'three.' 'One' would have meant you weren't playing the game, or you just jumped from the anticipation. 'Three' would have meant that you were waiting for the last second. 'Two' broke the pattern and threw him off. I still have my head thanks to you."

"B-But, are you alright?" Robby stammered as his hands tremored.

"What do I always say, Robby?" Jessica answered him as she started to painfully sit up. "There's no such thing as bullet-proof. There's only bullet resistant. No, the bullet didn't get through, but it definitely cracked something."

"Why don't you just sit for a while?" insisted Camilla as she supported Jessica's back.

"No time," Jessica answered. "Those shots just alerted everyone to where we are."

A sound of trotting footsteps began to emerge and grow louder.

CHAPTER 38
BLOOD BROTHERS

"JASON!" Paul yelled the name this time.

"Today is not your day, Paul," Avery antagonized as his light footsteps were gradually taking him away from Paul, but he stayed close enough to keep up the conversation. "You usually are much better at making deductions. Where do you think Jason acquired the enhancement you just saw?"

Paul could see just enough of Jason's face to notice that his mouth was set in a grim, unmoving line.

"Jason…" Paul started as if out of breath. "How long has this been going on?"

Jason finally spoke, but did so like it physically pained him. "Since we rescued you, and I killed the Rat. Avery came to me then. I was so confused that night. The Rat was… my dad. He didn't kill my mom like I thought. I misunderstood, and he kept up the ruse so I could become strong off of my path to vengeance. The people who really killed her… were Jackson's men.

Someone in A.R.C. connected my anima outburst from my awakening to the partner of an A.I.M. agent. They killed her in a scuffle, but the Rat drove them off. When I got into A.R.C. later, it was through a channel away from Jackson. He kept his eyes on me but could see that I didn't know my father and that I hated A.I.M. more than anything. That changed."

"Your revenge wasn't over then," Paul guessed. "When McGreevy and Howe from the strike force died, that was you, wasn't it? I knew from the files that they had been Jackson's men for years. Then, just now with Jackson…"

"That was all part of the plan," Jason admitted. "I won't ask you to understand, but I had to think of what was next, Paul. You and the others are actually the ones who got me thinking. After I killed everyone I wanted to kill, what was I supposed to do next if I was still standing? Well, Avery gave me the idea. Don't you get it, Paul? No one deserves to end up like me… or you. Think about what we've seen! Think about what we've had to do! Think about the world that did it to us! There are more people like Jackson. There are people like Jackson at the top of every government and corporation. The world is ruled by a spiderweb network of human filth upon human filth at the top. Avery's tearing it all down. I don't agree with everything he's done, but he's our only shot. With him, I have the opportunity to build a world that doesn't churn out people like me. There has never been a chance like this in history. With anima, it's all possible. I took the deal. You need to take it, too. Please come with us."

"Think about what you're saying!" Paul demanded. "Think hard! Avery's plans will only create more people like us! He's doing it already. Think about all the people he's killed directly and indirectly in his conspiracy. A lot of those people had loved ones. He's just going to take it further! Not only that, but he wants it to go on forever! There will be a never-ending stream of orphans out for revenge on both sides."

"It's not just a war," Jason justified. "It's a revolution. It's something that is going to change the minds of every person on the planet. People who think like Jackson will never exist again. We won't let it happen."

"You used to call me 'naïve' or an 'idealist,'" Paul reminisced bitterly. "Who's the one with the crazy ideals now? Look, I want the world to change, too. But it has to be by consensus or it won't work. People have to come together by themselves. You can't force them. I don't think the world needs human masters to dominate it. It needs guides and guardians to help it along and protect it."

Jason started walking hesitantly away from Paul. Paul rushed to catch up to him.

"I'm not going to let you do this!" Paul insisted. "I'm not going to let you make this mistake, even if I have to break your legs to stop you from walking away with him."

Paul angled to himself to cut off Jason's way.

"Step aside," Jason commanded.

Paul brought up his sword.

This is so counterintuitive! To point a sword at someone I want to help. I'm just too frazzled. I can't think of another way.

"I'm doing this for your sake and for the sake of the world," Paul pleaded as the emotion burst in his voice and he raised his sword.

"Stop aside," Jason repeated.

"N-No!"

Jason reluctantly took up his sword as well.

Avery, who was still just within earshot, called back. "You two do what you have to do. Just don't kill each other. I'll have you both on my team soon. You'll see, Paul."

Paul kept himself between Jason in the retreating Avery. He was not in a fighting stance exactly, but was trying to stretch his position to take up more of the hallway. His whole mind was focused on just stopping Jason.

There has to be something I can say.

However, Paul's throat was dry, and his words remained stuck in it. He put his sword in Jason's way.

In retaliation, Jason swung upward with his saber, batting Paul's Katana back. They both retreated several paces and eyed each other.

I never thought it would come to something like this. Even if we had our rivalry, I didn't think it would ever be anything more than that fight we had in Pittsburgh. I thought we were even starting to understand each other after that. I was too blinded by my own ambitions after I got this new crystal. I always forget to see what's in front of me.

They both charged in, almost mirroring each other. Each fighter angled slashes towards the chest. The blades slammed into each other, canceling the two attacks.

Jason dove in again aggressively. This time, Paul held back slightly. He twisted his body to block a sideways cut and let the opposing blade's length pass him. Paul shoved his shoulder upward as Jason's momentum carried him into it.

The result was only a painful bump to the chin that left Jason back-pedaling. Paul tried to follow up with an overhead strike powered by a strong stance but found himself unable to commit full strength into the attack. Jason swept the katana aside easily. Paul ended his advance and retreated before the other swordsman could counter.

They stared each other down again, waiting for the other to move and create an opening to pounce on.

It's no use. This is Jason. He's a friend… well, maybe not a close friend, but he's been my comrade-in-arms. He's even been my mentor at times. I just can't give everything I have. After all, I just want to capture him... not kill him. I'll do that and make him see...

Jason used Paul's indecision to press his attack again. His saber blade was now dyed completely in red light. Paul felt the anima sting his legs after dodging a low sweep.

Paul sent a green shock wave at Jason to push him back again.

He knows how unsure I am at the best of times. He's going to take advantage of that.

They launched forward in unison again.

The air was a whirl of dark silver metal. It buzzed with red and green sparks as if Christmas lights were exploding.

Paul gave just enough effort with his every action. He parried Jason's attacks just in time. His own advances were blocked at the last second. The feet of both fighters were constantly in motion as they shifted positions and stances.

These were two opponents that knew each other. They had trained together and fought alongside the other for months now. There was barely a tendency or flicker of movement that they had not seen before from the other.

It was beyond taxing. Paul felt himself becoming more drained than he had felt since inheriting his new crystal. He was beginning to feel the constant jarring of metal clanging into metal wearing on his arms.

They both pulled back again. Paul saw that Jason was also breathing heavily. With the sweat and bunches of small cuts and large bruises, they were mirror images of each other. The combatants both let the other catch their breath, almost as if there was an unspoken agreement.

"I don't think we'll get another chance at this," Jason said in the lull. "Come on. Show me everything you have! We owe it to each other, don't we? To go all out? Whatever happens, we were partners once. If we're going our separate ways, we should end it with a bang!"

Paul, oddly, thought that this was the most respect Jason had ever given him.

Jason grunted as he unleashed more red to surge around him. The energy darkened around its ethereal edges, becoming jet black. Dark veins started to bulge wherever Jason had exposed skin.

"Don't do it!" Paul shouted. "You can't control it! No one can! It just messes with your head!"

Jason sprang at him, even faster than before.

He's too out of control.

Seeing his enemy coming in high, Paul went low. He dove towards

Jason's legs with an outstretched, bent forearm. Jason was going too fast to stop quickly. He ended up tumbling over Paul's back.

I hate it, but I have to match the speed and power… especially if he gets it under control.

As Jason scrambled back to his feet, Paul called upon his own dark energy. As anima-enriched blood coursed faster through his veins, he felt something like screaming in his ears. The green energy around him grew dark and black in some spaces, as did the whites of his eyes.

There it was, in addition to the physical changes. All the emotion. It was rage. Rage at Jason for betraying him. Rage at him for making this fight so difficult. He hated Avery most of all. The manipulator. The mass-murderer.

He got his thoughts straight enough to dodge Jason's next attack. The displaced, dark anima cracked most of the drywall in the hallway. The last-second sidestep was just what Paul needed to shake up Jason's timing.

Seeing an opening, he aimed a strong, sideways cut. As his sword blasted through the air with the weight of anima behind it, he remembered to turn it at the last second. He would not allow the rage to consume and chop Jason in half.

The flat of Paul's blade caught Jason in the ribs. The dark-haired teenager bit his lip as he was sent flying the other way, sending rivulets of blood towards Paul. Jason smacked the wall but then bounced to his feet.

Paul's arms shook. *I need to get control! That was too close. If I hadn't changed the angle…*

Paul shook his head. Not wanting to even give himself the chance of another slip-up, he went completely unorthodox. He completely reversed the sword's grip in his hands. Now, the sharp length of the blade faced himself. The blunt side was toward Jason. The only sharp part facing his frenemy was now the curved tip.

The samurai and policeman, Hajime Saito, was supposed to have fought something like this. Only he did it to throw off his opponents. He still fought with the edge, but only on the upswing.

With Jason scrambling, Paul pressed the attack this time. He aimed to slam the dull part of the blade into Jason's head for a quick knockout.

Instead, Jason parried with force. Paul slid backward. More dark energy spiraled from Jason. It became a hurricane in the hallway.

Jason marched forward. His blade whirled in a confusing tornado pattern that matched his spiral anima. Paul found it difficult to decipher the sharp blade from its afterimage.

Paul moved to block, but at the wrong angle. Jason's saber slipped through, swiping Paul's forehead.

Paul recoiled as he still felt the singing hot metal scraping his head. Blood was now gushing forth. It mixed with sweat and burned his eyes.

Jason pressed his advantage. Paul's katana took a beating, barely warding off the attacks. Without a free hand, Paul had to shake the streams of blood away when they reached his eyes.

Paul started to feel desperation in a fight for the first time since Alice had given him the new crystal. Unlike his early battles with the Hunters and Carson Colter, he was not afraid of his imminent death. He now only feared what desperation would drive his subconscious mind and body to do.

Please, stop! he almost cried aloud, but the sound would have been lost over the clanging blades, anyway. *Please stop this, Jason! You don't know... I can feel it again...*

The horrifying blankness was beginning to cover his mind once again. It was chilling because he could feel it swooping in. He could feel himself losing it.

Jason... it's too much...

All the while, he had been defending on reflex.

Jason felt the anima pressure rising from Paul. It was intense, but he still had the advantage. He was whittling him down. The decisive blow could come soon.

"Stop it!"

The voice did not sound like Paul's usual meek tone. The growl was heavy with power.

There was an explosion of green that swept Jason backward. He braced himself but still skidded towards the opposing wall. Inside the maelstrom facing him, he could see that Paul's eyes were two unfocused, green and black orbs. His former friend and rival was no longer present at this moment. Jason realized that he had pushed too far. He may have been enhanced, but Paul had that power plus Alice's crystal. His intensity was beyond anything Jason had felt. As he was buffeted, he remarked internally that Paul had been holding this all back for months. The constant, internal pressure from that degree of anima would have long since shattered a lesser person's mind.

Jason finally understood. The Atlantean crystal was a cursed power. It was made of terror and pain. The anima alone was enough to damage enemies and also the mind of its user. No one who felt it survived unscathed.

Paul threw himself forward. Every heavy footstep burned away more carpet on the floor. Jason had no choice but to defend. He took a deep breath and aimed to match Paul's incoming stroke.

In the next moment, Jason's saber was sailing away as his hands went numb. He watched it clatter the length of the hallway. Shocked, he looked up to see Paul's blank face emerge from the fiery vortex.

Something like a bolt of lightning went through Jason's shoulder. Jason painfully turned his head to see Paul's ungripped katana. He tried to move but found he had no strength. It was as if all of his anima had fallen out of him, and he sank towards the floor. His body went limp, but he did not reach the ground. The sword in his shoulder had impaled him to the wall.

CHAPTER 39
THE RACE

THERE WAS a commotion down the street. The shouting, marching footsteps, and the grinding of tire trend were getting closer.

"Yellow bus, then the gunshot," Whaley summed up. "Not exactly conspicuous."

"What do we do?" Camilla questioned. "If we try to leave on the bus, they'll just blow it up!"

"We push them back," Jessica wheezed, still favoring her ribs. "They only seem to be going from one side. It's like before, we wait for a break and go. This time, we have wheels... well, more wheels."

"We're up against so many," Camilla pointed out.

"Nah," Colter brushed her off. "This is what I came here for. The fight's here!"

"Cam," Robby addressed her, appearing much more somber than she had ever seen him. "We'll just do what we can. Don't think about it."

Robby leaned over to help support his cousin.

"You can be the one on the bus," he planned. "Once Alice tells you we're in the clear, you gun it and pick us up. Keep it down the ramp until then. They won't reach it."

"I wish I could do more," Jessica admitted as Robby escorted her to the bus.

"You already did," Robby answered her.

"Don't forget about your bike," she reminded him, almost jokingly.

After helping Jessica inside, Robby opened the large emergency door on the back of the bus before stowing his lightweight motorcycle into the opening.

"Saving that for later," he noted for himself in a singsong voice.

Whaley clapped his hands together.

"Well, that has to be the plan since we're out of time. We *do* have three long-distance combat specialists. We can pick them off as they come. It will be urban, guerrilla warfare. Stay hidden where you can hit and not be hit. Each one of us is the most valuable of our assets right now."

"You should stay by the bus, too," Camilla told Robby. "You're out of ammo, right? Then, stay safe."

Robby shook his head. "I just thought of something. I'm heading up too."

He initially followed the Amuli before veering off to a separate area of the entrance floor.

"Robby..." she called after him but did not receive an answer.

Her leg twitched as she made a move to follow him before her brain decided against it. She told herself to remain mission focused.

"I daresay it is time!" Whaley declared. "We shall go to the front. Aim well. Fight well."

The five of them crept up the ramp. They each split off on their own, weaving through the concrete supports for cover. Alice and Whaley opted to use their enhanced speed to cross the street for a second sniping angle. Camilla remained on the garage side while Robby remained just inside, where Colter was prepping for a mad dash as soon as their cover was blown.

Then, a pair of masked patrollers rounded the corner. They went down after several flashes of anima. The enemy had been hit, but now they knew where the fugitives were. They charged forward against more violent blasts.

Colter, bouncing on his feet, left the safety of the parking garage to sprint straight towards the enemy line. His well-maintained anima barrier shrugged off a peppering of anima until he dove into the crowd, swinging his claymore in a large arc. Most of the front line was impacted, either by the blade itself or from the wave of anima that followed it.

"I just have to not hit him," Camilla muttered to herself as she kept up her purple shots from her pistol. "He's even crazier than I thought he would be."

Colter disappeared from view amidst the colorful explosions and mass of people.

"He's having the time of his life in there!" Camilla added to herself.

She stepped behind a concrete support for a moment to catch her breath and to see what Robby was up to.

Unlike Carson, there was no bounce in his step. He was getting straight to work in a no-nonsense manner that Camilla had never seen from him.

Early in the battle, Robby had smashed through the driver's side window of one of the garage's abandoned cars with his metal hand. Now, he was inside with the door open, using the increased strength of his robotic hand to fiddle with the shifter. Next, he had it in neutral, pushing it towards Camilla who looked at him quizzically.

"After I get it to the street, kick it and then shoot it once it gets to them," he ordered her.

Camilla nodded, understanding.

Robby pushed the car into the street, where Camilla gave it an anima-powered kick. The bumper split off, but the car barreled toward the enemy crowd but away from where she had seen Colter last. When it was close, she blasted the gas tank. The roaring fire took down the entire flank.

"I'll get another one," Robby told her.

Camilla nodded again before restarting her firing.

Each minute felt like a gut-wrenching eternity for the defensive group. Camilla, Alice, and Whaley all eyed the steadily advancing enemy line as they each took careful shots before slipping back behind cover. The enemy volleys were coming in more substantially now. The concrete supports on Camilla's side of the street were taking hits but holding.

Amidst the rain of concrete flakes, Robby readied what would have been his fourth car, but Camilla stopped him.

"They're getting too close," she warned him. "They'll just end up blowing up the next one in our faces!"

Robby paced around in frustration but took her advice.

A group of enemy agents was now forming a solid shield of anima around a slow-moving bus. The formation was coming like a patient battering ram. Further back, it looked like a couple of teams were about to circle the block of buildings to outflank the group. Their rates of fire were increasing as they gained ground. Camilla, Alice, and Whaley now had to duck behind cover much faster as streams of anima whizzed by them.

Camilla concentrated on the human shields, trying to wear them down. That was the key. She whipped up a near-constant barrage. Amid all the explosions and flying shrapnel, she could vaguely hear someone's voice. Her concentration, however, was only on the enemy.

Suddenly, Camilla felt a yank on the front of her collar, and then her vision went blank as a pop resounded in front of her.

Camilla skidded across the ground as her vision returned to see the aftermath of a red explosion. It had left burn marks on the pavement, as if the energy was now forever frozen in place. Even the nearest concrete support had been badly chipped. Camilla felt some of the smaller chips digging in where she lay on her elbows.

She sat up to assess herself. Her shirt collar was ripped and singed. Strangely, it had a piece of metal clamp hanging to it. She pulled it off to find it shaped like a finger.

"Robby!"

Robby had been lying motionless, facedown, but was now crawling back up to a sitting position. A mess of wires and broken metal hung from one of the wrists.

"Robby, your hand!"

He just looked down at the mangled metal and shrugged.

Camilla pieced together the moments before. She had been too drawn into the offensive to see how the enemy's own sharpshooters were getting closer to kill shots. Robby, even without enhanced senses, had noticed. He must have been the one yelling. Just in time, he had pulled her towards safety. At the same time, an anima bolt was about to strike Camilla right along the collarbone. Robby's false hand had accidentally gotten in the way.

"You saved me," she panted.

Not even close to being in the mood for one of his usual, snappy comments, he just nodded with a glint of a smile at the corners of his mouth.

Seeing the state of their team members and the pressing of the enemy, the others had enough of the current situation. It was time to switch strategy.

Cover me, Alice ordered Whaley before he stepped out with a thick, blue anima barrier.

Come back, she sent off a second thought transmission Colter's way, hoping it would get to him despite the confusion of pitched battle.

Alice waded into the street behind him. Next, she charged an arm until it dripped with what seem like liquid gold. Her eyes shown in the same color as the ends of her hair shot outward from the pressure in the air.

Alice whipped her arm around to produce a curved gold blast. At it its angle, it sheared the block of buildings to one side of the enemies. Bricks and dust spilled into the street in an avalanche. A cloud lingered over the surprised henchmen as they scrambled to regroup.

Go! Alice's thought screamed in succession to every member of her cobbled-together team.

The bus came roaring up the ramp, slowing just long enough to let Camilla and Robby climb on.

From the inside, Jessica was draped around the steering wheel.

"Cam… I'm not feeling great," she muttered weakly. "Take the wheel."

Without missing a beat, Camila slid into the driver's chair and maneuvered the bus toward Alice and Whaley. Jessica rested just above the bus's entrance stairs.

Alice dove in while Whaley waited for Colter, who was now sprinting back.

"Get in!" Camilla shouted desperately.

"I'm sorry," Whaley apologized.

"It's a 'no' from me, too," Colter added.

"What!"

Whaley and Colter eyed the figures moving out of the remnants of the building avalanche.

"They'll keep coming," Whaley explained. "You won't get far unless some of us stay behind. We will slow them down as long as we can."

"It's suicide!" Camilla warned them. "Why would you even do that for us? We barely know each other! We were just enemies!"

"Don't misunderstand," Whaley replied. "I'm doing this for me. I haven't felt as if I've done something worthwhile in a long time. This will be that thing. Besides, the enhancement is tough. It's so difficult to hold all that emotion and mental strain in enough to function in society. You probably know that all too well because of your friend. If this is the end, I'm ready. This is how I want to do it."

"First things first," Colter chimed in. "If you ever meet a kid named Jace Colter… er um… the ex-wife might change it to Jace Black 'cuz of her maiden name, tell him his dad died doing what he loved and to find a better father figure than the one I would have been."

He switched topic as he pointed intensely at Robby.

"I'll never be able to repay you, kid. It'll be a blaze of glory, just like I always wanted. Thank that frowny kid, too. Life's been so much more fun since I met him."

Camilla hesitated on the shifter.

"I don't… I don't…"

"Get out of here now, and you'll save at least the busload!" Whaley snapped at her.

With her head down and tears beginning to roll, Camilla shifted into gear and started closing the door before hastily hitting the gas pedal.

A figure rolled out of the door just before it closed.

Camilla, Robby, Alice, and the non-combatants in the bus swerved their heads to see the person who had jumped out as the bus remained moving.

Jessica slowly stood up on the pavement, still holding her tender ribs. Once on her feet, she swayed dazedly.

"Go back!" Robby screamed at Camilla. "Go back for her, now!"

Camilla shifted to reverse, but Colter stepped between the bus and Jessica. He hammered his huge claymore into the ground, cracking layers of pavement until there was a crater. He gave a final look to the bus's front window. His face was hard-set and sober. Camilla had to get into drive and speed up to prevent sliding back. She pulled out and kept going. The tears getting thicker on her face. She did not look back, but Robby started pounding at the back window.

"Go back!" Robby begged again, sobbing. "Go back!"

"I-I c-can't," Camilla cried as she shook. "He blocked us so we can't go back. Why? Oh, God, why?"

Robby slid to the bus floor, inconsolable.

The passengers in the back stared back in stunned silence.

At the other end of the crater, Jessica was wracked by a painful hacking fit that went on and on as she doubled over.

"You going back for the party, too?" Colter asked her.

When she stopped coughing, Jessica held up her bloody gloves.

"I didn't want to show anyone," she explained. "This has been going on for a while. That bullet… it cracked ribs, and I think one got into my lungs. Without a working hospital nearby, I didn't have much time, anyway. I would've just slowed them down. They're just a bunch of kids, but they're the future. I'll lay down my life for that."

Jessica pulled out her sidearm. "I won't do the same damage as you two, but I can do something if they get close enough."

Colter patted her shoulder.

"Honored," he addressed her solemnly. "We'll all be feasting and fighting for fun in Valhalla at the end of this."

CHAPTER 40
COLOR DRAIN

PAUL CRIED and grunted as he forced the dark energy back down. He doubled over, gripping the wall as he bit his lips and tongue to get some feeling back. The dark anima was not just rage. It was a numbness to the world. While the anger exploded outward, it left him just a husk inside. Finally, he snapped out of it, coughing spit mixed with blood as he caught his breath.

He looked at Jason in horror, not daring himself to breathe or his heart to beat.

The color had drained from Jason's face as his arms, and legs dangled. He was sweating profusely. He was not awake enough to talk and not numb enough to pass out. He just struggled with heavy breaths. The wound, with the sword still implanted, was pouring blood all over his arm and torso. His entire shirt was deep red.

Paul's arms shook. *He... he... he could die! I... just about killed him! Jason! My friend!*

Time and the blood flow seemed to be traveling too quickly, but Jason stayed in the same pale, sweating state.

Do I take out the sword? No... no! He would bleed faster! But how do I get him off the wall?

Paul was aware of how tired his body was. The dark energy had completely depleted him. The edges of his vision were fuzzy. Only his manic, guilty mind kept him going, albeit unhealthily and with paranoia.

I can't pass out! I can't pass out! He'll die! He'll...

Not knowing what else to do, Paul put pressure on Jason's shoulder Jason's glossy eyes were rolling back as his mouth opened and closed but formed no words. Only the severity of the situation stopped Paul's stomach from heaving from the guilt and shock.

"I thought I said not to kill each other!" Adam Avery repeated as he strode back down the hallway. "I was getting into my car, and I heard a war going on up here. It wasn't some friendly disagreement, was it? I thought Luper always taught you two to stop before someone got hurt."

Avery made for Jason, observed him quickly, and then put his hands around the katana.

"W-Wait!" Paul warned shakily.

Not listening, Avery yanked the sword out in one go before tossing it at Paul's feet. "That's still yours."

Knowing that it was his friend's blood on his own sword made Paul feel even sicker.

"He could bleed out now!" Paul stressed.

"The sword had to come out sometime," Avery shrugged. "I will get him help. If he doesn't make it, maybe he wasn't cut out for the tribulations that come from creating a new world."

He won't die if he has the chance, Paul assured himself. *He's way too stubborn for that.*

Avery hoisted up the now-unconscious Jason.

"Great. I'll need a heavy-duty shower now before I meet with the U.N. in a couple of hours," he complained exaggeratedly. "Are you coming with me now, Paul? You can keep an eye on your friend here. Trust me, you'll stumble towards this path, eventually. Why not take it now? In your current state, I could just capture you, but I would never do that. I only want people to follow me out of their own free will."

"And you'll crush anyone else," Paul added bitterly.

Avery smirked. "I'll take that as a 'no' for now. On the other hand, I'll have Alice with me soon. Maybe that will be a good time for you to join on as well. After all, things have been so crazy for you lately. I will give you time to get your head on straight. Just know, with my reach, I will never be far away."

Paul watched Avery carry Jason away.

He's too smart and too twisted. His words make things sound so good, but his actions do the opposite. He's so convincing and has everything that makes someone likable. There's the alluring voice, confident posture, handsome looks, youth, and all those accomplishments. He's just going to exploit that to become a demagogue.

Paul, allowing himself to feel the weariness, sank slowly on his knees.

Jason... why? I should have seen the signs. Were there signs? Have we really been so different all along? Sure, we were opposites at first, but our experiences turned very similar. I thought we were beginning to understand each other.

His body, mind, and spirit were now so exhausted. His midsection and arms were cramping badly as the effects of the battle were still catching up to him. He was face down on his stomach before he knew it. He could think of nothing else but to wallow there in the malaise and tiredness.

Paul was unsure how much time had passed before he could slowly and painfully stand up. He had been awake the whole time but could only now shake the daze. Finally walking, he stumbled around as if all his joints were frozen. He creakily made his way to the elevator at the other end of the hall. It had been relatively untouched by the battles. Once inside, he plopped down again as he took the long ride down to the hidden parking garage. It was just him and his thoughts for the duration. That was the problem. He saw Avery's face as he revealed his maniacal nature. He remembered Jason walking past him with his head down, almost ashamed. Most frequently and vividly, he pictured Jason's pale, sweating face as he gaped down at the sword impaled through his shoulder.

I thought I had it under control. That just proves that I know nothing. I didn't catch onto anything. Not Jason, and not Avery. I've always wondered why people think I'm so smart. Smart people pay attention to the important things. They don't get played like I did.

Paul became aware again of the blood still dribbling down his face. Seeing how his one sleeve was barely hanging on, he tore it off before tying it to his forehead as a makeshift bandage. The other cuts were not as deep. With his heightened healing ability, they were already scabbing over.

Paul suddenly noticed the familiar rush of darkness and whirling, shifting surroundings.

———

The sun was shining in the forms of large beams from the spacious windows. It lit up the shelves made of light-colored wood. A few books sat on display with their bright colors facing out. The older tomes sat deep in their shelves, which did little to hide the yellowed and brown pages.

It would have normally been a soft, comforting scene to Paul. At this moment, his blood stayed boiling, and a storm rolled in his mind. He saw a dark-haired, olive-skinned youth waiting patiently at one of the paneled tables.

Paul remembered the figure this time. The first time they had met, his mind had been aflutter. The current situation was just as uncomfortable, but he felt focused this time. *Maybe I'm getting used to it… all this anima-induced stress on my mind and these shifts to the mental plane and memories. These things are so strange. Should I get used to them?*

The Observer's expression seemed open but serious. Paul found it upsetting. *He knows what's been going on! How long has he been watching? Who has he been watching?*

Paul swung out the chair across from the observer before sitting down in haste.

"Did you know?" Paul demanded. "Did you see anything of this? Couldn't you have told me?"

"You are righteously angry," The Observer stated understandingly.

"You could have said something!" Paul insisted. "Avery's plan. Jackson's plays before that. Jason…"

"What would you have done if I had told you?" The Observer questioned. "Any one of those revelations would have been enough to tear your world asunder. It would have not stopped at your personal world. What would exposing Avery or Jackson had done? They have their own supporters. Would it have led to global civil war?"

"At least we wouldn't have all been manipulated!" Paul exclaimed. "I could have been cautious about it. I would have used that information to make informed decisions They could have been brought down slowly with help from the Council!"

"Perhaps," The Observer relented. "Who's to say what the rest of A.R.C. and A.I.M. would have done, or the world at large for that matter? It all would have come from my decisions. I have had quite enough of my good intentions leading to tragedy over the ages. You are not the first to converse with me. It is beyond understandable that you feel the way that you do. Your train of thought goes against my role. I am The Observer. I watch from beyond and provide insight. Nothing more. I have always shown you why things are. I send you visions of the past that show the memories of other people I have observed. I do not want to influence your choices one way or another."

"If you have this tool that can be used for good, why not use it for good?" Paul wondered.

"Good is a tricky thing," The Observer commented. "Surely this is no higher ideal, as I'm sure Plato would agree. But cannot evil arise from good? Isn't free will a good thing? Without it, we would be puppets of fate, and that would be terrible. However, when people have opportunities to choose, they may choose wrong. They may choose evil. How about another example? Love is a good thing, right? How about a love that leads to feelings of possession and jealously despite being pure in its conviction? Yes, good is good, but it may decay in time."

"What about Jason?" Paul countered. "We could have stopped him. We could have made him see-"

"People see what they wish," The Observer casually interrupted. "Jason was privy to more information than you in those matters and still made his decision. Could you have changed him? I have seen it countless times. Human actions are simply unpredictable. To be able to truly predict someone, you would think that knowing every moment of their life and experience would be enough to hazard a guess to their next action. Yet, how often do we do things on a whim which we cannot explain later? The strange, large brains that nature has given us have become in themselves the anthesis to the orderliness of nature."

Paul gritted his teeth, begging himself to come up with the words to prove this wise being wrong. The frustration within him was building.

"Another example," The Observer lectured. "I once had conversations in a similar manner with another young man centuries before you. This was a young man I saw as a hero. He was virtuous, just, and kind. He was trapped in a bitter struggle with his enemies, who had taken to hiding in a village. Seeing this young man as my champion, I gave him the information I had seen about his enemies' location. I may only be able to link with one person at a time like any other Psychic, but I knew who to seek out in this case for observation. And so, I told the hero exactly where they were. He and his allies found the village and easily rounded up the enemies and put them to the sword. That should have been it. That was the ending I foresaw. And yet, you can never truly understand the inside of someone's head... even if you can talk to it directly. No, that hero didn't stop with the enemies. In the heat and bitter mindset of war, he took revenge on the villagers who had hidden his enemies. They had been innocent of any ill will, only hiding the rogues under threat. I could tell a thousand other stories in the same vein. That is why I no longer interfere. I only observe and guide based on general information. You must draw the conclusions yourself."

"Then, what's the point of all this?" Paul questioned him. "Why observe?"

"I want to see it all to the end," The Observer explained. "In life, I studied Amuli and anima. It has been the most profound shaper of human history, pervading all cultures. What I do is selfish, I know. Likely, no one will ever hear or read my words. Yet, I must see it through. That was a promise I made. I will see what highs and lows Amuli reach until they no longer exist."

"Are we in danger of not existing?" Paul wondered.

"All things are possible in a world of anima, even a world where it ends."

"Cryptic," Paul muttered, not containing his frustration. "Always cryptic."

"If you had lived for eons, you too would have trouble conveying what you know."

"Eons," Paul realized. "You never explained it last time. Who are you?"

The Observer said words in a rhythmic manner. The vowel sounds were familiar enough. However, the accent and words were like nothing he had ever heard.

"That's who I am," The Observer related in English.

"You're messing with me," Paul fumed. "Is this really the time?"

"But that was my name," The Observer explained. "It doesn't translate very well, so that's why I go by 'The Observer.' There is a lot in a name, even if you can't understand the pronunciation. As for me, it shows where I come from. That is somewhere far beyond the experiences of every other person alive today. Those syllables came from the language of Atlantis."

Paul stroked his chin as he thought. The new piece of information was enough to jog his curiosity and distract him from his worries for a moment.

"I've been wondering how literal the term 'Atlantean' is," Paul thought aloud. "Was it a figure of speech or a legend made real? From what Avery said and what you're referring to, it's the real thing, isn't it? An ancient, forgotten civilization swallowed by the sea."

"Swallowed by the sea and hubris," The Observer elaborated. "Plato was right about that. On the other hand, I didn't really appreciate how he used my homeland's destruction to prove a philosophical point. Since it was used as an example in a mental exercise, no serious scholar thought it extended beyond the minds and legends of men. Few people seriously believed in it during Plato's time, and the number only shrunk as the ages passed. It was a blessing, I suppose. Atlantis should have stayed underneath the sea."

"Why didn't it?"

"Adam Avery," The Observer answered quickly. "You know the rest about him, so this is not a leading piece of information. He holds many of the same interests as A.I.M. Interests that A.R.C. members may consider occult or arcane. He and A.I.M. pressed deeper into legends and found one to be true."

"I somewhat gleaned that from what he said," Paul relayed. "The deaths of millions meant nothing to him."

"The danger has not yet passed," The Observer warned. "Atlantis may be even more destructive now."

"How can it be any more destructive?"

"I will have to answer your question with one of my own," The Observer apologized. "What do you know about crystals, especially the non-anima variety?"

"There are a few chemical reactions that can create them," Paul remembered. "Other than that, they tend to take on similar properties as the surrounding minerals."

The Observer nodded. "Anima crystals are no different. For example, an Amulus' crystal takes on its user's emotions and mood. It takes it and amplifies it until every other Amulus in the area can feel it as well. A similar reaction took place long ago. During the formation of the anima crystals, they took on the properties of the surrounding minerals."

Paul gulped as his mind's gears moved quickly. "You're talking about Atlantis. That's the source of the crystals, right? That's what you're implying. So, Atlantis is just like a giant anima crystal?"

"It's more accurate to say that it is the original anima catalyst," The Observer explained. "Its rocks and soil contain all the properties for the same reaction. It does not have the focus of a crystal, but the entire island is an anima amplifier. Every Amulus who sets foot on it goes beyond superhuman for the duration of their stay."

"And Avery has it," Paul added as he connected the dots. "He's plans don't seem as far-fetched now."

"Oh, it's far-fetched to believe that he can unite the world under him," The Observer commented. "His goal of assuming terrible power is achievable, however."

"How do I stop that?" Paul wondered.

"I told you that I will not use you as a puppet," The Observer reminded him. "I can guide you to the answers, but you have to find them yourself. Think! Use that impressive brain of yours. On the other hand, I will say this. Maybe you are asking the wrong question. Is it really just all on you?"

"Fine," Paul sighed. "It's how can we stop him."

"And that's why I've called you here," The Observer revealed. "Keep your mind moving and be flexible. What will hinder him?"

Paul reached deep into his thoughts for answers. He closed his eyes for a few moments before they shot back open.

"Alice is the first thing," Paul remembered. "He said that he needs her, if only for a little while. I can't let him get her. A good question is why he needs her."

"What is your guess on that?" queried The Observer.

"I'd say that it's because she is an Atlantean," Paul responded. "She is the last one we know of. I'm assuming that he has a plan to get his power and use the island. I got that from his confidence. He's just not sure if he can get everything without her."

"I would say that is a start," The Observer commended him. "Will you tell her?"

"A few weeks ago, when I was mired in my own head, I may not have," Paul admitted. "No, I have to tell her. She deserves to know. She's a player in this, and it's her life."

"Right," The Observer nodded. "What else is there to do now?"

Paul crossed his arms as he thought. His fingers absentmindedly tapped on his inner arms.

"Allies," Paul blurted. "Avery has numbers, but I don't know how many are loyal to him. There has to be a significant percentage of people who aren't. There are people who will feel just as fearful and betrayed as I do. Hamilton, Grady, and there have to be others. They wouldn't join him. Would they?"

"What does your gut say?"

"No. Definitely not."

"So, what are you saying?" The Observer. "Is your next step to keep Alice safe and to build an army of your own?"

"I thought you said that you weren't going to lead me on to anything," Paul shot back.

"Really?" teased The Observer. "Are those conclusions you just made something you wouldn't have come up with on your own? I think they would have been. I just expedited the process. I give information, and that tends to clear heads."

"I feel like you're pushing me," Paul said. "I'm just not sure if it's over a cliff or not."

"We'll call it a nudge," The Observer deflected. "Now, the real world awaits."

"The 'real world?'" Paul questioned.

"The physical one," The Observer corrected. "A place that is more substantial than a pocket of floating, unbound consciousness."

He waved Paul away.

———

Paul still felt bitter as the inside of the elevator came back into view. The only difference now was that he had something to focus and bitterness on.

Doing something this big isn't going to be easy. To say that I'm raising an army is one thing and doing it is another. The Observer is almost as smooth as Avery. They speak so convincingly that you think their words will just make things a reality. It's harder than that.

Paul tried taking in deep breaths as the doors opened.

How am I going to explain all this to the others? What do I say about Jason? I have to find them first. Avery said he had men moving in on them. His plan has gone so perfectly. I just need it to have a little crack, and then I can see everyone again.

Paul's body creaked again as he stood up. Walking hunched over, without straightening his back, was, strangely, the most comfortable way for him to move at the moment. He could worry about posture later.

"You bring a freakin' medic?"

I almost forgot.

Ben was still sitting in the same place, messaging one foot and the opposite shin. He had evidently taken off his shoes as his feet had begun to swell. Purple and gray bruises were visible through the white socks.

Paul sighed. "No, not right now. I don't have time for this."

"Oi! What's that supposed to mean?" shouted Ben back at him.

Paul slowly stooped down the assess the still-unconscious Brandon Robeson. He was also badly bloodied and bruised but not in any other danger.

"At least tell me what happened up there," Ben demanded. "It sounded like a bloody war!"

Paul did not know where to start or if he even wanted to.

"It was Avery," he gulped. "It's good he didn't come this way. You would both be dead... probably."

"What?"

Paul clenched his teeth and fists. He had enough of being frustrated. Jackson and Avery had both been playing him for months. Even Ben's relevant questions seemed annoying at the moment.

I'm just really tired of this all. Really tired...

"While Jackson was being a fascist," Paul started, "and we were all following his orders, Avery was sowing seeds. He got Jason and me to get rid of Jackson while he slowly undermined A.R.C. and A.I.M. at the same time."

"See!" Ben exclaimed. "You shouldn't have been fighting us."

"He had my family," Paul grunted through his teeth. "He's the one who kidnapped them to manipulate me. He ran experiments on Alice and other young Amuli. He's the one who kept her isolated and inhuman. Avery is evil but so was Jackson."

"So, where are those two?"

"Jackson's dead and Avery left," Paul relayed. "Turns out he was Red Mask and on the council all along. He used those positions to make those organizations crumble with infighting. Now, he's building something new on their ashes."

"You killed Jackson?" Ben asked. "I'll admit that's impressive."

"It was Jason."

"Where's he?"

"With Avery."

"What?"

Paul snapped. "I'm not explaining anymore. I need to get moving. If you want to live, you're coming, too. I'm assuming you have cars down here and a ramp leading to the surface."

"Yeah," Ben answered. "Can't get to them, though. Can't walk on account of you."

"What level?"

"A couple down, but-"

Paul wasted no more time. He grabbed Ben by the shirt and hoisted him over the shoulder. Next, he picked up Robeson and put him on the other shoulder. The sleeping young man's medicine shield hung from one of Paul's fingers.

We've never gotten along, but even he deserves a fighting chance in whatever crazy world Avery's actions will create.

Ben did not struggle but muttered angrily to himself. Robeson kept sleeping.

It was slow going to the car, but Paul could not think of another option. The muscle-cramping and spasms were worse with the added weight. He went on without dropping either passenger.

Finding the nondescript sedan, Paul slung Robeson into the backseat. He dropped Ben into the passenger side before stretching out his aching shoulders.

"Thought you were supposed to be stronger than all of us," Ben commented.

"I wasted everything in that 'war' up there, as you called it," Paul explained. "I'm assuming that you have a key."

Ben reached into his pocket and tossed it to him.

"Careful with her," he advised. "This one's mine."

Paul started it up and peeled out of the level and up the ramp.

"So, where are we going?" Ben wondered. "The way you told it, the whole world's coming down out there."

"We're going to some better people."

Please hold out! I'll be there soon.

CHAPTER 41
LEAVING TODAY

THE BUS HAD long since faded from view. It seemed like a long time, and yet, not enough. The further it got away the better.

Jessica could no longer stand. The bullets had quickly vanished from her gun. She had thrown that at an enemy as well. Even as blood dribbled out of her mouth, she held up her combat knife. In her weakness, she had to keep re-clutching it every time her hand started to go slack. Every breath was more a cough and a wheeze.

Whaley swayed on his feet. His forehead and upper face had so much blood on them, he could not see. For all he knew, his eyes could be gone. After all, the pain was there. He was an archer with no eyes, but he could feel the enemy crowd before him and that was enough. True accuracy did not matter at this point.

Colter still stood firm with his heavy frame. An eye had been taken out by a slash, and another slice had taken a chunk of ear. Somewhere along the line, he had lost all but a sleeve of his shirt.

There, they stared at the piles of bodies before them. It had created a ghastly barricade that had the terrible, metallic stink of blood.

The enemies held back for a moment, regrouping. They took up the whole width of the street while others had circled around to their backs. They could overwhelm them in sheer numbers, but the previous tries had shown that their first line, at least, would die. It took courage to charge in, and the enemy lines were still finding theirs. Presently, there was a commotion. Commanders were shouting, but their men were shouting back. There was shoving and pushing for position due to the indecisiveness. Some were wedging forward, while others tried to drudge toward the back amidst the mass of humanity.

Colter cackled through his parched throat. "Look at that, they're afraid of us! Dozens of them and three of us. This is bliss!"

The other two just tried to steady themselves. This was their end, and it was hard to find the words to sum up the whole of a life. Any words could be the last ones.

"Hey, Whaley," Colter shouted. "What was that one story about that Irish guy? Was it Chu Chu Train? Doesn't this ring a bell? Tell me, how does it go?"

"Cú Chulainn," Whaley croaked. "Cú Chulainn, the hero in the *Ulster Cycle*. He died after slaughtering so many enemies and forcing a retreat, he… tied himself to a rock to keep standing. For three days after he died, his enemies were… too afraid to approach him to see if he had… died. That's… until a raven landed on his shoulder, and he… didn't move. Only then… they knew he was dead, and it… was s-safe."

"Just like him," Colter chuckled, "we're legends."

The next enemy wave had assembled. Evidently, their commanders had passed on enough courage for another assault from all sides. The circle closed in until the defenders were swallowed in the sun-blocking sea of flesh and anima.

———

"What are we looking for?" Ben asked bluntly from the front seat as buildings blurred in the windows.

His nonchalant attitude about the situation was quickly wearing on Paul.

This abandoned area of the city was disconcertingly quiet. On a usual day, Paul could imagine the sidewalks being filled and the traffic being stifling. Now, it was just a ghostly silence.

And Avery did this, too.

Suddenly, there was a series of crashing sounds that seemed to thump the streets. Paul swore he felt the car shaking. He pushed on, turning through an alleyway as he felt his way around. Every time he heard the roaring thunder-like sound, he maneuvered towards it. Finally, there were flashes. They were well-hidden behind buildings at first but then seemed to burst around all structures.

"We're looking for something like that," Paul finally said stoically.

"You're driving right towards it?" Ben noticed worriedly.

Paul ignored him.

I just need to get there. I just need to get to wherever they are.

Out of nowhere, there was a rush of wind that shook the car along with the sound of a horn blaring repeatedly. A hulking yellow form raced past them in the opposite direction.

"*Paul!*"

Paul spun into a U-turn hard enough that Ben hit his head on the passenger side window. Robeson just rolled around in the backseat, still snoozing.

"Ow!" Ben grunted. "What the-"

"Alice," Paul interjected. "I felt her telepathy and her energy."

Soon enough, after pulling closer behind the fleeing bus, Paul could make out Camilla's anima signature as well as those less-powerful auras coming from non-Amuli. He also felt a third and fourth Amulus nearby. Both felt similar, but they were difficult to trace.

That better be Robby, Jessica, Antonio, and… everyone they were able to rescue.

Paul shook his head. *I know how badly I want to reunite with Aunt Morgan and Uncle Nick, but I just need to push that out of my mind to focus right now.*

Paul utilized a second lane to pull alongside the bus. Camilla, sitting at the wheel, nodded at him as he came into view. Paul waved slowly.

"*Alice,*" he tried sending the thought outward towards her as if she were a telephone receiver. "*What's the situation?*"

"*Paul!*" she returned the mental call. "*So much has happened! We… we just need to find a place to hide. A place far away.*"

"*There's so much I have to say, too! I-I… and Jason… Right, we just need to focus now. We can talk later.*"

With his eyes darting and observing all directions, Paul caught a glimpse of a gray-metallic vehicle coming up several streets behind them. It looked to be some kind of reinforced truck, like one that carried money or prison inmates.

"*One of ours?*" Paul questioned Alice across the distance between their two vehicles.

"*No.*"

Paul continued watching the truck gain ground through his rearview mirror. It's menacing, teeth-like grille appeared to Paul as an ever-growing scowl.

"*I have an idea,*" Paul informed Alice.

With one hand on the wheel and one eye on the road, he carefully slipped his sword out the side window. Its curved tip pointed back at the oncoming truck. Paul blazed his anima along the blade and let a spear-like projectile fly. It struck towards the bottom of the toothy grille with a flash of green.

The truck swerved slightly as if hitting a bump, but otherwise continued on.

Paul gritted his teeth in frustration. He was still tired, which meant his anima was weak. There was that and the fact his concentration was split between aiming and keeping the car steady.

"Take the wheel," he ordered Ben.

"What?"

"Take it!"

Paul pushed his body just outside the window so that his waist rested on the door. Ben half-fell over to latch his arms to the wheel. The car took a sickening wiggle before Ben got it steady.

"Of all the-" he complained as his words got lost in the rush of wind emanating from the open window.

This time, Paul could train his whole mind on his next blast. A second dart of green anima headed for one of the truck's front wheels. It careened into an outstretching of metal armor around the wheel well. The metal piece bent but not enough to point back into the wheel.

"I need more," Paul muttered.

He pushed himself farther out the window.

"You're taking the whole thing," he informed Ben.

Ben clumsily crawling over to the driver's seat.

"Need I remind you that my foot is broken!"

Paul ignored him. *His legs can still push down.*

Paul spread his arms wide as he made for the roof. The wind was intense and tore at his already bedraggled clothes. The surface was slick, but he cupped his whole arms around the roof to stay clinging to it. His legs dangled over the front window. When he was confident enough to raise his body slightly, he did so.

With his body freer and his range farther open. He aimed an entire slash. The shock wave spread out from one front wheel of the enemy truck to the other.

The truck bounced on its suspension on impact and the metal buckled even more. Despite that, it still kept coming at speed.

Paul noticed a glint of metal out of the side of the truck.

Someone was leaning out of that vehicle as well, learning from his truck. Only this Amulus had some type of antique handgun, primed for aiming. There was another glint. This one was red.

With nowhere to take cover, Paul skidded down toward the hood on instinct. There was a loud crack, and the car shook.

Paul just held on before surveying the damage. The back bumper was gone along with chunks of metal and plastic from the back of the car. Some type of liquid was splashing out, but the car kept running.

Ben yelled something out of the window. It was lost in the wind.

Paul scrambled back up the car's roof. Positioning himself, he put one foot on the roof, while the opposite knee rested on the window. It was the best leverage he could find at the moment.

The enemy in the vehicle had stopped shooting. It appeared that hitting a bump in the road had shaken the gunman's concentration for the moment.

Paul begged the last of his energy to encircle his blade as he pulled it back in anticipation of a final slash.

"Remember. I am here. I am with you."

Paul looked up to see Alice staring from the bus's nearest window. Her deep blue eyes were transfixed on him. He took a breath.

At that moment, he felt Alice on his wavelength. He could feel her anima resounding with his own. She was steadying the energy's fluctuations in him. His inner self had felt so chaotic for so long now. Gradually, he felt a burden being lifted. He was not shouldering it alone now. His right arm readied a final stroke. It felt as if Alice was steadying his sword arm. She was like his crutch.

No, Paul decided. *It is an equal relationship. We are supporting each other.*

Paul turned the anima wave loose. The wide band of anima battered the front end of the armored truck. The grille and hood caved in, sending smoke and sparks wafting through the air. Even the protected front wheel-wells loosened. The whole truck careened madly from side to side. Evidently, it veered onto a sidewalk. At this time, the driver must have hammered on the barely working brakes before striking a pole.

Paul kept staring, watchfully at the trailing street until the kicked-up dust and gravel settled. In the clear view, he could see no other pursuers.

In his relief and exhaustion, Paul's mind went blank and his body accidentally relaxed. His slackened body slid down the window and hood of the car. Ben yelled something out the window, while Alice cried out after pulling down her bus-seat window. Paul did not hear either of them. He felt sleep and a loss of conscious closing in. It felt enticing to his cloudy, weary mind. He had pushed himself too far for too long. His body was rebelling.

Sometime during his slide, he realized that he was moving downward. Instructively, his hand shot upward. It felt around until it touched the upper lip of the hood just below the front window. As his momentum caught up, his arm jarred but stayed in place. His own weight pulled his body taut as his feet hovered just above the rushing road. He hung there with his body on autopilot.

He gritted his teeth and squeezed his eyes as he fought just to hang there. Despite nearly dozing in place, he held his grip, even as the metal cut into his soft fingers. The rapid bobbing up-and-down of his body kept the fleshy parts bouncing painfully into the roof, cutting deeper each time.

How... how am I... going to get down?

Paul was too tired to come up with a solution. This time, he had to let someone else figure it out.

CHAPTER 42
REUNITE

PAUL AWOKE uncomfortable and aching in the front seat. The effects of his unplanned nap were less than pleasant. His neck ached terribly. Even when he straightened it, he still felt like it was bent from his sleeping position. He coughed and sniffled through a bunch of mucus. His eyes hurt from being pointed towards the sun, even while covered by his eyelids. It still felt like the sun was cooking them like eggs. The pain seemed to reach back into his head as well, forming a massive headache.

"We had to stop for gas," Ben informed him as he stirred groggily. "You may have noticed that you didn't end up on the road or under the car. You know, it's funny. I didn't know my arms could reach far enough to pull you back inside the car. I reckon you sprained my shoulder, even after what you did to my foot and shin. Still in constant pain, by the way."

Paul tried to shake his head back to lucidity, but moving like that made his head swim.

"The other funny thing is you had me so out of sorts that I started yelling things out loud instead of inside your head," Ben added.

"*Like this!*" the Psychic emphasized with an internal message.

It was not a pleasant-feeling transmission into Paul's throbbing head.

Ben opened his door, spilling a warm breeze into the car. The Australian then tapped him on the knee.

"Up. C'mon, you need to stretch your legs. God knows that I can't right now. Can't imagine what all that madcap driving did to my shattered foot and shin."

The prospect of that also made Paul anticipate discomfort. Sure enough, dizzily getting out of the car made his head spin and his stomach turn.

Come on. I have anima power stacked on top of anima power. I heal fast, but couldn't it be a little faster this time?

Noticing the yellow bus beside them at the gas stall beside him, he felt an odd sense of relief and nervousness. *Is everyone there? Did they all make it out? And why the heck is it a Schwert Academy bus? Wasn't it supposed to be A.R.C.?*

First, Paul let his practical mind guide him. He leaned down to assess the back end of the car. It was worse than he thought. Whole strips of plastic and metal were missing. The bottom bumper was completely gone, and the trunk was stuck open. The gas tank appeared to be the only thing back there that was intact.

Paul could not tell where they were exactly. They were definitely outside the city. The view was green with trees and long grass. He could see the gray concrete of a nearby town in the distance. The rest of the lot was empty. The connecting store to the gas station was devoid of people besides a single cashier at the counter.

Basically, no one to notice this nearly ruined car. Good. We don't need to stick out. A big yellow school bus with more than school-age kids on it does that enough.

He continued his survey of the car. Underneath the back end, he saw more battle scars in the metal. The concerning thing was the wheel axle. A lattice of cracks had appeared through the metal. Chunks were missing in one area, which made the still-connected pieces look needle-thin.

"Um," he called out to Ben. "We're going to have to ditch the car, I think. I'm not a mechanic, but the back axel is hanging by a literal thread."

"Great!" Ben shouted sarcastically. "Now, carry me to the bus then."

Paul was about to meet up with the bus riders when there was a chaotic banging at his side.

One of the sedan's back doors opened after two attempts. Robeson lurched out. Struggling with more vertigo than Paul and with dried blood caked all around his body, he looked like a zombie. Cursing, his shoes skidded around on the light gravel covering the old gas station pavement. He ended up bracing himself on the open car door.

He coughed and swore several times before growling, "Engel!"

Robeson was about to take a step forward when more dizziness and confusion halted him.

"Wait!" he cried in puzzlement. "Where the heck did you take me, and what the heck is going on?"

Paul raised his arms, partly to calm Robeson down and partly in reflex to the uncomfortable situation.

"I think I can explain," he indicated slowly.

"And what's with that face?" Robeson countered. "What ticks me off the most about you is that innocent look on your face. All that crap you just pulled-"

"Hey, Brandon," Ben interrupted as he leaned out the window. "You might want to listen. Believe me, I'm not happy either, but a lot of things just happened."

"And you," Robeson addressed him as he pointed at him. "What kind of noncommittal, wishy-washy attitude do you have? I mean… are you an A.R.C. agent or some kind of loser drifter who can't stick with the cause?"

"Well, the first option just went extinct," Ben answered mockingly. "Listen for a little, and we'll explain that."

"Extinct?"

"Jackson's dead," Paul stated succinctly. "A.R.C. is done for. A.I.M., too."

Robeson strode forward before yanking Paul towards him by his shirt. Paul offered little resistance.

"You killed him!" Robeson accused.

"It was Jason," Paul elaborated. "I'm sorry. I tried to stop him. I just wanted Jackson to answer for what he did. That's all. He had my family, Brandon."

Robeson shook his head. "It all started because you had to stir the pot. Yeah, it was a messed-up world, but we had lives!"

"It's not an excuse," Paul relented. "But we were played. You, me, Jackson, Ben, and… well… the rest of the world. It was Avery. I should have seen it, but I didn't. He pitted us against each other while he took down A.I.M. for the inside. He told me he was going to the UN to get backing for a new organization. He will be the only game in town."

Robeson released his grip, but only slightly. "Nothing you just said makes me hate you any less. Like I said, if you hadn't-"

"Yeah, what if," Ben interjected. "What if this. What if that. The thing is, we can't really change the past, can we? So, what about the present? Avery wants us all dead or to disappear, at least. We're all in the same boat. Lucky for us, it seems like a big boat, but we do need enough rowers."

"I'm not getting into close quarters with anyone I don't trust," Robeson scoffed.

"Take it easy now," Ben insisted gently. "Like I said, before this all started, I'm a survivor. When you think about what you want to do now, I think the best choice for survival is an easy one to make. I also said that I like the easy life, but that's spoiled now. I reserve the right to keep giving Paul crap for that. Other than that, let's all team up against Avery. It's like with A.R.C. and A.I.M. One superhuman is hard to stop. An organization of superhumans is impossible to stop."

Robeson started to walk off by himself.

"I just need to think," he sighed.

"You also need to clean up, mate," Ben informed him.

Robeson finally took notice of the dried blood all over his body. He made for the store and its restroom.

Leaving Ben, Paul slowly walked toward the bus. He felt his pulse beating rapidly in his neck.

I didn't think I would be so nervous. I will be seeing them after so long... Aunt Morgan and Uncle Nick... if they made it out. What could they possibly think? I'm a different person now. It doesn't matter how much I want to go back. And everyone else... why has no one stepped outside yet? Something's wrong.

Paul did not so much sense the unpleasant feeling from anima, but from his own anticipation.

Eventually, he found himself looking at his reflection in the glass door. There was that same boyish, innocent look that Robeson had complained out. That had not changed. Neither had the unruly hair. The eyes, however, were slightly different from what they had been months ago. There was a sternness there that seemed alien on the youthful face. He ended up brushing some of his own dried blood from his forehead.

The doors opened him. For some reason, he had imagined Robby or Camilla quickly running out to meet him. Inside, everything was quiet, aside from the squeaking door.

Camilla was the one in the front seat. She still had a hand on the door's lever. Paul was struck by the odd observation that she did not fit the usual profile of a bus driver, the ones Robby joked about loving Mountain Dew and country music. Like Paul, she had a tired look in her eyes, which were rimmed with red.

Paul gulped at that. He took it as a bad sign. Camilla looked as if she was going to say something, but was clearly struggling to find the words.

Robby came jogging down the stairs. He was even more misty-eyed than Camilla, and his mouth was more tightly drawn and serious than Paul had ever seen it. Without a word, he threw his arms around Paul.

Paul was taken aback and then felt his own sense of dread intensify. *Something's very wrong.*

"Jess," Robby whispered.

Paul felt his own tears welling.

Jessica Swanson. I used to see her at Robby's family barbeques. They used to have one every time the Steelers played. The whole time, she was a powerful young woman making the world safe by uniting Amuli and non-Amuli. She broke through decades of the Swanson's family ingrained hatred of superhumans nearly on her own. This world always seems to take the greatest people too soon.

"Avery," Camilla breathed shakily and bitterly. "He… do you know?"

Paul nodded. "I know. It's probably even worse than…"

He trailed off.

Camilla continued. "Antonio was on his payroll or whatever the whole time. He made everything go south."

"The bus?" Paul wondered.

For some reason, that was on his mind at the moment.

"Called Carson Colter for help earlier," Robby managed to get out. "He's gone, too. Same with Whaley who came with him."

I never would have thought Colter would have gone while saving my friends. Did I really ever pin him down after all? Was he really just a meathead who loved to fight and nothing else?

"Paul…"

Alice came to the stairs next. Robby gave her the space to hug Paul as well. Like Robby, she was trembling, even if her face did not show the same emotions.

"Jason?" was the other name she mouthed.

She could probably hear my thoughts screaming it out on my head.

"He…" Paul stumbled. "He's been with Avery's coup, too. It's been that way since he killed The Rat. Avery manipulated his sense of justice and duty. I-I just… didn't know how to get through to him."

Paul's three friends took the news the same way. Their eyes turned downcast as they tried to understand the new revelation, which was now piled on top of so many others.

"It's bad," Camilla admitted. "It's really bad, but there's some other news, too."

She climbed out of the bus to make way for the next group.

Without warning and barely a sound, a woman in a soft hoodie nearly plowed Paul over. He was being squeezed tightly when he felt a man's large hand on his shoulder.

Uncle Nick's face was scruffy and gaunt. His eyes were swept by waves of emotion. Paul could not even see Aunt Morgan's face. It was buried in his shoulder.

"Never again," she muttered huskily. "I never wanted to go through this again. Not after Michael. Not after Sam. Why our family?"

Paul was not sure how to respond, but knew that he was not meant to. Still, he felt guilty. *No, you don't know who am I am now, what I've become. I'm so sorry that the Paul you loved is gone.*

"I'm so sorry," Paul murmured through his choked-up throat. "I put you through all of it again."

"No, no, Paul!" Morgan shook her head. "It's not your fault. None of it is."

"Maybe not that," Paul responded. "There have been… so many other things. I don't feel the same anymore. I-I don't think I'm the person you raised anymore. I've done… so many things. I feel like everything's been just one big regret. There's so much blood on my hands and so many weights stacked on my shoulders. I wish I could be that person you knew again. I wish I could forget this all and go back to Palisville. At the same time, I don't think that would be fair to all the people I've wronged. But then, it's not fair to you. I'm so confused and so stuck."

Morgan just kept shaking her head.

"Do you remember when you were little? You asked me once if there was any way I would stop loving you. I said 'no' emphatically then. I'll say it again now."

"You weren't there all those times!" Paul cried.

"Maybe you can't see it in yourself," Morgan countered. "That's okay. It's hard to really see yourself. No, Paul. I think you are exactly the boy I know! You know how I know that? Look at all these people."

She waved her hand at the group at the front of the bus.

"If you were as terrible as you think you are, you wouldn't have these friends to support you. I can hear it in the way they talk about you. They all care about you, Paul. They know you always try your best. Is there any more anyone can ask? You can't be perfect. I know you, Paul. You're my nephew, but you're also my son."

Morgan then gestured to the bus's other occupants in the rear.

"Just look at what you've done here. You went up against a world power to rescue people. These people are now free because of you. You risked everything to do the right thing. How many other people would have done that? How many guards with a guilty conscience could have sprung us at any time? They didn't, but you and your friends did. You are committed to good. That's beyond admirable."

"Neutral good alignment, I would say," Robby commented through a weak smile.

It warmed Paul to know that Robby was at least trying to go back to his old self, even after suffering a tragedy. *It's selfish, but I wouldn't know what to do if he really changed. There would be no one to balance me out.*

Paul then noticed the others on the bus who had all quietly hung back during the reunions.

"I'm… uh… Ken," he introduced himself while rubbing the back of his neck. "This is weird. I feel like I just walked into a class or family reunion I don't belong in. Anyway, your friends rescued me. I guess I'm stuck with you guys then… not that I'm upset about that."

A thick-armed man with a balding head walked right up to Paul.

"Nice to see yah again, Mr. Green," he welcomed amusedly.

Paul felt the sinking guilt again, grinding in his stomach. *These two. After what I did to them…*

"Judging by your face, you didn't want the two of us again," Joe surmised.

"I-I just…" Paul stammered.

"Well, maybe you did us wrong, but then you did us right," Joe summed up. "Doesn't that mean we're back to even? Besides, I can't imagine being in a better situation right now, actually. We're free. That's what we really wanted."

"I still don't trust you," Kim warned as the dour girl came up beside Joe. "But thanks for not leaving us to rot."

"I-I'm still… I'm sorry," Paul apologized. "You would never have been locked up if it wasn't for me."

"Yeah," Kim agreed. "But the only reason we'll stick around is because you look so pathetically sorry for it."

Paul was unsure how to react, so he just nodded solemnly.

Brandon… he remembered with his heart sinking again. *If Joe and Kim even see Brandon…*

Paul left the bus for a moment to return to the nearly totaled car.

Robeson was sitting on the hood along with the odd mixture of a pile of bandages and disinfectant wipes on one side and a mound of hot dogs on the other. Ben was also chowing down in the front seat.

"I've been thinking," Robeson announced as Paul approached. "I want to take Avery down, but I don't think I want to do it with you. Not after what you did to Jackson. He was a man who could have sorted out this mess. To fix all this, I need to take out a lot of targets. You are going to like all of them. Jason's going down, too. Jason murdered Jackson, so he's going down for it. I know you're the sappy kind of guy who won't want to hurt his old friend. You'll preach and plead with him, even though he's already gone. I've always seen it in him. Jason's a killer, but I didn't know he was a rabid dog."

Paul picked some of the dried blood on his own forehead as he thought. It clung to the makeshift bandage-headband that was still stuck to his head.

"I think we can come to an agreement," Paul advised. "You disrupt Avery in your way, and we'll do it in ours. Just know this, if you ever call for help, we will be there. I don't abandon people... not anymore."

"Fair enough," Robeson exhaled. "Can't say I would always do the same. It just depends. Anyway, I have to find a ride now. Later."

Robeson finished another hot dog before scooting off of the road and leaving for the road by foot.

"Think we'll see him again?" Ben wondered.

We need fighters. Paul thought, somewhat dejectedly. *Even fighters like Brandon Robeson. On the other hand, I can't say that I wanted to reintroduce him to Joe and Kim.*

"What about you?" Paul asked, disregarding the question. "Are you leaving?"

"Leaving?" Ben questioned incredulously. "I can't walk, mate. Really shouldn't have been driving either."

"I'm being serious," Paul scolded. *With him, sometimes, it feels like I'm talking to Robby.*

"What have I been saying?" Ben answered with a question. "Strength in numbers. You and your friends don't have a lot of them, but that's better than none."

"Are you coming to the bus then?"

"Only if you carry me."

CHAPTER 43
NEW DAY

JASON STARED with disgust at his bandaged arm as it hung loosely in a sling. It was itchy and uncomfortable. More than that, he had to know. He had to know if there had been any lasting damage done. He had to know if he could fight like before. He wanted to rip through all the bandages. Even as an enhanced Amuli, the healing felt painfully slow and aggravating.

Jason felt an odd sense of pride and closure when he thought about how he had gotten the wound. That was the only bearable thing about it. Sure, it had come from a desperate, former ally who had felt betrayed, but Jason did not feel the guilt intensely. No, he considered himself closer to Paul now. Even on bitter, ideologically opposed sides, Jason now saw himself in him. Their fight had been honorable. Paul had stood up for what he thought was right, just as he had. There was no shame in it.

Adam Avery knocked on the glass door of the hospital-wing room with the back of his hand.

"Two different reconstructive surgeries," Avery summarized. "That is something for someone whose durability and healing ability is beyond superhuman. He really did some damage. Paul Engel. Who would have thought?"

"How long?" Jason asked gruffly.

"At least two weeks. Your surgeon, the top specialist on Amuli said-"

"Make it one," Jason demanded quickly.

Avery smiled. "If I forced you to wait any longer, you'd probably overthrow me, wouldn't you? I think I will avoid that."

"The political side," Jason changed the subject. "It's done?"

"It's done," confirmed Avery. "We have the complete cooperation of the UN and the world's major powers. As soon as you're ready, you can go back to doing what you do best."

Jason's face brightened slightly, but he did not smile.

"Oh, right," Avery said. "I have a visitor. Someone to remind you what you're doing all of this for."

Avery signaled with his hand to the doorway.

A slim girl with dark hair and a small face slowly walked into the hospital room. The girl's large eyes were missing irises so that her eyes were only white with black pupils. Like the color of her eyes, her expression was nonexistent. The way she moved, she looked like a marionette, with someone tugging on the strings. Tied into the back of her hair was an ornate comb with a crystal in the center. The red-rimmed the inside edges of the translucent crystal. Jason knew that the red had once been bright, almost scarlet.

"You really control her that easy?" Jason asked uncomfortably. "Through something like a back-channel?"

"A back-channel is a good way to describe it," Avery commented. "Usually in a Dead Eyes, there is one channel. It goes from the Psychic to the Dead Eyes in one direction. The Psychic is the signaler, and the Dead Eyes is a receiver. Ling was originally a Psychic who created numerous, untold of channels leading to her. I have picked up on one such channel. One that allows a Warrior with a strong connection with her, like me, to control her like a Dead Eyes. That was how I perpetrated the Red Mask disguise. I controlled Ling, who stayed hidden and made her cast her anima on my hands. I was able to appear like a Psychic. You can control her, too, if you wish."

"No," Jason answered emphatically and firmly. "You know, every time I see that little bit of red in the crystal, I know she's still in there."

"All the more reason to bring Alice into the fold," Avery added. "She made Ling into what she is, not by her own fault of course. Perhaps, we can work out a solution with her as a catalyst once again. That's not all. I told you that I found a channel to her. What if there are some leading from her? She could still be in there somewhere, you know. Speaking of Paul's group, I notice that you did not mention Ling's situation to Paul."

"No," Jason confirmed. "It's like you said. Anyone who joins us has to do it on their own terms. Paul is the type to be taken in by a sob story. If he helped us just to save Ling, he wouldn't truly be a part of the cause."

"He'll come around," Avery affirmed. "There's no other option for him. We are building a new world order. If he wants to be a part of the world, he'll have to see the light. The mechanisms can no longer be stopped."

"You seem so sure," Jason inferred. "Paul does have a stubborn streak."

"Oh, I didn't say he wouldn't drag his feet," Avery amended. "I've been studying him all these months. I see a sensitive soul in him. Sensitive means open, and open means malleable. His perspective of himself and the world has shifted so many times since he became an Amulus. It will only take a push to do it again."

"Why are you concentrating on him?" Jason wondered.

"He's a lynchpin," Avery answered. "He has a close connection to Alice, the Atlantean. He is close to the remnants of A.R.C.-Human. There is even a path to him through you. Human connections are what the world is built on. Play with those and you remake the world."

"Just promise me," Jason started. "You won't kill Paul, Alice, Cam, or their group. You stick to those notions you just mentioned. They are people who belong in this new world. They just don't see it yet."

"Of course," Avery replied. "Now, I should be going. The UN loves their paperwork. Should I take Ling with me or leave her here?"

Jason's face soured as he thought.

"She can go," Jason said meekly.

As Avery had her turn to leave, Jason's eyes were heavy with weary emotion.

"And I promise you," he declared to the breathing robot. "You will be back to normal someday. That is the goal I will not stop working towards. I swear it.

———

The interior of the bus was dead silent. Every passenger had his or her head facing out of the window. There was a lot to think about. It was time to think up solutions or to get stuck in the stagnant cesspool of negative thoughts. Paul thought that the latter option was all too easy to slip into. He had learned that it took real effort to escape the negative pull of his mind's magnet.

While the inside was quiet, sounds did pour in from outside. The tires cracked the occasional tree branch. The suspension creaked and rattled over every pothole. This long journey through the northeastern United States was made up primarily of weather-worn roads. Though the weather had been warm for months, the pavement perpetually bore the scars of winter.

It had crossed the mind of seemingly every passenger that a school bus running at odd hours with even stranger occupants inside might attract unwanted attention. However, this was not a usual time for the east coast, and disaster-relief vehicles were still the most common company on the road. Few things were strange or out-of-place in an area where the impossible had happened just months ago.

The radio, which had been just garbled buzzing, now played clearly.

"We're live from the newly reopened United Nations Headquarters in New York City," a radio-news reporter monologed. "Leaders from around the world are calling it a new day for how we treat superhumans in society. Just moments ago, the near-unanimous decision was made to dissolve the UN's two former Amuli control organizations, the Amulus Regional Containment, or A.R.C., and the Amulus International Medicine, otherwise known as A.I.M. This comes in the wake of the scandals that have rocked the world since the dumping of thousands of files from both organizations. Those files revealed articles relating to government and business black-mailing, assassinations, illegal imprisonments, torture, human experimentation, child soldiers, and a mafia-esque shadow war as well as possible links to the tidal waves and seismic activity that led to the deaths of tens of millions worldwide. In their place, a new organization has been created at the behest of the world's leading governments. It will be called The Order of the Amuli. Its chief duties shall be the apprehending of rogue Amuli. As per the newly enacted laws, former A.R.C. and A.I.M. agents will have to join this new organization or be marked as rogue Amuli. The Order of the Amuli, or The Order as some are already calling it, will be headed by Adam Avery. It was revealed, to the great surprise of many, that Avery was the figure known as Red Mask who started the data dump. This had already led him to gain much support as a whistleblower from those people outraged by the unsettling realizations. The UN said in part of their statement that Avery's appointment 'shows a true departure from the corruption of A.R.C. and A.I.M.' He has been lauded by leaders and private citizens alike for his bravery and honesty for coming forward with his revelations. In the UN chambers, Avery made the following statement-"

Camilla, still at the wheel, clicked the radio off. No one complained. Saying that they felt relief would have been going too far. They did not need to hear anymore. Avery's plan was coming to fruition. It was just as he had outlined to Paul.

Each passenger sat in a seat by themselves in the spacious bus. At some point, it had been implied that Camilla would drive as far into the country as possible. She knew the area the best out of the group, so no one offered to take her place. Everyone knew that lying low would be the first stage of whatever was coming next. They had left New York City's suburbs hours ago and were heading somewhere upstate.

When darkness has come, no one in the beleaguered crew felt like dozing off. There was far too much uncertainty and justified paranoia for that.

Another sound of buzzing and some clicking echoed in the bus's metal frame. In the quiet, it spread throughout the whole bus.

At first, Camilla checked the radio nobs again.

"Thought I turned it off," she murmured lowly to herself.

The former A.R.C. agents each checked their pockets and sitting areas. It was for not though. They had all smashed their A.R.C. hardline communicators hours ago out of fear of being tracked.

It was Robby who crept to the back of the bus, half-bouncing down the center aisle whenever they hit a bump.

He put an ear to his motorcycle as his hands rummaged through the maintenance pack that Blake had sent with it. After a moment, he straightened up, cursing at himself.

Camilla, who had been watching Robby from her large review window, called back as she pieced the situation together. "You didn't ditch the comms on your bike!"

"It was built in!" Robby explained as he readied a hammer and aimed it at a small box below the handlebars.

He suddenly stopped.

"Wait!"

His fingers twisted a knob that made the buzzing static grow.

"-hearing this… We… last time…"

Robby nimbly adjusted the settings as the muffled voice grew clearer.

"I repeat, this is our last attempt to reach you," a commanding voice announced. "It's too risky to try again. My team and I escaped The Order. Left Pittsburgh to hide in the surrounding hills for now. We're gathering everyone we can in secret… everyone who opposes him. Get close and we'll find you. Stay safe. Blake's cutting the signal for good…"

The transmission ended with more static.

"Grady!" Robby, Camilla, and Paul all cried in unison.

"Look at that!" Robby pumped his fist as he yelled. "Finally, some good news!"

"At least we know where we're heading now," Camilla realized. "We just need a map. Can't really risk a GPS, and we'll want to stay off the main roads, anyway."

"Hold on," Ben warned, with arms raised. "I don't even know this, Grady. Do I get a say in what we do?"

"Not really," Camilla scoffed at him.

"What's your thinking, Ben?" Paul asked, remaining magnanimous.

"I'm just thinking, what if it's a trick?" Ben commented. "How do we know that he hasn't gone over to Avery's side like your other friend?"

Robby and Camilla were both about to bark at him, but Paul raised a hand to stop them.

"What would you have us do? I'm sure we're open to ideas."

"Well," Ben said, "I don't really have anything concrete, but I'm still good with the Jackson... err former Jackson faction. Can't we team up with a few of them? I mean, especially if they know what Avery did to Jackson."

Paul finally disagreed. "Avery controls the story. Who knows what he's saying about Jackson's death? Even if they know the truth, they might be like Brandon. What if they want war?"

"And what do we want?" Ben questioned.

"Not world war," Camilla interjected. "I mean, not if we can help it."

"You don't know Grady," Robby added. "You don't become an Army Ranger out of a lack of loyalty to your friends. That's the type of background he comes from."

"Well, guess I'm outvoted," Ben conceded. "Should've known what I was signing up for. The easy days are behind me."

Camilla and Robby were content to leave Ben to his snark, but Paul spoke up. "If you're on this bus, you're a part of us. We're not going to do anything that isn't about what's best for us and the rest of the world. I'm sick of all the political games."

"So, what are we then?" Ben wondered. "They're 'The Order' or whatever. What are we?"

"We do need a cool group name," Robby agreed.

"I've been thinking about that," Paul started. "There is something that Jackson said near the end. He said that A.R.C. wasn't a 'charity.' Well, now, we aren't held back by all those politics and militarism. Why can't we just be a force for good? We'll just be a group of helpers. Sure, we'll try to take down Avery, but we all have amazing gifts. We'll do what we can. We can clean up disaster areas and run rescue missions. We can defend the weak and needy against oppression. We can show everyone that Amuli are just human beings like they are. We aren't predisposed to violence or power-hungriness. We can be that charity that Jackson didn't think A.R.C. could be."

"Charity," Alice repeated. "It is a good name."

With that, she, Paul, and Robby all left their personal seats to congregate behind Camilla's driver seat.

"Alright," Camilla sighed. "If it's the consensus, let's go find Grady."

CHAPTER 44
MEMORY FRAGMENT

"HOW ARE YOU FEELING?"

Veronica Mott, the non-Amuli coordinator of the base, set a Styrofoam cup of coffee down in front of Greg Luper.

Luper shrugged. He took the cup with a shaky hand, managing just not to spill any of the hot contents on himself.

Veronica nodded. "I figured as much."

"He was mad at the end... insane," he explained in a shaky voice.

"I don't suppose you can do what he just did without being that way," Veronica commented.

Luper shook his head. "You don't get it. He was never completely stable. He always had an edge. It was just never anything close to this. This is making me think about everything differently. Is this result for all of us? Is this what Amuli are doomed to? To lose all of our loved ones until we have a psychotic break. I lost her. Now, I feel like I'm losing it all as well."

"Come on," Veronica instructed him. "I need to show you something."

She led him to a hallway with a large window overlooking another clean-looking room with shining tile floors. Twin cribs rested side-by-side. One baby was a boy. He looked to be several months older than the other one. He seemed to be attempting to sit up but was continually half-rolling backward. He had an oddly full head of hair on his head, which was sticking up in several places.

It was difficult to catch a good glimpse of the second child. He or she was tightly wrapped in white. Luper craned his head toward the glass to see that the wrappings were a mix of blankets and bandages. To him, the latter seemed so foreign to be placed on someone so small. It made his stomach turn all the more.

"She pulled through," Veronica explained. "Can't say how, other than that Atlantean DNA. They thought she was dead. Honestly, what was Jackson thinking? Ordering an 'anima shootout' on two new parents. He had to know that the child could be there. Even if he's been drained of the human aspect, what good does it do? Aiden and Abigail were his best assets, and the girl was a potential asset."

"He is all about control now," Luper replied. "He couldn't control Aiden or Abby. In his eyes, they betrayed him when they escaped. You betray A.R.C. and you suffer his wrath. It is his method of keeping the organization together."

"I will always be curious as to why you didn't step up to lead," Veronica wondered. "You would have had the support. You still do."

"I don't do well with people," Luper explained before changing the subject. "Who is the boy?"

"He's Michael's," Veronica answered. "His sister was watching him and brought him here when she got worried. She's heard the news now, and she's not in any condition to be watching over a baby. Then, someone said that babies communicate with each other and to put these two together for a while. Not sure if that's true, but it's what we did. At least, he'll be out of here soon. We're setting up his aunt and her fiancé with a place out in the boonies. Although, with Michael and Sam both gone, I doubt any of our enemies will value him anymore."

"And the girl?" Luper queried.

Veronica shrugged. "Can't say yet. The doctors are a little worried about what happened to her head. They said she should be able to live a 'normal' life physically. They just aren't sure if her personality or other mental faculties will be affected."

Luper just continued to stare through a glass. A lump sat in his throat.

"They're two opposites, really," Veronica pointed out. "One is going to have a normal life. Two guardians, even if they aren't his parents, school, friends, and all of that. The other one… who knows? Yet here they are together, just babies who don't know any better… or anything at all, I guess. There's something poetic in that."

"I do not believe that children become their parents," Luper philoso-phized. "I sure did not. However, I think that we are often to pay for our parents' actions, whether they are triumphs, mistakes, or failures. It is an inherent injustice in the world. The hole Aiden dug for the girl is deep. As for Michael's son, the hole is shallow, but it can be hard to see that when you are standing in it. I doubt that I will be around to see either attempt their escape. The life expectancy is never long for a killer. Now, there is justice in that."

Luper slid his black jacket over his broad shoulders.

"Time for work?" Veronica asked him.

"For me, it is always time for that."

The End

ABOUT THE AUTHOR

LaTrobe has been a fan of science fiction and fantasy since his mom read him the Harry Potter series and his dad showed him Star Wars as a kid. He first took up writing as a hobby in middle school. Ever surrounded by books, he currently works as a librarian in rural, Western Pennsylvania. When he is not reading or writing, you can probably find him in the midst of an anime or video game binge. His current project seeks to blend the worlds of anime and YA fantasy fiction together in an action-pack novel. The Soul Crystals saga are his first publications.

Learn more about his past and future projects at his website:
Https://latrobebarnitz.com/